WOMEN OF UNCOMMON STRENGTH

A NOVEL OF THE REDEEMING POWER OF LOVE

Jacket credits: Front cover photos; (top row left to right) (c) Peter Forest/ Getty Images; Eric Audras/Getty Images; Sherrie Nickol/Citizen Stock; (bottom row left to right)(c) Blend Images/Trinette Reed/Getty Images; JGI/Getty Images; Nick Daly/Getty Images; Bottom photo: Dianne Avery Photography/Getty Images

Cover design by Laura Duffy
Book design by Elina Cohen

Published by Bridgehaven Books Publishing

ISBN: 978-0-9854832-9-6

www.facebook.com/gladneybdarroh

This book is dedicated to my mother,
Peggy Boyd Darroh, with love.
It is also dedicated to my children,
Ashley and Steven, my two greatest blessings—
kids, I love you very much.

ACKNOWLEDGMENTS

I wish to thank those who provided guidance, suggestions, and critical reading skills for this book, including Katie Sullivan, Samantha Lay, and she who wished to remain anonymous.

I would also like to thank my brothers, Will and Dick, for their support and encouragement over a lifetime.

Lastly, my thanks to the board and to the staff of the Boys and Girls Harbor in La Porte, Texas for their amazing dedication to the children and for the privilege of allowing me to be a part of the effort. Ten percent of the author's net royalties from the sale of this book is being donated to the Harbor for the care of children who have been abandoned, abused, or neglected.

For those wishing to make an additional donation, please visit: www.boysandgirlsharbor.org.

As a mother comforts her child, so will I comfort you;
and you will be comforted over Jerusalem.
—ISAIAH 66:13

CHAPTER ONE

Houston, Texas – November 5th, Modern Times

The earth had shifted again and sent another shock wave through her life, but what could a mother do? For this joy-filled reunion, the one thing this mother could do was purchase a new dress from an upscale department store—something she never did. But today is different. Today is special in every way, and she wants to look her very best, even if it means going considerably outside of her comfort zone with the choice of an expensive new dress to commemorate the occasion. What she could do to make a difference, some contribution, she did, and she was happy about it. Even so, she chose what women call a staple: a well-tailored classic piece with clean lines in navy blue that she knew she could wear again and again. Of course the designer shoes were stunning, but she just couldn't bring herself to purchase what the sales lady had recommended and settled instead, sensibly she thought, for navy leather pumps by Naturalizer with a decorative buckle strap across the toe. The woman accessorized with a double strand pearl necklace her husband had given to her after the birth of their second child and the pearl and gold broach he had bought for her on their tenth wedding anniversary. She wears gold clip earrings and on her left wrist is a flattering gold watch with a rectangular crystal that looks more expensive than it really is.

So, in her new dress and shoes, Mrs. Margaret McAllister, a pleasant-looking, petite woman in her fifties with a kind face and just-graying hair, peers anxiously out of the front window in her modest living room. Although her house and its furnishings clearly depict a lower-middle income family, Mrs. McAllister's simple, un–pretentious home is appointed tastefully and comfortably with a woman's touch for style and detail, even artfully so for someone always working on a limited budget. This morning, the white porch and railing are decorated festively with red, white, and blue "Welcome Home" banners and bunting, which billow out occasionally when gently stirred by the slight, steady November breeze. It is one of those perfect days in Houston just after a seasonal front has moved through the city: the sky is a clear expanse of brilliant blue, and the air is refreshingly cool and dry.

The phone on the living room lamp table rings. Mrs. McAllister glances quickly at it but is reluctant to give up her place at the window. On the third ring, she unwillingly leaves her post, walks a few short steps across the carpet, and answers the phone with a pleasant, "Hello?"

"Mom! Is he home yet? You promised you'd call as soon as he got there." The excited voice on the other end of the phone is her daughter, Kathryn.

The woman smiles when she hears her daughter on the line and replies patiently, "No sweetheart, your brother's not home yet. I checked, and his flight was on time, so he's probably just stuck in traffic. I'll call you as soon as he's home. I promise."

Kathryn's tone has a twinge of regret. "I was anxious to be there when he arrived, Mom. But he said he wanted it to be just you and him."

"You know how your brother is, sweetheart. I suppose he didn't want a big show over his homecoming. He didn't invite any of his friends here either."

"Sure Mom," Kathryn says, her voice softening. She knows her brother had everything well-planned, as he always did, with their best interests at heart. Her tone becomes concerned. "How about you, will you be all right?"

"I believe so. Yes sweetheart, I'll be fine."

"That's good."

Mrs. McAllister glances towards the window. "Seth has his reasons, Katie. I suppose he was only thinking of us when he said, 'Please don't come to Germany.' Let's trust him in this too."

Kathryn smiles to herself, thinking her mother doesn't know just how right she is about that. "I know Mom—sweet, beautiful Seth—our artist and man of the house. There's no one else like him."

"No dear, there's no one else like your brother. Please Katie, let me go now. I promise I'll call you as soon as he arrives."

"I'll be right here, waiting by the phone. Don't forget to call me. I love you."

"I won't forget. I love you too. Bye sweetheart."

"Bye Mom."

Mrs. McAllister always felt wonderfully blessed that her children loved each other the way they did. Of course, they had had the typical sister/brother spats growing up, but they were always short-lived, and soon after she'd see them sitting on the couch side by side watching a show and laughing together. Their close relationship had only deepened as they grew older. They not only cared for each other like best friends, they respected each other. Mrs. McAllister couldn't imagine how much more difficult life would have been if her children had felt any other way. That's not to say she never wondered what they were conspiring when she walked into a room and they immediately ceased talking, but she didn't think about it too much, not really.

Naturally though, like every good mother, she worried about them; in fact, she worried constantly about her children for real reasons and for no real reasons. Fortunately, when they were growing up, there were never any of those dreaded late night or early morning phone calls telling her that Katie or Seth were in trouble, hurt, or, God forbid, something worse. She had experienced a call like that once before in her life. The phone call about her husband had been a terrible shock. He was simply too young for something like that to happen, wasn't he? But the doctor explained that brain aneurysms can strike at any age, often come without warning, and are frequently fatal. They had been high school sweethearts and married soon after graduation. He called her Peggy and was the only person in her life to do so. Theirs was a wonderful marriage; two people had never been so perfectly matched. It had taken her years to get over his loss, but she never remarried. How could she? Her husband was the only man she would ever love, ever truly love. She knew that. She had known that from their very first kiss, as shy and awkward and innocent as it was for the both of them.

After losing her husband when Kathryn was twelve and Seth was nine, Mrs. McAllister found that the single thing that saw her through that tragic period was her love for her children. Once she paid off the mortgage with the proceeds of the life insurance to make sure her children would always have a home, there was still some money remaining. That money, plus the meager wages she earned at a part-time office job from nine in the morning to two-thirty in the afternoon, was enough for the family to live on if she scrupulously watched every penny, caught every sale, and collected every coupon. Yet despite the untimely loss of her husband and the economic hardship that ensued, Mrs. McAllister was a woman who remained strong in her faith and tithed weekly. She felt deeply grateful to have her children, her home, her church, and the part-time job that enabled her to make ends meet while offering work hours that allowed her to be home after school with the children. She was a demure woman who genuinely felt blessed and didn't want more from life than for her children to remain safe and to be healthy and happy. Her children always came first in everything she thought or did. Like all good mothers, she lived every day with unimaginable love and thankfulness for them, and she also lived every day with a constant fear that something tragic might befall them. If she had lost one of them, Mrs. McAllister knew that was the one loss she could never overcome. She had already learned how quickly life can change—a single phone call can change everything, as it did once before with her husband and as it did again with her son a few months ago. She had learned that one never knew when the earth might shake.

By the way she lived her life, all of Mrs. McAllister's virtues had been passed down to her children. They fully understood and appreciated their mother's sacrifices for them. To her children, she was a woman of character, courage, and uncommon strength.

They knew she was that special kind of mother who was there for them every day in countless ways, both small and large: protecting them, providing for them, encouraging them, hugging them, and loving them in every way she could and with whatever she had. They understood it was their mother's quiet, dependable strength of maternal purpose and her steady, unyielding force of faith that had kept things going for the family day after day and year after year following their father's death. Her life revolved around them and this was evident to Kathryn and Seth. But even so, this good and modest woman was always astonished that her children felt that she was not only the iron linchpin of their family but also believed that she, and every mother like her, were the iron linchpins of civilization. Theirs was a close and loving family.

After hanging up the phone with her daughter, Mrs. McAllister quickly moves across the living room to the front window just in time to see the taxi pull up to the curb. The circular logo on the cab door reads: Joseph and Sons Taxi Service. The woman feels the tears welling up in her eyes, and uninvited, her lower lip begins quivering. She has been preparing for this moment since she received the news and is determined to hold herself together. Straightening her back and using the white handkerchief she's holding to gently pat below both eyes, Mrs. McAllister hopes they haven't become red and puffy. As soon as she sees the young man exit the passenger side door, she smoothes her dress and brightens, and puts on her bravest face.

While backing out of the cab, the young man simultaneously reaches for a large, olive green duffel bag, standard army issue, and pulls it out. Through the car window, the cabbie hands him a clipboard. The soldier signs the paper on it and hands the clipboard back to the cabbie. The cabbie tears off a receipt and gives it to the young man, who politely takes it from him and puts it in his pants pocket. The cabbie says something to the soldier, who nods his head appreciatively, and the cab drives off, leaving the young man standing alone on the sidewalk. His back is to Mrs. McAllister. She has not been able to fully see him, not just yet, and her anxiety rises higher.

The young soldier turns and faces the house, taking it all in. The first thing anyone would notice about this young man is that he is remarkably handsome with broad shoulders, an angular face, strong chin, Nordic nose, and high cheekbones. But it is his eyes that always strike people the most: they are a clear, pale blue, the color of a cloudless summer sky, like glass crystals filled with a soft blue light. He is tall, trim, fit, and wearing his dress uniform, which displays an array of ribbons and medals. This soldier is Mrs. McAllister's son, Seth. He is twenty-six years old and back from the service. Protruding slightly below his left sleeve are two steel hooks. Mrs. McAllister looks at him with all the love and thankfulness that every mother in every century has ever felt when first looking upon a son who returns home safely from war. An anguished sob breaks from her throat, and she touches her heart when she sees his prosthesis for the first time. The woman buckles from a torrent of relief and joy and sorrow flooding in uncontrollably. Shaking her head slowly and sadly, her mother's pain is palpable. Mrs. McAllister carefully dabs her eyes with the handkerchief, and with strong determination, successfully regains her composure.

Feeling his mother's eyes on him, the soldier breaks into his trademark easy grin at the bright decorations she has carefully festooned across the porch. The young man takes a few steps forward and stops at the free-standing mailbox. Fixed atop a four-foot post, the aluminum box gleams in the sun. He looks up and down the street, appreciating in a new way the peaceful simplicity of his old neighborhood. Setting down his duffel bag, he grasps the little flag affixed to one side of the mailbox and playfully moves it up and down. Its familiar rusty squeak is reassuring. Seth picks up his bag and ambles slowly up the walk to the house. As he passes by the two pecan trees that flank the sidewalk he says good-naturedly, "Hello Eleven, hello Twelve." Unhurried, he mounts the four short steps to the top of the landing. Lightly stepping onto the porch, he sees the two person chair swing on the right and the small, metal patio table with two chairs on the left.

Everything is exactly the same now as it was on the day he left for basic training. It's somewhat surprising to him how these little items in their accustomed places give him such a deep sense of comfort and belonging. When he reaches the front door, his mother opens it and steps out, smiling warmly at him. He towers over her small frame. They stand facing each other. Right away, he notices that his mother has purchased a new dress and pair of shoes for his homecoming, and that she has been crying. The soldier quickly sets down his bag and removes his beret, exposing short, thick, curly blond hair. Then grinning in his relaxed way and looking directly into her loving eyes, Seth says pleasantly, like he's just returned from a leisurely stroll around the neighborhood, "Hi Mom."

"Son," she whispers wondrously and steps to him.

Seth leans down so his mother can reach her arms around him. Mrs. McAllister has her eyes closed and her face buried in his chest now, hugging her son and hanging onto him tightly. Seth hugs her gently in return and waits patiently for her to release him. He is willing to wait for as long as she needs. Seth understands his mother very well and knows that his homecoming will be hard on her. Mrs. McAllister finally steps back and gazes up smiling and feeling miraculously thankful.

"The decorations are terrific, Mom," he says. "Thanks a lot." And he sets his beret on top of his duffel bag.

"Son, you're too beautiful for words," Mrs. McAllister says quietly, and she hugs him again for a long moment with her face pressed against his chest. When she releases him and steps back, she notices that his uniform has darkened spots from her tears. "Oh, look what I've done," she says self-consciously and whisks at the spots with her handkerchief.

Seth catches her hand gently in his and squeezes it affectionately. "It's okay Mom," he says. "I like them there."

His mother stops and smiles up at him. The warmth of his hand and the sound of his voice reassure her. Mother and son look at each other, saying nothing but feeling everything.

Tilting his head slightly to one side, Seth playfully asks, "Is there a good place to eat around here? I'm starved."

"Of course you are!" she exclaims. "I made all your favorites."

"I was hoping you'd say that." Seth steps around her gingerly and quickly opens the door for his mother saying, "Ladies first."

"Thank you, sweetheart." Mrs. McAllister beams as she passes by him through the doorway.

The young man grasps his beret and grabs his duffel bag, glances once more around the neighborhood, and follows his mother inside the house. They walk through the living room and into the kitchen. He places his beret on the counter beside a small pile of unopened mail that is next to an acoustic radio he gave her as a gift last Christ-mas. There is a large cross on the wall above the stove, and on another wall hangs a round clock. To the lower right of the clock is a two foot by three foot chalkboard for writing messages. The kitchen and breakfast room were designed in such a way that the space was really one oversized room and had always been the main family gathering area. Here a table sits in front of a large bay window that looks out upon a surprisingly broad and deep backyard, at the far end of which sits an old swing set, and across from it is a children's playhouse, now faded and worn with time.

Made with loving care and sitting on the table are homemade chocolate chip cookies piled high on a plate. The centerpiece for the table is a lovely cut glass vase filled with beautiful yellow roses. At one end of the kitchen counter is another identical cut glass vase containing a unique combination of white silk daffodils and more yellow roses; it is as equally stunning as the centerpiece. The flowers are perfectly arranged for optimal creative effect, revealing the arranger's artistic talent.

At one end of the kitchen, a door leads through the utility room to the back door and beyond it to the extensive backyard. A few feet from the back door is a patio gate on the right, and on the other side of the gate is the driveway. Separating the patio from the driveway is a chain-link fence. It runs the short distance from the back door to the side door of the garage.

As Mrs. McAllister goes through the routine of retrieving her son's favorite lunch from the fridge and bringing it to the table—cold fried chicken, creamy coleslaw, and mushroom salad—Seth stands and observes her closely, keenly aware his mother has become very tense. In a sign he knows well, she chatters distractedly as she dutifully goes about her habit of setting food on the table.

"You see, you see," she says rapidly, "I knew you'd want your cold fried chicken." Jittery, Mrs. McAllister bumps the table with the serving dish and frowns.

"Mom, can I help?" Seth offers.

"No sweetheart," she answers agitated. "Sit down, now. I want everything to be just right."

"Always is."

Seth sits and waits patiently for what he knows is coming. Mrs.

McAllister smiles at him nervously as she brings the last item to the table, a large bowl of mushroom salad. As she places the bowl on the table, Seth reaches for a chocolate chip cookie and devours all of it in one bite.

Suddenly, Mrs. McAllister fusses at him. "Stop that! You'll spoil your appetite!"

Seth looks at his mother, unruffled. He offers her an apologetic smile.

His mother freezes, stunned and frustrated. "Oh! What am I saying? Eat them. Please, eat them all!" and she breaks down crying, covering her face with her hands.

Seth quickly stands and hugs his mother, pulling the woman closely to him and comforting her. He lays his cheek on top of her head, holding and rocking her gently. After a minute, he feels his mother's shoulders relax, and her sobs begin to quiet down.

Mrs. McAllister gathers herself and steps back. She finds the handkerchief she left on the counter and begins dabbing her eyes with it. Looking into the handkerchief as if talking to it, rather than to Seth, she says, "I was so scared . . . I was just so scared . . . if I'd lost you too." She covers her face. Her shoulders are shaking and soft, quiet sobs are coming from her.

Seth tenderly removes her hands from her face so she can see him. Utilizing his disarming grin, he speaks to her quietly and reassuringly.

"Mother, look at me. I'm here. I'm home now. I'm okay. Everything's fine."

"I told myself I wouldn't make a scene. And look at me," she says self-consciously, tears staining her face. "I'm afraid I'm spoiling your homecoming."

Seth nimbly takes the handkerchief from his mother's hands and carefully dries her tears as he reassures her in a gentle tone, "You're not spoiling anything, Mom. My homecoming couldn't be better. I grew up in a house with two females, remember? I'm used to the drama."

Her voice aching, she replies, "I couldn't stand knowing you were hurt, knowing I couldn't come to you, that I couldn't be with you when you needed me the most."

Seth raises his prosthesis slightly and says convincingly, "It didn't hurt, Mom. Never has. I just woke up in the hospital, and there it was, no big deal."

"You're not just saying that for my sake?" she asks hopefully.

"No, Mom. I'm not. Really, I'm not," he answers calmly, hoping to alleviate her anxiety.

Seth swiftly goes to the radio and switches it on. A waltz plays. He sweeps his mother up and begins dancing her around the kitchen. They are both excellent dancers and have danced together many times, a McAllister family tradition. After a few turns, Seth stops and gives his mother a quick kiss on the cheek. "You see? If I can dance the same as always there's not a thing in the world to worry about."

Mrs. McAllister is relieved by her son's reassurances. "All you McAllister men are natural born dancers," she says. "Your father was. He would've been so proud of you, son—a brave soldier and decorated hero."

Seth is pleased to see his mother is recovering. He responds warmly, "You've always been my hero. Did you know that?"

"I have?" she says, quietly surprised, raising her eyebrows.

"Absolutely you are, Mom. You were always there for me and Katie, sacrificing every day, doing it all, and doing it by yourself—never missed a school event, taxied us and our friends everywhere. You're the best mom in the whole world!"

His mother gazes at him tenderly. Revealing her life's ambition, she tells him with profound feeling, "All I ever wanted was to be a good mother."

"You're the best, Mom."

Mrs. McAllister continues to look lovingly at her beautiful son without saying a word. Grinning at her he teases, "Gee whizz, after dancing with this pretty girl I'm holding who bought a beautiful new dress and fancy pair of shoes for my homecoming, I'm even hungrier than before."

"Of course you are! Everything's ready." She is happy again, and thrilled that her son noticed her new purchases.

Seth pulls out a chair for his mother. "Ladies first."

"Thank you, sweetheart."

Mrs. McAllister serves her son's plate with generous, heaping portions. She hands the plate to him, and Seth thanks her. He politely waits for his mother to serve her own plate and only eats after she invites him to begin. With a mother's pure pleasure, Mrs. McAllister watches her son enjoy the food she has prepared before taking a bite herself.

"It's *so good*, Mom. Thank you." Seth gestures to the centerpiece. "Beautiful flowers, they must be from Mr. Nakamura."

"Yes. He brings them very early every Saturday morning. I set the empty vase out by the front door each Friday night, and in the morning the vase is full of fresh flowers again. I would like to thank him, but he comes so early and so quietly I never get the chance. The best I can do is to leave a sealed bag of chocolate chip cookies for him by the empty vase. I believe he likes them."

"Everyone loves your cookies. Mom, you never see Mr. Nakamura at all?"

"Well, I did once. There was a soft knock at the front door one afternoon. When I opened it, Mr. Nakamura was standing there with tears streaming down his face. He bowed, apologized for disturbing me, and asked about you. Somehow, he knew you'd been hurt."

Thinking about his mentor, his Shishou, Seth observes affectionately, "He always knows."

"When I told him you'd be coming home soon, Mr. Nakamura quietly said, 'Thank you, Mrs. McAllister.' Then he bowed again and left. I wanted to thank him for the flowers. But he left so quickly he was gone before I could."

"He knows you appreciate them."

Mrs. McAllister pleasantly adds, "Along with the cookies, I left him a note last week saying that you would be coming home today. Mr. Nakamura brought extra flowers this morning in a second vase. The ones on the counter are from him too. Seth, I believe that man loves you like a son."

"I'm seeing him later today."

"He'll be so pleased, sweetheart. Does he know you're coming?"

"It's a surprise, if that's possible."

The phone on the kitchen wall rings startling Mrs. McAllister and reminding her that she's forgotten to call her daughter. "Heavens, that's Katie! I forgot to call her."

Seth grins and gets up quickly, patting his mouth with a napkin.

He walks to the phone, picks up the receiver, sniffs twice very loudly into the mouthpiece, and answers with a perfect imitation of a snooty English butler.

"McAllister Manor, Jeeves speaking." He quickly extends the receiver at arm's length. From the other end comes a continuous, loud shriek. Returning the phone to his ear, he says affectionately, "Hi Katie."

His sister is ecstatic. "Seth, it's so good to hear your voice! I knew Mom would forget to call me."

"Good to hear yours too sis. You coming over soon?"

"Soon? I'm waiting outside in my car right now. I'll be there in two secs."

"Great. I'll tell Mom." Seth hangs up the phone and returns to the table.

"Was she put out with me?" Mrs. McAllister frets. "I should have remembered to call her."

"No, she wasn't. Katie already drove over. She's been waiting outside in the driveway. She'll be coming through the back door any second now."

Katie enters the back door. She is a lovely young woman, taller than her mother by a few inches, with a slender stature, shoulder length auburn hair, and hazel eyes framed by soft angled eyebrows. She wears a pair of black, Crepe Candace ankle pants, a French-purple Zenergy Francesco scoop tee, and pewter Missie Sport wedge sandals by AK. Her ears are garnished with small twist hoop silver earrings. Kathryn's casual chic appearance would be complete if not for the oversized Mickey Mouse watch she wears on her left wrist, a gift from her children. Seth's sister is highly intelligent, sensible, and practical—all of which is made more appealing by her outgoing, perky personality and a laugh that is as comfortable as a soft leather glove. Often when she speaks, her voice carries a tone of gentle authority, a tone that she has used quite effectively with Seth all of his life.

Seth stands. "Dr. Mason, I presume?"

"Seth!" Kathryn rushes to him, and they hug. Still holding him, Kathryn draws back and looks at her brother lovingly. "You're so handsome in your uniform—of course you would be." She hugs him tightly again and kisses him on the cheek. She releases Seth and takes a short step back.

Mrs. McAllister watches her two children. At this moment she has never been happier in her life.

Seth grins at his sister. "Congratulations, Katie. You graduated from med school while I was gone. How great is that?"

Grinning back at her brother, looking just like him, Katie says cheerfully, "Yep. A couple of years late with the twins and all, but I finally made it."

"You're amazing, sis. What's your specialty gonna be?"

"Pediatrics. You know I love kids."

"Yes, I know, but there's no way you can call yourself Dr. McAllister-Mason. The kids will never remember it. Call yourself . . . Dr. M&M. They'll remember *that*."

Katie laughs out loud. "That's really good." She deftly reaches and grasps her brother's prosthesis. "Let's take a look," and she examines it with great admiration. "Wow, Seth. Those military docs really know what they're doing."

"Yep, that's what they tell me," he says, a little too nonchalantly, Katie thinks. Katie and Seth sit down at the table close to each other.

Mrs. McAllister, who has been thoroughly enjoying her children's reunion, says with motherly delight, "Both my little sweethearts, home again. I'll get cold milk for the cookies."

"I love your special chocolate chip cookies, Mom." Katie compliments her.

"I'm glad you do, sweetheart."

Katie eagerly reaches for one. "Umm, these are *so* good, and I get to eat them without any sticky hands grabbing me."

Seth seizes the chance to tease his sister. "So, how is Perry?"

Amused, Katie quickly corrects Seth, "I was referring to the *twins*. And *Terry's* fine."

Puzzled, Mrs. McAllister asks her son, "Sweetheart, why do you always call Katie's husband, 'Perry'? You know his name is Terry."

"It's word association," Seth says lightly. "He's an attorney. His last name is Mason like Perry Mason, that big time T.V. attorney you like so much on *Retro*. Perry rhymes with Terry. That's how I remember it."

His mother is more baffled. "But that's just it, dear, you *don't* remember."

Seth cuts his eyes at his sister mischievously and replies, "It's close enough. Katie's had so many boyfriends in her life who can keep their names straight?"

Punching her brother playfully, Katie quickly replies, "A bunch of boyfriends but only one wonderful husband!"

Seth grins and devours another cookie in one quick bite.

Nostalgically recalling their teen years, Mrs. McAllister naïvely says, "Well, you two were never any trouble. Not like my friends' children. Most of them were worried sick all the time with their kids being out all hours; not my two little sweethearts though. You were always home between eleven and twelve. I never had to worry about my sweethearts, at least not when it came to that." Mrs. McAllister doesn't notice that Seth and Kathryn have just exchanged knowing glances, and Kathryn is biting her lower lip hard to keep from laughing.

Getting up from her place at the table, their mother says, "Don't mind me children. I'm going to check the mail. I'll be right back. You two probably want to talk by yourselves for a bit anyway." Mrs. McAllister makes her way through the living room and out the front door to the mailbox.

As soon as their mother is gone, Kathryn raises her eyebrows at Seth, grins, and asks impishly, "Should we ever tell Margaret the truth?" As teenagers, Katie and Seth had gotten into the habit of calling their mother by her given name whenever she wasn't in the room. But it was never out of disrespect because they adored her. They affectionately called her Margaret to give her a separate identity when talking about her. When they lived at home, it had somehow made it easier for Katie and Seth to see her as a person apart from "Mom" when comparing notes or complaining regularly to one another about how annoying she could be. In this way, their grievances seemed more impersonal and objective. Most of their teenage friends talked the same way about their parents. As young adults, Katie and Seth had continued this habit.

"No way!" Seth counters. "Why do that to her? Margaret would only worry now that she hadn't worried then. You know how she is."

Kathryn looks at her brother, her eyes dance with love and admiration for him. "That was pure genius, Seth. Naming those pecan trees Eleven and Twelve. We got away with murder!"

"Yep, we sure did. But at least we could honestly tell Margaret we came home between Eleven and Twelve whenever she asked. Good thing she was always asleep by ten-thirty. As exasperating as her routines were, they were always dependable—gave us some freedom and saved her a lot of worry."

Laughing, Katie adds, "And we saved ourselves a lot of repetitive writing. Can you imagine if she'd ever found out? We'd still be here at the kitchen table writing, *I will never again come home at two in the morning because my loving mother was worried sick an escaped convict had kidnapped me, chopped me up into little pieces, put me in a burlap bag, and threw it in Buffalo Bayou, and no one ever learned what happened to me. My poor mother was heartbroken and died from grief.* You know Margaret would have added that last line to make it about herself, too, and for the extra guilt effect."

Katie has Seth laughing now. She then points and says, "Look at that chalkboard on the wall. Can you believe she still has it up?"

"You know how Margaret hates change," Seth says. "I'm surprised there's not an old message up there instructing us to get our homework done by seven." Pointing to the thick phone book on the counter, he adds, "Do you even know anybody else who still keeps the White Pages around? I bet our old booster chair is still down there in the cabinet."

"You know it is," Katie laughs.

Seth eyes his sister. "Hey Katie—look!"

Kathryn looks at her brother. He opens his mouth wide, exposing a mouthful of chewed cookies. Katie tries not to laugh but can't help herself. "Men are such little boys," she quips.

Seth chuckles, pleased he got her. "Speaking of little boys, how are the twin terrors?"

"Tearing up, mostly," she answers in an exhausted tone. "They're sweet as can be, of course, but one hundred percent little boys. I didn't count on the terrible twos lasting until the fours."

"Might last until they're twenty-two," Seth teases.

Kathryn stops abruptly, and her brow furrows as a worried look crosses her face. "Oh, Seth, don't even say that. What if it's true?"

She contemplates that fate for a second but dismisses it, quickly convincing herself it couldn't possibly be true—it would be too frightening. She shakes it off and continues, "Terry's great with the boys. You should see him with them. I couldn't have made it through med school without him. He's always such a great support."

"Yep, that poor guy fell hard for you, sis. You flashed your patented come hither smile at him,"—Seth mimics a tree falling with his right arm—"and timberrr! Poor Perry, your smile cut him down like a chainsaw on steroids."

Kathryn casually takes a bite of cookie before coolly responding to her brother, "It's *Terry*. Men are such simple beasts. He was ready to fall. All I did was show him *how ready*. After that, he practically cranked up that ol' chain saw himself and handed it to me. Men need to be shown." Nodding smartly to Seth, she concludes in her practical way, "Luckiest day in that man's life," and she takes another bite of cookie, satisfied.

Seth grins at his sister, and they both have a sip of milk. "He's a good man, sis. I've liked Terry ever since you first introduced us."

"That's always meant a lot to me, Seth, thanks. Terry thinks the world of you too. So tell me, how did it go with Margaret today?"

"About like I expected; she put on a brave face at first, but finally broke down in tears—sort of like a dam giving way. I think I managed to get her over it."

Kathryn nods compassionately, thinking about her sweet mother. "That was a couple of years worth of saving up, Seth. She's never stopped worrying since the day you told her you enlisted. Actually, neither one of us has. But at least I had Terry and the children. When she got the news you were injured, she was all but inconsolable. You were so right not to let us come to Germany. She would have been too upset. And as much as I wanted to be here for your homecoming, you were right again about wanting the one-on-one time with her. If anyone's capable of comforting Mom, it's you. Margaret seems fine now." She looks tenderly at her brother. "I'm so glad you're back."

"Me too sis. It's good to be home. You really look great."

Kathryn smiles at him. "Thank you. Terry's hoping to see you later today. You are coming over, aren't you?"

"I'd love to, but I can't today. I'm meeting Alexis this afternoon and visiting Mr. Nakamura after that."

Kathryn frowns immediately. "What can you possibly see in that girl? She's not right for you."

Seth shrugs his shoulders. "I fell in love with her, sis. It just happened. I can't explain it."

More animated, Kathryn's tone is clipped. "She's gorgeous, I'll grant her that much. But no substance—Zero! Zip! Zilch! Nada! I would have screened her out in a nanosecond—one big red X!"

"Okay, okay. I think I get the picture," Seth replies good-naturedly.

Becoming more aggravated and emotional, Kathryn continues, "She didn't write you when you were convalescing, did she?" From Seth's reaction she has her answer. "No? I knew it. Alexis didn't meet you at the airport this morning, either. She's only going to hurt you, Seth. That girl better watch out for me!"

Seth shows his languid grin. "Looking out for little brother?"

"You bet. But I don't know who I'm madder at: that girl or *you* for letting her get to you the way she has."

Seth's only response is to shrug, and he continues looking at her with his easy grin and brilliant blue eyes. He couldn't be happier to see Kathryn. Seth has always been good at coaxing smiles out of his sister, and today is no different.

Despite herself, Kathryn cracks a smile and softens her tone. "Doggone it. I can't stay mad about anything with you sitting there grinning at me like that with those baby blues of yours." She pauses and then turns more serious, asking him gently, "How ya doin' with everything?"

"I'm good," he responds, again a little too dismissive to her thinking.

Arching her eyebrows, Katie asks concernedly, "Seriously, Seth. How ya really doin'? Tell me the truth now." She looks directly at him, her eyes insisting on an honest answer. Since they were children, Kathryn could stare down her brother until he caved and told her everything.

"My big sister is looking out for me again?" Seth asks mildly.

"Of course I am. Just like you've done for me about a bazillion times. All my heartaches, remember? You pulled me through every one. C'mon Seth, we've always talked to each other."

"I'm okay," he says, and he raises his prosthesis. "There's been some adjustment, mainly learning to be a righty. I'm good with it though."

Kathryn looks at him lovingly, but she's unconvinced. She knows her brother is not telling her everything, but she is not about to press her concern now. The sensible Katie decides to steer the conversation in a different direction while still letting him know she's not buying it, not altogether. Reaching out, she gently ruffles his hair. "That sounds like a telling-me-what-I-want-to-hear Seth answer. The kind you'd give me and Margaret when we'd go a little wacky at certain times of the month."

Seth angles his head and squints at her. "Whatta ya mean, *a little wacky?*"

"Oh, ha-ha," she responds, amused.

"Katie, you've no idea what it's like for a guy trying to broker the peace between two fractious females in close quarters. The drama: it wasn't *As the World Turns;* it was *As the World Spins Wildly Out of Control for No Apparent Reason.*"

Protesting, Kathryn declares, "That was Mother."

Seth folds his arms and looks at her skeptically, "Really?"

Smirking, she responds sheepishly, "Well, it *was* Mom . . . I mean . . . it was *mostly* her."

Seth realizes that Katie has given him the perfect opportunity to get her goat and says, "What? You're just like Mom."

"Not true!" she wails. "You take that back! Besides, we couldn't have been *that* bad."

"No? My C.O. was the father of three daughters. When he found out I grew up with two women, he had me teach the class on survival skills under hostile conditions to the entire regiment."

Kathryn laughs out loud at her brother's joke. She realizes he got her good, and she knows there's a lot of truth in what he just said. Katie sympathizes with what Seth had to put up with for years between her and Margaret.

His sister lightly pats him and says, "She'll be a lucky girl, the one who gets you, little brother—such a handsome, well-trained man."

Tipping his head towards her, Seth replies with no small degree of satisfaction, "That's okay, sis. With three men at home *you're* the one who's about to find out what life's like when you get outvoted all the time."

"Never happen," Kathryn says sprightly, "my vote counts for four."

Seth laughs, "Why doesn't that surprise me."

They munch their cookies and sip their milk. With her sisterly knowledge and doctor's training, Katie searches Seth's face for signs of stress. He is aware she is observing him but doesn't let on. His facial expression won't betray any of his feelings. Seth has a practiced way of appearing open to his sister and mother while masking his true feelings completely. Katie is aware of this, of course.

"Promise me please," she says, "you'll call me if things start bothering you too much."

"Sure."

Arching her eyebrows for emphasis, she counters, "You didn't say, '*promise.*'"

Seth salutes her. "I promise I'll call."

Kathryn reaches and ruffles her brother's hair again. "I'm gonna hold you to it. You know I will." She glances at her watch and gets up from the table saying, "Time for me to get back home." Kathryn leans forward and hugs Seth tightly, kissing him lightly on the cheek. She steps back and looks tenderly at him. "You *really* do make that uniform look good." She pauses, then adds emotionally, "I know you've had a hard go, Seth. I'm so sorry. I'm really proud of you and what you did. I want you to know that. We're all proud of you." Katie ruffles his hair again. Beginning to tear up, she says, "I love you so much I could cry."

"Please don't do that," he says. "I've had about all the female drama I can handle for one day. You're a doctor now, sis. It's a terrific accomplishment—Dr. M&M."

"That really is catchy," she laughs. "And it's special because you thought of it. From now on, yes, it's Dr. M&M!"

Mrs. McAllister comes back into the kitchen with a handful of mail. She smiles at her children as she places the mail on the counter. "Going so soon, dear?" she asks her daughter.

"Yes, Mom, gotta run. I need to get back to Terry and the

kids. I'll call you later. Seth, don't forget about our 'Day-Before-Thanksgiving Day' holiday party. I want you there."

"I'll be there."

"Great. Bye. Love you both." Kathryn pops another cookie in her mouth and gives them each a last quick hug. When she reaches the back door, she stops and turns around. "Hey Seth!" she calls.

Seth looks at her. Kathryn opens her mouth wide, exposing the remains of the cookie. They both laugh, and Katie quickly covers her mouth to prevent cookie crumbs from spraying out. She turns and walks out the door, closing it lightly behind her.

"Mom. Okay if I borrow the car?" Seth asks.

Mrs. McAllister has begun cleaning up the dishes. Her habit is to wash them in the sink thoroughly before stacking them in the dishwasher to cycle. "Of course you can," she replies. "Seeing Mr. Nakamura?"

"A little later, I am. I'm meeting Alexis first."

Preoccupied with her work, his mother comments, "That girl's always seemed a bit frivolous to me."

"She's okay, Mom. Sheltered a little too much, that's all."

"Well then, go and have a good time, sweetheart. The car keys are in the candy dish on the counter where they always are, whenever you're ready. Will you be home for supper? I'll have everything on the table at seven, as usual."

"I'm planning on it, Mom." Seth observes his mother's behavior. He is pleased to see she is once again wrapped comfortably inside her cocoon of routine.

"Wouldn't you like to freshen up? I put clean towels out."

"Thanks, Mom. I think I will go throw some water on my face."

Seth retrieves his beret, kisses his mother lightly on the cheek, and picks up his duffel bag. Reaching the hall doorway that leads to his bedroom, he pauses and looks back at his mother standing at the kitchen sink, working there as she has always done for as long as he can remember. He thinks how remarkable it is that such common acts like rinsing dishes at the sink, doing the laundry, cutting up fruit, fixing school lunches, and heaping praise on children for all minor and major achievements are just a few of the countless examples of motherly acts of love and devotion. Performed every day and night with unwavering dependability over the years, these simple, single acts of love, when added up, were the real cement that binds a family together and the solder that bonds society. Mrs. McAllister notices her son looking at her and smiles warmly at him.

"Thanks for everything, Mom. It couldn't have been better," Seth tells her.

His mother stops her work at the sink, gazes at her son, and says, "Since the day you left for training, this is the first time I haven't been afraid. I'm grateful to God you're home safely." She pauses, looking at him affectionately. "Standing there in the doorway like that, son, you look just like your father did when he was your age. You're so like him. I love you very much."

"I love you too, Mom." Seth turns and ambles down the hall to his bedroom, his tall frame filling up the narrow hallway. He is listing a little to the right due to the heavy burden of the duffel bag in his hand. But there are other heavier burdens he carries with him, much heavier: one is a deep sense of loss; the other is excruciating guilt. Both burdens press down on him profoundly, sinking his spirits, pushing him under, and threatening to drown him.

o   o   o

Entering his bedroom, Seth drops his duffel bag on the floor by the chest of drawers, removes his beret and sets it on the dresser, slips off his jacket, and loosens his tie. He looks around the familiar setting where he spent so many happy hours by himself, peacefully working on his designs and constructing his models. This room was his refuge away from the women. It was his quiet place where he could be alone. And to their credit, his mother and sister always respected that Seth's bedroom was his domain and left him alone in there unless invited to join him.

His mother is a consummate, fastidious cleaner. "Cleanliness is next to godliness" is one of her favorite and most annoying quotes. He knew there wouldn't be a speck of dust anywhere in his room— or in the house for that matter—and he genuinely appreciated how she had assiduously kept his bedroom exactly the way he had left it on the day he departed for basic. He could picture her in there cautiously lifting and carefully dusting underneath every fragile model and paper figure, then placing each back in exactly the same spot as before. He thought, "Man, it must have taken her hours every week." But Seth also knew that she wanted to do it, in fact needed to do it, because it was one of the important ways she had of feeling close to him. For his kind-spirited mother, this work was one more routine that comforted her. It made her feel like she was helping. Even though he was six thousand miles away at his army base in a war she didn't really understand, it was his mother's way of making some kind of meaningful contribution. Moreover, Mrs. McAllister had become famous among his army buddies for the dozens of chocolate chip cookies she shipped to him like clockwork. As a result, he was one of the most popular people at mail call. Even his C.O. had a standing order for Mrs. McAllister's cookies. Once, when the mail was late, Seth opened his door to find the C.O.'s top aide standing there inquiring about his mother's cookies. They were that good.

Seth's room is virtually an art gallery. On every wall hang beautiful posters of some of the most famous buildings in the world: among them, St. Denis Church in Saint-Denis, The Louvre in Paris, Jefferson's Monticello in Virginia, The Wainwright Building in St. Louis, the Taj Mahal in India, Palladio's Basilica in Italy, the Chartres Cathedral in France, and The Forbidden City in Beijing.

Seth has a special love of bridges. So in spaces on the wall between these posters are color photo reproductions of many spectacular bridges: the Sydney Harbor Bridge, with its dramatic arch providing a magnificent view of the harbor, the blue waters it spans, and the breathtaking, beautiful Sydney Opera House beyond; a midnight shot of the Brooklyn Bridge—one of the oldest suspension bridges in America—with its pearl-like strings of light strung gracefully between tall girders, glowing lustrously in the cold night air beneath a gold October moon; the resplendent Golden Gate Bridge stretching like a leviathan over the white caps and swirling tides and swift currents of a churning San Francisco Bay, its world famous orange hue framed against a brilliant blue sky, stunning the senses; the unique Rialto Bridge spanning the Grand Canal in Venice, built in 1255, whose vaulted, avant-garde design for its time made everyone think it would fall down, which it did, only to be rebuilt again, only to fall down again, and to be rebuilt again (how Seth loved the Italians); the Île Sainte-Hèléne Bridge looming starkly across the Saint Lawrence River in Montreal with its massive iron girders looking like a behemoth exoskeleton protecting the asphalt arteries below through which a busy stream of traffic flowed; and the splendid Kentai Bridge in Iwakuni at the foot of Mt. Yokoyama, its delicately curved arches like poetry in wood, beautifully mirrored by the meandering waters of the Nishiki River passing peacefully beneath.

The walls in Seth's bedroom are crowded with these and many other posters and photos of the world's most magnificent and beautiful structures. Seth could look at them all day long and never cease marveling at their beauty and the creative geniuses that conceived and brought them to life. He copied all of them, drawing and sketching them with studied care hour upon delightful hour, filling dozens upon dozens of sketchbooks. He treasured every one of his sketchbooks and kept them neatly on his bookshelf, along with his many books on art and architecture.

All of the shelves and most of the flat spaces in Seth's room were filled with balsa wood structures. Some of these structures were complete, and others were in various stages of completion. Some were perfect reproductions of the buildings on the posters and of the bridges in the photos on the walls, and others were original designs that Seth had painstakingly and lovingly glued together, having taken inspiration from the famous art that surrounded him in his room. The incomplete pieces are the most interesting, for one can see that Seth did not intend to complete them. He was intentionally constructing a single facet of the structure so he could better examine its design and better understand its form, function, and fit to the finished work. He was like a Michelangelo, spending months studying a single finger to understand its relation to the human hand so he could reproduce it perfectly in the finished masterpiece. This was art to Seth.

Equally impressive are the fantastic number of origami pieces that hang from the ceiling and rest in all the remaining flat spaces on his bookshelf, lamp table, dresser, and chest of drawers. The shapes and sizes and colors are amazing. He has constructed entire origami bridges and buildings. There are brilliant origami hot air balloons and a parade of origami magic carpets that hang from threads and are so cleverly suspended that they appear to float across his room, ferried by an unfelt breeze. Above them are an origami yellow moon and orange sun and a hundred origami golden stars scattered across the ceiling—his own starry sky. There are animals of every sort, and not just the usual lions, horses, giraffes, and elephants, but also splendid sea creatures: whales, dolphins, and sailfishes of every size and color, jumping and swimming. His room is a bright palette of bold primary colors and pleasing pastels. There are so many of these paper figures in his room that his mother often fretted out loud that they could be a fire hazard, which only made her children laugh and tease her genially.

His mother and sister knew Seth had a special talent as an artist. But it was really much more than a special talent; he was truly gifted. Growing up, he simply observed the natural world with more vision than other children and most adults. He intuited the relationships between things and perceived the meanings behind them: like the way the sunlight fell in winter and caused a tree's shadow to look differently on the ground, or against a stone wall, or upon a wooden fence, than the way these shadows looked in the summer when the sunlight fell upon the same tree. Innately, he knew it was Mother Nature's timeless way of mixing pigments from an eternal palette and layering her seasonal colors over the landscape. He felt that light and objects were not inanimate at all but living things that expressed themselves in myriad ways with the movement of the planets and the ageless passing of the seasons. "To know the truth," he often thought, "that everything in the universe is connected, all one has to do is stop and look. It is in plain view for anyone to see who takes the time to notice." Seth believed that sun and shadow, stars and seasons, were all notes in the same symphony. Soul and sentiment and sensitivity, Seth was a true artist. In art, he found complete harmony. It was when he was immersed in his art that he felt closest to God.

But this sensitive young man hadn't spent every day alone in his room working on art projects; no, not at all. He had been outgoing and popular at school. His sports passion was Ultimate, and he enjoyed hanging with his teammates, thoroughly relishing the male companionship. He also loved playing his guitar and listening to music. Seth had always thought of himself as just a regular guy, and that's how he wanted to be seen by his buddies. Naturally, his good looks and reputation for being the best dancer in school attracted legions of girls. But despite living in a household with two women every day (or perhaps because of it), Seth was typically shy around girls, which only enhanced his allure. And if these fine qualities alone weren't enough, Seth's appeal to the ladies was amplified by his polite consideration and old-fashioned, respectful manners that his mother had imbued in him. When it came to the opposite sex, he always opened doors, pulled out chairs, stood when being introduced, waited for a lady to offer her hand to him before offering his own, and did his best to avoid hurting their feelings. He enjoyed doing this and felt it was the proper way to treat women. Because he adored his sister and was her chief comforter whenever some jerk broke her heart, Seth was especially sensitive to a girl's emotional need for continuous reinforcement and confirmation of her value, her intelligence, her beauty, and her desirability. As a result, there was a constant clamor of females vying for a date with Seth. Yet, the reality was, he dated only a few girls in his life because he was a one-girl-kind-of-guy and because of his sister's ever-present influence. Without asking his permission, Kathryn had conveniently appointed herself Sergeant at Arms in charge of screening female prospects for her brother. She promptly screened out ninety-nine and a half percent of them. Regardless of how charming or wily they were, it was practically impossible for any girl to get past Kathryn's stiff gauntlet of strict qualifications to gain access to her brother. They had to satisfy her first, and this was well-known among the girls at school. Contrary to what one might think about it, Seth was happy with this arrangement. He trusted his sister's judgment, and, with her as referee, it relieved him from bearing the onus of blame when an interested female wasn't successful. In fact, he noted curiously, girls didn't seem to take it nearly as hard when the rejection came from another girl; tender feelings were spared, thankfully. "Just a girl thing," he thought. So with Kathryn as the go-between guard and with Seth's charming manners, in the end, he managed to stay friends with all of the girls at school, which was really pretty remarkable.

After graduating from high school, Kathryn lived at home and worked part-time while attending college to earn her undergraduate degree. During these years, she remained sentry at her self-appointed post, protecting Seth from unsuitable females. Kathryn, in her forthright way, would be the first to say that after she moved out to attend medical school and could no longer act as her brother's gatekeeper was precisely the time when some unwelcome, ne'er-do-well female moved in on Seth. As much as Kathryn loved her brother, she knew he was still a man and easy prey for a beautiful huntress like Alexis. It hadn't taken long for this sultry girl to sink and set her claws steadfastly into Seth's heart. Kathryn knew Alexis was the spoiled only child of a wealthy father who indulged her while her mother travelled to Europe six months out of every year. She hadn't liked her from the first moment Seth introduced them. Kathryn had no use for people like Alexis, who didn't think about, much less know or care about, what the real world was like. She felt the silly girl was completely devoid of compassion for the plight of people far less fortunate. It was true, Alexis would be the heiress to a family fortune one day, but Kathryn knew that fortune had already ruined any chance she had of living a life that mattered. Whenever she discussed this girlfriend of Seth's with her mother, the sharp-witted Katie referred to Alexis as the "heirhead," and that was only on those days when Katie was feeling particularly charitable towards her. On those days when she wasn't feeling charitable, Seth's sister had other names for Alexis that made her mother blush. The sensible, practical, and keenly intelligent Kathryn knew, intellectually, that Alexis was a sad case and wasn't really to blame for being a spoiled and self-centered person. After all, she thought, what chance did the girl have with a mother who selfishly neglected her and with a father who thought writing a check was the only affection he needed to show his daughter? But emotionally, it really pained Kathryn to know that this ninny-headed lioness was going to break Seth's heart. This was enough to incur her wrath, despite the failings of Alexis' parents.

Now, as Seth stands in his room thinking about everything that has happened to him, he casually retrieves his prized guitar leaning against the wall, reconsiders, and returns it. He goes to his bed, sits on one side, and picks up a gold and white Frisbee that's lying on top of the lamp table. It's a memento from his team's trip to the Nationals his junior year in college. He tosses it lightly in the air once and puts it down, disinterested. He picks up and examines a bright orange origami figure from his lamp table. It's the figure of a phoenix, and Seth contemplates its symbolism before putting it back in its proper place. As he gazes at the many drawings in his room and various reproductions of art work on the wall, his thoughts stray elsewhere.

At this moment, the young man feels lost and doesn't know what to do. Seth hopes that after being home for a few days, after he and Alexis are together for a while, when the newness of civilian life wears off, that things will simply sort themselves out somehow, that things will start to make sense again, and he'll finally be able to sleep through the night. That's what he hopes. But despite this hope, Seth drops his head, covers his face with his right hand, and sobs.

CHAPTER TWO

Later that day, Seth enters a neighborhood sports bar wearing his dress uniform. It's four thirty in the afternoon. The establishment is nearly empty of patrons. He feels thankful that it is. It will give him and Alexis a better opportunity to talk in private. Meeting at this time and place had been Alexis's idea. He walks across the floor and sits at a four-top table, facing the entrance to the bar. Seth's excitement about seeing his girlfriend shows in the way he sits on the edge of his chair, leaning forward with eager anticipation.

In front and above him are two large T. V. screens side by side, the high definition models that are popular in sports bars. The screens are not turned on at the moment. He removes his beret and hangs it on the chair to his left. A young waitress approaches his table. She is polite and friendly towards him, thinking how attractive he is.

"Hi. What'll you have?"

"A strawberry malt, please, extra thick if you don't mind, and a French vanilla one for my girlfriend. Not thick though. She doesn't like 'em thick." Seth is excited.

The waitress is amused by his exuberance. "Been a while since you've seen her, huh?"

"Yep," he says, smiling broadly.

"I thought so. I'll make sure they're right. Need wings?"

"Thank you, but no," he replies politely, looking at her, and then returns his gaze to the front door.

The waitress smiles at him, appreciating his good manners and turns and walks away to place his order. Seth continues watching the front entrance with anxious anticipation. The time is now four forty-five. He knows Alexis will come through the door any minute because he's learned to expect her customary fifteen minutes of fashionable tardiness.

His anticipation changes to elation the moment he sees Alexis walk in. Seth is completely captivated by her. She is tall, slender, and gorgeous with straight, recently highlighted shoulder length blond hair and dark-blue eyes with long lashes, above which are a pair of rich mahogany eyebrows, perfectly bowed and remarkably expressive. Her pouty lips are a rich dark-red, moist and inviting, full and sensuous. The dark-red coat of her perfectly manicured nails matches her sumptuous lips. Alexis is wearing sexy, four-inch, leather Prada heels, and a short, trendy, espresso-colored wool skirt by Christian Dior; her skirt is beautifully complimented by a Fendi, open neck cream blouse. Gracing her neck is a sparkling platinum necklace that mirrors the platinum earrings that shine from her earlobes. On one wrist is a thin, silver Cartier watch and on the other is a delicate diamond tennis bracelet from Tiffany's. Alexis sports Jackie O sunglasses that are scooted to the top of her head and she carries a large Chanel handbag over her right shoulder. Protruding from the handbag's side pocket is a copy of *Glamour*. Despite it being November, Alexis has a lovely, even tan. Her makeup is the essence of perfection. This girl looks like a top model who just stepped out of the best fashion magazine.

She eagerly talks on her cell phone. "Really? No! You think so? He's so sketchy!" she giggles. Listening to her girlfriend intently, she looks around the bar nervously while her eyes adjust to the different light. Alexis finally sees Seth. She waves and kisses the air in his direction, but continues talking into the phone. Seth waves back, but a hint of uncertainty crosses his face. He remains seated. Alexis is smiling, absorbed by the gossip. She chatters back to her girlfriend, ending her sentences with a rising tone.

"Back to you soon, ciao!" Alexis says. She slips the cell phone into her Chanel bag, takes a deep breath, and walks stiffly toward Seth with a tense, forced smile.

Seth stands and steps around the table to greet her, consciously pulling out the chair closest to him to his right. Obviously he expects a lover's greeting. His prosthesis is clearly visible. He has made no attempt to hide it. In fact, he has forgotten all about it in his pure joy of seeing his girlfriend.

Alexis, now just a few feet away from Seth, immediately diverts her eyes and stares at his prosthesis, riveted. She stops abruptly. Her forced smile evaporates instantly. Alexis is visibly repulsed by what she sees. Her shoulders sag; she closes her eyes for a moment and works hard at steadying herself.

Seth is completely unprepared for her reaction. He's suddenly embarrassed and self-conscious and quickly hides his prosthesis behind him.

Alexis opens her eyes and steps closer to him, bends forward, and gives Seth a weak hug while pressing her cheek quickly to one side of his face and kissing the air. Avoiding the chair that Seth has offered next to him, she sits directly across the table, which is the farthest chair from Seth.

Feeling awkward, Seth sits down. Alexis looks around the room apprehensively. Her eyes are looking everywhere but at him.

Despite how self-conscious Alexis made him feel just now, Seth is still elated to see her. He can't help himself. He wants desperately to get past the moment's clumsiness, and he works at being buoyant. "You really look great, Alexis. You're all I thought about on the plane home from Germany."

Immediately, the girl is defensive and pouty. "About Germany . . . I'm sorry I stopped writing. It was mean of me, I know."

"It's okay," he reassures her. "I understand."

"I just didn't like thinking about it. You know . . . your little accident," and she looks down at the table, "and what it must feel like now to be an invalid and everything." She lifts her head and looks past him. "It was just too awful to think about. So I stopped . . . just stopped writing. Do you forgive me?" she purrs.

Although stung by her invalid comment, Seth's reply is neither harsh nor condemning. "Sure I do. Please don't make a big thing out of it. I'm just happy to see you."

Alexis begins patting her eyes with a Kleenex she has plucked from her purse and smiles weakly at him. "You're always so nice, Seth, the perfect gentleman in every situation. I must look a mess." She fishes in her bag, finds her compact, checks herself in the mirror, frowns, fusses with her hair, and continues talking, airily, "I'll just never understand why you enlisted."

"I thought it was the right thing to do. We talked about it," the man responds evenly.

Clicking her compact shut, she retorts, "But you'd finished grad school—graduated first in your class. Everybody wanted to hire you."

Seth calmly observes her. "It wasn't about jobs or money, Alexis. I felt it was the right thing to do."

Alexis is petulant. "Right thing! Right thing, Seth? What could possibly have been right about it? Look what's happened to us. Nothing's perfect anymore. You gave up everything on a whim."

"It wasn't a whim. And I didn't give up anything. I just postponed things for a while."

"Daddy wanted to hire you," she pouts. "You would've started as a Vice President with his company. It'd been so much fun."

Seth remains calm. "I met a lot of great men and women in the Army, Alexis. All of them were outstanding soldiers. I'm glad I volunteered."

"At least someone's glad about something!" she snaps.

"You knew I wouldn't work for your father. He runs a great company, but I had plans of my own. I thought we agreed on this."

"Of course I remember. I'm not senile, you know. I thought I could change your mind, that's all."

Seth maintains his composure. "The important thing is that I'm home."

"You're just so stubborn, Seth," Alexis chides. "Things could've been perfect. Why can't you understand that?"

Seth doesn't reply. He simply nods his head slightly and continues looking at Alexis, measuring her and thinking about what she said.

She sighs, "I was proud of one thing though. Daddy showed me the story in the paper. You got a medal for saving that guy. My girlfriends were *so* jealous when I showed them." She points to his uniform and asks glibly, "Which one is it? The medal you got for saving that guy?"

Seth is reserved about her request. He shows signs of impatience. Alexis is blithely unaware of this. "It's this one," he answers, emotionless, "the Distinguished Service Cross. He wasn't a guy, Alexis. He was a soldier."

Coquettish and flippant, she presses, "Tell me what happened. You know, the day of your little accident. Just leave out the gory stuff, okay?"

Clearly uncomfortable with her request, Seth shifts in his chair and says, "I'd rather not talk—"

Alexis's cell phone chimes. Holding up one finger to Seth as if saying, "Hold that thought," she hunts for her cell phone in her purse, pulls it out, and a smile broadens across her lips as she reads the text message. Alexis taps a quick reply. Smiling and pleased with herself, she finishes her text message and places the phone next to her on the table.

Looking at Seth again and raising her eyebrows, coaxing, she asks, "So? Are you going to tell me what happened?"

"It's not something you really want to hear about."

"It is too," she says, frowning.

Relenting, Seth begins reluctantly, "All right. It started off like any other day—"

Alexis's cell phone sounds again. She shrugs and answers it. She listens intently, giggling several times.

"No way! Can you believe it?" she snickers. "Listen, I'm a little busy right now. Call you back in a few. Ciao!" Alexis ends the conversation and keeps her phone beside her. Smiling vacuously at him, she says, "Sorry 'bout that. There's just *so* much going on in my life right now."

The waitress returns and sets the malts on the table: the vanilla in front of Alexis and the strawberry in front of Seth. They have straws in them. She offers Seth a friendly smile and asks sociably, "Anything else? Sure you don't need wings?"

Seth gives her eye contact. "No, but thanks for checking again," he says. The waitress smiles at him and she glances at Alexis, then turns and leaves.

Annoyed at the waitress, Alexis complains, "She could have been more polite. She's just a waitress." Then grimacing and pointing at her malt, she demands, "What's this?"

Surprised by her question, Seth simply says, "A malt . . . French vanilla . . . your favorite. I remembered how you like 'em, not too thick."

"I *can see* it's a malt Seth," she says with disgust. "I wouldn't drink that—the carbs! Why would you remember such a little thing anyway?" Ungrateful, Alexis shoves the malt away.

Seth stares at her and answers quietly, "I remember everything about you, Alexis."

"Ohhh, that's so sweet," she coos, patronizing him. "Now, tell me about the day you had your little accident, won't you, *pretty please?*"

The man finally loses his patience and barks sternly at her, "Stop it, Alexis. Stop it now!" He lifts his prosthesis in plain view of her. "This was no little accident. That sniper intended to shoot me. That's what they enjoy doing—shooting and killing American soldiers. Not guys, Alexis, *United States soldiers!*"

The girl bursts into tears. She is genuinely frightened. "Keep it away from me," she cries.

Seth lowers his prosthesis below the table. He already regrets he'd lost his temper, something he rarely did.

Alexis is hanging her head, dropping her eyes to the table, and sniffling. She fishes another Kleenex from her bag and blows her nose dramatically. "You don't have to be mean to me, you know." She pats her eyes, tearfully explaining, "You just don't understand. It took all of my courage to come here today . . . I mean . . . things just aren't perfect anymore . . . and . . . and you might as well know, my life has taken a different direction now." Sounding little girlish, she stammers pathetically. "What I came here to say . . . what I'm trying to say . . ." Alexis is unable to complete her sentence. She stares silently down, trembling. Beneath her face a large tear splatters on the table.

Seth is crushed. He realizes that things are over between them. But neither harsh nor condemning in his tone, he says, as if comprehending it himself for the first time, "The truth is, Alexis, I'm not perfect. Not anymore. I'm an invalid in your eyes."

Alexis doesn't respond; she simply looks down at the table in silence.

"What you're trying to say," Seth continues, "is that things are over between us. We won't be seeing each other again. But you hope we'll always stay friends."

Too faint-hearted to lift her eyes to meet his, Alexis whimpers, "Y-yes . . ." Her cell phone sounds. She stares at it, biting her lower lip.

Seth knows she desperately needs a way out. He says evenly, "Alexis, it's probably best if you go now."

Relieved, Alexis grabs her cell phone and bag and quickly rises from her chair. Without looking at Seth, she turns and hastily walks toward the front door. As she leaves, she answers her phone, exclaiming in a near panic, "I just had the most awful experience ever!"

After she is gone, Seth continues looking in her direction a moment longer. He drops his head, heartbroken. He slowly raises his prosthesis, looks at it briefly, and lowers it again beneath the table. Considering his malt, he pushes it forward until it is even with hers; both are untouched. The light has grown darker in the room. As he sits staring at the malts, the twin screens above him begin flickering and come to life. Seth looks up at them. What the screens televise have nothing to do with sports.

On the left screen is Senator Abe Solomon, and a nameplate sits in front of him with the title "Chairman" embossed on it. He is a panel member with several other senators to his right and left. Senator Abe Solomon is in his early seventies, lean and stately, with a full head of gray hair and eagle-like gray eyes.

On the right screen is a documentary about American soldiers and their families. At this point in the documentary, there is a silent, continuous parade of slides moving across the screen, and each dramatic picture slowly follows the next, telling its own special story.

Sitting at a desk below and in front of the Senate panel is an executive of a prominent Wall Street investment banking firm. The Wall Street executive's nameplate reads "J. P. Horman." Beneath his name are the letters "CEO," and beneath the letters is the name of his firm, "Ghoulman Styx." Horman is pasty-looking with a pudgy pink face, weak chin, fat lips, a whiskery little round trembling nose, and small rodent-like ears. Shifty and conniving, his eyes are like two black BBs in a glass Petri dish that roll around crazily as he restlessly surveys the room. His head moves in quick, jerky motions, and he habitually rubs his hands together in little frenzied spates. The man is completely bald with the exception of a few threads of oily, black strands that are groomed with care and combed fastidiously to the left. Outwardly nervous and holding a large, once white handkerchief in his right hand, Mr. Horman continuously mops his face and head. He is dressed in an expensive black suit that nevertheless appears ill-fitting on him. Sweat bleeds outwardly from his shirt collar, staining the neckline. His tie is solid silver. There is a large glass of water sitting in front of him, and alongside it is a pewter pitcher with drops of condensation sliding down its sides.

His attorney, sitting stiffly to his right, is dressed completely in dark gray: suit, shirt, tie, and silk handkerchief. For some mysterious reason, this man cannot be readily seen, not completely. He remains a hazy figure, shrouded and opaque. Even in the glare of camera lights, he cannot be captured clearly. It's as if this man is from the netherworld and has the power to bend light around him and stay half hidden, outlined by the altered light but remaining a murky hulk, perpetually in shadow.

The gallery is crammed with spectators and reporters sitting in rows behind Horman and his attorney. The room is filled with news cameras rolling. The hearing is being televised nationally.

Senator Solomon begins formally. "Ladies and gentlemen, after that short break we'll continue now with Mr. Horman's testimony."

On the right screen is a picture of a soldier having dinner at home with his adoring family.

The senator focuses a laser-like stare at Horman and says sternly, "Mr. Horman, we've established that Ghoulman Styx sold billions of dollars of subprime mortgage securities to unsuspecting buyers, knowing full well the enormous risks they posed. Your firm never disclosed these risks. Even more dishonest, while pushing these risky securities on the public and extolling their value and safety, in reality, Ghoulman Styx was secretly betting these same securities would go down in value. In other words, it was selling them short. What do you have to say about this?"

Mr. Horman confers with his attorney, licks his lips, and answers innocently, "The term 'disclose' is a matter of interpretation, Senator. And I can honestly say that we believed in these securities. Remember Senator," he emphasizes, "they did come with the highest investment grade ratings from the most reputable rating agencies in the country."

Irritated by the man's demeaning testimony, Senator Solomon impatiently counters, "We've already established the rating agencies were being paid by Ghoulman Styx and the rest of the investment banking community for these so-called 'highest ratings.' Here, I'll quote from the earlier testimony of your former Senior Vice President of Marketing: 'We knew the ratings were completely bogus—bought and paid for—and those mortgage securities were nothing but worthless junk.'" The senator looks at Horman angrily and says accusingly, "Your firm reaped billions of dollars in profits, ultimately at this country's expense. These facts are undeniable."

A slide appears on the right screen of soldiers on a crowded dock, hugging and kissing and saying their goodbyes to their husbands, wives, children, and sweethearts.

After whispering heatedly to his attorney, Mr. Horman smiles unctuously; his anxious eyes roam the room. "In my mind, we did nothing wrong, Senator. We were fully convinced these securities were a sound and safe investment opportunity."

"You didn't believe that for one moment!" exclaims Senator Solomon lividly. "While you were dumping subprime securities as fast as you could on the public with high pressure sales tactics, your firm was secretly betting they would go down in value. You were selling them short as fast as you were selling them to gullible buyers. Ghoulman Styx never disclosed that material fact to the buyers. This was clearly an enormous conflict of interest and represented monumental, gross self-dealing at your customers' expense."

Failing to confer with his attorney, Horman responds combat–ively, "We at Ghoulman Styx didn't do anything wrong! We don't disclose our own trading strategies. Look here, Senator, every security is an investment risk. People take risks, and sometimes they lose. Losses are a fact of life. It's not my fault. I don't feel sorry for anyone. Why should I? Everybody knows we're in business to make money!"

Horman's lawyer is forcefully tapping him on the arm. The investment banker turns on him fiercely and freezes, instantly realizing he has made a serious mistake. Horman cringes in his chair, and curiously, appears genuinely frightened of his own attorney. The banker blots his head and face with his damp handkerchief and scrubs his hands together briskly, as if determined to wash them clean. His beady eyes dart wildly, and his little round nose pulsates rapidly.

Observing Horman with a critical stare, Senator Solomon says austerely, "Being in business to make money has never been the issue at all. It's *how* you make your money that's the issue. The 'how' is the only difference between running an honest business and running a crooked enterprise. Ghoulman Styx knows very well the difference between the two. Yet you and your partners, Mr. Horman, not only have chosen to live a life of moral turpitude, but you've also chosen to promote and reward it within your company. The dollar sign has become your soul's only moral compass, and it houses a needle that points to unbridled greed as its true north, south, east, and west. Poisoned by avarice, your firm nurtures a culture whose everyday practices are to mislead, betray, lie, and abuse customer trust. It is a business culture that borders on criminality and often crosses that border, in my judgment. I assure you, this committee will be thoroughly investigating these practices of yours over the next few months. And one notable thing more, Mr. Horman; losses are a fact of life for the rest of us, but Ghoulman Styx never lost, did it? Even when things went terribly wrong for you, the United States government, meaning the average taxpayer, changed the rules for your benefit and bailed your company out at one hundred cents on the dollar. Without the change of rules and the bailout there wouldn't be a Ghoulman Styx today. You'd be out of a job. All of you would be. Isn't that right?"

"I suppose so," a subdued Horman answers.

Senator Solomon continues harshly, "It is obvious to me and this panel that you have no regard for the millions of families that were wiped out financially because of what your firm did. You don't care one bit about your customers. You don't care one bit about the ordinary hard-working citizens who can't afford to send their children to college now. You have no feelings whatsoever for the many American citizens who are just hoping to hold on to their homes. Do you even think about the charities that can no longer fund their worthy causes because their endowments have been wiped out? All of this misery caused because of greed—your greed, Mr. Horman, and other people like you. What do you have to say to this?"

Horman confers dutifully with his attorney. There are agitated whispers and bobbing heads. Looking up, Horman offers a phony smile and replies in a buttery tone, "With all due respect Senator, I repeat, we did nothing wrong."

The right screen now shows pictures of soldiers riding in Humvees and deploying to the battlefield.

With open disgust, Senator Solomon says, "I just have a few more questions for you. Mr. Horman, how much money did Ghoulman Styx make selling subprime mortgage securities?"

After glancing at his attorney for permission, Horman answers, "Fifty billion dollars."

"How much money did Ghoulman Styx make betting these securities would go down in value?"

The investment banker smiles, rubs his hands together, and smacks his lips, "Another fifty billion dollars, Senator."

"One hundred billion dollars in all," observes Senator Solomon. "And how much money would Ghoulman Styx have lost if the taxpayers hadn't bailed it out?"

Horman suddenly becomes alarmed by the very thought of such a calamity. He mops his face nervously, jerks his head, and his little round nose quivers rapidly. Answering in a squeaky, high-pitched voice, he repeats, "If the taxpayers hadn't given us the money?"

"That's right," Senator Solomon says flatly. "I said if the taxpayers hadn't given you the money."

Turning ashen, Horman fashions a weak smile, clears his throat, and leans into the microphone, saying anxiously, "I believe, Senator, that figure would be one hundred and fifty billion dollars."

"A fifty billion dollar loss for Ghoulman Styx," the Senator summarizes succinctly. "Would your firm have survived such a loss, Mr. Horman?" Senator Solomon's eyes drill into the Wall Street executive, demanding the truth.

The investment banker bends into the microphone again. But

no longer is there a smile on his face of any kind, only a grim, gray countenance. He is physically sickened by the thought of financial ruin and the calamitous consequences for him and his partners. "No, Senator. It would have bankrupted us." He mops his face, licks his lips, and squirms uncomfortably in his chair.

"That's right," Senator Solomon says severely. "Ghoulman Styx, the wunderkind of financial engineering, wiped out completely. Financial engineering indeed! That term is nothing more than Wall Street code for disguising debt, swindling customers, and committing massive fraud. Your firm, and others just like it, turned the world's financial system into a global casino and usurped for yourselves the role of House, taking things over like a gang of riverboat gamblers carelessly wagering and wasting the savings of the unsuspecting masses. But even then, with everything stacked in your favor, your greed became too addictive, too insatiable, and, in the end, Ghoulman Styx overreached and was doomed. Despite your ill-conceived chicanery and your legions of smarmy MBAs from top universities, your firm would have been bankrupted by its own avarice if not for its rescue by the common, hardworking American taxpayer."

The slides on the right screen are now sobering images of soldiers huddled in fox holes, of men and women in uniform with bloody wounds and faces twisted in pain being rushed off the battlefield in stretchers with IVs hooked-up to their broken bodies.

The senator pauses and observes the investment banker who is now hunched in his chair and sweating profusely. "This hearing is being televised nationally," Senator Solomon says. "Here's your opportunity to make some redeeming statement to the American people for what you've done. Go ahead, Mr. Horman, in your own words."

The picture on the right screen is now a single slide of several dozen pairs of combat boots lying on the ground, laced and tied together in separate pairs with a tiny American flag stationed next to each.

Mr. Horman begins conferring with his attorney, whispering to him frantically and looking at him with fear on his face. His beady eyes bug and roll crazily. The investment banker takes a quick sip of water, clears his throat, adjusts his tie, taps the microphone, and slopes forward awkwardly. Horman's tone is revoltingly patronizing as he begins. "On behalf of Ghoulman Styx, I want everyone to know we believe in fairness and the American way. We believe in honesty and integrity and customer care. We believe people should pull themselves up by their own bootstraps. I know you've had to tighten your belts some. Trust me; I feel your pain. Here at Ghoulman Styx, we've taken dramatic steps to tighten our belts, too. We've suspended hiring summer interns, withdrawn every single job offer to spring graduates, and frozen the entertainment budgets of all of our junior executives. Why, we even fired one third of the waitstaff in our executive dining room. In these trying times, I can sympathize with all Americans. And to show you how much I really care about all of you and your families, I want to say that I'm very grateful today to have this opportunity to talk to you and to personally thank everyone out there. So let me say right now, thank you; thank you all from the bottom of my heart for my twenty million dollar bonus this year. Of course, I wanted more. I deserved more! But, in these trying times, I believe all of us good people must sacrifice and share in the pain together. Because in the end, we're just one big, happy family, aren't we?"

The Wall Street banker leans back from the microphone and sinks into his chair with a moony grin, satiated with self-satisfaction. Swiping his sweaty bald head, he glances nervously at his attorney, hoping this dark figure approves of his performance. The banker is relieved by what he sees and, positively glowing now, stuffs his handkerchief into his pants pocket.

Reaching over, Horman's lawyer gives him an affectionate pat on his lapel, leaving his hand on his coat as if comforting him. In the bright camera lights, the spectacle of this hand reclining on Horman's suit is frightening; it is scaly with stiletto nails curved claw-like. Appearing more reptilian than human, it looks to be part of something prehistoric that crawled out of the ancient shallows one primal afternoon to tan on the volcanic sand and wait, motionless, for a meal. There on the front edge of his coat, crouched croc-like and playing its deadly game of possum, the lawyer's appendage basks on the bank of the soft fold of the banker's tailored suit, slyly still, sunning itself and soaking up the man's soul, while Mr. J. P. Horman sits comfortably in his chair, beaming stupidly.

The right T. V. screen now shows a picture of row after row of American flag-draped coffins.

Senator Solomon has listened closely to Horman's speech to the nation. He is thoroughly appalled and says with disgust, "In my thirty years in the United States Senate, I've never met anyone who is as devoid of personal scruples, business ethics, and human compassion as you, Mr. Horman. Like so many privileged professionals in this country, you've let love of money and a systemic corruption corrode your soul. The kind of concentration of power you and your cronies enjoy is very dangerous and always leads to abuse. Now, we must hold the criminals accountable for their crimes because accountability is essential to democracy. And we must correct the system that spawned them. Because if we don't do both, the same thing will happen again and again. I have one final question for you, Mr. Horman. How can you possibly sleep at night?"

Horman looks agape at the Senator, surprised. He doesn't think he heard the man right at all. With beady eyes bewildered, the investment banker saws his hands together in a quick spate, jerks his head sideways, and pokes his quivering nose into the air, sniffing. He is truly perplexed by the Senator's question, and repeats, mystified, "How do I sleep at night? I sleep very well, Senator. Why wouldn't I?"

The left screen freezes with a frame of Horman's perverted face, black eyes, and quivering nose filling the screen.

On the right, the slow moving slides now show stark images of row after row of white markers over the graves of brave, fallen American soldiers. Their memorials show that these men and women were of many different faiths: Christian, Jewish, Islamic, and more. There are several slides of families in mourning. They are standing at the grave sites praying, hugging, and crying. Babies are held in the arms of most, and small children cling to their mother's dresses. The final image is of Arlington Cemetery from a long distance, showing the enormity of the cemetery and the thousands upon thousands of white markers set against an emerald green lawn on a cloudless, bright blue day. It is serenely beautiful. The slide show ends with this frame remaining on the screen.

Lost in uneasy thought, Seth gazes at the right screen. Doubts about his choices and beliefs had crept in some months ago while he was recuperating. Seth had not been truthful with his mother about his injury. He remembered, quite clearly, what it felt like to have his hand blown off by a high-powered bullet. After blacking out initially from the shock, he had woken up and found himself lying on the ground in a small depression with the battle still raging around him. The depression provided just enough cover if he didn't budge, and even with that, bullets whizzed past his head and kicked up dirt only a few inches beyond. He had lain there for hours in agony before the field medics could finally get to him. He was fortunate he hadn't bled to death.

His injury proved problematic and required numerous painful operations over several months. The rehabilitation process had been long and excruciating. When he wasn't doing rehab, Seth passed the long hours in the Army hospital in Germany watching U.S. cable news programs and documentaries on T.V. He was disgusted by the sight of corporate executives flying to Washington in their company jets, and with hats in hands, snaking their way up to Capitol Hill and begging for billions to keep their businesses afloat. He was appalled by the support they received from government regulators who had failed in their duty to protect the public. He was equally appalled by politicians who gave these executives all they asked for and more without demanding real answers or accountability. No doubt, this was because many of these congressmen and department secretaries were former classmates, frat brothers, and business colleagues of these rogues, and a number of them still belonged to the same country clubs.

These self-important men had left their comfortable mansions snug and secure behind thick walls in gated communities to fly to Washington in their private planes to plead pathetically. Until recently, they had seen themselves as the chosen few, who in a faint blue haze of aromatic cigar smoke, swirled, sniffed, and sipped Napoleon brandy after a pleasant evening of feasting on pheasant under glass. Congratulating themselves for being brilliant, they opined reasonably on the misguided missions and misspent monies on social safety nets for the poor in society, all of which amounted to nothing more than reckless public spending that must stop.

It was these same egocentric men who were now elbowing and bullying their way frantically to the front of the welfare line for a government bailout with cold panic in their eyes.

Seth could see no difference between corporate welfare and social welfare except the shamefully obvious: corporations got more—a lot more—and the executives kept their jobs, kept their mansions, and kept their fortunes whole, while workers lost everything. He was sickened by the hypocrisy that these very same executives, their companies restored through public assistance, were now demanding, "Get the government off our backs! They're mucking up our companies and our compensation schemes!" He had asked himself, "Could their companies have been any more mucked-up than they already were before these executives came wailing with gnashing teeth to the public trough crying for mercy?" Reading about their stories, it was clear to him that these corporations had come to their sorry ends by their own devices after years of mismanagement when there was no government involvement. Their own smart executives, with golden parachutes strapped tightly to their backs, had run them into the ground, destroying the business, destroying jobs, pensions, and livelihoods, while executives floated to earth safe and secure. But in the end, the problems these executives created were so large, even they found themselves bereft of golden parachutes, and thus bereaved, looked and sounded like everybody else who needed help, even in their Italian suits.

Seth remembered studying the economic theory of creative destruction in free markets. Someone really smart at some fancy university had gotten a Nobel Prize for devising this theory. He knew all of these executives who had pounded on the table for public relief counted themselves strident capitalists who con-scientiously championed creative destruction. Creative destruc-tion, a Darwinian acceptance that free markets, like nature itself, evolve, and with their evolution comes the inevitable destruction of old, inefficient companies and the loss of jobs that went with their rightful extinction. These businessmen had reveled in the sophisticated vision that creative destruction was not only inevitable in free markets but also a necessary, beneficial, and progressive feature of free markets: the economic equivalent of older species who couldn't adapt being replaced with newer, smarter ones that could. Sure, many of the erstwhile employed would never find good jobs again, but this simply meant it was their appointed time on the evolutionary clock to stumble into their own version of the La Brea Tar Pits. These pirates of industry felt it was a small price for other people to pay to ensure the progress of markets and society. As technology advanced and demand shifted from a lower to a higher skilled labor force, new, superior paying jobs replaced the Jurassic occupations of the past. It was inescapable; it was unavoidable; it was Darwinian; it was progress!

Seth knew these executives in their custom-made suits steadfastly believed in creative destruction right up until the very moment that their own inevitable date with destruction arrived. But then they quickly rationalized that this enlightened, creative destruction talk was all right for everybody else but certainly not for them. They were the privileged few who were entitled to have their princely positions preserved as a matter of public policy at public expense for the public good. After all, as a society, we needed them, they told us. It was plainly apparent to Seth that these aristocratic executives had paid and politicked to preserve a playing field that should have been even for everyone but in reality had been duplicitously tipped in favor of their species. They had rigged evolution and shrewdly sidestepped their own appointed plunge into the tar pit. The problem was, he thought, now saved, who's to say these derelict, meat-eating dinosaurs wouldn't bloody the ground all over again? If history was to be believed, he knew they would. Left to survive and roam loose on the landscape, these T-Rex relics would still go lumbering about the countryside feeding on the flesh of whole communities.

The young man feels Senator Solomon is right: accountability is essential to democracy. But it didn't appear to Seth that anyone in authority or leadership took responsibility for anything, except when it came to collecting rapacious bonuses or generous stock grants or juicy dividends or fat campaign donations or kicking the can as far down the road as possible. They were all cronies, and the system stunk to high heaven. It also occurred to him that accountability is much more than essential to democracy, it is essential to morality. For without accountability as an uncompromising minder meting out swift and certain consequences for immoral acts, people will be guided by impunity, and when people are guided by impunity, people will do anything. Seth angrily thinks, "United States soldiers on far away battlefields are dying for men like these! Why?"

At this moment in the sports bar, Seth feels the America he had grown up loving has somehow gone astray. This is not the America he believed in and fought for alongside his buddies. What happened to the country that stood for freedom, democracy, equality, fairness, humanity, morality, charity, sacrifice, and the common good? He believes the country has gotten itself lost, just as he himself feels lost. "Is it possible I've only been fooling myself all of this time?" he asks himself. This morning, deep down, he knew Katie was telling him the truth about Alexis. But he had refused to admit it to himself—he hadn't wanted to face the reality of it. If this were true, then maybe he had been fooling himself about the reasons he volunteered in the first place. Had Alexis been right after all? Had he given up everything on a whim? Or worse, had he given up everything on a myth? Had all of the sacrifices been in vain? These thoughts were crushing him.

While Seth is gazing at the screens and having these troubling thoughts, the left screen goes dark and Horman's distorted face disappears. The right screen remains on. Seth rises slowly from his chair and picks up his beret. His eyes are cast downward, his heart is broken, and his spirits are smashed. He places more dollar bills on the table than are necessary. He stands and stares at the field of white grave markers that speak solemnly and eloquently of the brave souls slumbering beneath America's most sacred ground. The young soldier fixes his beret on his head, straightens to attention, and soberly salutes his fallen comrades.

Seth turns and, weighed down by a fresh burden of doubts, makes his way to the front door. As he leaves, the frame on the right screen vanishes, and the white markers disappear into a golden eternity. The establishment is nearly empty of patrons.

CHAPTER THREE

Seth stands before the front door of a small cottage. The porch light above the door is shining down on him. The light is soft and welcoming.

He gently knocks on the door. Seth hears a lock turning, and the door opens slowly. Standing before him is a diminutive Japanese man in his mid-eighties. He is slightly stooped and wearing simple, loose-fitting clothes that are in harmony with the peacefulness the old man radiates. The moment the man sees Seth, he smiles broadly. There is a mixture of tremendous joy in his eyes and pride on his face. Seth smiles back at him warmly. This gentleman is Mr. Nakamura. Since he was a boy, Seth has looked to him as his teacher and mentor.

Bowing in Japanese tradition, Seth greets him respectfully. "Shishou," he says quietly.

Mr. Nakamura returns the bow. "Deshi," he replies softly. After this short ritual, Mr. Nakamura steps forward and takes Seth's hand in both of his. He retains a Japanese accent, but speaks English quite well. "Welcome home, Seth. You honor me with your distinguished presence. It has been too long, surely."

"And you, Mr. Nakamura, honor me with your kind words and generous friendship."

Mr. Nakamura nods approvingly. "Please, come in." Stepping aside, he motions for Seth to enter his home. Seth slips off his shoes when he steps inside the doorway. His teacher leads the way through his small cottage, which is neatly and sparsely appointed. The rooms are decorated with simple, beautiful Japanese furnishings that are meant to calm and inspire reflection and tranquility. There are vases of varying sizes and shapes and colors that array the rooms. All are filled with many of the same kind of lovely roses that were in Mrs. McAllister's kitchen for Seth's homecoming. But here there is a greater variety, including Abraham Darby, American Beauty, and Blush Rose in a multitude of vibrant colors in deep red, soft pink, cream, yellow and multi-colored hybrids, all raised in Mr. Nakamura's greenhouse, which is an ever-changing habitat for new botanical creations and a testament to the man's horticultural genius.

As the senior gentleman makes his way with Seth following, the young man observes with concern that his esteemed teacher has become noticeably frailer since he last saw him two years ago. The elderly man leads Seth to an inner room with a small table and two chairs. On the table is a pot of hot tea and two white porcelain cups with colorful red and gold dragons hand painted on each.

"Please, please have a seat, Seth."

Seth bows, thanking him, but considerately waits for Mr. Nakamura to sit first and then takes a seat himself. Mr. Nakamura begins pouring tea in the delicate round cups. While he is serving the tea, his intelligent eyes shine with pleasure at the sight of Seth.

Mr. Nakamura says, "I remember when your wonderful mother, Mrs. McAllister, first brought you to my studio. You were only nine years old. You wanted to learn the art of origami, so she brought you to me," and he smiles and chuckles, recalling that first day.

"Yes, I remember too," Seth says.

Mr. Nakamura continues, "In a short time, you became my best pupil. In a few years, you exceeded the talents of your poor teacher." He laughs quietly again as he remembers, his penetrating eyes fixed on Seth.

Seth politely raises his hand to protest.

Mr. Nakamura will have none of it. "Yes, this is quite accurate," he insists. "You were a true virtuoso. A person gifted by God with an artistic talent surpassing all others. I never saw the like of it nor do I ever expect to again."

Seth studies his beloved teacher and is concerned about the man's failing health. He answers, "Without my wise teacher's guidance, whatever talent I possessed would not have blossomed. You nurtured me like you do your prize flowers. Are you developing any new hybrids?"

Appreciating Seth's respectful reply, and with his eyes glowing and still focused on Seth, he responds enthusiastically and happily explains, "This year, I am working on something new—an Easter lily!"

"I know your new variety will be very beautiful," Seth compliments.

Mr. Nakamura nods gratefully and then changes the topic. He says, "I read about you. What I read made me very proud. You saved your fellow soldier. It was a selfless act of courage."

Seth does not readily respond to his teacher. Instead, his brow furrows, and his eyes are cast downward, troubled. The old man waits patiently and regards Seth with fatherly affection.

"You are troubled, Deshi?"

Seth answers, subdued, "Mr. Nakamura, I do not deserve this praise."

His Shishou observes him closely. "You are wearing the Distinguished Service Cross, second only to the Medal of Honor. It was awarded to you by a grateful country. May I ask why you feel undeserving of this recognition?"

There is anguish in Seth voice when he answers. "We were all soldiers together. The one who died was a good friend of mine. He had as much right to live and come home as I did."

With deep compassion, Mr. Nakamura speaks kindly to this young man for whom he feels such paternal-like love. "War is indifferent. However, this indifference does not diminish your individual act of courage."

Seth replies with growing distress, "Maybe war's indifferent. But God shouldn't be."

"I see," his teacher replies calmly. "In this, God has disappointed you?"

Seth is now edgy. "I didn't see Him on the battlefield, if He exists at all."

"Because you didn't see Him, you believe He wasn't there?" Mr. Nakamura gently inquires.

"I suppose—yes!" Seth responds with undisguised disillusion.

His mentor simply nods and gazes kindly at him. He waits patiently for Seth to continue.

Seth's eyes are full of pain as he explains, "Mr. Nakamura, I enlisted because I believed I was fighting the good fight, for a good country, for good causes. I couldn't just stand by any longer and let others do it for me. I wanted to do my part too. But now . . . now, I don't know . . ."

"What has changed your mind?

With torment mixed equally with confusion, Seth is fiery when he answers, "Why are we fighting? Who are we fighting for? Corrupt Wall Street bankers who loot the country? Crooked politicians who protect and profit by them? The powerful and greedy who steal billions yet go unpunished?"

"Not for the corrupt, Seth," Mr. Nakamura quietly replies. "You have fought for the freedom of your mother and your sister and for other people just like them."

Seth shakes his head in protest. "While the powerful keep piling up their vulgar fortunes? Wealth built on the backs of the dispossessed."

"The rain falls on the good and evil alike, Deshi. The sacrifice of gallant soldiers falls on the righteous and the unrighteous alike. But in the end, only the righteous receive righteousness, the wicked are vanquished, and God's scales are justly balanced for all eternity."

Still conflicted and his voice cracking, Seth replies, "But in the mean time, nothing's changed. What difference have our sacrifices made?"

With conviction and compassion Mr. Nakamura assures him, "A great difference, Seth, a very great difference. It takes a big sacrifice to preserve freedom. The sacrifice of each soldier—every wound and every death—is a weld fused in the shield that protects the people's freedom: their freedom to go about their everyday lives to school, to work, to play, to fall in love, to marry, to have children, to grow old in peace—all without oppression. Freedom is a precious gift, Seth. It is given time and again by the blood of courageous men and women. You are one of these. It is why you deserve honor. I am pleased to welcome you into my home. It is a great honor for me that one such as you is here. It is an honor for anyone." He leans back, gazing steadily at Seth.

Seth is despairing, "I thought more people would care."

His teacher nods his head in understanding and says calmly, "Many people care, Deshi. Others do not, to their great shame. But their shame doesn't concern the gallant. The gallant do what they do with no thought of changing the hearts of corrupt men or for the notice of fools and the feckless. Noble principles alone are their reasons. Sacred truths are all that matter to them. You understood this, Seth. It is why you volunteered. Do not ever forget that."

Seth continues to be deeply troubled. Mr. Nakamura regards him and quietly observes, "You are wrong to say that nothing has changed. You have changed."

Perplexed, Seth asks, "Have I? For better or worse, Mr. Naka-mura? I'd like to know at least that much."

"You have always been a good and gifted person, Seth. Nothing in this world could ever change these true qualities about you."

"But you said I've changed?"

"Yes. You have changed for the better."

"How?"

Mr. Nakamura pleasantly answers, "This is something you will discover for yourself, Deshi."

Seth doesn't understand. His wise teacher lifts his teacup and gestures to Seth to join him in a sip of tea. They each have a taste of the fragrant, jasmine tea. Then, Mr. Nakamura gently inquires, "What will you do now that you are home?"

Seth slowly shakes his head. "I don't know."

"That is a most reasonable answer for any young man of your age." The elderly gentleman pauses and then adds, "Trust God,

Seth. In time, He will reveal the reasons for the journey you are on. Of this, I am most certain."

Seth shrugs. "I have serious doubts about that, Mr. Nakamura."

"In Japan, we have a proverb: Do you need proof of God? Does one light a torch to see the sun?"

"I didn't save my friend," Seth says despondently. "The girl I loved was revolted by the sight of me today." He raises his prosthesis. "She was repulsed by this. We won't be seeing each other again."

The old man nimbly grasps his prosthesis, raises it, and declares with passion, "This is a symbol of great courage. It is sacrifice made tangible!"

"It's not so beautiful though," Seth says glumly, "and not so useful." He nods to his steel hooks. "Once, there was feeling here. Once, inspiration flowed through the tips of fingers and became beautiful images on paper. But there's no feeling in this steel. No art can come from it. It frightens people. It frightens me . . ."

Mr. Nakamura releases Seth and sits back in his chair. He folds his hands together on the table and gazes at the soldier. His voice is serene, and his words rise peacefully and with certainty from deep within him. "Your words are not true, Seth. Your art flows from your heart and always has. Because of this, it will flow as easily through steel as it did through flesh. Do not be frightened that your gift as a great artist is lost. God would not permit it."

With a bitter edge to his voice, Seth answers, "Why wouldn't He? If there is a God, He knows I seriously doubt His existence."

The gentle teacher studies the young man's face before replying softly, "God understands every person will doubt His existence at one time or another during the course of a life. But His patience and love exceed even our deepest doubts. There is a good reason why God brought you home, Seth. In time, this reason will be revealed to you. When it is, your faith will be renewed and become stronger."

"Faith?" the young man declares skeptically, "if God desires my faith why does He test me so?"

Mr. Nakamura considers the harshness in the young man's voice, and he answers with quiet certainty, "God does not test your faith, Seth, the world does."

There is a pause in the men's conversation. They take time to consider their exchange. They reflect and have another sip of tea.

The old man suddenly smiles broadly and becomes energetic. "I have a gift for you," he says. Mr. Nakamura rises unsteadily, walks with some difficulty a few steps across the room, opens a desk drawer, and retrieves a gift wrapped package. He returns to the table, places the gift on it, and sits down again. His eyes glowing with eager anticipation and gesturing to Seth, he says, "Please, please open it."

Seth nods his appreciation but is hesitant. "Thank you, Mr. Nakamura. I wasn't expecting a—"

Mr. Nakamura raises one hand to silence the young man. He motions again for Seth to open his present.

Seth begins to unwrap the gift. It is a small, thin leather case. He opens the case and discovers that it contains a set of expensive drawing pens and pencils, and a sheaf of extraordinary drawing paper.

Seth is humbled and truly grateful. "Thank you, Mr. Nakamura. The instruments are beautiful, and the drawing paper is exquisite. They are the finest I've ever seen. I don't know what to say."

Pleased, Mr. Nakamura graciously replies, "You have already said it, Deshi."

Halting and unsure, Seth stammers, "I truly appreciate your gifts . . . only . . . I don't know if I'll ever use them."

"We shall see, Deshi."

Seth glances at his watch. "I must be going. Mr. Nakamura, I appreciate the flowers you bring my mother every week. She loves them. She told me you brought extra ones today for my homecoming. Thank you."

"It brings me great pleasure; as do your mother's delicious cookies," he laughs. "Please tell Kathryn—Dr. McAllister-Mason now—that I am very proud of her. Please give your mother my best regards and thank her for me for her wonderful treats. Your mother is a very wise woman, a woman of uncommon strength, truly a remarkable person. She is to be greatly admired."

The two men rise and bow to each other. Seth picks up his gift and gestures with an acknowledging nod his appreciation again to Mr. Nakamura for his thoughtfulness. They walk to the front door where Seth's shoes are on the floor. Without hesitating, Mr. Nakamura kneels down on both knees to help Seth with his shoes.

"Mr. Nakamura," Seth protests, "no. *Please*, I can manage . . ."

Mr. Nakamura waves him off and looks up at Seth, serenely. "Please allow your ancient teacher this special honor." He carefully places Seth's right foot in one shoe, ties the shoe laces with care, and then repeats the action with the left. When he is done, he gazes up at Seth, offers his right arm, and says affably with self-deprecation, "However, now I will ask you to help this old man off the floor. Otherwise, he may very well remain here to greet the morning sun."

Seth smiles fondly at him and helps his esteemed teacher to his feet. The two men stand in the open doorway looking at each other affectionately.

"Follow your heart first, Seth. Soon after, the reasons will follow," Mr. Nakamura says.

Seth nods politely, but it remains plain to the old man that the boy is still troubled. "Mr. Nakamura," Seth says, "thank you for your abundant hospitality and your generous gifts."

"You are most welcome. Life holds many good things for you, Seth. Please return soon and honor me again with your presence, Deshi."

The young man bows, replying softly, "Shishou."

Seth turns and leaves. Mr. Nakamura watches him from inside the doorway until Seth is out of sight. Then he gently closes the front door of his cottage and switches off the porch light.

CHAPTER FOUR

Seth has returned home from Mr. Nakamura's. He sits at the kitchen table while his mother sets out dinner. Mrs. McAllister sees that her son is deeply troubled, and she is very concerned about him. Seth stands and pulls out her chair for her when she approaches the table. His mother sits, thanking him.

Mrs. McAllister inquires, doing her best to sound cheerful, "Did you visit Mr. Nakamura this afternoon?"

Without any life in his voice, Seth answers, "Yes Mom. He gave me that case on the counter. They're drawing pens and paper."

"He's so fond of you, Seth. I really believe he loves you like a son. Since our first visit to his studio he has taken a special interest in you. Being a great artist himself, he recognized your talent right away."

"I know, Mom," Seth responds listlessly.

"I think we're sort of his family in a way," she continues. "The poor man lost all of his own family in World War Two. I heard he came to this country shortly after the war ended and never returned to Japan. Still, Mr. Nakamura is a man of great faith."

Seth doesn't answer his mother. Distracted, he picks at his food.

Tentatively, Mrs. McAllister asks, "Did you see Alexis, dear?"

Seth's voice is hollow. "It's over between us." He places his prosthesis on the table. "She couldn't handle it, Mom. That's all there is to say."

"I'm so sorry. I know you had great hopes for her."

"So much for hope," he says, heartbroken and bitter. Seth nods towards the prosthesis. "I should have expected it, given the way I am now."

His mother's heart breaks for him. She says lovingly, "I see the same Seth I've always seen, and I'm truly thankful."

Seth's voice is tense. "But things have changed. They've changed a lot. We both know that."

"Life wounds every person, son," she replies quietly. "It's what we do with our wounds that matters."

"Mom, I know you mean well. But this is reality." Seth has become more upset and strains for emotional control.

His mother speaks gently to him, "Son, nothing is different about your true self. Your injury doesn't define you. Only you alone do that. When you stop thinking of yourself as wounded other people will too. They'll only see the person you believe you are, the person you know you are. They'll only see the same person that I do."

He shrugs dismally, "I wish that were true." The young man suddenly holds up his prosthesis and cries out in anguish, "Mom, what girl is going to love me now?"

With the profound love that only a mother feels for her hurting child, Mrs. McAllister says softly, assuring him, "The right girl, son . . . the right girl."

CHAPTER FIVE

At the same moment that Mrs. McAllister is looking at her anguished son over dinner, sitting at another kitchen table across town is a thin man of average height with lanky features, an Armenian nose, flaring ears, and a prominent Adam's apple that bobs emphatically in his long neck whenever he swallows. He has kind eyes that radiate quiet patience and compassionate wisdom. This man is fiftyish, Anglo, and his name is Father Michael. Father Michael is well known throughout his parish for two principal things: his unending benevolence and his voracious appetite. His parishioners dearly love him and think it is a small miracle that the man never gains an ounce.

This priest talks amiably to a plump and pleasant looking Mexican woman of about his same age, whose long, black hair is carefully fixed in a tight bun. She wears a colorful apron and busies herself at the stove. The kitchen has a rich Mexican décor with a heavy Catholic theme; there are crucifixes on several walls including a large cross above the stove, images of Jesus, Mary, and Joseph, and a prominent photo of Pope John Paul II neatly framed and sitting in a place of honor on the counter by the refrigerator. The long, tiled counter next to the stove is filled with individual slices of tres leches cake and numerous cinnamon churros, a favorite Mexican pastry, on small paper plates. There is a shiny stainless steel coffee pot on the counter steaming with fresh coffee.

The priest sits near the end of the table close to the stove. He indulges in a piece of cake and drinks a large mug of coffee. There are several empty paper plates scattered next to him on the table, proving the priest has enjoyed more than one serving of dessert this night. The Mexican woman stands at the stove, leisurely stirring the skillet with a long-handled cooking spoon and occasionally checking the two boiling pots on the twin back burners.

"Yesenia, your tres leches cake is the best!" the priest says heartily. "And you can't get coffee this good anywhere else except down in Old Mexico."

"Thank you, Father Michael," replies the Mexican woman pleasantly. "Please Father, let me refresh your cup," and she pours the priest more pungent coffee. He smiles gratefully as she returns to her skillet.

"I can't thank you enough for all you do for the church," the priest tells her. "The bazaar is sure to be a much bigger success because of your casseroles, cakes, and churros."

"Do they know what damaged the roof?" asks Yesenia.

"The high wind from the recent storm," Father Michael answers. "There's just no money for it," he sighs. "The bazaar will help, of course. But wood's gotten so expensive. I've been told it'll take a full load of two-by-sixes to repair it. Still, God will provide."

With her eyes cast Heavenward, Yesenia nods solemnly and crosses herself reverently. She returns to stirring her skillet.

The back door of the kitchen abruptly opens. Backing into the room is a Mexican man in his mid-fifties. He is approximately five feet eight inches tall, is heavy set, and has round facial features, deep-set eyes, and wavy black hair laden with streaks of gray. His face is lined and weathered from working outdoors most of his life. He wears khaki work clothes and an old, battered, and soiled fedora. His name is Humberto Hernandez, husband to Yesenia.

Humberto is turned away from his wife and the priest and is speaking heatedly on the phone to the other person, really giving him a good chewing out. The priest is shocked. The woman is shocked. In a panic, Yesenia quickly moves the iron skillet to a cold burner and rushes to the priest, clasping her hands over his ears. Horrified by her husband's language, she presses the priest's ears tightly, turning them white, and hopes she blocks out any sound of Humberto's voice.

Still facing away from them, Humberto is completely unaware anyone is in the kitchen behind him. "And if you don't send it back first thing Monday morning," he says harshly, "I'm going to run your skinny, brown behind all the way back to Mexico! What will you do then? Hey!" Humberto is all but shouting.

The voice on the other end is passive and submissive. He speaks with a bit of a lisp and with an effeminate signature. On the receiving end of the heated words is Juan-Carlos. Juan-Carlos is the receptionist, secretary, bookkeeper, office manager, and interior designer for the Humberto Hernandez Design and Construction Company. Juan-Carlos also performs special projects, as needed.

"Yes boss." Juan-Carlos says meekly, "Boss? I'm a citizen now, remember? It's been two years."

Humberto grimaces and complains loudly into the phone, "How did the idiot gringos ever let you become a citizen?"

"You boss," Juan-Carlos explains plaintively. "You make every–one who works for you go to class to become citizens. I went to class to become a citizen, just like you said." Then he proudly adds, "Thanks to you, boss, I'm the citizen!"

Humberto roars, "Then I'm going to un-citizen you if you don't take care of it first thing Monday morning! You hear me?"

Wearily, as though he's heard this tone many times before, Juan-Carlos replies submissively, "Yes boss. Monday morning. First thing. I will do this."

Humberto snaps his phone shut, slips it into his shirt pocket, turns around, and sees the priest sitting at the table with his wife pressing her hands tightly over the priest's ears. He looks at them quizzically and raises his hands, palms up, questioningly.

The priest's face has turned pale like his ears, and Humberto's wife looks mortified. Humberto is totally unaware that his phone language was offensive. Using his pet name for her, Humberto says to his wife in a tone of incredulity, "Yes, what is this?"

Staring stonily at her husband, Yesenia slowly releases her hands from the priest's ears that are now comically white, pats his shoulders reassuringly, and looks accusingly at her husband. "Humberto Hernandez! You should be ashamed—talking like that!"

"Like what?" Humberto asks innocently.

"And with good Father Michael sitting in our kitchen hearing every word." She looks at the priest apologetically, consoling him with another motherly pat. "And you know I don't like you using that G word. It's not nice."

Annoyed, Humberto says, "How was I to know this hungry priest would be sitting in my kitchen?" Turning to the priest, "How you doing, priest? What brings you around tonight? Hungry again, I see."

Yesenia glares at her husband and says cursorily, "Father Michael's here to thank me for my cooking."

Humberto pooches his lips together and observes, "Looks like he's sampling to me, Yes, not thanking."

Yesenia snorts at her husband and returns to the stove, busying herself over the iron skillet. Humberto doesn't pay her any mind. The priest has quietly been observing them. His customary pious look has returned; the one that his flock knows so well.

Wearily, Humberto pulls out a chair across the table from the priest and sits in it. Standing at the stove, Yesenia stirs her skillet and lifts the lid off one of the boiling pots, looks into it carefully, and stirs it too. She taps the long cooking spoon lightly on the top of the pot, replaces the lid, and turns her attention again to the iron skillet. Humberto takes off his battered hat and hangs it on the back of his chair. His cell phone rings. He fishes it out of his shirt pocket, agilely lifting it past the two stubby pencils that are stuffed beside it.

"Sí," answers Humberto.

"Humberto. Casey here. That idiot nephew of mine got the deliveries mixed up. Juan-Carlos just called me."

"I know, amigo," Humberto replies with an exhausted sigh. "His twin idiot at my place unloaded it without checking the order."

"I'll send the truck back with the right order. Pick up the other."

"Nah," Humberto says, "just as much our fault. Besides, we lost the job. Would've had to return it anyhow."

"Sorry you lost the work," Casey says. "Business is terrible. The Robinson's company went under, did you hear? That family's been in business over thirty years."

"No, I hadn't heard," Humberto responds, surprised. "I bought a lot of tile from them. Good people. You holding up okay?"

"Barely hangin' on to be honest, ol' friend. Down to the one truck from four. Applied for a loan. Got turned down flat. Funny, been banking there over twenty years. Never missed a payment on any loans before and don't owe them any money now. I know my credit's good."

"That doesn't seem to mean much these days," Humberto says. "I'll send the wood back Monday morning."

"Thanks. You've been a good customer, and better friend, for twenty-five years. You've always paid me on time, Humberto, and I always appreciated it. Receivables are running way behind now. I'll probably have to write-off quite a few of them. We'd be fine if I had a dozen more customers just like you. It's okay to bring the order back whenever it's convenient. It doesn't have to be Monday morning."

"Thanks, Casey, I appreciate it," Humberto tells him. "Adios amigo."

"Don't mention it. Goodbye amigo."

Humberto closes his cell phone, puts it in his shirt pocket, and sighs, thinking about his best friend, Casey. He surveys the kitchen scene, curious about what his wife is cooking and showing great interest in the desserts. Looking at the priest unassumingly, he says, "Hungry priest. Did you hear the one about the young priest and the old priest?"

In protest, Yesenia bangs her long spoon on the edge of the heavy iron skillet and glares disapprovingly at her husband. Humberto looks at her and says disarmingly, "Yes, this one's really harmless."

"It's all right, Yesenia," the priest says amiably. "I enjoy hearing a good joke about the clergy. Go ahead, Humberto, let's hear it."

Yesenia looks sharply at her husband and shakes her spoon at him. "Harmless? The man can't be trusted," she says knowingly.

Smiling, Father Michael waves her off. Yesenia huffs and pretends to focus on the skillet, but secretly listens very closely.

Having permission now, Humberto begins with relish. "A young priest is very nervous about hearing confessions for the first time. So, he asks the old priest to sit in, which the old priest happily does. The new priest hears a few confessions. After a while, the old priest asks him to step out of the confessional. The old priest says, 'Now I want you to cross your arms over your chest like this and rub your chin with one hand like this.' The young priest does these things. Next, the old priest says, 'Now, try saying things like: I see . . . yes . . . please go on . . . I understand . . . and, how did you feel about that?' The new priest recites these things perfectly. The old priest then advises him, 'Now, don't you think that's a little better than slapping your knee and saying, Holy crap! What happened next?'"

Humberto howls with laughter. The priest's first reaction is to laugh, but he quickly stifles himself and frowns. Yesenia bangs her cooking spoon several times on the rim of the iron skillet then points it accusingly at her husband. "You see? The man cannot be trusted! Humberto, you should be ashamed!"

Father Michael smiles faintly and says, "That was an interesting one, Humberto."

Yesenia scowls at her husband. "Perhaps if I feed you there'll be no room in your mouth for foolish words."

Humberto clasps his hands together, smacks his lips and says, "It looks like a feast tonight, Yes. And do I smell my favorite dish, chicken ranchero?"

She lovingly replies, "Yes, mi amor, you do." Putting a few things on a plate, Yesenia brings the food and places it on the table before her husband.

Humberto looks down with eager anticipation. On his dinner plate is a small green salad, steamed carrots, and four ounces of poached tilapia. His face drops, and he looks up at his wife, frowning. She smiles at him demurely. He demands, "Yes, what is this?"

"Your dinner, mi amor," she replies

"Dinner? A rabbit couldn't live on this!" he protests.

Patiently, Yesenia says, "Maybe not a rabbit, but you will have to, mi amor. The doctor says so."

Humberto thunders, "What doctor? A veterinarian?

"Dr. Fuentes. He's concerned about your weight and cholesterol. Tonight you start to eat the healthy way." Yesenia's pleasantness is quite irritating to Humberto, and of course she knows this.

Looking again at his plate, Humberto complains, "Healthy way? Eating like this will be the slow death of me woman."

Yesenia has anticipated all of Humberto's complaining and responds very patiently, "You will get used to it in a few weeks. The doctor says so. Tonight you begin. It won't do you any good to argue with me." She gives Humberto "the look," which means he can't win.

Father Michael watches, amused. Humberto, looking forlornly at his plate and then at her, begins bargaining, "Yes, a little more meat? With rice and beans, please? There's plenty."

"No," his wife says flatly.

"I see you made your special bread," he says gratuitously. Then flattering her, he adds, "*Only you* can make it so wonderful—a small slice?"

"No."

Becoming irritated, Humberto says, "Some coffee then? To wash down this food for rabbits!"

"No. You use too much cream and sugar."

Growing desperate, Humberto pleads, "Yes, surely a piece of your tres leches for dessert? It's my favorite." He pinches his thumb and finger to indicate a small portion. "Muy pequeño."

Yesenia scrunches up her face. "Certainly not! That's for the church. Besides, Dr. Fuentes says we need to tame your sweet tooth."

"Fuentes! Fuentes!" Humberto grumbles. "The man's a quack! Got his degree from the back of a comic book! I don't know why I call you Yes, Yesenia, when all you ever tell me is 'no'."

"It's not always 'no,' mi amor," she responds.

Resigned to his fate, Humberto picks up his fork, reluctantly takes a first bite, and makes a face.

His eyes twinkling mischievously, Father Michael asks, "Yesenia, I can't resist any longer. May I have some more cake and coffee, please?"

Humberto glares at the priest as Yesenia serves him more cake and coffee. Morosely, he looks down at his own plate.

Standing by the stove over the skillet, Yesenia casually asks Humberto, "Who were you fussing at on the phone?"

"Juan-Carlos," he replies dejectedly, picking at his food.

"Juan-Carlos? Why were you so angry with Juan-Carlos?"

"Casey's place sent the wrong wood. Juan-Carlos unloaded it without checking the order ticket. Makes no difference now, we lost the job anyway. I'm sending it back first thing Monday morning. I won't have any more work for the crew for at least another week."

"What was wrong with it?" she asks.

Humberto sounds exhausted when he answers, "I ordered two-by-fours. They delivered two-by-sixes. Juan-Carlos *always* checks the order ticket. I can't understand why he didn't do it this time. It's never happened before."

Father Michael and Yesenia immediately look at each other as if a miracle has taken place. Yesenia quickly crosses herself, the priest folds his hands, and they both look up towards Heaven, believing a prayer has just been answered. Humberto doesn't notice this, absorbed in picking at his rabbit food.

Overly polite, Father Michael inquires, "Did you say two-by-sixes, Humberto?"

Distracted by other thoughts, Humberto half-heartedly responds, "Yes, priest, lousy two-by-sixes."

Father Michael chooses his words carefully while Yesenia looks on, anxiously. "Hmm . . . well . . . you know Humberto, I've always admired our church's beautiful sanctuary. Being something of a carpenter myself, I've often said so. Your design was truly inspired. The detailing and finish are like works of art."

Humberto looks up from his plate and eyes the priest sus—piciously, asking in a low voice, "What do you want, priest?"

"Oh, nothing . . . nothing at all," the priest responds airily, rolling his eyes towards Yesenia. He continues, cautiously choosing his words, "But you see, Humberto, the church's roof was damaged by the high wind from the storm last week."

"What's that got to do with me, priest?" he asks flatly.

"Nothing directly; nothing at all as they say," Father Michael answers benignly. Yesenia looks on expectantly. She is scarcely able to contain her excitement at this moment. The priest continues agreeably, "But that's the reason for the bazaar tomorrow—to raise money to repair the roof."

"Good luck," Humberto answers, emotionless.

It becomes impossible for Yesenia to restrain her child-like enthusiasm any longer, and she bursts out, "It's not luck, mi amor! It's a sign! A sign from Heaven!"

Humberto drops his fork, annoyed and irritated. "What are you talking about, woman? Can't a rabbit eat in peace?"

"Don't you see?" she says enthusiastically. "The church needs two-by-sixes; Father Michael said so. It's a sign! Humberto, God sent you this wood!"

Becoming more aggravated, Humberto replies pointedly, "No, Yesenia. God did not send me this wood. It was sent by Casey's idiot nephew on one end and unloaded by a Mexican moron on the other."

"The good Lord uses the foolish and the wise alike," Yesenia replies reverently.

"Well said, Yesenia," Father Michael compliments.

Looking up at the ceiling in amazement, Yesenia continues, "This wood was delivered into *our* hands straight from Heaven. I know it was." She crosses herself with her cooking spoon and adds wondrously, "Thanks be to God."

Humberto, seeing how this is going and beginning to feel trapped, fidgets uncomfortably in his chair and becomes more animated. "Wait a minute. Wait a minute! Everybody just *wait one minute*! Now listen, Yesenia, there hasn't been any wood delivered into *our* hands. It's been delivered into *my* hands. And it's going back where it came from first thing Monday morning—to Casey O'Toole's lumber yard."

Casting her eyes upward again, Yesenia announces, awestruck, "It came from Casey's, but it was sent by God."

Rubbing the back of his neck, Humberto declares, "And I'd send it back to God Monday morning, but our truck doesn't make deliveries to the Almighty."

Staring at her husband, Yesenia calmly shakes her head, saying decisively, "No . . . you're . . . not. God sent you this wood for the church. And now Angel and Tomás can repair the roof."

Shocked, Humberto cries, "What, woman? You want my wood *and my crew?*"

"And why not?" she asks forthrightly. "There's no work for them next week. You said so yourself."

Humberto knows she's cornered him with words from his own mouth. He begins to panic. "Yesenia, you and this . . . this hungry priest are tricking me! Besides, we can't afford it."

"We've seen tougher times than these, mi amor," she replies patiently.

Yesenia puts her hands on her ample hips and stares at her husband. Humberto sags and slowly pushes his food around his plate, knowing he is close to defeat. Father Michael and Yesenia watch him closely.

Humberto attempts a last appeal, "We'll end up in the poor house, Yesenia. And what does it matter to this priest? He took a vow of poverty—the man likes being poor."

Yesenia's only response is to say gently, "I know you'll do the right thing, mi amor." She has a way of winning by simply putting her husband on his honor. She knows him so well. Humberto has always found this tactic of hers to be particularly irritating. Try as he might, throughout their long marriage, he's never been able to figure out a way to defend against it.

Humberto sighs dramatically and finally gives in, "All right, Yesenia. I'll think about it."

Yesenia and Father Michael clap their hands in joy. Yesenia hurries to her husband and hugs his neck enthusiastically. "Oh, thank you, mi amor por siempre!"

Humberto grimaces. "Yesenia, would you stop *hugging* me." Then trying to salvage some dignity, he adds, "And don't get so excited. I'm not saying I will, and I'm not saying I won't. All I'm saying is, I'll think about it." He sighs again and decides it's a good time to barter while his wife is in such a good mood. "Yes? It might help me decide if I could have some real food and maybe a churro, por favor?"

"Always bargaining, mi amor," his wife answers affectionately. "And using God and the church this time, you should be ashamed. No, querido. Remember, it's for your own good. I want you around for a long time."

Humberto pouts, "Why, woman? Just so you'll have someone to aggravate?"

Smiling at him lovingly, she replies, "Not just someone; *you*, mi amor por siempre."

Humberto is about to reply to his wife when the back door opens and in breezes a beautiful, energetic young woman in her mid-twenties carrying a folder in her hands. She is five feet six inches tall and slender with a graceful figure that she keeps modestly concealed. She wears a casual camel-colored wool dress that comes down to her ankles. It is as stylish as it is conservative and was purchased at a rare seventy percent off sale at an uptown dress shop. Complimenting her dress to perfection are the classy leather pumps that she picked-up from a resale shop at a remarkably good price. This lovely creature has large, intelligent, dark brown eyes and stunning black hair that falls in gentle folds and half-twists below her shoulders. Her heart shaped face has a comely straight nose, and her lips are exquisite twin waves with an inherent rose tint. She has flawless skin the color of alabaster and delicate hands with perfectly manicured nails finished in clear coat polish. Her makeup is practically nonexistent, as anything more would only detract from her natural beauty. But it is her smile that is totally unforgettable: it's like summer sunshine and as refreshing as spring rain. The term "like a breath of fresh air" was invented to describe someone just like her. Everything about this young lady is wonderful and uplifting and full of the optimistic energy of youth—she literally radiates the joy of life and infuses every room with it the moment she enters. This lovely young woman is Humberto's and Yesenia's daughter, Elena. She is the delight of their lives.

"Hi Mama! Hi Papa! Hello Father Michael!" She gives her papa a hug and a kiss on the cheek, leaving one hand lovingly on her father's shoulder. Humberto reaches up and pats her hand.

"Niña bonita," he says affectionately, "you're just in time to save me from these two."

Elena rolls her lovely eyes and dramatically bats her naturally long eyelashes. She walks to her mom, gives her a hug and a kiss, and stands next to her, facing the men, leaning casually against the counter.

"Need some help, Mom?" she offers cordially.

"No thank you, cariño."

"Poor Papi," Elena says sympathetically. "What are they doing to you this time?"

Humberto points to his plate and complains, "Elena, look at this. Your mother would starve me. And this hungry priest would bankrupt me."

Elena glances at her mother, eyes twinkling. "Oh, now I understand why you're so grumpy. Mama's started you on Dr. Fuentes' diet. It's about time."

"Niña, you've deserted to the enemy. And I'm not grumpy!"

Elena lightly dismisses her father's remark and addresses Father Michael. "Father, what is Papa talking about? Bankrupting him?"

Humberto interrupts, eagerly wanting to stake out his case first. "I'll tell you myself. That moron Juan-Carlos took delivery of the wrong wood. I ordered two-by-fours. Casey sent two-by-sixes by mistake. Juan-Carlos didn't check the order ticket—just signed the ticket and unloaded it. He's never done that before, but it could happen to anyone, isn't that so?"

Father Michael speaks cordially. "Elena, the wood's the wrong size for your father. But it's just the right size for the repairs we need for the church's roof."

"The damage from last week's storm and high wind?" she asks. "You mean Papa's wrong wood is the right wood for the church?"

"Yes, niña, yes!" says Yesenia breaking into the conversation excitedly. "It's a gift from God! Can these things be coincidence?"

Humberto says defensively, "Now stop, Yesenia. Stop trying to influence her. I would never try to do that."

Humberto pleads with Elena, "You see how they conspire? The wood was delivered by mistake. Now, this starving priest and your mother think God sent it to me for the church. If He had wanted this wood to go to the church, He would have sent it there in the first place, right? You can see it was just a little mistake. You agree with me, don't you?"

Yesenia quickly offers Elena a churro. She takes the delicate treat with her fingers and has a bite. "*Umm*, Mama, this is *so* good!"

Annoyed that his daughter is enjoying dessert that he can't have,

Humberto says impatiently, "Elena, enough about dessert. What do you think about the wood?"

Leaning against the counter Elena finishes off the churro, licking her fingers clean, relishing the taste, and smacking her lips just to tease her father. "Well Papa, let me see . . ." She folds her arms and furrows her brows, pretending to think hard. "You ordered two-by-fours. Mr. O'Toole's lumber yard got the deliveries mixed up and delivered two-by-sixes instead. You said Juan-Carlos has never made a mistake like this before. You can't use the two-by-sixes, but that's exactly what the church needs. Am I correct so far?"

"Yes, yes," her father says anxiously. "Just a simple mistake, you can see that, right?"

Yesenia frowns at Humberto for attempting to lead their daughter.

Elena purses her lips and furrows her lovely curved brows again, studiously focusing on the floor. Finishing her deliberation, she looks seriously at her mother, then seriously at the priest, and then seriously at her father. All of them look at her anxiously and wait for her pronouncement. Elena reaches her decision and says conclusively, "Papi, I think it's a sign."

Father Michael and Yesenia smile and nod knowingly at each other with pleasure.

"Elena . . ." her father whines, "I thought of all people my muchacha bonita would be on my side."

Elena steps over and kisses her father on the cheek and hugs him. "Papa, I'm always on your side," she says lightheartedly. Showing him the folder she brought with her, she changes the subject. "I brought you this government application. Would you look at it, please?"

"What is it, cariño?"

Elena takes a chair at the table next to her father and explains, "An application, an application to become a HUB."

"A what?"

"A HUB. It's a government program that can help your business."

"The best thing for my business is for the government to stay out of it," he says skeptically.

"Papa, please just listen for a minute," Elena says patiently. "HUB stands for 'Historically Under-Utilized Business.' It's for minorities and women owned companies. It gives them a better chance to compete."

Her father replies in a deadpan tone, "I don't need a HUB application, Elena. What I need is a HUM application."

"What's a HUM?" she asks intrigued.

"Historically Under-Utilized Mexican," her father replies.

Elena laughs out loud, appreciating her father's quick humor. "That was a good one!"

Humberto brightens. "If you thought that was good, I've got a new one about a young priest . . ."

Like she's ringing a bell, Yesenia bangs her long spoon several quick times against the heavy iron skillet, complaining loudly, "Humberto! Elena, you know better than to encourage your father."

Elena wrinkles her nose, grins at her father, and shrugs her shoulders. "C'mon Papa, I'm serious."

"I'm serious too, cariño. But leave the government forms. I'll look at them later."

"Promise?"

"Sure."

She raises her eyebrows and sounding a lot like Dr. Kathryn McAllister-Mason says, "You didn't say, 'promise.'"

"I promise."

"Thank you, Papi."

"Elena," Father Michael asks politely, "may I read about this government program?"

"Of course, Father." She hands him the file.

"Thank you."

"Priest," says Humberto, "there's not a government program for HUP: Historically Underfed Priests. They don't exist."

Father Michael smiles and waves his hand airily. After making a face at Humberto for that last remark, Yesenia begins wrapping individual cake slices. Elena gets up from her chair by her father and leans against the counter next to her mother while Father Michael becomes absorbed reading the documents. Yesenia opens the oven door and lifts out a large rectangular pan of chicken ranchero that she sets on the counter to cool. Immediately, the kitchen is filled with the spicy aroma of her husband's favorite dish.

Humberto spies it immediately and gestures toward the priest, saying petulantly, "At least that one won't be getting any of *my* chicken ranchero tonight. He stuffed himself on cake and churros."

The priest looks up from the folder, saying mildly, "Oh, but I did. I had some earlier. It was just wonderful, Yesenia. It'll sell like *crazy* tomorrow."

Yesenia says sweetly, just to annoy her husband, "This is my second batch, mi amor. And it's not *your* chicken ranchero, it's *mine*, and it's for the bazaar tomorrow."

Humberto grumbles and scratches his chin. He picks up the sports section from the newspaper that his wife leaves for him on the table every night and begins reading it. While studying the paper, he snaps it lightly and begins talking into it. "Elena, it's Saturday night," he says. "You should have a date. It's time you were married."

Elena looks at her mother and rolls her eyes dramatically. She's heard this from her father a thousand times before. Respectfully, she says, "Papa, when I meet the right boy I'll get married."

Still focused on his paper, her father continues, "What about that young man in medical school?" he asks. "Wasn't his name Jaime Gonzales or Morales or something?"

Elena sticks her finger in her mouth pretending to gag. Too absorbed in the sports story he is reading, her father doesn't notice his daughter's antics.

"Enrique Calderon?" Humberto says. "What about him? A lawyer, wasn't he?"

Elena sticks a finger in her mouth twice and bends over for emphasis.

Humberto lowers his paper an inch. Looking out over the top of it, away from the women, he stares ahead and thinks out loud. "There was a Robert somebody or other, too. Wasn't there?"

Melodramatically, Elena rolls her eyes, grabs her throat, and falls backwards into her mother's waiting arms as if she fainted.

Still unaware of Elena's antics, Humberto shakes his paper,

looks around, and turns to his daughter. Elena quickly pops up and assumes a serious demeanor before her father catches on.

"Papa," she says courteously, "Jaime Gonzales could have won first prize for being the most uninteresting man in the world. Enrique Calderon was a creep. He chased everything in a skirt. I wouldn't go out with him, not ever! And Robert Johnson was a very sweet boy, but so shy and lovestruck around me he couldn't even remember his own name."

"That's what happens to people who are lovestruck, niña," Yesenia says knowingly.

Elena winces. "Mama, that's ridiculous. Love doesn't do that to people."

"It's one of the signs, Elena," her mother says, nodding her head in confirmation.

"Forgetting your own name?" Elena says skeptically. "Maybe that's what happened in the olden days when you and Papa met, but not anymore."

Yesenia and Humberto exchange amused glances at "olden days."

Humberto comments, "You're so picky-picky-picky, niña. You have to give these boys a chance."

"The *right* boy will have a chance," Elena patiently responds.

Humberto continues his fatherly advice, "It seems to me all these young men were good marriage material. And it wouldn't hurt if you learned to cook like your mother. A man loves a woman who can cook."

"You're such a male chauvinist," his daughter teases.

Looking wistfully at the pan of chicken ranchero cooling on the counter, Humberto says, "I'm only saying, if you learned a few good recipes, like your mother's wonderful chicken ranchero,"—he nods and smiles at his wife—"the men would fall all over you."

"Thank you, mi amor," Yesenia says lovingly. "But the answer is still no."

Humberto grimaces and grumbles.

Elena laughs good-naturedly at them.

The priest studies the folder.

"Papa," Elena says, "I don't want men falling all over me. I just want one, the right one. And besides, I do have a fantastic recipe."

Her father is impressed. "You do? That's *good* . . . that's very *good*, muchacha bonita. What is this fantastic recipe?"

Lightly Elena replies, "555-840-9922."

"What kind of recipe is this?" he asks, perplexed.

Grinning at him, she says, "It's the best kind—the phone number for my favorite takeout."

Humberto frowns, "She gets that from you, Yesenia," he accuses.

Elena laughs and says, "Never in a million years could I cook like Mama. She spoils you so."

Humberto's tone is instructive. "All I'm saying, niña, is a young woman of your age can't be throwing away good prospects. You'll be twenty-six next year. Most American girls of Mexican heritage are married by that time."

Elena dramatically places the back of one hand to her forehead and laments, "Oh, no! Twenty-six! The other side of twenty-five and sliding helplessly towards the great abyss—thirty! My poor, sad, miserable life will be over with then." She pretends to sob mournfully. "And worse still . . . I'll be an old maid!" She sobs harder, playfully. "But even worse than that. Oh, the inhumanity of it all! I'll be—*sob!* I'll be—*sob!* I'll be an old American maid—*sob! sob!* Of Mexican heritage!" Wailing, she throws herself into her mother's arms.

Seeing no one is taking him seriously, Humberto gives up and says to Yesenia, "Woman, you see what kind of daughter you've raised?"

Her mother proudly places her arms affectionately around Elena's shoulders. "Yes, we both have a wonderful daughter who is smart, confident, and beautiful. She'll get married when she's ready and to whomever she chooses."

Humberto acts annoyed. "Well, marry who and when you want, niña. No one cares what I think around this casa anyway."

Elena grins, wrinkles her nose, and says respectfully, "Thank you, Papa. And I do care very much about what you think. The man I marry must have your approval." She walks to her father, kisses him on his cheek, and caresses his shoulder.

"Just promise me this: you'll marry a real man," Humberto says.

Exasperated with him, Elena asks her mother, "Is he always like this?"

"Pretty much," Yesenia answers.

Elena pats her father on the shoulder. "Of course, I'll make sure he rides a horse, wears a six shooter, and chews tobacco."

"That's good," her father comments amiably.

Dreamily, Elena muses, "Mama, I want to fall in love just like you and Papa did. It was like lightning striking, wasn't it? The moment your eyes met, you both knew."

Yesenia moves to Humberto and places both her hands on his shoulders, patting him lovingly. "I'll never forget. One night your father came to our neighborhood dance. The moment he walked in the door, I saw him. He was looking around the room, checking out all the girls," she chuckles, remembering. "Our eyes locked. He strode across the room to me and said, 'Let's dance.' He didn't exactly ask, and he didn't exactly demand. But I knew he wasn't going to take 'no,' for an answer." She pats Humberto's shoulder again. "You were so handsome, mi amor, and such a *good* dancer— the best!"

"And you were the prettiest girl in the room, Yes," Humberto recalls fondly.

Yesenia becomes wistful. "As we danced, I looked into his eyes and saw a man I could spend forever with. It was our first dance, Elena, and we've been dancing together ever since. I was hopelessly in love. And you were too, weren't you, mi amor? The lightning struck."

Humberto reaches up and affectionately places his hand on hers. "I fell in love with you instantly, mi amor," he says. "Sí, the lightning struck. It was only after we were married that I heard your roaring thunder. It's gotten louder every year," he teases.

Yesenia lightly raps him on his shoulder. "Usted!" she says, and walks back to the stove by her lovely daughter.

Elena laughs gaily at her parents. "Mama's right, Papa, you are a terrific dancer. I'm glad you taught me. None of the boys I meet are nearly as good as you. Most of the time, I have to teach them." Elena twirls around the kitchen dancing lightly on her feet and stops, bringing her delicate hands up to her mouth, laughing. "We had so much fun, remember? We won all the father and daughter dance contests."

Humberto smiles, remembering the many evenings he spent with his muchacha bonita in the kitchen teaching her every dance step he knew. As a little girl, she placed her feet on top of his shoes, and he danced her over the floor with her holding him tightly around his waist, looking up at him in her pigtails and smiling brightly. She was a quick learner. "Yes, niña, I remember it well." Humberto sighs and says to his daughter in an offhanded way, "Well, maybe God will deliver you a man. He seems to be delivering everything else these days."

"Listen to you, Papi," she teases. "You're such a male chauvinist. I don't know how Mama puts up with you."

"Me? A male chauvinist?" he says, surprised. "No, not me. What makes you say that?"

"You just said to me, 'Maybe God will deliver you a man. He seems to be delivering everything else these days.' *He,* Papa,—*He?* You see, that proves you are just a male chauvinist. What makes you think God is a *He?* Why couldn't God just as easily be a *She?*"

"God is male, daughter. He has to be. Everybody knows that," Humberto says conclusively.

Yesenia casually stirs the pot on the stove and pretends not to be paying any attention to this father/daughter discourse. Of course, she listens carefully.

Father Michael looks up from the folder he's been reading. This subject has caught his attention. Humberto notices that the priest is listening to them now.

"Priest," Humberto says, "maybe you can be useful here, and for once, earn your unjust desserts."

Elena laughs out loud again. Then she folds her arms, leans against the counter nonchalantly, and with her big brown eyes shining, she challenges him respectfully. "Okay Papa, I'll bite. Why does God have to be a male?"

"Priest," Humberto says, "Hebrews 8:12, what does it say?"

Father Michael answers, "Well, the Lord is speaking and the verse says, 'For I will forgive their wickedness and remember their sins no more.'"

"You see, niña, this proves God is male." Humberto folds his arms across his chest and smiles knowingly and contentedly.

"What?" Elena says incredulously. "Why that's ridiculous! That doesn't prove a thing!"

Annoyingly smug, Humberto answers, "Ohhh yes it does . . . it proves it beyond any doubt."

Aggravated with her father, Elena looks at her mother in disbe—lief and then back at her father. "Papa, you can be *so* frustrating sometimes."

Tending the skillet and without looking up, Yesenia says to anyone who is listening, "What do you mean, *sometimes?*"

Elena grins at her mother's comment. "Okay Papa," she says considerately, "I'll play along. How does that verse prove God is male?"

Looking like the cat that swallowed the canary, Humberto answers, "Cariño, the verse says, 'I will *remember* their sins no more.' God must be male because a woman may forgive,"—wagging his finger for emphasis—"but a woman *never* forgets." Now pointing at Yesenia, he adds, "*Especially* that one."

Despite herself, Elena grins, admitting with her body language that she knows her father has a reasonably good point. With her arms still folded across her chest, she begins slowly rocking back and forth trying to think of a clever comeback. However, realizing she is stumped for a quick-witted reply, she appeals to her mother for help. "Mama?" she says plaintively.

Yesenia glances at her daughter, unconcerned. She coolly looks at Humberto and continues slowly stirring the contents of the skillet. She is accustomed to his tricks. Yesenia says, "Maybe you're right, husband. Yes . . . now that I think about it, God must be male." She turns and points her cooking spoon at him. "Only a male would cause so much trouble by creating a mate that suffers hot flashes. Do you like living with that? It serves you right! It serves all of you right!" and she shakes the long spoon at him for emphasis.

Elena bursts out laughing. "Mama, that was terrific!"

Not wanting to be outmaneuvered, Humberto responds too quickly before thinking it through. He holds up his thumb and forefinger and pinches them nearly together. "One itsy, bitsy, tiny, little mistake, that's all."

Yesenia pounces, sweetly, "Ohhh, I see, mi amor, a little mistake?" She turns to the priest. "Father Michael," she asks innocently, "is God capable of making a mistake?"

The priest answers emphatically, "No child. God is infallible."

Coyly, Yesenia pinches her thumb and forefinger almost together and asks, "Not even an itsy, bitsy, tiny, little mistake?"

Again, the priest responds authoritatively, "Impossible!"

Cooing sweetly to tease her husband all the more, Yesenia says to Humberto, "You see, cariño, by your very own words you have proven that God cannot be male because God cannot make mistakes." Then pinching her fingers together again for emphasis and shimmying her hips slightly, "Not even one *itsy, bitsy, tiny, little mistake*. If God is *not* male, then God *must* be female."

Elena claps her hands for her mother. "Yay, Mama!"

Humberto moans, "You see what I have to live with, priest?"

Still, Humberto is not ready to give up. "Father Michael, what do you think?" he asks wryly. "Is God male or female? Catechism only refers to God in the masculine, isn't that right?" Humberto knows he has the priest trapped. Yesenia observes that Humberto is up to his tricks; it was the first time all evening that her husband had addressed Father Michael as Father Michael, instead of "priest."

Father Michael is hesitant to answer. He doesn't want to let the ladies down, but he knows he must answer truthfully. The priest looks at Yesenia, apologizing to her with his eyes. She simply smiles innocently at him. He decides to stall for time. "Well . . . of course, we've always . . . I mean . . . the Catechism of the Catholic Church teaches . . . traditionally the Church . . ."

"Please have another churro, Father Michael," Yesenia offers. She quickly puts the pastry in front of him on a paper plate.

"And more fresh coffee too," Elena adds and smiles charmingly at him as she pours a generous amount of the steaming liquid into Father Michael's mug. The priest nods appreciatively at the women and quickly takes a large bite of the pastry.

Humberto grimaces, but prods agreeably, "Don't let those two bribe you, Father Michael. Go ahead, you were about to say?"

With his mouth half full of the pastry, Father Michael lifts his eyebrows in surprise and says modestly, "Me? Was I about to say something?"

Desperately restraining his impatience, Humberto says, "Yes, yes—you were saying traditionally the Church . . ." and he motions, encouraging the priest to finish his sentence.

Father Michael looks at the women for help, who continue to smile sweetly at him in silence. He gulps his coffee to wash back the last bit of pastry which causes his bulbous Adam's apple to swim up and down in his throat looking like a whale as it plows ahead bowing the water before it, then answers cheerfully, "Oh yes . . . I remember now. What I was saying was that God is a Spirit, and therefore is neither male nor female in the human sense, although God might choose to be revealed as a male; and traditionally, when a priest is a guest in the homes of parishioners, the Church doesn't approve of them taking sides in a family's private philosophical discussions." As he finishes a small burp escapes from his mouth. "Oh! Pardon me," he apologizes and lightly pats his lips with his napkin.

Humberto scowls, "The conspiracy continues."

The women smile and nod their heads agreeably at Father Michael. Yesenia places another delicious-smelling, warm cinna–mon pastry before the priest as a reward, and he tips his head ap–preciatively.

Yesenia changes the subject and asks her daughter, "Elena, how's school? Are the children doing well?"

If Helen's was the face that launched a thousand ships in Homer's *Iliad*, Elena's was the face that launched a thousand hopes in the hearts of children. Helen of Troy did it once; Elena Her–nandez did it every day in her classroom. But Elena did much more than teach—she inspired her students to believe that they *could* learn. With all of her heart, she felt that every one of them was capable, if given the right opportunity, and she was determined to do just that. Because the school's budget was disgracefully paltry, Elena relied on her incredible teaching talents, creativity, energy, and imagination to give her students what she knew they needed. Every day she read aloud from a textbook to the classroom, engaged the children by asking them questions as she went along, and wrote words on the chalkboard for visual comprehension. To build their confidence, Elena played number games with them and created simple puzzles she knew they could solve. She cleverly put them into smaller learning groups that she oversaw and made certain each group had two higher performers paired with a counterpart who was struggling. This made learning a fun, collaborative effort where everyone showed progress and prevented classroom cliques from forming that were harmful to self-esteem. Elena tested her students regularly with little quizzes to stay current on where extra help and extra praise were needed. Most of all, she loved reading them classic children's stories that were set to music, like *Peter and the Wolf.* The children loved it when she assigned parts to them that they read aloud and acted out while the music played on the portable disc player—a disc player and discs that she bought for the classroom with her own meager salary.

On two weekends every month Elena had a standing arrange–ment with several other teacher friends who shared her dedication. Together, they took her entire classroom on field trips to local fire stations, the zoo, the Children's Museum, outdoor concerts, or special events at public libraries. None of this was ever entirely free, as there was always the need to pay for incidentals such as gas, food, drinks, and special little treats like snow cones and train rides, all of which Elena paid for out of her own funds. As a result of her "special calling," as she fondly described it, Elena was dearly loved by her students and completely broke. Living paycheck-to-paycheck, Elena was once thrilled that her checkbook showed a balance at the end of the month of a whopping twenty-five dollars. She laughed when she got her statement and saw that the bank had charged her a service fee of twenty-five dollars for failing to maintain a minimum monthly amount in her account, and her balance was reduced to exactly zero—again. Elena was relaxed, free, and easy about everything, and this was especially true about money. She didn't care about money. She cared about teaching, and her only concern was to put forth her best effort and give the most to her students. Like the miracle of feeding the five thousand with five loaves and two fishes, Elena worked a similar miracle in her classroom with the little she had at hand, feeding her students' appetite for learning and filling their eager minds with knowledge.

Appreciating her mother's interest in her students, Elena replies warmly and proudly, "Very well, Mama. I'm giving them a new assignment for Thanksgiving. They must write something that was special to them about the holiday."

"That's so nice, niña," Yesenia says.

In a caring, fatherly tone, Humberto says, "You spend the day teaching orphans, Elena, nights grading their papers and preparing lessons, weekends taking them on field trips. You don't make time for yourself, cariño."

"Papa," Elena says with feeling, "the children aren't orphans at The Children's Sanctuary. They're terrific children whose parents have failed them." With rising passion in her voice she continues earnestly, "These poor children are wonderful, but through no fault of their own, they've been neglected or abandoned or abused. It would break your heart to know some of their tragic stories." Elena looks at the priest with hurt in her eyes. "How can the world be so cruel?"

"It's terribly sad, child," Father Michael replies sympathetically.

"You've always told me to follow my heart, Papa. That's what I'm doing."

"I'm sorry, cariño. You're right," Humberto agrees. "It's wonderful work you're doing."

"We're both very, very proud of you, Elena," assures her mother.

"I just worry about you," her father says. "With your master's degree, you could be working around other young people like yourself, having fun, making more money."

Elena smiles tenderly at her father's concern and answers sincerely, "My heart's with the children. And I am having fun. There's time for money later. The children are out of time. They need me now."

Looking at his daughter adoringly, Humberto says, "The children are lucky they have you, niña."

Elena smiles back at her father, pleased that he is proud of her. She loves him very much.

"Elena, I'm almost done with the angel costumes," her mother says enthusiastically. "Would you like to see them?"

"Already? Of course, I'd love to see them." The two women walk out of the kitchen, leaving Humberto and Father Michael alone at the table.

After the women have gone, Father Michael says, "You have a lovely daughter, Humberto, and your wonderful wife is an angel herself. The church couldn't do without Yesenia."

Lowering his voice, Humberto replies guardedly, "They are the light of my life."

"Yes," the priest observes, "I see that they are. You have a very special family."

With suspicion laced with irreverence, Humberto challenges, "What do you want, priest? My wood and my crew aren't enough for one evening?"

Compassionately, the priest responds, "My son, the church needs you. Our parishioners respect you as a leader. The church owes its beautiful sanctuary to you. Won't you consider coming back?"

"The church owes me nothing! Leave it be, priest. Leave me be," Humberto answers bitterly.

The priest is not offended. He simply nods with understanding. Getting up from the table, he says, "Please tell your lovely wife and daughter I look forward to seeing them at Mass in the morning."

"I'll tell them."

Reaching the back door, Father Michael turns to Humberto and says with kindly concern, "You were once a man of great faith. I hope you haven't stopped believing."

Humberto's voice is harsh. "Not entirely, not yet, priest. That's what makes it so hard."

The priest nods sympathetically, turns, and leaves, closing the back door quietly behind him. Humberto is left alone sitting at the table, staring silently into space with a terrible strain on his face. He is remembering and mourning an unbearable loss.

o o o

After leaving Father Michael and Humberto in the kitchen, Yesenia and Elena enter the sewing room. They are sitting together on a small sofa and her mother is showing Elena a pattern. This is the second year Yesenia has made angel costumes for the younger children who are in The Children's Sanctuary's Christmas program. On a stand nearby is a completed costume with a wire halo so cleverly attached it appears to float.

"Mama, the children will love their costumes. They're just darling. Thank you so much," Elena says.

"I enjoy doing these things for the children."

"Mama?"

"Yes, cariño?"

"Papa seems better tonight."

"Your father's always better when you're here."

"Is it true?" Elena asks concernedly. "What he said? Men fall in love with women who can cook?"

Her mother chuckles at her daughter's innocent question. "Of course not, Elena. When your father was courting me, it wasn't the kitchen he had on his mind."

Surprised by her mother's candor, Elena exclaims, "Mama!"

Her mother laughs saying, "Men fall in love with us because we are women, and they are men. Still, cooking is a good thing when it comes to men."

"What do you mean?" asks Elena.

"They like the nurturing."

"The nurturing?"

Thoughtfully, Yesenia explains, "Men never lose their longing for a woman's nurturing. I suppose it makes sense when you stop and think about it, as much as anything can make sense about a man. We nurture them in our bodies, birth them into this world, nurse and bathe and swaddle them, sing them to sleep with lullabies, and kiss away their tears. Then, one day, they break away from us to follow their manly ways. But deep inside, the men, they never lose their longing for a woman's nurturing. That's why they like the cooking, niña; it's the nurturing."

Absorbing her mother's sensible words, Elena softly asks, "That's why you're such a wonderful cook?"

"Not only that," her mother says expressively, "it's another way I show love for my family. Preparing and sharing a good meal brings a family closer. Do you recall all the wonderful times we had around the dinner table together?"

"I do. I remember all of us laughing so hard at Papa's funny stories."

"Yes, niña, we enjoyed many wonderful times around the family table. When your father pesters you with his talk of marriage, please remember he only wants your happiness."

"I know he does."

"It's just that he is still so afraid. He's afraid that something might happen again—to you, or to me."

With loving concern for her father, Elena says, "Sometimes I'm so sad for Papa. It's been nearly three years. I miss the way he used to be."

Yesenia nods with understanding. "We are always at the heart of your father's thoughts. Everything he does, he does for us. You must never forget that."

"But he can't seem to get over his grief. It's so hard on him, on you too."

"He loves you more than anything, Elena. You'll always be his muchacha bonita. But your father dreamed of the day when Javier would join him in his business. When he was a little boy, your father would tell him: 'Today, Javier, the sign says: Humberto Hernandez, Design and Construction. But one day, one day when you grow up, we'll be partners. Then, the sign will say: Humberto Hernandez and Son, Design and Construction. How do you like that?' And Javier would grin and shout, 'We'll be partners, Papa!' But it wasn't to be, cariño. It broke your father's heart."

Quietly, Elena asks, "You're at peace . . . aren't you, Mama?"

Her mother thinks about her daughter's question for a long moment before answering softly, "Yes, Elena, I am at peace. Even though I cannot see him, I feel Javier's presence every day. The same way I felt his presence from the moment he was conceived and growing inside me. I couldn't feel or see him in those first few days, but I knew he was there. A mother's love is eternal and overcomes all for her children. Even death cannot separate us, not entirely. I know I'll see Javier again. He will welcome me into Heaven. He'll be smiling and handsome, and as sweet and loving as always. Fathers can't understand this the same way mothers do."

"Oh Mother . . ." Elena whispers tenderly and pats her mother's hand affectionately.

Yesenia smiles weakly and continues, "But I couldn't bear to lose your father too. He needs my strength, my patience, my love. He even needs my teasing, cariño. Your father is my life."

"Will he ever go to church again?" Elena asks emotionally.

Her mother answers quietly, "I hope so. Your father is still angry with God for taking Javier from us. This is why I'm hopeful."

Elena doesn't understand her mother's meaning. "You're hopeful because Papa is angry with God?"

Wisely, her mother says, "Yes, niña. Your father's anger means he still has some belief, however small. Where there is small belief, there is great hope." Yesenia squeezes her daughter's hand lovingly.

Elena takes her mother's hand in hers and says with deep feeling, "Papa is wonderful, isn't he?"

"Your father is a very good man. A man of true virtue. The three happiest days of his life were when he became an American citizen, when Javier was born, and when you were born."

"There was a fourth, Mama. It was the day he married you."

"Yes," her mother says remembering, "I suppose that's true, niña. But I was the lucky one."

Elena looks at her mother anxiously. "I want to love someone the way you love Papa. Will I ever meet him?"

Yesenia reassures her beautiful daughter, "Of course you will. One day you'll walk into a room, and your life will change forever. He'll be in that room, and you will know. You both will know. You both will know instantly. He's hoping to find you too, cariño. He's searching for you right now. God will bring you together."

"I hope so," Elena says wistfully.

"Elena," her mother says, "the government paper you want your father to sign?"

"You mean about the HUB?"

"Yes. He will never sign it."

"Why not?" Elena asks. "It could help his business."

"Your father's a very proud man; you know that. He believes the quality of his designs, his hard work, and fair prices are enough to earn him the business. He understands you mean well, but he sees something like that as a handout. Do you understand?"

Elena knows her mother is right. Now that she thinks about it, she knows it's one of the many fine qualities she loves and admires about her father. "Yes, I understand." Smiling at her mother, she says, "You and Papa are so sweet together."

Yesenia sighs, "It's a good thing we are. That man drives me crazy half the time."

Elena laughs out loud. "Mama, you two were *meant* for each other."

"I suppose we were," Yesenia says, sighing again. She stands and takes her daughter's hands. "Come, niña. Let's go see what those men are up to."

The two women walk back to the kitchen together. When they enter, Elena has her arm around her mother's waist.

"Father Michael has left?" Yesenia asks.

Subdued, her husband answers, "A moment ago. He said he'd see you and Elena at Mass in the morning."

Yesenia is immediately sensitive to her husband's somber mood. "Was there anything else, mi amor?"

"No, there was nothing else."

"Time for me to go," Elena says cheerfully. "Homework needs checking." She kisses her mother and goes to her father. Placing an arm around his shoulder, she kisses him on the cheek. "I love you," she says. Then, leaning down, she whispers conspiringly in his ear, "You can tell me that new joke later, Papa. I really want to hear it."

He looks up at her and smiles weakly. "I love you too, cariño."

Elena pats her father on the shoulder, kisses her mother one last time, and leaves. Once she is gone Humberto casually scans the government folder, turns a few pages, and places it to one side. His dinner plate is still in front of him.

Yesenia quietly goes to the counter and fixes him another plate, this time with all of his favorite foods. She brings it to Humberto, moves the other plate aside, sets the new one in front of him, and takes a seat beside her husband. "Mi amor, we will start the diet another time," she says softly.

"Thank you, Yes," he says, but Humberto makes no effort to eat.

Affectionately, Yesenia places a hand on his and rises from the chair. She looks compassionately at her husband, worried about him. "I'll get ready for bed now. Don't stay up too late, mi amor."

"I'll be along soon," he answers in a whisper.

Yesenia kisses him on the cheek and leaves the room. After she is gone, Humberto slowly pushes away the new plate of food. He sits in the chair breathing deeply, thinking and brooding. He releases a long, tired sigh. He straightens up, pulls his cell phone from his shirt pocket, flips it open, and punches in a number. Juan-Carlos can be heard on the other end.

"Hello-ohhh!" he answers dramatically.

"Juan-Carlos," Humberto says dryly. "Don't send the wood back to Casey's Monday morning."

Juan-Carlos is surprised and apologetic. "Boss! I wasn't expecting you. What did you say?"

"Don't send the wood back. I've changed my mind."

"Boss, you never change your mind."

"I just did," says Humberto flatly. "Now listen. Deliver the wood to my wife's church on Monday morning. Call the men. Tell them to go over there. Father Michael will show Tomás and Angel what to do. They can take care of it in a few days."

Juan-Carlos gushes, "This is such a beautiful thing you're doing, boss! This is why I work for you! All the time you do these wonderful things!"

Humberto rubs his forehead wearily and says in a fatigued tone, "You work for me because I'm the only Mexican dumb enough to hire you."

That remark doesn't register with Juan-Carlos. He is overly excited. "Right, boss! No, boss! Not about being dumb! I mean . . . I mean . . . I'm just so happy I don't know what I am saying!"

"Juan-Carlos!" Humberto growls.

"Yes boss?" he answers defensively.

Humberto breathes hard, collects himself, and softens his tone, "Goodnight Juan-Carlos."

Juan-Carlos is relieved. "Goodnight boss."

Closing his cell phone, Humberto says to himself, "I must be the dumbest Mexican in the world. I hope the bank believes in signs."

Exhausted from his work day, Humberto slowly gets up from the table, leaving his favorite foods untouched. He is no longer hungry; nothing could possibly appeal to him now. This kind man walks through the kitchen into the living room. On the mantle is a picture of Elena as a little girl in her white communion dress and another one of her in her quinceañera gown. Beside Elena's pictures are two others: one is of a darling little boy in a green and gold soccer uniform, smiling broadly, with his right foot resting on top of a soccer ball; the other is a photograph of this same boy as a young man dressed in marine fatigues. He is staring directly into the camera with serious dark eyes. The young soldier is exceptionally handsome. These pictures are of Humberto's and Yesenia's son, Javier.

Humberto gazes at the pictures of Elena for a moment. Then, he stares at the pictures of his son. He picks up the picture of Javier as a little boy. Dispirited, he sits down in an overstuffed chair by the mantle. He holds the picture of his son adoringly in both hands near his lap. Tears are rolling down his cheeks now. Humberto hears his young son happily shouting, *"Papa, we're gonna be partners!"*

Yesenia silently enters the living room. She is dressed in a full length nightgown, and her hair is braided. She stands observing her husband. Her heart breaks for this man she has been married to for thirty-five years. She approaches his side and touches him lightly on the shoulder. Humberto gazes up at his wife, tears spilling from his eyes. "He was so beautiful," he says.

"Yes, mi amor, our son was very beautiful," Yesenia answers softly, looking into his eyes.

Humberto's cheeks are now tracked with tears, and he says with a catch in his throat, "How can this be fair?"

His wife answers him tenderly. "We must try to remember that fairness is God's providence; faith is ours." She pauses before speaking again and then adds quietly, "Mi amor, won't you come to bed now?"

Humberto slowly nods his head. Yesenia kisses him lightly on the cheek, affectionately pats his shoulder, and returns to their bed–room.

Humberto stares at the picture of his son a moment longer, unwilling to give it up. He presses the picture to his chest and a sob breaks from his heart. He rises slowly, wipes the tears from his eyes with the back of one sleeve, and meticulously and lovingly places the picture of his son in its sacred place on the mantle. With a broken heart, this good man makes his way through the living room in the direction of his uncommonly strong and loving wife. As he leaves the living room, he turns off the light.

CHAPTER SIX

On the same evening of the same day of Seth McAllister's homecoming and the Humberto Hernandez's family discussion about the gender of God, a different family meeting takes place in another part of town. It is much later now, around midnight. An oafish looking, heavy set, middle-aged Anglo man is standing before a door in a gleaming high-rise office tower. He is disheveled with a bull-like neck, bushy eyebrows, a nose that is a lumpy wreck from being broken in barroom brawls several times too often, and coarse, unkempt, unwashed black hair. His face is ruddy and flushed. His teeth are stained yellow from nicotine, and his eyes are black and soulless. The man is unshaven with two day's growth of dark stubble. Shabbily dressed, he wears a junky sports coat and ill-fitting black trousers that hang loose and baggy around his big belly. His scuffed leather shoes are worn-out and the heels are run over. A furtive, animal-like demeanor makes him seem out of place in this sleek office building. He sways slightly because he has been drinking heavily. His face is pressed close to the door, and he strains to read the letters on it. Satisfied he is at the proper place, the man raises his bear-like right hand to knock on the door. On the ring finger of this beefy hand is a massive, heavy, brass ring. In the center of the ring is the crest of a growling gargoyle with a twisted, maniacal mouth, its lips curled and stretched back grinning in an eternal, frozen scream. This grotesque man doesn't knock; he pounds on the door, calling out impatiently and slurring his words.

"Hey in there! I said hey! It's me!"

From somewhere behind the door comes the muffled sound of an equally impatient voice.

"Coming, I'm coming!"

The door opens, and standing in the doorway is a tall, emaciated man with a narrow, chalky face that contrasts starkly with his slicked back, jet black hair. He is impeccably dressed, wearing a dark gray suit, a dark gray dress shirt with French cuffs fastened with flashy silver cuff links, and a silver silk tie. Stuffed in the left top pocket of his coat is a gray silk handkerchief. The man's pinched pallid face, contrasted with his shellacked black hair, makes him look like an immaculate, creepy undertaker that stepped off the screen of a freaky, B-rated horror flick shown on a Saturday matinee. Along with his powdery appearance, the man is afflicted with an obsessive compulsive disorder that causes him to tidy himself neurotically: he whisks his clothes constantly, checks his fingernails continually, and cleans his teeth incessantly by raking his tongue over them. Upset at the sight of this uncouth man standing outside his office door, the neatly-dressed man nervously glances past him in hopes they haven't been seen. He shudders when, unexpectedly, the barbarous man places his sweaty palm on his fine lapel and leans his face forward saying, "Brother Wickham, Attorney . . . at . . . Law. Ha!" he crudely mocks.

"Emond, you fool!" Wickham responds impatiently. "Get in here before you attract attention!" The lawyer pulls his brother inside his office and closes the door quickly. He fishes a large white cloth akin to a handkerchief from his pants pocket and hastily bushes the spot on his lapel where the foul man just touched him. "Follow me," he orders.

The men go through the front reception area of the law office down a long hall. The lawyer walks briskly ahead. Liquored and limping, Emond lunges forward as he struggles to keep up. They enter the attorney's richly appointed private office. It is dominated by a large, black topped desk. Behind the desk there is an impressive, wingback leather chair, solid black and throne-like. It is raised on a dais so the person sitting in it looks down on those seated in front. There are two wooden chairs before the desk that are plain and rigid, lacquered in solid black and highly polished. These chairs look uncomfortable. An overstuffed couch sits against the wall a short distance and to the left of the wingback leather chair. Neatly spaced on the walls are diplomas, letters of recognition, and gilded-framed paintings of scantily clad women and mythological nymphs. Glowing, gold sconces adorn the walls and ornate lamps sit on lamp tables expertly placed around the room for seductive effect. The office lighting is low, and there is a bawdy ambiance about the room.

Wickham takes a seat in the wingback chair and gestures for his brother to sit in one of the black lacquered chairs facing him. Sitting before the polished black desk, its semigloss finish reflects ghostly images of the men's watery faces shimmering on its surface. Emond surveys the room suspiciously, his cold eyes darting from side to side as if guarding against something unearthly he expects to spring from the shadows and go for his throat. He is tense, and despite his smallish stature, there is an absolute brute force about him that is terrifying.

"Emond," the tall man begins harshly, "you're late, as usual," he admonishes.

Emond glares up menacingly at his brother on his dais. He taps his heavy ring on the desk, warning him, "Watch your tone, brother. I ain't never liked that tone."

A shadow darkens Wickham's cadaverous face. He grimaces and peers at the spot where the heavy ring struck the desk, straining to see if it left a scratch. Taking heed of his brother's warning, the lawyer continues in a grudging tone, "All right. We've got to work together on this thing, Emond. We can't afford any mistakes, that's all. There's too much at stake here for anything to go wrong. Five million is a lot of money."

His brother Emond curls his lips back into a grotesque smile, exposing his yellow teeth and splotchy gums. Contemplating the money, he rubs his hands together and laughs low, sounding beastlike and fearsome. "Could live awful good on that, hey Wickham," he says. "What's your plan?"

With nothing short of evil glee, Wickham eagerly explains. "It's so simple, brother Emond. It's absolutely failsafe. Once we get custody of those kids, it'll be easy enough to get control of their trust. After that, we ship the little darlings off to a boarding school. I've found the perfect one for them on the coast of West Africa. Only thing, they have a terrible problem with malaria there. Children die by the thousands every year, pity them. We send those kids over there, somehow an inoculation is sadly missed, and they're as good as dead. Our little mosquito friends are quite dependable. You and Nadine inherit the trust money. We split it."

Emond applauds the simplicity of it. "Brother Wickham, that's brilliant. Whar we go from here?"

Counseling his brother, Wickham peers down at him from his dais. "First, while you're on probation, stay away from those girls. The court orders say a thousand feet."

Snorting and sneering, Emond replies, "Ha! That's easy enough. Them pesky kids ain't been nothin' but trouble." He backhands the air with his heavy ring. "Jest a little tap to keep her in line. I'm in jail three months. On probation fer a year!"

Warning him, Wickham says, "You were lucky, Emond. You could've killed that little girl. Then, unlucky, you got the toughest judge, Judge Peters. If I hadn't bribed my friends into writing letters on your behalf, that judge would've put you in jail for a year, on probation for five. It cost me a bundle."

His brother grouses, "Cost you a bundle? I was the one in jail. You fergotten that?"

Wickham is indifferent to his brother's complaint and continues, "And if that judge knew the truth? That it wasn't the bed frame at all, it was that heavy ring of yours that cut her? You'd be in prison now for God knows how long. You ought to get rid of that thing."

"Yeah. Your generosity," Emond snarls contemptuously. "Ain't got nothin' to do with the five million, I guess? And this ring and me ain't partin' company. It's brought me nothin' but luck."

Wickham scoots his tongue over his teeth, flicks something imaginary from his lapel, and glances at his nails. "I admit it, I'm after the money," he answers coldly. "But I'm warning you, Emond. You mess up once—*just once*—and it's five to ten for sure. Judge Peters has got you pegged for a child abuser. It's the worst form of criminality in his mind, short of murder."

Emond casually waves his heavy ring in the air, complaining and ruminating, without feeling one scintilla of guilt. "A light backhand to the child's head . . . wern't hardly nothin' . . . And it wern't even my fault. I wern't tryin' to hit that little girl. If'n she hadn't a jumped thatta way . . ." He taps his lower lip, reflectively. "Just . . . plain . . . bad . . . luck. That's all it was, Wickham . . . bad luck. Catched her in the upper eyebrow," he says, now tapping his left eyebrow. "Ya know, in this soft, fleshy part here. She burst open like a pastry shell. I cain't hep if'n she jumped in the way, now can I? How was I to ah know'd she'd go and do a fool thing like that? I'm tellin' ya, it weren't my fault. None of it were my fault."

Wickham yawns, "Maybe so."

Justifying himself, Emond continues malevolently, "Ya gotta keep'em in line. Ya know what I mean, Wickham: spare the rod, spoil the child." He waves his heavy ring in the air with a flourishing backhand swing. "Works the same way for wives too, ya know. It didn't take the Missus long to learn, neither."

Wickham's tone is eerily ominous as he recounts, "Yeah, that's what the old man bellowed when he beat us: 'Spare the rod, spoil the child!' I remember. He sure took that verse to heart. Or better said, to his belt and to our backs. And even more so when he'd been drinking. I can still smell his stinking breath."

Emond's eyes widen and look haunted. "Sometimes, Wickham, in my dreams . . . I can still hear him raging." He points to his left ear. "Still cain't hear so good from whar he walloped me that one time."

Raking his tongue across his teeth and chuckling fiendishly, Wickham recalls with chilling satisfaction, "What I remember best is the sweet sound of his neck breaking as he tumbled down those hard wooden stairs. *Crack! Crack! Crack! Snap!* That old man sure did bounce."

Emond snickers, "Yeah. Got his all right and none too soon. Come up them staars a swing'n his leather belt and iron buckle a time too often. Drunk as he was, he still know'd what was happenin' to 'em. Funny thing, in the end, that ol' man wern't much like I'da feared all them years."

Darkly, Wickham observes, "No. We were just a couple of scared kids for a long time. But we grew up. The fool just didn't notice. I'm glad he knew it was us. He had plenty of time to think about it the few hours he lingered on his back at the bottom of those stairs, murmuring on the floor and staring blankly up at the ceiling, pleading for help that was never coming."

"Yeah," Emond says, "and jest like you said, the next mornin' them cops thought he'd got drunk and fell down them staars all by hisself."

"Dumb cops," Wickham notes, his tone icy with contempt.

Looking around his brother's office admiringly, Emond says, "Don't look like ya hurtin' fer much in this here law bizness. You expensive?"

"Yeah, I am," Wickham answers and adds, "thirty thousand retainer and five hundred an hour. My specialty is family law. I represent the fairer sex. Now there's an oxymoron for you."

Emond looks at his brother with envy. "You've always been the clever one, brother Wickham. Must be somethin' really special fer ya bout this family law."

Coldly sarcastic, Wickham laughs, "A cozy clan are we. Emond, you wouldn't believe what a churning cesspool of cronyism, money, greed, politics, and corruption the whole thing is. But Christ, how the money rolls in!"

Emond narrows his eyes and cocks his head at an angle. "It cain't be so easy."

Grinning knowingly, Wickham says, "Listen brother. The couple's already at each other's throats by the time little wifey pooh shows up here. And if they have a kid or two it's even better. It guarantees my fees will double. Maybe triple, if I can keep the fight going long enough. It's not my fault she came to me."

Emond tugs thoughtfully at his chin. "But what if they ain't at each other's throats?"

Wickham pats the table confidently. "I never let that happen. Once I give her a little of the right 'legal advice,' she's out for blood. Of course, they never realize it's their own blood, not until it's too late."

Emond's eyes grow large, and he licks his lips. "Too late?"

Wickham giggles demonically. "Yeah, too late; between me, the ad litem, investigators, a couple of shrinks, and whichever lawyer buddy of mine's working the hubby over, we pick 'em cleaner than a pack of hungry piranhas out for a family picnic. By the time we're done with them, there's nothing left but two pale skeletons drifting somewhere in the backwash bumping along the bottom."

Emond leans forward in awe. "They don't never catch on?"

"Nah," Wickham snorts, "The fools actually believe we're on their side. They never get we're just everyday mercenaries sporting silk suits and slinky smiles. It's whoever's got the thirty pieces of silver."

Impressed and eager to hear more, Emond asks, "And after the money's gone?"

"We settle," the lawyer answers vainly with a smirk.

Scratching his bull neck thoughtfully, Emond tilts his head to one side, squints at Wickham, and asks slyly, "But what if she *cain't* afford you?"

His eyes are smugly evil as Wickham laughs and responds re–morselessly, "Oh, there's ways to work around that important little detail. If she's old and ugly, my secretary makes sure she never sees me." He jerks his thumb toward the overstuffed couch, "If she's young and pretty? She's shown in, and I show her the couch."

"She refuses?" Emond asks.

"I show her the door. There's always another pretty one who's desperate enough to be willing."

"Ah," Emond ruefully opines, "the sheep to slaughter, mighty sweet." Then something occurs to him, "But what 'bout their kids? They care about 'em, don't they?"

"Their kids?" Wickham chortles sarcastically. "No! Listen Emond, you take two otherwise perfectly normal, intelligent people and really get them going at each other? You'd be surprised how quick they are to forget about little Tommy and little Susie. Do they think about their children? Ha!"

"What happens to 'em, brother?"

"Call it collateral damage from friendly fire," the lawyer answers coolly. "But don't you see? Friendly fire sprays shrapnel that maims and kills just the same. The parents, too selfish and hell-bent on destroying each other, are like wild beasts so consumed by the battle that they trample their young." Thinking about it, Wickham begins to giggle. "Human frailty, you gotta love it. I can count on it every time. It's great for billable hours!" and his giggling becomes ribald laughter.

"What a racket," says Emond, admiringly. He points to his brother's suit. "What's all this gray about, Wickham?"

Wickham fastidiously arranges his silk handkerchief and briskly whisks his lapel. He skates his tongue over his teeth before answering. "It's a lawyer's favorite color." Wickham quickly switches to a business-like tone and continues, "Okay, let's finish up. While you're on probation you've got to stay out of trouble and keep away from those children."

"Will do," Emond says dutifully.

"That's the spirit, brother. Now, what about that mousy wife of yours, Nadine?"

"She don't know nothin', and she ain't gonna give us no trouble," Emond says cockily. He places the heavy ring against his cheek and taps it several times for emphasis, "*if* ya know what I mean."

"Good," Wickham sneers. "Now, there are just a few more things to think about. Stay off the booze, if you can, and no drugs. Both are violations of your probation. I see you've been drinking. Smoked any dope?"

"Yeah, a little," Emond admits.

"Stop the dope, Emond," Wickham warns. "At least do that much. It stays in your system for weeks. You'll be tested soon."

Concerned, Emond asks, "What'll we do?"

His brother grins conceitedly, "I figured you'd smoke a joint. The lab guy's in big time trouble with the bookies. We've struck the right bargain. Your test will come out clean as a whistle, guar . . . an . . . teed!"

Emond is very impressed with his brother's efficiency. "You do get them bases covered."

"I do my best," Wickham gloats. "The other thing is the court appointed psychologist. She'll be evaluating you and Nadine and making her recommendation. We were lucky with the rotation. She's a broken down old biddy who hits the bottle too hard. Her practice has been failing for years. Without me and my cronies funneling her business, she couldn't afford to pay her office rent. We can count on her for a stellar recommendation."

Emond nods, "What about that other group, Child Protective Services? They was out at the place when I was locked up."

Wickham scoffs, "Good people. But understaffed, overworked, and overwhelmed, pity them. All you and Nadine have to do is act normal when they visit. Once they know you completed probation successfully, read the court appointed shrink's report, and see your clean drug screen, they'll be more than glad to close your case and get you off their crowded books."

"Anything else?" Emond asks.

"Yeah, and this one's the most critical," Wickham emphasizes, "so pay very close attention, brother, to what I'm about to say. The day after your probation ends—I mean the very next morning now—you've got to hurry over and see those girls. It's important to establish your record of love and concern for them for the upcoming hearing. I'm certain we can get on the docket in April. There won't be any challenges. It shouldn't take more than half an hour to wrap up."

Emond nods agreeably, "I understand. Is that it?"

Wickham's voice turns cautious. "Judge Peters concerns me some. He's heading up the state's special committee on legal ethics and reform. They're nosing around. It'll blow over in time, always does. Then back to business as usual." Ridiculing, he complains, "He thinks he's so high and mighty! But stay out of trouble, Emond, and that judge can't touch us."

"He's that bad, huh?"

"Emond, I can fashion a hook that will catch most men. They're caught easily enough on the barb of their own vices. Most practically jump on the hook. To tell you the truth, it still surprises me how little bait it often takes."

"What's the bait for that Judge Peters?"

Aggravated, Wickham tugs at his chin and says, "None that

I know of . . . at least not yet. Emond, you serve on some judge's campaigns, donate money to them, and they'll always find enough wiggle room for rulings favorable to their friends. Christ! We're talking about the law here." He ponders for a moment. "But you could write a check for a million dollars to Judge Peters' re-election campaign, go before him the next day, and he'll rule against you if it's the law. There's no friendly reciprocation in his court."

Emond grunts, annoyed by the description his brother paints of Judge Peters. He feels coldly malevolent towards the man already.

The lawyer continues, disgusted, "He's part of that crowd that's got a hard streak of stubborn morality down their spines." Wickham pauses, strokes his neck thoughtfully with his polished nails, and speaks contemptuously, "When the time comes, I'm going to take that hard back bone of pious morality of his and hit him right between the eyes with it."

Emond is suddenly very curious about something his brother said and probes Wickham, asking, "Whatta ya mean, 'Serve on them judges' campaigns?' Donate money to 'em?"

"I told you, Emond. We're a cozy clan. We lawyers serve on judges' election committees and donate heavily to their campaigns. Why man, they depend on us to fund their re-elections and keep them in their jobs. Later, they appoint us to lucrative ad litem roles, shade their rulings favorably, and approve our fees. Nice cycle, hey?"

Emond shakes his head in disbelief, observing with morbid admiration, "You lawyers give 'm money. Them judges decide things and approve your fees. Leaves a lot of latitude for larceny, don't it?"

Aroused by his brother's insight and fevered eyes wild with demonic glee, Wickham shouts, "Bingo! You should've been a lawyer, brother. Like I always say: it's good enough to have the law on your side, but pure ecstasy to have the law in your pocket!"

Emond looks at Wickham approvingly, nodding and grinning. "And like I always say, brother Wickham, you're the clever one."

Leaning far back in his black, throne-like leather chair with his hands clasped comfortably behind his neck, deeply satisfied, Wickham waxes philosophical and observes, "Yes, brother Emond, I was born to this low business. It's perfectly suited to all of my talents. And this whole financial crisis mess couldn't have come along at a better time for us. If the bank handling the children's trust hadn't failed right after you got the letter, and the acquiring bank weren't so inept, this opportunity never would've dropped in our laps. In all the confusion, nobody knows what's going on but us. By the time they find out, it'll all be over." Wickham, smiling and content, sweeps his tongue across his teeth and directs his eyes down at his brother. "Remind me again, Emond. Your probation is over with, when?"

"The end of February," Emond replies offhandedly.

"Good," Wickham muses, "the shortest month of the year—a real blessing. And what are you going to do the very next day after that, brother?"

Curling back his lips in a grisly grin and baring his nicotine-stained teeth Emond gloats, "First thing that next mornin' I'ma hurryin' over to see them darlin' girls."

Wickham brings his hands to his front and claps them twice in giddy, demonic joy, squealing, "Brother Emond, the money's as good as ours!"

The brothers begin laughing spontaneously in devilish cackles. They are like two demons deep in a fiend-infested forest at the bewitching hour, hopping and howling and leaping into the cold night air as they dance wildly round a roaring bonfire, its sweeping hot flames sending masses of red embers swirling skyward in a ferocious vortex, whirling away-away-away! Swept away! Swept high into the black starless sky, the blazing embers soar like swarming fireflies glowing and crackling and popping; their little stern lights the color of blood, zigzagging and blinking out one by one as they are swallowed up for eternity by the gaping maw of midnight. These men worship pure evil.

CHAPTER SEVEN

It is three weeks later, the day before Thanksgiving. Mrs. McAllister is fixing breakfast for Seth when the phone rings.

"Hello?" she answers pleasantly.

"Hi, Mom." It's Kathryn's voice.

"Good morning, sweetheart. How's everyone?"

"Everyone's good. Please don't forget the potato salad today. It's a favorite."

"It's ready and in the fridge."

"Has Seth said anything to you about coming?" Kathryn asks, concerned.

Her mother lowers her voice, "Not to me, to you?"

"I've tried to pin him down," Kathryn sighs. "He's been so noncommittal."

Mrs. McAllister frowns, and worry lines etch her face. "I hope he'll go. Be good for him to get out. Your brother hasn't wanted to do much lately, I'm afraid."

"I think he's depressed Mom. It may be a form of PTS—post-traumatic stress."

Mrs. McAllister becomes very concerned. "What can we do, Katie?"

Kathryn's voice takes on a more professional tone, and she sounds like the caring physician advising a patient's worried family member. "Just encourage him; that's the best thing we can do for him now, Mom. I believe the depression is a mild form. We need to remember that Seth has a solid emotional core. He's always been our rock."

"Yes, he has been," Mrs. McAllister replies. "Since he was nine years old, he's felt he had to be the man of the house."

As the two women talk, Seth enters the kitchen. He is dressed in his bathrobe, his hair is disheveled, and his face is dark with stubble. As she listens on the phone, his mother smiles at him, mouths that she is talking to Katie, and pours him a cup of coffee.

"Thanks, Mom," he says, subdued.

"I heard Seth," Katie says. "Please put him on."

Mrs. McAllister hands the phone to her son. "Katie wants to talk to you," she says brightly.

Seth takes the phone from his mother and says listlessly, "Hey, sis."

Kathryn is cheerful. "Seth, please come this afternoon. Terry and the kids really want to see you. Please come, *please*."

"I don't have anything to wear." Seth is making excuses, and his sister knows it.

Kathryn maintains an encouraging tone. "Wear your uniform. The kids will love it."

"I'm no fun these days, Katie," Seth stalls.

"Fun or not, we want you here," Katie insists. "Mom won't stay long. She has packing to do. Please Seth, please do it for me?"

He relents, "Okay, Katie. What can I bring?"

Kathryn replies warmly, "Bring that easy grin I love so much."

"I'll try."

"Great. See you at five. Bye now."

"Bye sis."

CHAPTER EIGHT

Mrs. McAllister and Seth stand at the front door of Kathryn's and Terry's home. Mrs. McAllister is dressed conservatively, and Seth is wearing his uniform absent his beret. He is looking tense and is holding a large bowl of potato salad in the crook of his left arm. Mrs. McAllister rings the doorbell. Momentarily, the door opens, and it is Kathryn's husband, Terry, who welcomes them. Terry is Seth's height, with a medium build, friendly amber-colored eyes, a handsome face with a rakish cleft chin, and an easy demeanor much like Seth's. He wears taupe True Chino Relaxed-Fit Dockers, chocolate brown Coronado slip-on driving shoes, and a wheat-colored cotton sweater. On it is a large comical turkey whose colorful feathers are displayed in full fan with a caption next to its goofy eyes that reads: I gobble for vegans. Several years before, when Katie first introduced them, these two men had liked each other immediately. Seth had always thought Terry was the perfect match for his sensible sister. Behind his brother-in-law is a room full of people talking and children running about. Terry is delighted to see Seth and his mother-in-law. He hugs Mrs. McAllister and grins widely at Seth as he reaches to shake his hand and hug him.

"Seth! You're lookin' good!" Terry says enthusiastically.

Seth relaxes a bit and says, "Thanks Terry, you too. How's the environmental law business?"

"A little harder to get off the ground than I first thought," Terry laughs. "But Katie's been a great support. I'm sticking with it."

"You'll get there," says Seth.

Terry reaches for the bowl of potato salad. "Here, let me take that bowl from you. Margaret, you and Seth join the party. I'll stick this in the fridge, for now. Seth, as soon as the twins see you, get ready to rumble."

"I'll be on my guard," says Seth. He instinctively moves his prosthesis slightly behind his back so people will not easily see it.

Terry holds the bowl of potato salad, and Mrs. McAllister says, "I'll go with you, Terry. It still needs a little more of this and that." Terry and Mrs. McAllister disappear into the kitchen.

Seth is left alone. He nervously surveys the room, which buzzes with a pleasant, festive holiday mood. Standing in the middle of the living room in a pair of goldenrod Lexxi booties, Kathryn is dressed attractively in a cinnamon wool pantsuit that is paired beautifully with an autumn colored silk blouse. A narrow herringbone belt completes the pantsuit and small gold hoops grace her ears. She is laughing at something her friend has just said. When her companion walks away, Kathryn looks Seth's way, sees him, and eagerly beckons him to join her. Seth goes to Katie and she gives her brother a big hug.

"Seth, I'm so glad you came," she says. "Welcome to our 'Day-Before-Thanksgiving Day' party. It's becoming quite a tradition. Better watch out though, you'll get the sticky hands treatment as soon as the twins see you."

Seth keeps his prosthesis self-consciously behind him. Still, he feels his spirits brighten standing next to his sister. "Yep," he says, "Terry's warned me already."

Seth then notices that there is a young girl standing shyly and slightly behind Kathryn, as if she is purposefully obscuring herself. She appears to be about nine or ten years old, is slender, tall for her age, and dressed plainly, except for a lovely white sweater. She has expressive, emerald green eyes and delicate features. On one side of her head a white barrette holds back her blonde, shoulder length hair, exposing more of her classic face and framing it nicely. Seth observes a scar that begins in the top of her left eyebrow and extends in a slight curve to the left about one and a half inches. Although this scar is noticeable and her clothes are plain, neither detracts from the fact that she is a beautiful little girl. He observes that she stands gracefully. She is very poised and, although close to him, there is an air of aloofness about her, reminding him of a ballerina. Moreover, despite her delicate features, there is a sense of strength about her that is beyond her years.

Seth is somewhat surprised when he realizes that the little girl is not just looking at him but studying him in a way that implies she is sizing him up. This stirs his curiosity and he becomes more intrigued. In turn, the little girl realizes that Seth is looking at her, and she deftly takes a half step back behind Kathryn, shyly shielding more of herself. She places her hands lightly in the small of Kathryn's back and leans out, gazing at Seth with her expressive green eyes and with an inquisitive, candid stare.

Kathryn is well aware of what is taking place between Seth and the little girl, but says nothing. She prefers to wait and let things play out between them.

Seth gazes back at the little girl for a moment and then turns to his sister. "A friend's daughter?" he asks, curiously.

Katie smiles at him without parting her lips and gently shakes her head.

"Okay, she is . . . ?" Seth inquires.

"Why don't you ask her?" Kathryn lightly encourages him.

Seth looks at his sister quizzically. Then, keeping his prosthesis hidden behind him, he drops down on one knee, meeting the girl at eye level.

"And who is this angel?" he asks in a friendly tone.

The girl's response is to take another half step back behind Kathryn. She continues to watch Seth steadily, without saying a word.

For a long moment she and Seth gaze at each other, neither of them moving or speaking, as if they are both patiently waiting for the other to act first. But even so, there isn't any feeling of awkwardness between them as they stare and wait.

Seth looks up at Kathryn, pleading for guidance with his eyes, but she only offers him a smile. Seth turns again to this quiet girl who continues to silently observe him. She is clearly in the process of making some decision about him.

Uncertain, Seth grins self-consciously and begins to stand up when suddenly the girl offers him her right hand. At this, Seth loosens and appears relieved. He extends his hand in return and sees that even fully extended his hand is still short of hers by a few inches. Seth realizes this curious girl is fully aware of it, but she makes no move and waits without budging with her hand extended. Instantly, Seth understands she expects him to bridge the gap between them. Somewhat amused by her expectation, he grins more easily now. Looking into her eyes which remain fixed on his, he reaches forward. Just as their fingers are about to touch, Seth hesitates for a brief moment, and then follows through, grasping her hand gently.

The little girl smiles at him, a Mona Lisa-like smile that appears to be a sign of encouragement. The girl takes his hand and squeezes it with a firmness he didn't expect, but she doesn't say a word. She continues gazing steadily at Seth, now with a hint of acceptance in her eyes.

Seth smiles back at her in his leisurely way. "Hi. My name's Seth," he says, and motions up towards Kathryn, "and that's my big sister, Kathryn. I call her Katie."

The girl's response is to give him a slight nod of acknowledgement, nothing more. She gently withdraws her hand from his, looks up at Kathryn, and smiles graciously. The girl then turns her head and looks across the room, seeming to search for someone.

In a soft voice, she says politely, "Excuse me, Mrs. Mason," and she walks away in the direction of children playing.

As she goes, Seth watches her and notices that she moves gracefully across the room, even artistically so. She reminds him again of an agile ballerina. Seth stands up and grins self-consciously at Kathryn, who looks both pleased and more than a little surprised.

"Wow! That's never happened before," Katie says, amazed.

"What hasn't?" Seth asks.

"That hasn't. You should feel very flattered."

"Why?"

"You just met Emily Fleming," Katie says. "She isn't accepting of strangers, Seth. I've never seen her do that before. Usually, Emily is very good at making herself invisible. It's astonishing she offered you her hand."

"Guess I've got some of that ol' charm left," Seth replies.

Kathryn pats his chest playfully. "Don't kid yourself, little brother. The truth is, right now you're still very much under review. A final decision is pending."

"She's never done that before, huh?" Seth says, thoughtfully. "I wonder what she saw in me."

Kathryn reaches out and gently ruffles his hair. "The same thing we all do."

Seth looks at his sister appreciatively. He feels more relaxed. The outing is agreeing with him. Unconsciously, he still holds his prosthesis behind him.

"Why didn't you say something when I looked up at you?" Seth asks.

"I never coax Emily with people," Katie tells him. "I believe it's completely up to her."

"I'm under review, you say?" Seth asks, wondering what that really means.

"Trust is not something Emily bestows easily," Kathryn informs him. "It takes time."

Looking in the direction Emily went, he says reflectively, "Time is the one thing I have."

Kathryn tilts her head at her brother and teases, "Why Seth McAllister. I believe you're smitten."

He grins and shrugs. "Not smitten, sis. But there *is* something about her. Something special that draws your attention. She moves like a well-schooled ballerina. Who are her parents?"

The teasing look on Kathryn's face is replaced by a serious one. "It's a heartrending story," she says. "Her parents were killed a year ago by a drunk driver. Both were doctors attending a conference out of town when it happened."

Seth shakes his head sadly. "Unbelievable."

Kathryn continues, "CPS placed Emily with her only living relative, a distant cousin and her husband. Turns out, we believe there's spousal abuse. The husband's an alcoholic, maybe other substance abuse as well. One night he came home drunk and threw Emily to the floor. She hit the bed frame, and her head was cut badly. The man's wife ran out for help. The police arrived a short time later."

Seth's voice has a hint of emotional outrage in it when he says, "The scar above her left eyebrow? That's how she got it?"

"Yes. The police found the brute passed out against a wall in the girl's bedroom. He had a large contusion under one eye, and his upper lip had been split. They found Emily under the bed. She was shielding her little sister."

"She has a little sister?"

"Yes, her name is Chloë. The police theorize the girls were together when Emily was assaulted. After Emily was cut, she still managed to get her sister under the bed and as far back against the wall as possible. She then placed herself between her sister and the side of the bed that was open to attack."

"She was assaulted?" Seth says, his emotions rising.

Kathryn keeps her voice steady. "There were multiple hema—tomas covering her legs. Apparently, the man was grabbing at Emily, forcibly trying to pull her out. She's a fighter though and fought back hard. Emily got in a few good kicks to the man's face with a pair of tap shoes she was wearing at the time. The tap shoes probably saved her."

"That's when the police arrived?" Seth asks.

"Yes. Chloë slept through the whole thing cuddled with her doll. No doubt that was her defense mechanism, as petrified as she must have been. There was so much blood they thought both of them had been hurt. But it was Emily's alone. Intent on shielding Chloë, the poor child bled all over her sister."

Stunned, Seth quietly says, "My God."

"Emily was in the hospital for a week. The bruising was so severe that the doctors were concerned about blood clots, and they kept her under close observation the entire time. She remembers being in the hospital but not the assault itself. She's blocked it out completely."

"What happened to the man who assaulted her," Seth asks, "and to his wife?"

"He was arrested," Kathryn says. "Went to jail for a few months. Nothing happened to the wife. The police concluded she wasn't involved."

Seth looks incredulous. "Are you kidding, a few months? Then what happened?"

"CPS removed the children and placed them with The Children's Sanctuary. I volunteer there. That's how I got to know them. Emily never lets her sister out of her sight for more than a minute. She left to go see about Chloë."

"The Children's Sanctuary. Is that an orphanage?" Seth asks.

"No," Kathryn says. "It's a place for children who've been abused, neglected, or abandoned. They have a campus with individual cottages and house parents. There's even a school on the grounds. They do an extraordinary job."

"So, why are they here with you?" he asks.

"We're 'Guest Parents,'" she says. "We're allowed to take children on weekends and holidays. Emily and Chloë stay with us often. We've grown quite fond of them. They'll be with us over Thanksgiving."

Seth looks at his sister with awe and admiration. "With all you've got to do, you're incredible, sis. What are they like?"

Kathryn responds affectionately, "Emily will be ten in February, but she's way beyond her years. She's reserved, introspective, and keenly observant. There's an amazing, deep reservoir of strength inside of her. Emily gets discouraged, but she never gives up or gives in."

"She moves so gracefully," says Seth.

"That's because she's been classically trained. Her mother enrolled her in ballet school when she was four. Emily excelled from the first day. She was something of a prodigy. She's happiest when she's dancing and loves every genre. Dancing is where Emily loses herself."

"What about Chloë?" Seth asks.

Kathryn laughs. "Miss Chloë is five. She's lively, free-spirited, and impetuous. Emily's done an incredible job of protecting her."

"Katie," Seth says, "I noticed Emily called you Mrs. Mason and not Dr. McAllister-Mason?"

Katie grins at him. "You mean, Dr. M&M. That's who I am now thanks to you. But here at home I prefer Mom, Mrs. Mason, or Honey."

At that moment, Terry and Mrs. McAllister arrive at their sides.

Terry says affably, "C'mon Seth, let's get caught up," and they walk away from the group.

Kathryn hugs her mother and says, "Thanks for bringing Seth, Mom. I think he's made a new friend."

Mrs. McAllister is pleased. "That's nice, sweetheart. He does seem to be enjoying himself."

"You ready for your holiday mission service?" Kathryn asks. "How many weekends is it, Mom?"

"Four in a row," Mrs. McAllister says enthusiastically. "Each weekend my ladies group is visiting different towns nearby. We'll be cooking and serving meals at the homeless shelters. I'm leaving early this Saturday morning for our first one. We're also planning more trips right after the new year."

"Mom, you and your church lady friends are the greatest. By the way, will you and Seth be joining us for Thanksgiving tomorrow?"

"Thank you, sweetheart, but no. Seth wants a simple Thanksgiving at home. It'll be good for him to have the house all to himself this weekend, don't you think?"

"Sure, that's a terrific idea," Kathryn encourages. "Mom, step over here with me, please. I want you to meet some new neighbors."

CHAPTER NINE

It is the Saturday after Thanksgiving. The clock on the wall in the McAllister kitchen reads eleven forty-five a.m. Seth sits at the kitchen table in his bathrobe leisurely drinking coffee and sorting through the mail. His hair is unkempt, and his face is unshaven. The phone on the wall rings. He glances at it and continues to lazily sort through the mail. On the third ring, he reluctantly gets up and answers the phone. Kathryn's anxious voice is on the other line.

"Seth. Thank goodness you're there."

Seth yawns and stretches. "What's up, sis?"

"Seth McAllister!" Kathryn says impatiently. "It's Saturday, almost noon. You still in your bathrobe?"

Languidly, he replies, "Yep, I'm still digesting from Thanks–giving, takin' it easy the rest of the weekend. Thanks for calling to check on things, but there's no need to worry about me."

"It's not you I'm worried about, knucklehead!" she barks. "Here's a news flash little brother: your 'takin' it easy weekend' just crashed and burned. I've got an emergency over here. The twins have come down with a bug and high fevers. Terry got an unexpected call from his most important client—actually his only client—and is working the rest of the weekend. You have to take care of the girls for me until Sunday afternoon. Shower, shave, and get dressed.

Stunned, Seth stammers, "What? Take care of the girls? Katie, what are you talking about?"

In a crisp tone she quips, "Emily and Chloë, of course."

Seth tries to wrap his mind around things. "Emily?" he says slowly. "Oh, you mean the little girl I met at your party?"

"That's who I mean all right, and Chloë, her younger sister."

"C'mon, Katie!" Seth exclaims. "You can't be serious. What do I know about little girls?"

"Plenty," Katie instructs. "You grew up with two women, remember? These are just younger versions."

"Just take 'em back to that children's place. Problem solved."

"Can't," Katie says, growing irritated with him. "It's a holiday weekend. Not enough staff there. But you'll be glad to know, little brother, I just got their permission to let the girls stay with you."

"No! I mean, what will they eat? Where will they sleep? Katie, what am I supposed to do with them?" Seth is in panic mode now.

In the no-nonsense manner Seth is familiar with, Kathryn is methodical. "Listen mister, I'm sure Margaret left you a mountain of food in the fridge. They'll sleep in my room. Mom still washes my bed linens every week, and my room's full of my old dolls, toys, and children's books. Even my dress-up box is there. Chloë will love that. The fact is, you really won't have to do much. Emily will run things; she acts like a mother to her little sister. And what she doesn't run, Chloë will, I can assure you."

"But, Katie!" Seth protests.

"No buts, little brother. I'm bringing them over in two hours, and that's that."

Resigned, Seth sighs, "Okay, sis. I know that tone. I'll get moving. What should I do to get things started off right?"

Kathryn's voice softens; she teases him, "C'mon, Seth. It's just not that complicated. Children aren't space aliens."

"We were," he answers laconically.

Kathryn laughs. "Look in the fridge, Seth. See how you're doing on food. Oh, and check if Margaret left you a bowl of chocolate chip cookie dough."

Seth opens the fridge. "Yep, there's a ton of food all right. Here's the cookie dough."

"Great. You're home free," she says. "Make some cookies. Chloë loves warm chocolate chip cookies. She can't resist 'em."

"So how do I make 'em?"

Exasperated, Kathryn says, "Seth, you're such a *guy*! I thought I raised you better than that. All the work's done. Just preheat the oven to 375 degrees, spoon out the dough in globs on a cookie sheet two inches apart, and stick 'em in the oven for 15–20 minutes. Chloë likes 'em on the soft side. Got that?"

He scratches his neck lazily. "Yep, I got it. See ya in a couple of hours . . . Katie?"

"Yes?"

"I hope you know what you're doing."

"You'll be fine. Bye Seth . . . and thanks."

"You're welcome . . . I guess."

CHAPTER TEN

Seth is in the kitchen, neat and clean shaven, casually dressed in blue jeans and a white, long-sleeve, open-collar cotton shirt, and brown Hush Puppies Consensus. He sits at the table, waiting anxiously. There is a rapid knock at the back door and he hears Katie coming in. Seth quickly gets up and instinctively hides his prosthesis behind him.

Kathryn enters with the two little girls in tow. She is dressed casually in jeans, a light blue wool blouse, and a pair of white Pumas. Both girls carry small backpacks in their hands. Emily is dressed neatly but plainly in simple, brown slacks, an inexpensive, ivory blouse, and cream-colored tennis shoes. Over her blouse she wears a lovely, light, long-sleeve, white sweater. Chloë wears blue jeans arrayed with pink hearts and yellow butterflies and has on a pink pullover shirt also covered with butterflies. She sports pink tennis shoes whose heels flash whenever she takes a step. The little pink jacket over her pullover shirt completes the rest of what she calls her "outfit."

Chloë holds a large doll in the crook of her left arm. Seth has never seen a doll like this one before. His sister certainly never had one like it. The doll is about eighteen inches long and resembles something akin to a well-worn Raggedy Ann, but it's not a red-headed Raggedy Ann; rather, it's like a well-worn, raggedy Shirley Temple with more than a few ringlets of hair missing. The doll's eyes look a little spacey, and its fixed facial expression appears to be something akin to perpetual surprise. But despite wearing a threadbare faded pink and white frock that has been patched multiple times in several critical places, the doll magically overcomes its missing curls and sartorial shortcomings and manages to be completely adorable and totally lifelike.

Unlike her sister Emily, who is tall for her age, lissome with high cheekbones, green eyes, and shoulder-length, blonde hair, Chloë is of average size for her years with round cheeks that have a rouge glow, a sweet little nose with an upturned tilt, and a head of hair that is a curly brown mop whose spun yarn ends taper into a thicket of spirals that spill across the little girl's forehead and frolic above her eyebrows. Chloë's eyes are a luminous brown, and they always shine with an impish fascination and love of life.

Kathryn is hurried but cheerful. "Here are the girls," she says to Seth. Then turning to Emily and Chloë she continues brightly, "This is my little brother, Seth. Not so little though, is he?" she laughs. "He's going to take good care of you until Sunday afternoon. Seth, this is Chloë Fleming. You met Emily at the party."

Tentatively, Seth says, "Hi ladies," and he offers a weak smile. The girls do not respond. Emily gazes at Seth in her appraising way. Chloë's eyes shine, looking at him with delightful expectations.

Kathryn gives them a quick hug and says gaily, "Gotta go! Have fun everyone!" and she hurries through the kitchen and out the back door before Seth can say another word.

Seth is left alone in the kitchen with Emily and Chloë, feeling clumsy. The girls look at Seth, he at them, and not a word is spoken. In unison, the girls drop their backpacks, and they hit the floor with a thud. Seth swallows uneasily, shifts his feet, and feels a little silly. Chloë moves in front of Emily and leans against her, hugging her doll closely to her and staring at Seth curiously. Emily places her long arms crisscross over Chloë's front and gives her a reassuring pat. Both girls continue to look at the man, neither saying a word.

Seth, tentative and unsure, attempts to break the ice. "Emily," he begins awkwardly, "we met at Katie's party, remember?"

Emily nods almost imperceptibly but doesn't respond verbally. She continues to regard Seth with her appraising look.

"I guess we didn't really meet though, did we?" Seth continues nervously. "We just sort of shook hands, and you went to find your sister. So we never really introduced ourselves . . . because . . . because you went looking for your sister . . . like I said." He shifts uncomfortably and now looks a little silly.

Chloë casually tilts her head back and rolls her large brown eyes up at her sister. Emily gives her another supportive pat. Chloë returns her merry gaze to Seth. Neither child says a word; they simply continue to look at the man, staring at him and waiting.

Seth struggles with the situation. He decides on another tactic, works up a smile, and kneels down, smiling at Chloë. "Hi Chloë, I see you have a little friend with you. Does she have a name?" Seth reaches towards the doll in a friendly gesture.

Chloë reacts quickly and pulls the doll away protectively, leaning harder into Emily. Emily hugs her sister to her lovingly, but neither girl shows any sign of being frightened of Seth. They simply look at him curiously.

Realizing his mistake, Seth immediately withdraws his hand and says apologetically, "I'm so sorry, Chloë. When you're ready, I'd like to meet her. I'm sure she's very special . . . very special just like you."

Chloë cracks a friendly smile at Seth. She rolls her head back again and looks up at Emily. Emily responds by giving her two gentle pats.

Chloë returns her gaze to Seth and in an excited voice suddenly says, "Her name is Gracie Ann. I'm her mommy!" She holds out one of Gracie Ann's little hands for Seth to shake.

Relieved, Seth gently shakes the doll's hand and says, "So nice to meet you, Gracie Ann, and also very nice to meet you too, Miss Chloë. I know you're a very good mommy."

"I am!" she replies and giggles. Emily watches Seth carefully.

"Miss Chloë," Seth says, "can you please tell me something about yourself that I should know? I want us to be really good friends."

Chloë responds fearlessly, "I don't get cold, and I don't take naps!"

Seth is amused. He is a little uncertain how to respond to such a plucky declaration of independence from this five-year-old little girl whose curls crowd across her forehead and tumble nearly to her eyes. "O . . . kay . . ." he slowly says, "I guess I can go with that."

Emily quietly observes Seth's interplay with her sister. Chloë's nostrils widen, and she begins sniffing the air. Her eyes get bigger as she recognizes the pleasant aroma.

Seth smiles, "I bet you smell the little surprise I have for you. A little fairy told me that chocolate chip cookies are your favorite. They should be *just about ready*. Would you like some?"

Wide-eyed, Chloë whispers in awe, "A fairy told you . . . really?" Then remembering the cookies she exclaims, "Yes!" and nods en–thusiastically, her big, brown curls bouncing energetically. Chloë suddenly stops and rolls her eyes up slowly at her sister, eyes that have become hopeful orbs, pleading for permission.

Emily smiles down at her sister affectionately and then looks at Seth. "Thank you," Emily says quietly. "That would be very nice."

"Yippee!" Chloë shouts.

"Wonderful!" Seth says. "Now ladies, allow me to seat you at the table." Still deftly concealing his prosthesis, he goes to the table and pulls out a chair for Chloë. He motions for her to come to the table. Giggling and holding Gracie Ann tightly, Chloë skips to the chair and sits in it. She grins up at Seth as he scoots the chair forward. Discovering that Chloë is not tall enough for the table, Seth immediately feigns a perfect French accent.

"Sacré bleu! The lovely mademoiselle needs the booster accommodations royale, oui?" He grabs the thick phone book from the counter and places it underneath Chloë. Next, he bows to Emily. "Mademoiselle Chloë should not dine alone, oui?"

Emily smiles without parting her lips and walks aesthetically to the chair. She allows Seth to pull her chair out and seat her, saying, as he does, "Thank you."

There are dessert plates, two glasses and a plastic tumbler, forks, and spoons already on the table that Seth had set out for the arriving company. All in one quick motion, he goes to the fridge and opens it, grabs a pitcher of cold milk, closes the door with a bounce of his hip, and returns to the table.

He says to Chloë in his French accent, "Mademoiselle, may I pour you the milk from the finest cow in all of Franz?" Chloë, giggling, nods enthusiastically. With a flourish, Seth fills her tumbler three quarters full. He then turns to Emily, "And the other beautiful Mademoiselle? May I?" Emily nods her assent. She remains formal with her shoulders back, holding herself at the table as gracefully as a swan. She is pleased with Seth's entertainment and is playing along for her sister's sake. With another flourish, Seth fills Emily's glass and dramatically places the pitcher on the table. With heightened drama, he announces, "Now Mademoiselles, la pièce de résistance! Aha! Ho! Ho!"

The girls watch intently, enjoying Seth's show. Seth is now caught up in his own antics, so much so that he forgets about his prosthesis. He whirls on his heels, pulls opens the wall oven door with his right hand, and quickly reaches in with his left, grabbing the hot cookie sheet.

"You'll burn yourself!" both girls shout in alarm.

Seth stops, his right hand holding open the oven door, his left inside the oven. He turns, looking sheepishly at the girls who are wide-eyed with concern, and says reassuringly in his heavy French accent, "Mademoiselles, do not be alarmed. Chef Seth *nevoor* burns himself. He has the grand secret. It is the envy of all the chefs in Franz!" He pulls out the cookie sheet from the oven. He is holding it between his steel hooks.

For the first time the girls see his prosthesis. From his expression, Seth is very apprehensive that the children will be frightened by it. But on the contrary, Emily and Chloë seem fascinated.

Seth deftly places the hot cookie sheet on the stove top to cool and quickly sits at the table. Encouraged, he decides to rest his prosthesis on the table in plain view. The children whisper to each other excitedly.

Chloë, with a child's directness, is the first to speak. "You're made of steel," she gasps. "Just like Superman!"

Seth laughs nervously and says, "At least part of me."

Chloë studies his prosthesis, trying to comprehend it. "Wow-wee . . ." she whispers. Suddenly, a thought pops in her head, and animated, she asks, "Can you fly?"

Seth laughs again saying, "You never know." He then adds ten–tatively, "Does Mademoiselle wish to see the grand secret . . . more closely?"

Chloë is clearly interested but unsure. She turns to Emily, who cautiously gives her approval. Chloë looks at Seth with uncertainty, and though hesitant, she slowly nods her head in the affirmative.

Still fearing rejection, Seth raises his prosthesis and guardedly dips it towards Chloë to within a few inches of her. Chloë is very curious about it and not the least bit frightened. Fascinated, she leans forward and studies it closely. Emily is looking on intently. There is a brief moment of suspense as Chloë carefully examines it with her eyes. Suddenly, the little girl grabs her spoon and bangs it rapidly on the steel hooks. *Clang! Clang! Clang!* Surprised, Seth bursts out laughing, as much in relief as at the child's innocent antics. Emily quickly reaches and places her hand gently over Chloë's and gravely shakes her head. Reluctantly, Chloë puts down the spoon.

"Awesome! You are made of steel!" Chloë exclaims.

Seth laughs and says, "Mademoiselles must keep the grand secret, no?" He leaves his chair and takes the cookie sheet between his hooks and with a spatula pushes the cookies onto a platter. They slide off in bulk. He places the platter on the table in front of the girls.

Chloë, with eager anticipation and glowing eyes, looks hungrily at the cookies. Her expression of joy immediately becomes a frown, and she turns to Gracie Ann, distressed. "Ohhh-noo," Chloë groans, "they've all run together . . . and they're mostly black." She moans dramatically, "Oh, Gracie Ann! What is there to do?" Putting her elbows on the table and plopping her little chin in her cupped hands, she observes forlornly, "Chef Seth never burns himself, but he sure burns the cookies."

In a sweet, motherly tone, Emily says, "I think there's a couple of good ones in here, Chloë. Please take your elbows off the table and sit up nicely like a little lady." Carefully trimming the blackened edges from two cookies on the platter with the end of her spoon, Emily reassures Chloë, "You see, here are two perfectly good ones just for you." Emily places the repaired cookies on Chloë's plate. Chloë is instantly happy and takes a bite from one, relishing it.

Gazing at the platter Seth says mournfully, "Sacré bleu."

Emily says, "Thank you, Chef Seth. You did a good job, mostly."

Playing his part well, Seth slowly shakes his head. "Mademoiselle is too kind. Sadly, Chef Seth sees he has failed."

Without thinking about it, Seth has rested his left arm on the table and his prosthesis is within easy reach of Chloë. Chloë, hearing the pretend sadness in Seth's voice, believes he is truly sad. She reaches out and gently pats his steel hooks. "Oh, there, there," she says with genuine sympathy. "We forgive you. Don't we, Gracie Ann? Don't we, Emily?"

"Of course we do," Emily agrees.

Leaving her small hand on his steel hooks, Chloë says reas–suringly, "See? It's all right."

Seth's eyes drop down to Chloë's small hand resting on his prosthesis. He is nearly moved to tears by her unconditional acceptance of him. Chloë, happily unaware, withdraws her hand and reaches for her tumbler of milk.

Regaining his composure, Seth employs his wonderful French accent saying, "Mais oui? Ha! Ha! It is the day of luck for the lovely Mademoiselles. Chef Seth has the dough for to make more cookies!"

Both children glance at each other gravely. Emily says quickly but politely, "Later please, Chef Seth. And we'd like to help, wouldn't we Chloë?"

Chloë eagerly nods her head in agreement and brushes curls away from her eyes, leaving a little smear of chocolate on her forehead.

"What do Mademoiselles wish to do?" Seth asks.

Emily gazes out the kitchen bay window. "We like to play outside," she says.

"Please! Please! *Please!*" Chloë begs.

"But of course!" Seth replies in his French accent. "Allow moi." He pulls the chair out for Chloë and helps her down.

Without waiting for assistance, Emily rises gracefully from her chair and is immediately at Chloë's side. Emily takes her napkin and cleans Chloë's mouth and hands and the chocolate streak from her forehead. Chloë doesn't like it and protests, making a face.

When her sister finishes scrubbing her, Chloë turns to Gracie Ann, who is lying face up on the table, and says sweetly, "Mommy is going outside to play. You be a good girl while Mommy is gone." Gracie Ann's feelings are hurt. She frowns when her mommy doesn't invite her to play with them outside.

Seth opens the back door for the children. As she passes through, Emily politely thanks Seth. They walk out into the backyard. Emily is holding Chloë's hand, reluctant to give her too much freedom right away.

The patio is a small, half-moon concrete slab covered by an awning. Sitting empty on the slab is a large, mesh wire cage. Beyond it, potted plants are arranged around the perimeter of the patio where it meets the edge of the grass. On the right side of the patio a dirt and gravel pathway winds through the backyard. On either side of the pathway, spaced nicely apart, are sycamore and pecan trees, with islands of round and rectangular flower beds nestled among them. A concrete bird bath is stationed ten yards down the path, and by it on the left is a concrete garden bench for sitting. The little trail continues deeper into the backyard and stops just short of a swing set. This swing set is made on a wooden A-frame and is a combination of two swings, a glider, a trapeze bar, and a slide. Aside from one sturdy swing still intact, the swing set is in sad condition: one swing seat is gone with just the ropes dangling loosely from the frame; the trapeze bar hangs vertically, pointing at the ground from one chain; the glider lies on its side in the grass; the slide looks rickety, and one of its ladder rungs is broken. Once stained a rich chocolate brown, the swing set is now faded, weathered, and grayish.

Directly across from the swing set but slightly further back in the yard is a playhouse crafted to look like an English castle. It has obviously been custom made by someone who was very skilled. There are two doors on its front: one is the size for a child to enter, the other is the size for an adult. There is a small window on either side of each door, one of which is broken, and there is a large four-paned window on the far side facing the swings. Above, on the roof at either end, are parapets on the castle walls where pennant flags once flew in the breeze. The castle had been painted pink and white, but like the swing set, it is blanched terribly with age and neglect. One can readily see the entire backyard was once a children's paradise for play and imagination, but now that paradise has faded into near obscurity along with the happy echoes of children's laughter.

The Fleming children are holding hands and gazing around, interested in all the sights. Chloë is anxious to break loose and run down the path to explore, but Emily, ever cautious, is not ready to release her. Pointing at the big cage, Chloë is the first to speak.

"Was something in it?" she asks amazed.

"My sister and I kept little birds in it called diamond doves," Seth answers.

"Awesome!" Chloë says.

Seth grins at her and continues, "We started with just two little diamond doves, Bobby and Nellie, and soon we had a whole bunch. They kept having babies."

"They had babies?" Chloë responds enthralled.

Seth chuckles. "Well, they laid eggs, and the babies hatched from the eggs."

"Wow! What happened to them?"

"We gave most of them to our friends."

Chloë turns to Emily and says, "Did you hear that, Em? Suddenly crestfallen she adds, "We had a bird, didn't we? He was a real nice one. What happened to Bluebonnet, Em?"

Tenderly, Emily replies, "When we moved, we gave him to our friends, Chlo. They had lots of other birds for Bluebonnet to play with. He's very happy."

The sudden sadness in Chloë's tone catches Seth's attention. He listens intently to the poignant exchange between the sisters.

Sadly, Chloë answers, "Oh, I'd forgotten that part. I miss him Em . . ."

To distract her sister, Emily says brightly, "Do you want to go exploring, Chloë?"

"Yes!" Chloë says excitedly.

Releasing her hand, Emily gives Chloë her freedom, and her sister bounds off. Chloë stops at the bird bath and looks in. She turns to Seth and shouts, "There's no water! The birds can't take a bath if there's no water!" Chloë races further down the path.

Both Seth and Emily are watching Chloë from the patio. Emily hasn't taken her eyes off of her sister. Deciding to be unassuming about it, Seth casually asks, "You and Chloë had birds?"

Her eyes focused on Chloë, Emily answers without emotion. "We had a blue parakeet. Chloë named him Bluebonnet."

"It was nice you found a home for him when you moved," Seth says compassionately.

"We didn't move," Emily responds pointedly. "They wouldn't let us bring him. I don't know what happened to Bluebonnet. It doesn't matter." Her eyes haven't strayed from Chloë.

Seth is caught off guard by Emily's frank statement. "Emily," he says sympathetically, "I'm sorry."

Emotionless, Emily responds, "Why?" and she says it in a tone of such finality that Seth understands she is not expecting an answer from him nor does she invite one. Before Seth can say anything more, Emily calls out, "Wait, Chlo. Stay right there. I'm coming."

Chloë is squatting down, looking at something in the grass. "Hurry, Em, hurry!" When Emily reaches her, Chloë says, "Look Em, a grasshopper." Chloë quickly looks up. "There's a squirrel in that tree. And a bunch of birds! You see 'em all, Em?"

Enjoying her sister's excitement, Emily looks up and points, "Yes, Chlo, I do! And I see a red bird. Do you?"

"I do! I do!"

"How does a red bird go, Chlo?"

"Tweet-Tweet! Tweet-Tweet!"

Emily hugs her, praising, "That's right, Chlo. That's right."

Then Chloë sees the swing set, excitedly grabs Emily's hand, and starts tugging her towards the swing. "C'mon, Em. Let's go swing! Seth can push us!"

Emily glances quickly over her shoulder to Seth, signaling him to follow them. When they arrive at the swing set Chloë stops abruptly, surveying its poor condition. She looks at Seth coolly. "It's kind of wrecked," she says, mildly accusing him.

Seth stammers apologetically, "It hasn't been used in a long time, Chlo." He checks the intact swing for sturdiness. "But this one still works fine," he says, cheerfully.

Chloë immediately brightens and turns to Emily. "Let's swing together, Em. Seth'll push us."

Laughing at Chloë's audacity, Seth says, "Ladies, it would be my pleasure. Hop on!"

Emily is cautious. She is the first to sit on the swing, and she pulls hard on the ropes to make certain they are strong. She looks at Seth questioningly.

Standing behind the swing Seth tugs on the ropes again and reassures her, "It's perfectly safe, Emily."

Emily pats her lap for an impatient Chloë to come join her. Chloë climbs onto her sister's lap front-wise. She reaches her arms around Emily's back, and leans into her, laying her face to one side against her sister's chest. Emily is holding onto the ropes tightly. For a moment nothing happens. Chloë promptly lifts up her head and commands, "Push!"

Seth assumes an English accent, "Of course, m'lady."

He pushes them slowly with gathering momentum, higher and higher. With her head thrown back and her brown curls flying in the wind, Chloë laughs more gaily with each strong push. She brings her head forward and buries her face in Emily's blouse, giggling. Emily looks ahead with a controlled smile, holding onto the ropes firmly and enjoying the thrill of the air rushing by and the squeals of delight coming from Chloë.

Daringly, Chloë now tilts from Emily, inclining her head far back, looking up at the sky and laughing. "Seth, make us go higher! Higher and *faster*!" she shouts.

"This is high enough. Seth can't push us any higher," Emily calls out cautiously.

"Yes he can!" Chloë yells with glee. "He's made of steel! Higher, Seth! Faster and *higher*." With her head dropped back she suddenly glimpses the playhouse. "Wait! Stop! What's that over there?" she calls.

Quickly Seth stops the swing. Chloë jumps off and runs over to the playhouse. "C'mon, Em! Let's go see! What is it?"

Emily and Seth follow Chloë to the front of the playhouse. "This was my sister's playhouse," Seth explains. "Our dad built it."

"Awesome! Can we see it?" Chloë asks, her eyes glowing with curiosity.

"Sure," says Seth.

"Why's it got two doors?" Chloë asks.

"One's for little people and one's for big people," Seth answers.

"Can we go inside?" Chloë asks.

"Probably pretty dusty in there," Seth warns.

Chloë turns to Emily, "You go first."

"I'll go first," Seth laughs. "Make sure there aren't any bee's nests." The children nod their heads in agreement. Seth turns the knob on the larger door and pushes on it. It sticks, and he gently pushes on it twice more before it gives way and opens. A shower of dust rains down. Once the dust has settled, Seth enters the playhouse. He checks out the inside and then comes back out. "Everything's okay," he says, "just a little dusty, but not as much as I thought it would be."

He pushes the smaller door open for the children to enter. Emily goes in with Chloë glued to her side, and Seth returns through the adult door. With amazed expressions on their faces one would think the children had just entered a secret hidden cave filled with treasure chests. Inside the playhouse there's an old table with several children's chairs around it, a small vanity, a cupboard with dust-coated tiny cups and saucers and dishes stacked on its shelves, and a play stove.

Chloë, bright with curiosity but cautious, grabs Emily's hand. "It's kinda scary in here," she says apprehensively, "but it's really neat."

"When my sister was little, she and all of her friends spent hours playing in here," Seth says.

"Did you play in here?" Chloë whispers.

"No," Seth laughs. "My sister had a sign on the door outside that said, 'No Boys Allowed.' My sister's rule—and believe me, she ruled."

"If it was ours, we would play in it all the time," says Emily. "It's safe in here."

Seth is struck by Emily's words. He understands the deeper meaning they carry.

"I'm thirsty, Em," Chloë whines.

Emily squeezes her hand. "Okay, Chlo. We'll go back now."

"That's a good idea," Seth agrees. "We'll get something to drink. I'll make more cookies."

"Can Emily make the cookies? She's really good at it," Chloë says. It's more of an appeal than a question.

Grinning, Seth replies, "Sure. While Emily's making the cookies, Chlo, I'll show you how to take a dollar bill and turn it into a rhinoceros."

"You can do that? Awesome!" Chloë says.

Emily watches Seth again, carefully studying him. She is forming a favorable opinion of the man.

"Sure can!" Seth brags. "And an elephant and a giraffe, too."

"Uh-uh . . . really?" says Chloë wondrously.

"Absolutely, really can," Seth assures her. "C'mon, let's go, and I'll show you."

They leave the playhouse; the girls exit through the children's door and Seth goes out through the adult's door. Once outside, Emily stoops down, allowing Chloë to hop onto her back, piggyback style. As they walk to the house Chloë clings happily to her sister, kissing her sweetly on her neck and laying one side of her face on Emily's shoulder, feeling content and secure.

When they enter the kitchen, Chloë hops off and bounces up and down in excitement. "I wanna see the rhinoceros. I wanna *see!*"

Emily pulls out the chair with the phone book on it and helps Chloë to sit down at the table.

Gracie Ann lies on the table where Chloë left her. It appears to Seth that the doll, somehow, appears to have an unhappy expression on her face.

Picking up the doll gently, Chloë says, "Hi, Gracie Ann. I told you Mommy would be right back." She hugs Gracie Ann tightly.

Standing by the counter next to the kitchen sink, Emily assumes control and says, "Seth, please make the rhinoceros for Chloë. I'll make the cookies."

"Don't you want to watch too?" asks Seth.

"I'll be watching," Emily replies politely.

Seth sits down at the table next to Chloë. Emily looks in the cabinet and finds another plastic cup for her sister and a water glass for Seth. She draws water from the tap and brings their cups to them; her sister's is half filled and Seth's is filled to the top. Next, she goes to the fridge, takes out the bowl of cookie dough, and sets it on the counter by the stove. Taking the platter from the table with its sad remains, Emily finds the garbage can underneath the sink and unceremoniously dumps the burnt cookies into the trash. She goes about her business very purposefully but always with grace and poise.

Seth plucks a crisp dollar bill from his pants pocket. Chloë watches him, wondrous and wide-eyed. He turns it over, telling her, "Just a normal, ordinary one dollar bill, see?"

Chloë, mesmerized, nods her head enthusiastically, her big curls bouncing out of control. She crosses her arms on the table and rests her chin on them, watching Seth carefully while swinging one leg under the table. Gracie Ann is propped up next to her mommy, watching too.

"Now," says Seth with magician-like showmanship, "watch *very, very* closely."

He begins meticulously folding the dollar bill. He works methodically and is pleasantly surprised that his hooks don't impede his progress like he thought they might. He expertly folds the dollar, crafting it carefully.

Chloë's eyes follow his every move and stay riveted on the dollar bill as its shape changes. Under the table, her leg is swinging faster.

The grand finale has arrived, and Seth says, "Close your eyes Chlo . . . hold out your hand."

Chloë closes her eyes tightly and sucks in a deep breath. She holds out her palm, keeping it as still as she possibly can.

Seth places the dollar bill in Chloë's palm. "Now, open your eyes."

Chloë opens her eyes and squeals, "A rhinoceros! Look, Em! See what Seth did! It's like magic!"

Emily steps over and looks at Seth's work. "That's really good." She smiles at Seth and pats Chloë on the head affectionately. Emily returns to the oven, checks the temperature setting, walks back to the cookie sheet, and begins preparing it.

"Do some more magic!" Chloë demands.

"What would you like? An elephant or a giraffe?" Seth asks.

"An elephant!" Chloë giggles.

"An elephant, please," corrects Emily in a motherly tone.

"An elephant, please," echoes Chloë dutifully.

"One elephant coming up," says Seth.

Taking another dollar bill from his pocket, Seth begins again. While he fashions an elephant, Emily spoons out the last of the dough, pops the cookies in the oven using a hot pad, and sets the timer. Emily comes and sits at the table next to her sister just as Seth places the finished elephant in Chloë's palm.

Chloë squeals with delight again. She places the elephant on the table next to the rhinoceros. "They can be friends," she says sweetly.

"Yes, best friends. Will you take good care of them, please?" asks Seth.

Breathless, her eyes like brown saucers, Chloë whispers, "They're mine?"

"Of course they are. I made them *especially* for you," he says.

Chloë beams and drops her head low to the table and begins talking in a motherly fashion to the elephant and the rhinoceros. "I'm your new mommy," she says. "I'm going to take real good care of you. And this is your big sister, Gracie Ann." She plays with them, totally absorbed.

Emily has been quietly observing Seth and Chloë during this exchange, just as she has been appraising Seth's interplay with Chloë since they arrived. In an approving way she says, "Thank you for being so nice to Chloë. What do you call that?"

"It's a Japanese art form called origami," Seth says. "I started learning it when I was your age."

"In school?" Emily asks.

"No, after school. My mom took me to a special place. I was taught by a true Japanese master. His name is Mr. Nakamura."

"Was it hard to learn?" Emily asks, interested.

"I've always had a knack for making and drawing things, Emily. It didn't take me long to learn the basics. But it takes a long time to learn how to make the more difficult shapes."

Ever perceptive, Emily observes, "Not you, though. You were the best student, weren't you Seth?"

Surprised by her insight and a bit bashful, Seth admits, "Origami came more easily to me than it did to others."

"You have more than a knack. You have a gift," she says.

"Some people think so," Seth answers. "I could show you how to make something if you like."

"Thank you, no," she replies, reserved. "But Chloë would like it."

Chloë looks up excitedly, "Show me, please."

Seth pulls out another dollar bill, saying agreeably, "Okay, one more. I'm running out of money here. I'll show you how to make a little dog."

Emily suddenly looks concerned and quickly asks, "Could you make something else, please?"

"We used to have a dog," Chloë says, "a big red dog, like Clifford. Her name was Blossom." The little girl becomes teary-eyed as she remembers their favorite family pet. "What happened to our dog, Em? She was a nice dog. A real nice one. I liked her."

Emily hugs Chloë, saying cheerfully, "Oh, Chloë, don't you remember? Blossom's living in the best home ever with lots of little children who play with her all the time. We'll see her soon." She looks at Seth and says, "Maybe something else, please?" Scrambling to distract Chloë, Emily says sweetly, "Warm cookies coming up, Chlo. You ready?"

"Yay! Milk, too?"

"Milk, too!" and Emily takes her tumbler to the counter.

Seth has picked up on Emily's concern and quickly switches to another figure. "I'll teach you how to make a star," he says cheerily. "Would you like that?"

"A star? Awesome!" Chloë responds.

Seth folds the dollar several times and presents Chloë with a star. She is awestruck. He hands her another dollar bill and encourages her, "Now, you try it. It'll take a while to learn, but just keep trying. You'll do it, Chlo. I promise. I'll be here to help you."

"Okay," Chloë says eagerly. Beaming with excitement, she begins working on the dollar bill with Seth overseeing her.

While Chloë attempts to make a star, Emily retrieves the cookies from the oven and places the cookie sheet on the stove to cool. She turns to observe Seth and Chloë at the table. Watching her sister, Emily stands there like a mother contentedly looking at her child. She is relieved that Chloë is now playing happily, distracted from her thoughts about their beloved family dog, Blossom. Emily forces herself to hold back her own tears as she remembers Blossom and their home. So practiced is she with her emotional control, no one would ever guess Emily's true feelings at this moment.

Emily opens the fridge door, pulls out the pitcher of milk, and pours a child's size amount for Chloë in the tumbler. She then scoops up the cookies with a spatula and slides them onto a plate. She takes the plate of cookies and the tumbler of milk to the table and sits by her sister across from Seth. Just as she sits down, Chloë looks up happily and gushes.

"Look, Em. I'm learning to make a star! Seth says I'll do it if I keep trying."

"You'll do it, Chlo," encourages Emily. "I know you will."

Chloë takes two cookies from the plate that Emily offers her. Emily then offers the plate to Seth. As she does so, she gives him a look that says, "thank you" and asks, "Would you like some milk too? I'd be happy to get it for you."

"Yes, please," he says. Emily takes his glass, goes to the counter, pours him milk, returns to the table, and hands it to him.

"Thank you," he says.

"You're welcome," she responds, and she sits down ladylike with perfect posture next to her sister. She watches her enjoy her cookies and milk.

"These are good!" Chloë says happily.

"A lot better than mine," Seth agrees.

"Thank you," Emily says.

Chloë finishes her second cookie and asks, "Can we go play?"

Emily looks at Seth and says, "Mrs. Mason told us we could play in her room. Is that all right?"

"Sure," he says. "You'll be sleeping in there, too. Chloë, you'll really like my sister's room. It's awesome."

"Let's go!" exclaims Chloë.

"You two go," Emily says. "I need to see about dinner."

"My mom left a ton of food in the refrigerator," Seth says.

"Okay, I'll look at what your mother left." She glances at the clock on the wall. "It's four p.m. Dinner will be ready at six. Seth, will you play with Chloë?"

"You don't have to do dinner, Emily. I'll do it," Seth says.

Emily gives Seth a considerate smile. "Chef Seth, thank you, but I enjoy making dinner. You and Chloë go have fun, please."

Chloë jumps from the chair and bounces excitedly. "Yay! Come play with me. Please! Please! *Please!*"

Seth chuckles, "Okay, Chloë, I'll grab the backpacks."

Asking permission, Chloë says, "Can I leave my dollar on the table with her friends?"

"Sure you can," Seth answers lightly. "It's the best place for it. We'll work on it some more later." Chloë and Seth walk out of the kitchen and go down the hall to Kathryn's bedroom. Emily opens the fridge door, takes an inventory of its contents, and begins setting out a few covered dishes that Mrs. McAllister had lovingly prepared. Lastly, she checks the freezer and discovers a frozen apple pie that she decides Seth and her sister would enjoy for dessert.

CHAPTER ELEVEN

Emily has been so busy in the kitchen preparing dinner she hasn't noticed the time. At five forty-five p.m., Seth walks back into the kitchen alone. Emily stands over the stove stirring a steaming pot. She removes the spoon, taps it lightly on the edge of the pot, and places it on the spoon holder. Emily turns and goes to the wall oven, opens the door, quickly checks its contents, and closes the door. When Emily sees Seth come in alone, she's immediately concerned and asks, "Where's Chloë?"

Lightly, Seth replies, "She's still playing in Katie's room. Chlo discovered my sister's dress-up box. I know boys can't stay in a room where girls are dressing so I asked Chloë's permission to leave. Does she ever run out of energy?"

"She goes until she conks out," Emily answers.

"Can I help?" Seth offers.

Emily graciously nods at him and says, "Yes, please set the table. Dinner will be ready in a few minutes."

"What's for dinner?"

"Really, your mom did it all. You're very lucky to have her, you know. I did the pie first. The rest I just warmed up. There's meatloaf and mashed potatoes in the oven, and green beans and gravy on the stove. Chloë doesn't like green beans—she'll protest for sure. But she needs to eat something green."

"I'm with Chloë," Seth declares. "I hate green beans. I'm sur—prised Mom even made them."

Stirring the pot on the stove, Emily looks at Seth and pointedly says in a no-nonsense tone, "Your mother fixed them because she knows they're good for you."

Seth shrugs, "She's not here though. Mom will never know."

Elevating her eyebrows and looking directly at him, Emily says instructively, "Moms always know. I expect you to eat your green beans and pretend to like them. Chloë won't eat hers if you don't." She looks disapprovingly at his table setting. "The knife goes next to the plate on the right with the spoon, the fork on the left. Fold the napkin neatly under the fork. No knife for Chloë."

Grinning and thinking to himself that Emily sounds just like Katie did when she was her age, Seth dutifully answers, "Yes, ma'am," and rearranges the flatware as instructed.

"Thank you," Emily says. She goes to the wall oven, removes the food, and places the hot dishes on the stove while Seth finishes with the table settings. Once everything is out, she asks Seth, "It's safer to serve from the stove. Do you mind doing that?"

"My pleasure," he responds.

Emily goes to the door leading to the hallway and calls out sweetly to Chloë, "Chlo? Chlo? Dinner's ready. Stop playing, and come to the table, please."

A muffled voice answers from the distance, "Okay. I'm coming."

Emily turns from the hallway door and walks back to the kitchen table. Seth pulls the chair out for her. Emily nods, smiles, and sits with perfect posture. "Thank you," she says softly.

Emily's chair is facing the door that leads to the hallway. Seth stands directly behind her next to the counter. There is a rustle as Chloë enters the room with a clop, clop of her shoes. She is dressed in a long, blue-sequined gown, a string of clunky Wilma Flintstone-like plastic pearls adorn her neck, and a large rhinestone ring sparkles on her right ring finger. Her shoulders are caressed by a feathery white boa, and on each wrist there are several gleam—ing bangles that clank when she moves. Her shoes are absolutely stunning. Chloë is wearing dazzling, low-heeled, red patent shoes two sizes too big that look exactly like Dorothy's red slippers from *The Wizard of Oz*. Her costume is splendidly capped by the wide-brimmed, purple hat that's angled smartly atop her little head. It sports a prominent orange feather that juts a foot above the right crown. Tonight's Haute couture is finished off dramatically with over-sized, glittery, white-framed sunglasses that want to slide off her nose, causing Chloë to keep her face permanently tilted up to prevent it from happening. In the crook of her right arm is Gracie Ann, whom Chloë has managed to dress-up in clothes she stripped from one of Kathryn's old dolls. Gracie Ann appears to be a princess from some strange realm where tailors and seamstresses have been horribly trained or simply don't exist at all. Due to Gracie Ann's stature, the doll's clothes are comically tight and small on her: the buttons across her front threaten to burst at any second, which would be horribly embarrassing should it happen. Chloë enters the kitchen dramatically, stops abruptly, preens, and waits to be admired.

"Oh Chloë, what a beautiful lady you are!" Emily exclaims.

Keeping her little face pointed skyward lest her sunglasses slide off, Chloë announces breathlessly, "I'm . . . a Princess Lady!"

Seth pulls out the chair for Chloë with the telephone book on it, and makes a sweeping gesture saying, "Your royal throne, Princess Lady."

In oddly elegant fashion, Chloë clop-clops to the table, nearly bumping into it. Seth reaches down and lifts Chloë up into the chair. Emily motions to Chloë, instructing her to remove her sunglasses, which she does. Emily places the napkin in her lap and nods to Chloë to do the same.

Seth plays his part well. Reverting to his English butler accent, he says, "Miss Emily and Miss Princess Lady, if you will permit me? I will serve your entrées from the manor's high kitchen." Ever dramatic, Seth takes their plates, serves from the stove, and places the full plates in front of the children. While he is serving his own plate, Chloë notices her green beans and frowns. Seth returns to the table with his plate and sits down.

Emily offers a hand to Seth and her other hand to Chloë.

They hold hands around the table as Emily says grace. "Dear Lord, thank you for our many blessings and our new friend, Seth. Thank you for Chloë, my wonderful sister. Please bless this food to the nourishment of our bodies. Amen."

The moment Chloë opens her eyes she seizes the chance to complain, "Green beans? Ohhh . . . I hate green beans!" and she makes a yucky face.

"You only have a few," Emily says motherly. "They're good for you. We're all having some."

To satisfy herself that they all have an equal serving of green beans, Chloë looks at Emily's plate and then at Seth's. Irate, she complains, "Not fair! Seth doesn't have as many green beans as I do!"

Emily immediately looks at Seth's plate and then at him, purses her lips, and raises her eyebrows in disapproval.

Seth eyes his plate and then looks up at the girls. His face is a mug shot; there is guilt written all over it. "Gee whizz . . ." he says sheepishly. "How did that happen?" He looks innocently from Chloë to Emily.

Emily gives Seth another disapproving glance, and he drops his head in shame, but not in remorse. He really hates green beans.

"You're right, Chlo," Emily says, agreeing with her. "Seth was just being nice. Making sure there were enough green beans for us." She rises gracefully from the table and, taking Seth's plate, says, "Thank you, Seth. I'll get you some more."

Almost blushing, Seth nods, knowing he has been caught. Emily goes to the stove and spoons more green beans onto his plate. As she does so, Seth and Chloë stare at each other across the table. Chloë's little arms are crossed, and she challenges him with her eyes. She casts a wary glance at her sister, and once sure Emily won't catch her, she quickly sticks her tongue out at Seth. Seth grins and shakes his head, smiling to himself, and thinking how comic this is. Emily returns to the table, sets Seth's plate in front of him, and takes her seat again ever so lithely. Chloë eases up from her chair and surveys Seth's plate hawk-like, satisfying herself that he now has the right amount of green beans to make things fair.

Seth looks around the table and feigns a cheerful smile. "I

just love green beans. Doesn't everyone?" He stabs a few with his fork and begins chewing them, forcing a half smile at Chloë, who watches him suspiciously, squinting at him with skeptical eyes. He looks over at Emily who nods her head approvingly, teacher-like.

As the dinner progresses, Emily finishes her dinner first. Seth has eaten his meatloaf and mashed potatoes with gravy, but he has eaten only a few green beans. Although Chloë has eaten well enough, she hasn't touched a single green bean on her plate.

"Chlo, please eat your green beans," Emily directs her.

Chloë puts her left elbow on the table, plops her chin in her hand, rolls her eyes mournfully, and guides the green beans dolefully from one end of her plate to the other with her fork, hoping somehow they will just disappear. "Ohhh . . . I really hate green beans," she moans. She looks at Emily glumly, pokes out her bottom lip, and says petulantly, "You're so bossy!"

Motherly in tone, Emily patiently instructs her, "Chloë, please take your elbow off the table, and remember to sit up straight with your shoulders back, like a little lady. Start by eating just one green bean. Just one, please, I know you can do it."

Chloë slides her elbow from the table. Sucking in her breath dramatically, she drops her eyes, frowns miserably, and now herds the green beans round and round on her plate.

Trying to encourage her, Seth says energetically, "Chloë, green beans will help you grow up to be pretty and strong."

That comment is the last straw for Chloë, who hasn't forgotten about Seth's earlier trickery by a long shot. She looks at Seth detached, totally unimpressed. Slowly, she puts down her fork, leans back in her chair, and crosses her arms over her chest. She narrows her eyes and gives Seth a steely stare. With her little mouth pursed up, she challenges him, "You're just saying that!" Looking directly in his eyes, she adds defiantly, drawing out each word for emphasis, "I . . . hate . . . green . . . beans. And . . . I'm-not-going-to-eat-any!"

The gloves are off.

"Chloë . . ." says Emily, issuing a mother-like warning.

Seth thinks to himself, "You've got to be kidding me? I can't let myself be bullied by a five year old, particularly one dressed-up in a silly white boa, plastic pearls, and an oversized purple hat with that ridiculous orange feather!" Not to be outdone, Seth stares straight back at Chloë and says deliberately in a perfect German accent, "I see . . . hmm . . . Fraulein Princess Lady refuses to eat her green beans, ya? Green beans that will help her grow up to be a very pretty and strong Fraulein, ya? Vell . . . I have my vays . . . very persuasive vays of convincing little Frauleins to eat their green beans."

"*Do not!*" Chloë retorts, now downright sassy. Her eyes are shining brightly though. She senses a game.

Emily chooses to observe patiently and remains quiet. Her confidence in Seth is growing. She sits elegantly with her shoulders back and her head held high.

Seth rises stiffly from his chair. Taking his time, he rocks his chair on its back legs as he walks it under the table. He eyes Chloë as he slowly marches to one wall and stops.

Chloë watches him with insubordinate eyes that follow his every step. The clever little girl wonders why Seth stopped next to the chalkboard.

"Vone last warning," Seth cautions. "Please, Fraulein Princess Lady, eat your green beans . . . or else!"

Chloë rapidly shakes her head no, causing her pearls to rattle, her dress to rustle, and her hat to fly off. She is fixated on Seth, and her brown eyes gleam with anticipation.

Dramatically, Seth says, "Fraulein Princess Lady, you leave me no choice. See how you like this! Ha-ha!" Seth places his steel hooks high up on the slate board and drags them down achingly slowly. As he does, they make a bone chilling, high-pitched grating sound.

The children's hands fly up to their ears, covering them. "Stop!" Chloë laughs. "Stop! I'll eat one."

Seth raises his eyebrows, stops, and watches her closely while leaving his hooks pressed firmly on the chalkboard. "Very goot, Fraulein."

Forgetting her table manners, Chloë picks up one green bean with her fingers, carefully places it in her mouth, and chews it slowly, never taking her mischievous eyes off Seth.

"And another Fraulein?" Seth commands.

Chloë looks at him and cracks a smile. She is teasing him now and cautiously shakes her head, no. Without her hat, Chloë's ringlets rock and swing.

Seth drags his hand down an inch more making the horrible sound again—*screech!*

Chloë instantly stops shaking her head.

Seth stops instantly.

Eyeing him, Chloë gives a quick half shake of her head.

Seth drags his hooks an inch—*screech!*

There proceeds a quick series of exchanges between them like a tennis ball volleying rocket-like back and forth at Wimbledon: half-shake—*screech!* Half-shake—*screech!* Half shake—*screech!* By now, Chloë is giggling out loud.

Then Seth delivers his coup de grâce. Pressing harder, he drags his steel hooks down the chalkboard six inches creating a mega decibel rusty iron hinge sound.

Chloë surrenders, laughing and shouting, "Okay! Okay! I'll eat all my green beans!" Chloë immediately picks up one green bean after another and quickly finishes them off. Emily had put only five on her plate in the first place. Seth had served himself two.

Seth lifts his hooks from the slate board and returns to his seat. "A little child psychology works every time," he thinks, congratulating himself on his victory over a five-year-old little girl. He looks at her triumphantly and says, "Fraulein Princess Lady, very goot!"

Emily is pleasantly pleased with Seth's antics. She gives him her approval with her eyes.

Chloë says sweetly, "Em, can we have dessert now, please? I finished all of my green beans."

"And you did a very good job, Chlo," Emily praises. "Yes, I'll get dessert now."

Scrutinizing Seth closely, Chloë says indignantly, "None for Seth!"

"What?" he protests. "Why not?"

Chloë eyes become half slits. "Because *you* haven't finished *your* green beans—like I have!"

Glancing at Seth, Emily says pointedly, "But he will, Chlo. And as soon as he finishes his green beans there'll be dessert for everyone." She tilts her head, stares at Seth, and waits. He must obey.

Seth caves and confesses, "I was just about to. Really, I was." And he thinks to himself, "Emily is Katie all over again. I'm right back where I started in this house."

"Hurry up!" Chloë demands. Then looking at *him* triumphantly she adds in a sing-song tone, "I'm wait . . . *ting* . . ."

CHAPTER TWELVE

An hour after dinner, Seth is sitting comfortably on the living room couch. Emily has gotten herself and Chloë into their bedtime routine. The children have brushed their teeth and have had their baths. They come into the living room dressed in their pajamas. Chloë has Gracie Ann under one arm, and in one hand, she is carrying a book from Kathryn's bookshelf—*The Runaway Bunny*.

"Will you read me a bedtime story, please?" Chloë asks.

Seth smiles at her and says, "Sure Chlo, climb up on the couch, and we'll read together."

Chloë hands him the book, and she climbs up on the couch on Seth's left side. She picks up his left arm, drapes it over her shoulder, and nuzzles into him. Again Seth observes that Chloë has no fear of his prosthesis. To the contrary, he can see that she believes it will keep her safe and secure.

Emily takes the chair across from them and observes Seth and Chloë's comfortable relationship. She sits with perfect posture and poise: her shoulders are back, her head is held high, and her hands are folded daintily in her lap.

"*The Runaway Bunny*, I haven't seen this one in a long time," Seth says affably.

"I like looking at the pictures," Chloë says, sounding tired.

"Me too," Seth agrees. He begins turning the pages slowly without reading. As he comes to the end of the book, Chloë yawns.

Emily rises from her chair. She comes to Chloë and says affectionately, "It's time for bed, Chlo."

"Will you carry me?" she asks.

"Of course I will." Emily picks up Chloë and rests her on her right hip. Chloë has her arms around her sister's neck, and she places her head on Emily's shoulder. She has mistakenly left Gracie Ann on the couch sitting next to Seth.

"Let's say goodnight to Seth, okay Chlo?" and Emily kisses her lightly.

"Goodnight Seth," Chloë says sleepily.

"Goodnight," he chimes.

"Goodnight," says Emily. She turns to walk out of the room.

Chloë whispers something in her ear, and she stops.

Seth watches them, wondering why they stopped. Emily nods her head, walks back to Seth, and stands next to him.

"Lean this way, please," Emily says.

Not knowing what to expect, Seth bends towards Emily. As he does so, Emily tilts towards him, and Chloë leans out and quickly kisses him on the cheek. Chloë immediately buries her face in her sister's shoulder, hiding. Emily turns and walks towards the bedroom. Keeping her head hidden behind her sister's shoulder, Chloë raises her small hand and waves goodnight to Seth by flapping her little fingers up and down.

Seth waves back even though he knows she can't see him. When they are gone, Seth thoughtfully touches the spot on his cheek where Chloë kissed him.

A moment later, Emily returns to the living room. "She left Gracie Ann," Emily explains. "Chlo can't sleep without her."

"She's right here," Seth says and gently hands Gracie Ann to Emily.

"Thank you," she says softly and starts to leave.

"Emily?"

Emily stops and looks at him with a question in her eyes.

"Earlier," Seth begins apologetically, "I didn't mean to make Chloë sad about her dog. I'm really sorry. I just didn't know."

Quietly, Emily explains, "Blossom was our Golden. We got her in the spring when Mommy's flowers were blooming. Mommy loved her flowers. That's why we named her Blossom. When they took us away, they made us leave her."

Seth is stung by Emily's story. With wholehearted sympathy he offers, "Emily, I'm so very sorry."

"It doesn't matter," Emily says without any trace of feeling, surprising Seth again with her controlled, unemotional response. She turns and leaves.

Seth remains on the couch thinking deeply about the children and how their lives have been shattered. Especially, he thinks about Emily. He didn't pick up on it at the time, but the full meaning of Emily's earlier comment about his mother suddenly strikes him with the force of an avalanche: *"You're very lucky to have her, you know."* He realizes he *is* lucky to have such a good mother. He fully comprehends that for Emily and her sister, the loss of their mother is an incalculable loss, immeasurable by any standard on earth, just like the loss of his father was for him and his sister. "How insensitive of me," he faults himself, "not to have given it more thought before." With the loss of both her mother and her father, Seth wonders how this little girl can cope at all, and his admiration of and respect for her grows exponentially when he reflects on Emily's determination and devotion to her sister.

o o o

Emily brings Gracie Ann to Chloë, who is already in bed and under the covers. "Here she is, Chlo," Emily says sweetly. "You know Gracie Ann can't sleep without you." Emily sits on the edge of the bed next to Chloë and strokes her hair, gazing lovingly at her sister.

Chloë whispers, "Em, I like Seth. Don't you?"

"Yes Chlo. He's very nice."

"Can we come live here? Can this be our new home?" Chloë asks hopefully.

"We'll see." Emily tucks the covers more tightly under her sister's chin. She strokes her hair gently and kisses her on the cheek. "It's time to go to sleep now, Chlo."

"Will you hold me, Em? Will you hold me until I go to sleep?"

"Of course I will. You'll be my little bunny." Emily slides into bed next to her sister, drapes a willowy arm around Chloë, and says softly, "I'll keep holding you long after you're asleep and dreaming sweet dreams. And when you wake up in the morning I'll be right here, holding you."

Drifting off to sleep, Chloë says dreamily, "I bet he can fly, Em . . . I just know he can . . ."

Emily whispers, "Go to sleep now, little bunny," and she kisses Chloë lightly on her forehead as she reaches and turns off the table lamp.

CHAPTER THIRTEEN

The next morning, Sunday morning, Seth and the children are in the kitchen. It is raining outside. Emily wears spearmint colored cotton twill pants, a simple cream blouse, and her cream colored tennis shoes. Chloë is proud of her Hello Kitty pullover shirt and Hello Kitty jeans that go so nicely with her pink tennis shoes that flash at the heels. Seth is comfortably dressed in a long sleeve blue denim shirt, black jeans, and brush suede loafers.

Refusing Seth's offer to help, Emily has taken charge again and is busy doing two things: cleaning up after breakfast and giving Chloë a lesson in being a "Little Lady."

Sitting at the table, Seth is casually sorting through the mail and glancing at Chloë. He is trying to retain a serious expression. Next to him, Gracie Ann is propped up on the table, watching and listening with great interest and hoping to learn something very important about becoming a little lady herself.

Chloë, standing very still and looking quite unhappy, has a book balanced on her head. Emily is standing directly behind her. Concentrating, Chloë begins walking methodically towards the chair that's facing them that Emily has placed approximately six feet away. The little girl always struggles with her lessons in etiquette, and to say she was annoyed today with the whole exercise would be like saying the passengers on the *Titanic* were annoyed their ship was soon sinking straight to the seafloor. Chloë rolls her eyes up anxiously at the book, hoping beyond hope that it will stay balanced on her head and silently huffs, "I wish my head was flat!"

"Remember?" Emily encourages her, "shoulders back . . . eyes forward now . . . head held high . . . that's *very* good."

Chloë carefully moves forward one slow, excruciating step at a time. Her arms are outstretched at shoulder height as if she's balancing on a high wire. Doing her best to stay focused on the task, she chants, "Oh . . . ohh . . . ohhh." Just before she reaches the chair, the book slips from her head and hits the floor with a bang. "Oh!" Chloë exclaims. Frustrated, she jumps, stamps one foot, and gives the dumb book a swift, soccer-like kick, sending it skittering across the tile floor.

Emily sighs but remains patient as she instructs, "That wasn't very ladylike, Chlo. Now, please pick up the book, come over here, and let's try again."

"You're so bossy!" Chloë complains. She scoops up the book and stomps over to Emily.

Calmly, Emily takes the book from her. Informing the world with her body language that she is aggravated with everybody and everything in it, Chloë turns to face the chair, and Emily carefully balances the book on her sister's head once again. "You almost made it last time. I know you can do it," Emily reassures her.

Chloë carefully repeats the process, this time with success. She sits perfectly still; the book teeters on her head; her eyes stare straight ahead; her lips are tightly puckered. She holds herself in ladylike form stiffly still, corseted by convention. As the little girl sits motionless, captured and tied to her seat by Miss Manners, she looks like a subdued Tinkerbell, tethered and temporarily grounded. Even so, within her young heart a coltish spirit blazes that would buck the social saddle, and it shows: her rosy cheeks bloom in full rebellion, her little nostrils flare, and her feisty eyes glint with fire for want of unfettered flight.

Emily nods approvingly and instructs, "Knees together now . . . shoulders back . . . hold your head high . . . fold your hands in your lap. Hold it . . . hold it . . . very good Chloë!" Emily and Seth clap enthusiastically for her.

"Can I get up now, please?" Chloë pines.

Emily grants permission.

Chloë tips her head, the book slides off, and she catches it in midair. She skips over to the table and sits beside Seth, tossing the book carelessly to one side. Sitting on Seth's left, she puts both elbows on the table, plops her chin in her hands, blows a spiral of hair away from an eye and asks, "Whatcha doin'?"

"Just looking at yesterday's mail," he replies. He sees Chloë studying his prosthesis. "Would you like to ask me something?"

Standing by the sink and drying a plate with a dish towel, Emily watches them. Looking up at Seth brightly, Chloë responds with innocent curiosity. "What's it like?"

"Kinda like any other ol' hand," Seth replies casually.

Chloë's eyes grow large. "Can you feel things?"

Seth is amused by the child's interest. "I can feel the weight of things, and I can tell if something's wood, or paper, or glass," he says.

"Wow-wee," Chloë whispers in awe.

Seth grins. "And would you believe it, Chlo? It even itches sometimes. In fact, it itches right now. Would you scratch it for me, please?" He offers his hooks to Chloë.

Without hesitancy or fear, Chloë gently scratches the curved top of one of the hooks.

Dramatically, Seth pants, "Oh! That feels so good. Now the sides, please. Give it a real good scratching!"

Her eyes shining, Chloë scratches more vigorously, giggling with delight.

Seth becomes more theatrical, thumping his foot and craning his neck like a big sheep dog. "Oh! Oh! Oh! That feels so *really, really* good! Thank you!"

"That was fun," Chloë says delighted. "I like your steel hand."

Seth considers what this lovely child said and thoughtfully replies, "Me too, Chlo."

Emily continues to observe them from the sink. Chloë's chin rests in her hands, and her elbows are on the table. Emily notices but doesn't correct her.

Chloë sighs and rolls her eyes pathetically. "It's gonna rain forever and ever. . ." she moans. She picks up Gracie Ann and laments, "No outside today. Oh, Gracie Ann. What are we going to do?" and she presses her face in the doll's face and rocks sadly back and forth.

Emily and Seth smile at each other. They can't help but be entertained by Chloë's melodramatics.

Seth says briskly, "Chloë, how would you like to go on a roller coaster ride?"

Chloë springs up from Gracie Ann's face and brightens immediately. "Yes! Let's go!" Holding Gracie Ann, she excitedly jumps down from her chair.

Emily watches now with curiosity. She maintains her perfect poise.

Seth is a bit surprised. "You've been on a roller coaster before Chloë?"

"Not really. But I've seen 'em on cartoons. They look like fun. Let's go!"

"Let's go?" Seth laughs. "We don't have to go anywhere, Chlo. It's right here in the kitchen."

Chloë looks around. "Uh-uh. Not either," she says doubtfully.

"Sure it is, Chlo. All you have to do is use your imagination." Seth gets up, goes to a cabinet beneath the counter where his mother always kept the booster chair, opens it, and, sure enough, he retrieves the leather booster seat stowed within. He sits in the chair that Chloë had sat in for her etiquette lesson and places the booster chair in his lap. "C'mon Chlo, come sit in the roller coaster chair."

Chloë gleefully rushes over to Seth and turns around, waiting for him to lift her and Gracie Ann onto the roller coaster seat. Seth lifts Chloë, and as he seats her in the booster chair, he says, "Ker plop!"

Chloë giggles. "What should I do?" she asks, thrilled.

"Just grab on tight," Seth encourages, and he holds out his two arms on either side of Chloë. She can only latch onto one arm because she's holding Gracie Ann, so Seth wraps his free arm across the child's tummy for stability. "Okay girls and boys, here we go. Remember, you better hold on tight now."

Chloë giggles with excitement. She is fearless.

"And off we go!" exclaims Seth. "Up, up, up! Higher . . . and higher . . . and *higher.* Chloë, can we go any higher?"

"Let's go as high as we can!" she squeals.

With a slow, dramatic count that gets ever slower as they ap–proach the imaginary crest, Seth begins, "Higher . . . and higher . . . and high-errr . . . we're almost at the tippy-tippy-*top.* Just about there . . . Chloë, look down," he says. "See how small the people look way down there on the ground? They look like ants."

Chloë leans forward and looks down. "They *do* look like ants!" she yells. "The cars look like toys!"

"And there's a zoo way over there." Seth whoops. "I can see animals walking around. You see it?"

"I see a rhinoceros and an elephant!" Chloë cries, her brown eyes shimmering.

"I see a giraffe!" Seth shouts. Then he says cautiously, "Uh-oh, uh-oh . . . we're at the very top . . . and down we go!" At this he begins to bounce his knees wildly, and Chloë flies up and down. He leans forward to give Chloë the sensation she is headed down.

Chloë is shrieking with delight, and her curls are flying.

"First turn!" he cries out, swinging Chloë to the right. "Second turn!" He swings her to the left. "Sharp bend!" He swings her to the right again. "Another!" He swings her to the left.

Chloë is completely enthralled and screams with joy.

Seth leans back and pretends to start climbing the next hill, talking slowly, "Up, up, up again. Nearly . . . to . . . the . . . tippy-tippy . . . *top.* " And then without warning, he suddenly takes Chloë through the ride again, madly bouncing her up-and-down on his lap and swinging her back and forth as they dive down drops and fly around curves.

Chloë is having the time of her life, and the kitchen walls echo with her squealing and screaming.

"Oh no!" Seth exclaims. "Chlo, there's an elephant standing on the tracks. How did he get there?"

"He escaped from the zoo!" she shrieks.

"Duck!" Seth yells. "We just ran under his legs!"

"Lucky for us!" Chloë shouts.

Seth pretends to glide and then suddenly jerks forward and

back, simulating the roller coaster car coming to an abrupt halt. He looks down at Chloë. "Okay, girls and boys, ride's over. Have to buy another ticket if you want to ride again. How did you like it, Chlo?"

Chloë jumps off the booster chair and bounces up and down, shouting, "Awesome! That was fun. Your turn, Em."

Emily smiles at her sister and shakes her head, politely declining. "You can go again," she says.

Chloë spins to Seth. "Can I have Emily's turn?"

Seth chuckles, "You're wearing me out, Miss Chloë. You'll have another turn later, okay? I need a little break for now."

"Okay," Chloë says happily and skips over to her sister. "You should've gone. It was really awesome. Me and Gracie Ann had fun. What are we going to do next, Em?" Her sister's only answer is to pat Chloë lovingly on her shoulder.

Seth stands up with the booster chair, stretches, and places the booster chair out of the way under the table. "I'll be back in a few minutes, ladies." He leaves the kitchen and goes down the hall.

While he is gone, Emily notices the acoustic radio on the counter. She hesitates for a second and then switches it on. The radio is tuned to Mrs. McAllister's favorite classical station, and a slow waltz is playing. Emily looks at Chloë, and they both frown and shake their heads.

"Okay Chlo," Emily says excitedly, "let's take off our shoes." First, Chloë takes Gracie Ann to the table and props her up so she can watch. Then the girls quickly get out of their shoes. Emily pushes the play forward button, and a new song, "Everybody Dance Now" by C + C Music Factory blasts out. Grabbing Chloë's hand, Emily says gaily, "C'mon Chlo, let's dance," and leads her to the middle of the kitchen floor in front of the table.

"Chloë," Emily says, thrilled, "do you remember how I showed you to rock to this song?"

Chloë's eyes are shining like the sun. "Kinda," she says eagerly. "Show me again, please."

Emily laughs, "Remember our starting position: stand with our feet together, arms down by our sides like this, and knees bent a little like this. Watch me, Chlo, there are just four really easy steps: cross the right foot over the left, step back, step to the side, and step front again. You see?" Emily quickly repeats the steps again, and Chloë catches on immediately, giggling with anticipation. "Now, one more thing," Emily says, energized. "When we do these steps we want to act really sassy! So swing your hips and shake your shoulders and snap your fingers and move your feet double quick to the beat of the music. It's okay to be wild. And sometimes it helps to close your eyes and forget about everything. Just let the music take you where it wants to go." Emily is excited. "It's really easy; just feel the music and do anything you want!"

The girls instantly jump to the rhythm of the song, gyrating to the tempo, and dancing in their socks to the steely electric guitar, the booming bass, and pounding drum beats. Calling Emily a good dancer would be like calling Ginger Rogers a pretty good hoofer. Emily's natural gift for understanding rhythm, tempo, timing, and interpretation of music was extraordinary. When she danced, Emily and the music were truly one element. And she knew how to have fun with it too.

The girls are so enthralled with the music and dancing that they haven't noticed that Seth has come back into the kitchen and is leaning against the hallway door, watching them. When the music ends, Seth applauds. Instead of being shy, both girls turn and grin at Seth, not the least bit self-conscious. Emily goes to the radio and switches it off.

"Oh, please don't do that, Emily," Seth says cheerfully. "I was hoping I could have the next dance with one of you ladies."

Chloë begins bouncing up and down. "Em!" Chloë shouts, "Let's play 'Dancing with My Girls!' Please? Can I push the button? Please! Please! *Please!*"

"What's it called, Chlo?" Seth asks curiously.

"You tell 'em Em. You can tell 'em better."

"It's a game Daddy played with Mommy and us," Emily says. "He called it 'Dancing with My Girls.' The person at the radio pushes the fast forward button. When it lands on a song, we dance to it, whatever it is."

"Please, Em, *please?*" Chloë begs.

Emily smiles at her sister, considering her request. She gazes at Seth appraisingly for a moment and turns to Chloë. "Yes, Chlo, we'll play."

"Yippee!" shouts Chloë.

"You need a safe chair to stand on by the radio," Emily tells her.

"I'll get it," Seth says. He places a chair from the kitchen table by the radio and helps Chloë up. Seth and Emily position themselves in front of the table, facing each other a few feet apart. Seth bows politely to Emily, and Emily curtsies politely to him. Emily nods for Chloë to begin. Chloë switches on the radio, giggles, and pushes the play forward button.

The radio stops on the fast-paced "Playing with the Queen of Hearts" by Juice Newton. Surprising Seth with her agility, Emily is suddenly there in front of him, waiting. He takes her in his arms, and they begin dancing to the lively tempo of this country-pop classic. The pair looks like they've danced as partners for years. Seth can't believe Emily's ability. She's as light as a feather and follows him so effortlessly that she seems to know his next step before he does. He was the best dancer in school and danced with dozens of girls but never anyone like Emily. They do open turns, reverse turns, and even the more confusing outside turns, and she is flawless. Ninety seconds into the song it suddenly changes and becomes "Living on a Prayer" by Bon Jovi.

Surprised, Seth stops and says, "Hey, what happened?"

Emily and Chloë giggle. "I forgot to tell you," Emily says, "the person at the radio can push the button at any time. It's part of the fun!" Emily begins dancing to the rock music around Seth and shouts merrily, "C'mon Seth, you're missing the music!"

Seth shakes his head and does his best to keep up with this girl whom he realizes is light years his better. He can see that Emily is totally lost in the music. All thoughts of sorrow are subdued by her love of rhythm, tempo, beat, and melody as she dances in perfect time.

Chloë suddenly changes the music again. "She's In Love with the Boy" by Tricia Yearwood booms from the speaker, and Emily and Seth set off whirling, dipping, and spinning. Seth can't remember when he's had so much fun. This little girl is magic to dance with, and it's exhilarating. Emily's love of dance and abandon to the joyful music is infectious. Like Emily, Seth has become completely immersed in it, and any regrets about the last two years are silenced for now, relegated to a far corner of his mind. He can only hear the music, feel its beat, and somewhere in his consciousness faintly hear the sound of a five-year-old little girl giggling.

Without warning, Tricia Yearwood is replaced by the Bee Gees' hit, "Stayin' Alive." Seth really hits his stride with this piece, or so he believes. He breaks from Emily and begins swaggering to the beat around the kitchen, mimicking John Travolta's famous dance scene, strutting, pointing, and gyrating.

Emily stops abruptly, staring at Seth. She looks at her sister quizzically and quickly joins Chloë by the radio, where they both watch Seth curiously, uncertain of what to make of this spectacle.

Seth is taking himself seriously and is very proud of performing such a great imitation of Travolta. "Maybe even better than ol' John himself," he thinks.

The girls start laughing uncontrollably.

Seth stops. "Hey, what's so funny?" he asks.

The girls can't answer because they're laughing so hard and pointing at him.

"What?" Seth asks again, clueless.

"You look so silly!" Chloë says, and she and Emily continue laughing.

"I thought I was pretty good," he protests mildly. "I was John Travolta from *Saturday Night Fever*."

Both girls ask, "Who's that?" and keep laughing at him.

Seth grins and shrugs his shoulders. "Never mind," he says. "Ol' John was a little bit before my time, too. C'mon, Emily. Let's go!"

"Not if you're going to dance like that," Emily teases.

"Okay, I won't," he agrees, poking fun at himself.

Emily rejoins him, and Chloë pushes the fast-forward button. It lands on a station playing classical ballet music: "The Lilac Fairy" solo from *The Sleeping Beauty*. Immediately, Emily is up on her toes dancing deftly around Seth, her willowy arms sweeping gracefully through the air and her head held beautifully high.

"No way can I do this one," Seth confesses.

Chloë shouts, "Emily can! She's gonna be a ballerina when she grows up!"

Seth bows quickly. "Be my guest," he says to Emily, who nods as she dances past him without saying a word. She's now in character, and ballerinas, as everyone knows, never speak.

Seth joins Chloë by the radio. If he was impressed with Emily's dancing skills before, he is astonished by her astounding talent on display to a classical mainstay. Up on her toes, Emily's poise and grace are a pleasure to behold. Her acrobatic movements flow precisely, and Emily's face is wonderfully expressive. The music seems written for her, or it seems that she was born for it, or both. "This girl is a prodigy, just like Katie said," Seth thinks.

The truth is, as much as Seth is an artist with design, Emily is an artist with dance. At that moment Seth realizes how similar he and Emily are to each other. But not just as kindred artists, he understands they both have lost something that is irreplaceable.

Made starry-eyed by her sister's performance, Chloë lets the music continue to its completion. Then, with eager delight, she quickly pushes the fast-forward button again. Chloë relishes being in control of *something*, as she feels it's totally unfair that, at her age, it so seldom occurs.

The radio plays a C&W line dance. Emily waves to Chloë and Seth to quickly join her. They line up in a row with Chloë in the middle, and dance in perfect unison to the music. Seth sticks his right thumb in his back pocket, hangs a hook through a belt loop, and throws his head back pompously. Both girls imitate him, giggling. They step in rhythm to the front. They step to the back, turn to the right, and repeat the process to the music's lively tempo.

As the trio dances, Kathryn walks into the kitchen, having entered through the back door. She's arrived for the children. Seth motions for his sister to join them, which she eagerly does, next to Emily. They line dance until the music ends. Laughing and giggling they stop. Emily moves nimbly to the radio and switches it off.

"It looks like everyone's had a good time," Kathryn says, happily surprised.

"We have," says Seth, grinning. "Haven't we, ladies?"

"Do we have to go?" Chloë pines.

Kathryn looks at Seth amused, and then reminds Chloë, "You and Emily have school tomorrow, Chlo."

"Can we come back after school tomorrow?" Chloë asks hopefully.

Kathryn tussles her hair, "Not tomorrow, Chlo. But you and

Emily are supposed to spend the weekend with us in two weeks. You could stay with Seth instead, if you'd like."

"Yippee!" Chloë shouts.

"Mrs. Mason," Emily quickly says, courteously, "we always like being with you and your family."

Kathryn hugs her. "I know you do, sweetheart. We love having you and Chlo with us." She grins at Seth. "But Seth would really like another turn."

"Yes, I really would," Seth says excitedly.

"Please, Em! *Please!*" Chloë pleads, tugging on her arm.

Emily smiles and says graciously, "Thank you, Mrs. Mason. That would be very nice, Seth."

Chloë bounces so excitedly that it looks as if her big curls might fly off her head. "Yippee! Yippee! *Yippee!*"

Kathryn laughs lightly and says, "Okay, children. Please go and gather your things." As the girls run off down the hall to the bedroom, Kathryn looks at Seth with a twinkle in her eye. "I see I've been replaced. You're such a charmer, little brother," she teases.

"It was the other way around, really. They're wonderful, Katie."

"Well," Kathryn says, "I'll make sure The Children's Sanctuary knows you're coming. There'll be some paperwork to sign. The director's name is Mrs. King. I'll e-mail you directions."

"Katie," Seth says gratefully, "I'm really glad you talked me into watching the children. It was the greatest thing. Thank you." He hugs his sister.

Kathryn playfully replies, "I didn't talk you into anything. I commanded you."

Seth laughs, "Yep, some things never change. But guess what, sis? I went inside your playhouse yesterday, nana-nana-naaan-nah!"

Katie responds indignantly, "No Boys Allowed!" and impishly sticks her tongue out at him.

"You know, you're the second female in twenty-four hours to do that to me," Seth says. "The first one was five years old, now you. Why do girls of all ages do that?"

"Because boys of all ages can be so annoying."

"Or maybe it's because you can't think of anything clever to say," Seth teases.

"Certainly not!" Katie rejoins. "It's our saucy way of telling boys they're being annoying without bothering to talk to them, that's all. It sums up all of our feelings at the moment very nicely. Think of it as an exclamation point."

Just then the children return to the kitchen with their backpacks. With Gracie Ann under one arm, Chloë proudly shows Kathryn the rhinoceros and the elephant origami figures and tells her about the star she is working on. Emily wears her white, long-sleeve sweater and Chloë her little pink jacket. They walk to the back door and are about to leave when Chloë turns to Seth and wiggles a finger for him to bend down. When he does, Chloë gives him a hug, then presses Gracie Ann's face to his right cheek—*smack*! Gracie Ann feels she could just melt with embarrassment.

Seth encourages her, "Keep working on that star, Chloë." He straightens and looks at Emily. He bows formally, and she curtsies formally in return. Kathryn and the children leave. He hears car doors opening and closing, the motor starting, and the car backing out of the driveway.

Seth gazes at the closed door for a moment and then turns and goes back to the kitchen counter. He takes the chair by the radio, places it at the table, and sits down in it. His prosthesis rests on the table. He lifts it up, contemplates it for a moment, grabs a spoon from the table, and strikes it rapidly against his steel hooks three times. *Clang! Clang! Clang!* Seth leans back in his chair and roars with laughter. From this moment forward in his life, his prosthesis never concerns him again.

CHAPTER FOURTEEN

It is the Monday after Thanksgiving and the children's big weekend with Seth. Emily sits at her desk in a small classroom with fifteen other children. She is in the front row, and the children are all writing in their notebooks. There is a large clock on the wall that reads three o'clock.

Miss Elena Hernandez, their teacher, is standing by her desk and speaking sweetly to the class. "Children, it's time for me to collect your Thanksgiving papers." She stops by Emily's desk, who hands her paper to Miss Hernandez. "Thank you, Emily. I could see you were working really hard on it."

"You're welcome, Miss Hernandez," Emily says and smiles up at her, shyly.

The bell rings and the children get up to leave. Elena goes to the door, and as each one of her students passes by her, she smiles and calls them by name, saying lovingly, "Have a great day. I'll see you tomorrow. Can't wait."

After all the children have gone, Elena returns to her desk and sits down. She looks at the clock and then gazes at the stack of papers on her desk that she gathered from the children. They are the children's reports on what they thought was special about their holiday. She picks up the first one and begins to read. An hour later she comes to Emily's paper. "Emily Fleming," Elena says to herself, "let's read about your Thanksgiving holiday. You and Chloë certainly deserved a special one. Hmm . . . what an interesting title."

Our Man of Steel
by Emily Fleming

Thanksgiving was really fun. We went to Mrs. Mason's home. Her children got sick. Mrs. Mason took us to her brother's house. His name is Seth. He doesn't cook very well. He has a hand that is made of steel. At first he seemed sad, but then he was happy. Sometimes he talked funny. He pushed us on a swing. We saw a playhouse Mrs. Mason played in when she was little. It was just for girls. She wouldn't let Seth play in it because he's a boy. Seth made zoo animals for Chloë with dollar bills. At night he and Chloë looked at the pictures in The Runaway Bunny. When it was raining, he took Chloë on a pretend roller coaster ride in the kitchen to make her happy. Seth is a real good dancer. He is almost as good as my daddy. Seth is a very nice man. We are going to stay with him again in two weeks. I circled the day on my calendar. Chloë thinks he can fly. But we didn't see him do that so maybe he can't, but Chloë thinks he can. We have a secret name for Seth. We call him, Our Man of Steel.

Elena looks up from the paper and smiles to herself, saying out loud, "I think you're right, Emily. Seth sounds like a very nice man."

CHAPTER FIFTEEN

It is two weeks later, the Friday afternoon that Seth is to pick up Emily and Chloë from The Children's Sanctuary. Mrs. McAllister is on the kitchen phone with Kathryn.

"Katie, I just don't know what's changed your brother," says Mrs. McAllister excitedly.

"I have a good idea," Kathryn answers.

"Well, if it's those two little girls I could just kiss 'em both 'til their ears fall off! Seth's back to his old self. And my goodness, he hasn't stopped working."

"He sure sounds great over the phone," says Kathryn. "I've tried to get him to come over a couple of times, but he said he was too busy. Mom, I heard you're leaving for your mission trip this afternoon instead of in the morning."

"Yes, dear, in a few minutes. Will Seth be all right with the children? There's plenty of food."

"Sure, Mom, he'll be fine. Is he leaving for The Children's Sanctuary soon?"

"He's been ready for hours. Says he's going over right after I leave. My ride should be here any minute now."

"Great, Mom. I have a patient waiting, gotta go. Bye."

"Bye sweetheart."

CHAPTER SIXTEEN

Seth has arrived at The Children's Sanctuary and is waiting patiently in the outer office for Mrs. King, the Director. She comes out of her office to greet Seth. Mrs. King is a charismatic, well-spoken, and keenly intelligent African-American woman in her late-fifties with stylish, short silver hair and an extraordinarily kind and caring face. She comports herself as a consummate professional, and her demeanor is welcoming and personable.

"Hello, Seth. I'm Mrs. King," she says warmly, extending her hand to him. "I'm the Director of The Children's Sanctuary. It's so nice to meet you."

"And you too, Mrs. King," Seth says energetically. "Katie has told me so many wonderful things about you and your staff. I couldn't wait to meet you."

"Dr. Kathryn McAllister-Mason," Mrs. King says cordially, "better known out here as Dr. M&M. She's a real angel. How she manages her work and family and still finds time to be a sponsor parent I'll never know. I could use a dozen more just like her. Come on Seth, let's go in my office."

"I agree with you, Mrs. King, Katie's very special." He follows the director into her sparse office. She sits behind her plain desk in a wooden swivel chair with a thick, worn seat pad.

"Please take a seat, Seth," she invites him. "Katie has filled out these forms for you already. Just sign in the spaces, please." She hands him the forms across her desk.

Taking the forms from her, Seth says, "Thank you, Mrs. King." He signs them and hands them back to her.

"We'll take a tour of the campus in just a few minutes. But first, we feel it's important for our guest parents to understand the background of the children they're sponsoring." Mrs. King's tone becomes serious as she offers Seth a manila folder. "Here is the file for the Fleming children, Emily and Chloë. I must warn you Seth. There are graphic pictures of Emily in there that are quite disturbing. The pictures were taken at the hospital right after she was assaulted."

Feeling some trepidation, Seth takes the file from her. "Katie told me about it," he says gravely. Seth opens the manila file and begins reading through it, turning the pages slowly.

Mrs. King observes him closely.

Seth comes to the photos of Emily that were taken at the hospital soon after she arrived by ambulance. He becomes visibly upset and shakes his head sadly as he looks carefully at each photograph. He looks up at Mrs. King. "How could anyone do this?" he asks, incredulous.

"It happens more than you think," Mrs. King answers. "In a way, Emily was lucky, Seth. She was badly cut over her left eye. There were multiple bruises and deep contusions on both legs. As traumatic as that experience was for Emily, nothing more traumatic occurred. Do you understand what I mean?"

Seth has become subdued and answers quietly, "Yes, Mrs. King, I do. Thank you for telling me that." He continues to read through the file and strives to regain his composure. He stops and peers at another photo. Holding up the manila folder and pointing to the picture, he shows it to Mrs. King. "Is this the man who assaulted her?"

"Yes," Mrs. King says. "His name is Emond Slagg. His wife's name is Nadine. Nadine was the children's only living relative. That's why CPS placed them with her. Relatives always take precedence. It's the law."

Seth thinks it's nearly incomprehensible. "Unbelievable," is all he can manage to say.

Mrs. King continues. "His wife ran for help. From what we know about her, we have every good reason to believe that Nadine has been repeatedly abused by her husband. But she's never filed formal charges against him, and without formal charges, the law can do nothing.

"Then why does she stay with him?" Seth asks, bewildered.

"It's hard for people to understand," Mrs. King observes. "Do–mestic violence involving physical abuse by a partner often causes the abused person to become depressed. He or she is unable to take any independent action to escape the abuse."

"You said *he* or she. Men can be victims, too?" Seth asks.

"They can be, but the vast majority of abused partners are women. What's saddest is that because of a sufferer's low self-esteem, they often believe the abuse is their own fault. They refuse to press criminal charges against their abuser, refuse all offers of help, and even seek out their abuser for comfort shortly after an episode of abuse."

Seth is confounded by what he's just heard. "That's incredible."

"It's true though," Mrs. King tells him. "A person can suffer abuse for years and never leave. It finally ends when the abuser becomes more emboldened and the violence escalates to a point where the sufferer is permanently injured or killed."

Seth breathes hard. "So Nadine hasn't left him because she can't, psychologically?"

"That's probably correct," Mrs. King concludes.

Seth is having a hard time understanding the violence. He carefully closes the file and hands it back to Mrs. King.

"Seth," she says, "children are remarkable in their ability to recover if given the chance. That's what we do here at The Children's Sanctuary, we give them that chance."

Seth asks hopefully, "Do you think Emily will recover, Mrs. King? I mean, fully?"

Mrs. King considers the young man's question and answers, "She doesn't remember the assault itself, Seth. Emily has blocked it from her mind entirely. But one day something will trigger that memory, and it'll all come flooding back. If she's had the right care, I think she'll deal with it successfully. Emily is a strong little girl, well-advanced beyond her years. But there's something else about her that transcends her fortitude and determination, something much more profound that I really can't explain, nor do I fully understand. The best way I can put it is that there's some secret place from within where she draws her strength and courage, a source that surpasses all human understanding."

"I noticed that about her right away," Seth says. "She is far beyond her years in so many ways and has managed to cope with circumstances that would have crushed most children, even many adults. Where do you think this ability comes from, Mrs. King?"

"It always comes from the same wellspring," Mrs. King replies. "It begins and ends with the family. Emily had remarkable parents who were in a stable, loving marriage, and they loved their children dearly. There is no doubt that the family is the greatest influence on children. Seth, it's who the parents are, how they support and interact with each other and with their children, that's most important. The children will grow up to be like their parents, for good or for bad. A loving, healthy home environment is the key ingredient to a child's success; a loveless, unhealthy one is the root of their failure. Exceptions to this rule are very rare. Emily's mother must have been an amazing woman who was married to an equally amazing man. Emily has had the benefit of two exceptional parents; that, and now the mystical assistance whose origin is known only to her."

"I'm sure all of that is true, Mrs. King," Seth agrees. "Emily and Chloë are terrific children."

Mrs. King smiles kindly at him. "I can see you really care about them. Seth, this is what I believe: Emily's courage, her strength of will, and her extraordinary character, together with her fierce love for Chloë, will sustain her. She's quite an exceptional child. Yes, in the end I believe she'll be fine. And because Emily will be fine, Chloë will be fine too."

Seth nods thoughtfully and says, "Mrs. King, I can see why Katie thinks so highly of you."

"Thank you." Mrs. King rises from her chair. "Would you like to see the campus now?"

Seth stands as well, "Yes, very much. Thank you."

"Come with me, then, and I'll give you the grand tour. I think you'll be impressed by all the things we do here."

They walk outside to the grounds of The Children's Sanctuary. As Mrs. King shows Seth their facilities, she explains, "Our mission is to provide a family environment in a home setting filled with warmth and care. We want children to feel perfectly safe and know they are surrounded by people who love them. We have ten cottages, and each cottage can hold eight children and a set of house parents. Of course, we're always trying to add more cottages. Sadly, there's never a shortage of children who need us."

Seth notices the school. "They go to school here?"

"Oh, yes. We have a wonderful school. The children have all of the normal school programs and the extra-curricular activities, too. They participate in scouts, baseball, volleyball, and they even raise farm animals."

Seth is very impressed. "This place is really great," he says.

Mrs. King is grateful for Seth's enthusiasm. "We think it is. Our larger mission is to help children learn to overcome self-destructive patterns, break cycles of abuse, learn responsibility, and develop the right social skills to become healthy, happy, and responsible adults."

"Mrs. King," Seth asks, "how does all the abuse get started?"

"Ninety-five percent of the cause is substance abuse," she answers. "Basically, drugs and alcohol are the culprits. Once the abuse takes hold in a family, it's often passed down from one generation to another. It's a terrible cycle of violence. The children who are placed with us are often victims of abuse; or, its ugly first cousins, neglect and abandonment."

"I never knew that," Seth says, astonished.

They stop in front of an empty lot where a foundation has been poured.

"A new cottage?" Seth asks.

"It was supposed to be," Mrs. King says. "After pouring the foundation, the builder went broke in the recession and disappeared. All the building material is still over in our barn."

Seth is surprised. "You mean you have all of the construction material to build it?"

"That's right," she answers. "The construction material was

donated to us. Such a shame, we have a long waiting list of children. Another home would have helped eight more needy children."

Curious, Seth inquires, "Mrs. King, where are the design plans?"

"They disappeared along with the builder. Apparently the contractor never filed anything with the city or the county. We looked, but no one could find them."

"I see. That is unusual," Seth observes thoughtfully.

"Shall we go back to the office? The children will be there shortly. Chloë's been a little chatterbox about you for two weeks."

They walk back to the office. Once they enter the reception area, Mrs. King turns to Seth and says appreciatively, "Seth, her teacher told me since coming back from Thanksgiving Emily's been much happier and hopeful. Emily turned an important corner. You helped her do that."

"Thank you, Mrs. King," Seth says sincerely. "But the truth is I'm much happier and more hopeful too. You might say Emily and I turned that corner together."

She nods and observes sagely, "It was a true Thanksgiving then." Mrs. King smiles at him. "Emily and Chloë will be here soon. I have more paperwork to do. Three more children coming in tonight." She extends her hand cordially, "Very nice to meet you, Seth. You and Katie are quite alike."

"Thank you, Mrs. King. That's a real compliment. Very nice to meet you too."

Mrs. King leaves Seth in the reception area and returns to her office. In less than a minute, the children enter the reception room with their backpacks. Chloë is wearing her "outfit." She carries Gracie Ann crooked in her left arm. Chloë's mop of unruly curls cluster around her ears, spill across her forehead, and drape above her eyebrows. Seth notices that Gracie Ann has a new patch on her worn blouse. Emily is neatly dressed and perfectly groomed. She somehow manages to look as graceful as a swan in clothes that would look decidedly plain on any other child. Seth notices she is not wearing her beautiful white sweater, even though the autumn afternoon air is cool. As soon as Chloë sees Seth, she drops her backpack and runs to him, jumping into his arms, squealing. She kisses him on the cheek and then presses Gracie Ann's face to Seth's other cheek. *Smack!* Gracie Ann wishes she was invisible. Sometimes her mother embarrasses her *so* much.

"Seth! Seth! Seth!" Chloë shouts happily.

"Hi Chloë! Hi Gracie Ann!" replies Seth.

Emily, poised and formal as ever, stands a few feet away, observing them. After his enthusiastic reunion with Chloë and Gracie Ann, Seth puts Chloë down, straightens, and smiles at Emily. He bows formally to her. Emily smiles shyly back and curtsies.

"Hi Emily," Seth says warmly.

"Hi Seth," she answers quietly, her face showing she is clearly pleased to see him.

Chloë stands by Seth, holding his hand and looking up at him with her large, shiny brown eyes, eager to go. Seth is about to say something to her when the door opens and Elena Hernandez walks into the reception area carrying Emily's white sweater.

"Emily, sweetheart, you left your sweater in the classroom—" Elena stops in mid-sentence, her voice trailing off. She locks eyes with Seth. He stares at her, mesmerized. There is instant electricity between them. Uncharacteristically, Elena is totally flustered. She is caught off guard and looks around self-consciously and then back at Seth. She can't stop herself; she cannot take her eyes off of him. Emily is watching them closely, and observing what is happening between them.

Chloë immediately drops Seth's hand and rushes over to Elena. She grabs both of Elena's hands in hers and begins tugging her towards Seth, shouting, "Miss Hernandez! Miss Hernandez! This is Seth! He's our friend! You have to meet him!"

Chloë drags Elena to where she is now standing directly in front of Seth. They are no more than a foot apart. Elena is even more bewildered than before. Seth is enchanted. Chloë suddenly lets go, takes the sweater from Elena's limp hand, and runs to her sister with it, stopping and leaning into Emily.

Emily places her willowy arms crisscross over her, giving her sister an affectionate pat. Elena and Seth are standing close and looking at each other. Neither one can say a word. Both are starstruck.

Finally, Seth manages to say, dreamlike, "Hi. I'm Emily's and Chloë's friend Seth, Seth McAllister."

Elena can't answer. She slowly extends her hand to Seth. Seth takes her hand in his and holds it tenderly while gazing into her eyes. Her heart jumps at the touch of his hand.

Elena was woozy from her first look at Seth. Being within inches of the man now and looking into his blue eyes, she has felt the final knockout punch. Dazed and staggering around somewhere inside those beautiful eyes of his, Elena hears herself saying from faraway, "Hi. I'm Elena Sanctuary. I'm Emily's teacher here at the Hernandez school."

Hearing Miss Hernandez, Chloë tilts her face up to Emily with a questioning expression. Emily motions for her to be quiet.

"Elena Sanctuary . . ." Seth repeats, spellbound. "Such a lovely name . . ."

"No . . . no," Elena answers, bewildered. "No . . . not Elena Sanctuary, I'm Emily Hernandez. Elena's teacher." She smiles at him wanly.

Totally moonstruck, Seth says, "Oh . . . Emily Hernandez . . . lovelier still . . . Elena's teacher . . . how incredibly wonderful."

Elena sighs. She's unable to tear her eyes from him. But she is painfully aware she hasn't gotten anything quite right in this introduction. She is puzzled and annoyed with herself and thinks, "What's the matter with me? This gorgeous man must think I'm totally daffy!"

She tries to look away from him but she can't, she simply can't. Desperate to gather her wits, Elena gazes directly into Seth's eyes and says slowly and deliberately, "No . . . no . . . what I meant to say . . . what I'm trying to say . . . I'm Elena Hernandez . . . Emily's teacher . . . at the Sanctuary school . . . I think." She sighs again, not wanting to do anything except look at this handsome man who is standing directly before her like a dream come true.

Seth is so spellbound he never realizes Elena's mistakes. He can't take his eyes off of her either. He thinks she's the most beautiful creature he has ever seen, and the sound of her voice is like a Vienna waltz, lilting and perfectly timed.

The truth is, if Elena only knew it, that Seth had heard just two words. He thinks the reception room has turned into another Shangri-La over two words: *Miss Hernandez.*

"That's absolutely amazing," Seth whispers. "Miss Hernandez. It was *Miss* Hernandez, wasn't it? *Miss?*" he asks hopefully.

Unable to say a word, Elena just nods several times in the affirmative.

Seth gazes at her, waiting for Elena to say something. "Have I scared her off?" he wonders, "by saying about the dumbest thing in the whole world I could possibly say at this moment?"

Elena shakes her head gently, as if clearing it of cobwebs, and says, "Yes, it's *'Miss.'* It's definitely, *'Miss.'* It's *'Miss'* all right." Unconsciously, she bats her eyes at him.

Seth grins, looking relieved. "Miss Hernandez. *Miss* Hernandez," he repeats.

They are both oblivious to the fact that they are holding hands. They even begin to sway them.

"Please, it's Elena. I want you to call me Elena," she says ardently, having cleared the cobwebs. "I know who you are," she teases, "you're Seth McAllister, *Our Man of Steel.*"

"Our Man of Steel?" Seth replies, puzzled.

"Yes," Elena says brightly. "I read about you in Emily's Thanksgiving paper. That's what she and Chloë call you, secretly, that is."

"I got an A+ on it," Emily announces, pleased.

The sound of Emily's voice brings Elena and Seth back to reality. They suddenly realize they are holding hands and reluctantly release, both blushing.

Seth chuckles and taps his head. "My sister Katie would say my head's a lot harder."

Elena perks up. "Katie? Your sister's Katie? Katie McAllister-Mason. Dr. M&M! Yes, I see the resemblance now."

Seth laughs out loud. "One and the same. I've reported to her all of my life."

"I just adore Katie," Elena says. "She's out here every two weeks doing checkups and physicals for the children without charge. She's the most wonderful person imaginable."

Before Seth can say more, Chloë runs to him and starts pulling on his arm. "Seth! C'mon! *C'mon!* Let's go! I'm ready to go!"

Playfully, Elena tilts her head and cuts her eyes at Seth, teasing him. "Well, Mr. Seth McAllister, *Our Man of Steel*, you certainly are in demand with the ladies. Probably always have been, haven't you?"

Seth shrugs and grins at her. Chloë stops tugging on him but still holds onto Seth firmly.

Innocently, Elena inquires, "You'll have the children all weekend?"

"Yes, until three on Sunday afternoon." Seth wants to say more, but hesitates.

"Miss Hernandez?" Emily asks. "Please come see us this weekend?" She looks at Seth. "Would that be all right?"

Chloë bounces up and down. "Please! Please! *Please* Miss Hernandez!"

Seth quickly adds, "I hope you will, Elena." Then concerned he's overstepped, he drops his voice an octave lower, sounding apologetic. "But I understand it's short notice, and you're probably too busy . . ."

"I'm not busy!" Elena eagerly responds. Embarrassed, she catches herself, clears her throat, and says in a ladylike manner, "I mean . . . I'll double check my calendar . . . if memory serves me right I don't believe I'm too busy to stop by for just a little while." She brings a hand up and twirls her hair distractedly.

In his leisurely way, Seth says, "That's great, Elena. Would one-thirty tomorrow work? Come casual. We'll just be hanging out. I've got a surprise . . ." He stops short and rolls his eyes. "Oops, didn't mean to let that out," he says.

Hearing about a surprise, Chloë bolts forward, tugging hard on Seth and shouting, "Seth has a surprise, Em! I bet it's for us! Let's go! Let's go! *Let's go!*"

Elena laughs. "You'd better go, Mr. Seth McAllister. I'll be there tomorrow at one-thirty."

As Seth is being dragged out the door by Chloë, he calls back to Elena over his shoulder, "But I haven't given you my address. You don't have my number."

"Your address is in the file. No problem," Elena says. Then, she lightly adds, "I've already got your number, mister."

Chloë has pulled Seth halfway out the door, and in the com–

motion Seth didn't hear Elena clearly. "Sorry, what'd you say?"

Elena's dark eyes are glowing. "I said your number is in your file, too, Mr. Seth McAllister."

Chloë has gone behind Seth, and she and Gracie Ann are literally pushing him out the door with Emily following, carrying both backpacks and wearing her sweater.

After they have gone, Elena reaches in her pocket, pulls out her cell phone, and calls her mother. She starts pacing back and forth with nervous energy while the phone rings. She is animated, happy, and excited. She picks up a magazine from the coffee table in the reception room and begins fanning herself. Her mother answers the phone.

"Sí?"

"Hi, Mama!"

"Hello, cariño. How are you?"

Elena breathes rapidly, fanning herself briskly. "Mama," she says excitedly, "you know what you've always told me? How I would walk into a room one day and suddenly my life would change forever?"

Her mother is all ears now. "Yes. That's how it happens."

Breathlessly, Elena says, "This is the day. I just walked into that room!" and she squeals with delight.

"Tell me about it," Yesenia says, overjoyed.

"I will. But first, I've got this huge favor to ask."

"Of course, what is it, niña?"

"You know that dish you make for Papa that he loves so much, chicken ranchero? Can you make it veggie style? And the beans and salad you fix to go with it? Oh, and your tres leches is just to die for. Could you make those for me tomorrow and have everything ready by noon? I'll come over and help."

Yesenia sounds amused. "This must have something to do with that room you just walked into? Yes, cariño, I'll be happy to do it. I just made two fresh cakes today and churros, too. The rest will only take a few hours."

Sounding incredulous, Elena says, "A few hours? That long?"

Yesenia chuckles at Elena's lack of culinary knowledge. "Yes, dear daughter. It takes that long to do things right."

"I'll come over early and help," Elena eagerly offers.

"Don't worry," her mother says sweetly, "it'll all be ready in time. Just come around eleven. Can you tell me anything now?"

"Mama, I just met the most wonderful man. He's invited me to his home tomorrow afternoon . . ." She squeals with delight again. "And I'm staying for dinner!"

Now her mother sounds concerned. "That's wonderful news. But . . . you've just met him? He's invited you to his house for dinner? And you're going?"

"No, not exactly," she says. "He invited me to visit him and the children. He doesn't know I'm staying for dinner, but I am." She jumps in the air.

"He has children? He doesn't know you're staying for dinner? At his own house? Niña, what are you talking about?"

Giddy with excitement, she answers, "No, he doesn't have children. Why would you think that?"

"Didn't you just say he has children?" her mother asks, puzzled.

"Occasionally . . ." Elena responds, dizzy with joy.

"He has children *occasionally?*" Yesenia is now alarmed.

"Mo-therrr! He doesn't have children at all. Why do you keep saying that?"

"Ai, yai yai," Yesenia cries and slaps her palm to her forehead. "Elena, are you all right?"

"All right? I'm wonderful. I just met the man I'm going to marry!"

Yesenia sighs, "In that case, be here at eight in the morning."

Elena is in Heaven. "I will," she says dreamily. "Isn't everything just wonderful? The world has never been so wonderful."

"Yes," her mother says patiently. "But should your father happen to call you, let's not say anything to him about this . . . not just yet, okay?"

"Sure, Mama. I've gotta go. Bye."

"Bye, cariño."

Elena closes her cell phone. She smiles broadly with a look of pure joy on her face. This young woman feels she has been waiting all of her life for the young man she met today in the most unexpected way. He had finally arrived. "Everything about him is perfect," she thinks. She returns the magazine to the coffee table that she used as a fan, and notices it's a copy of *Family Circle*. She smiles, saying to herself out loud, "Now *that's* a sign. I'll have to remember to tell Mama about it tomorrow."

Elena twirls lightly. When she leaves the reception room, the young woman skips down the sidewalk back to her classroom and dances a few ecstatic steps along the way.

CHAPTER SEVENTEEN

As Elena skips and dances her way back to her classroom, Seth enters the front door of his home with the children. Chloë begins bouncing up and down with excitement, yelling, "I'm ready for my surprise! Where is it? *Where?*"

Chloë drops her backpack on the floor and looks around the living room expectantly. Emily picks up her sister's backpack and hands it to her, instructing Chloë to remember her manners.

Seth is excited too. "Let's go to the kitchen. Bring your stuff. The surprise is in the backyard."

Once in the kitchen, Chloë looks eagerly at Emily for permission to go outside. With her customary poise, Emily regards Seth and raises her eyebrows. Seth walks over to the back door and opens it. "Ladies, be my guests."

Chloë puts Gracie Ann on the table, telling her, "Mommy will be right back, don't worry."

Gracie Ann frowns. Once again, she feels like she's being left out of all the fun just because she's little. It's not fair!

Chloë runs to Emily, grabs her hand, and begins tugging her frantically towards the back door, shouting, "C'mon, Em! C'mon! Let's go see!"

The children go through the back door, followed by Seth. They abruptly stop on the patio, astonished by what they see. Over the last two weeks, Seth has completely transformed the backyard to the state it was in when he and Kathryn were children. Everything looks new again. The wire cage is freshly painted white with a pair of diamond doves occupying it, cooing softly. The gravel pathway is lined with cyclamens in bright reds, pinks, and whites. The bird bath fountain bubbles. The swing set is completely restored and stained a rich chocolate brown. Most important of all, the playhouse has been newly painted pink and white and its broken window has been repaired. It is vibrant, warm, and inviting. Two pink and white pennants dip and snap in the breeze on each turret above the castle walls. Everything about the backyard is now, once again, a children's paradise.

"Wow-wee!" exclaims Chloë. "Wow-wee! Look, Em! See the tiny birds!"

The children approach the cage in awe. "They're so cute," Emily says, amazed.

"They're diamond doves," Seth explains. "And would you believe they're already grown?"

Emily looks surprised. "Aren't they too little to be grown?"

"They're grown all right," says Seth, assuring her.

"Why do they live in such a big house?" whispers Chloë.

"Because they'll have children Chlo," Seth says chuckling. Pretty soon, their big house will be filled with lots and lots of diamond doves."

"They're married?" asks Chloë, surprised.

"Yep, they sure are," Seth replies.

Chloë skips down the path. She stops and smells the flowers. She scampers to the birdbath, looks in, and then waves back to Emily and Seth, yelling, "It's got water! The birds can take a bath now!" She runs to the swing set, calling, "C'mon, Em. Let's swing!"

Emily runs ahead of Seth to join her sister.

It's the first time he's seen Emily act anything like a nine year old, Seth thinks to himself, pleased. He trots to the swing set and joins the girls.

The girls are already swinging. Chloë is holding on tightly

to her ropes; her head tilts far back as she looks up into the sky giggling wildly. Her ringlets blow freely in the wind. Emily swings higher than before. Her usual closed-lip smile has flowered into a beautiful, open smile.

Once the girls finish swinging, Chloë jumps off and runs to the playhouse with Emily following closely behind. The children enter through the children's door, and Seth enters through the adult door. It is here that the children are truly astounded. Inside, the playhouse has been meticulously cleaned and freshly painted a pastel spring green. It is furnished with a small yellow couch large enough for several children to sit on, a white table with four little chairs all a different pastel color, a bookshelf filled with children's books, a vanity with a mirror, and a play stove with little dishes in the rack above it. With Chloë in mind, Seth has decorated the walls with large, framed, colorful posters of scenes from classic fairy tales, including *Sleeping Beauty, Goldilocks and the Three Bears, The Frog Prince, Cinderella, Snow White,* and *Rapunzel.* Between them are dozens of smaller framed prints of characters from beloved stories like *Peter Rabbit* and *The Little Prince.* For Emily, an entire wall displays an array of former and current ballet stars from the best known ballet companies: Bolshoi, Kirov, Paris, London, New York City, and Houston. In scenes from all the ballet classics, the ballerinas are dressed in their stunning costumes, posed solo and paired with their dance partners. This wall appears to be in motion. Seth has cleverly hidden track lighting in the ceiling so that all of the dazzling posters are wonderfully highlighted, and the characters seem so vibrant that one wouldn't be surprised if they spoke out loud.

Chloë is so overwhelmed by the enchantment of the room she is frozen in place. "Chlo," Seth says, nodding towards the vanity, "go take a look in the drawers over there."

Catching her breath at his words, Chloë looks wondrously at Seth and then runs to the vanity, opens a drawer, and takes out a new hairbrush that Seth purchased. "Look, Em! A hairbrush!" Beside herself with excitement, she pulls open another drawer. "And bows and hair bands! There's everything in here! Can we play?"

"Of course we can," Emily says happily. She pulls out a chair from the little table and stands by it. "Pick out some bows and bring the brush. Come over here and sit down. I'll fix your hair."

Chloë begins digging for bows. Emily turns to Seth and smiles appreciatively, not having lost her manners or her poise in all of the excitement. "Thank you, Seth," she says softly. Except for her father, Emily has never known such kindness from an important male figure in her life.

Seth smiles back, nods, and bows with a flourish. Emily curtsies in return.

"You ladies have fun," he says. "Play as long as you like. I'll be in the house taking care of a few things."

CHAPTER EIGHTEEN

Emily and Chloë had a wonderful time playing all afternoon in the backyard and in the newly refurbished playhouse. It is now eight p.m. on that same day. The children have had their dinner, baths, and are dressed for bed. It is story time. Emily sits classically in the chair in the living room across from the couch. Her shoulders are back and her hands are folded neatly in her lap. As before, Chloë has snuggled up to Seth's left side and has taken his arm and draped it over her shoulders, protectively. She holds Gracie Ann in her lap. Seth is dressed in a navy blue sweat suit and is wearing white tennis shoes. Chloë has just handed him a book to read that she has brought from Kathryn's bedroom.

"*Clifford, the Big Red Dog*," Seth reads. "Chloë, you sure you want to read this one?" he asks.

Chloë yawns, "Yes. But let's just look at the pictures, please."

Seth glances at Emily, and she cautiously nods her approval. Seth begins turning the pages for Chloë. It doesn't take them long to finish the book.

Chloë begins to sniffle. "I like Clifford. He's big and red. Just like Blossom. Em, when are we going to see her again?"

Emily rises immediately and sits next to Chloë on the couch, pulling her close and putting her arm over her shoulders. Chloë leans into her sister and rests her head against her.

Seth is already regretting the story selection. He knows he could have convinced Chloë to look at another book that didn't come with hurtful memories attached to it.

Chloë hugs Gracie Ann. "I miss Blossom," she says tearfully. "Em, why did we have to leave her?"

Emily kisses Chloë lightly on top of her head and hugs her more tightly.

"There, there," Emily consoles her sister. "Blossom's safe, Chlo. She's having fun. We'll see her soon."

Chloë wipes a tear away and says sadly, "I hope so . . ."

Seth gets up from the couch and excuses himself, leaving the book on the cushion.

Chloë picks up the Clifford book and looks longingly at the cover, a full picture of the big, red, friendly looking Clifford. Emily caresses her sister and strokes her hair.

Quietly, Seth reenters the room and stands in front of the couch. The girls do not notice he has returned. Seth lightly clears his throat.

Emily is the first to look up. She sees that he is holding a little red puppy. It's a Golden Retriever that's a fluffy ball of fuzz, just six weeks old.

Chloë remains unaware. She is too absorbed in the book's cover. With one finger she traces an imaginary outline around Clifford.

Emily smiles broadly at the sight but doesn't say a word. She gently nudges Chloë, who doesn't look up at first. Emily gently nudges her again and whispers, "Chlo, Chlo, look what Seth has."

Chloë looks at her sister who nods towards Seth. Chloë turns her eyes to Seth and for a moment she doesn't comprehend what she sees. Then, the little girl explodes off the couch, bouncing up and down and squealing, "A puppy! A puppy! A red one! Just like Blossom! Just like Clifford! Can I hold her? Can I? Please! Please! Please! Please! *Please!*"

"Sure," says Seth laughing. "But calm down a little, Chlo. Sit next to your sister, please. We have to be very gentle with a puppy."

Chloë jumps onto the couch and scoots against Emily. She puts

Gracie Ann to one side. Seth gently places the puppy in Chloë's lap. Chloë kisses its head, and nuzzles its cheek. She is beside herself with joy and strokes the puppy gently. "Is she ours?" Chloë asks hopefully.

"Of course," Seth replies, thrilled with Chloë's reaction.

"Did you hear that, Em?" Chloë whispers. "She's ours! Em, she's ours!" Chloë gushes, "She's the prettiest puppy in the whole world! And the smartest, too! I'm going to name her Samantha. Em, can I name her Samantha? Don't you think Samantha's the best name ever?" Chloë's eyes have never shined more brightly.

Lovingly, Emily replies, "Yes, Chloë. Samantha is a wonderful name, the best ever. And you thought of it, so it's extra special."

Chloë kisses the puppy on the head again. She carefully passes the little dog to her sister. "Em, it's your turn to hold Samantha."

Emily gently takes the puppy and places it in her lap, stroking it softly. She turns it over and scratches its belly and then turns it back up scratching behind its ear. The little puppy becomes more animated with all the attention and begins licking her hand and squeaking a cute little bark.

"Samantha is a wonderful name, Chlo," Emily says, "a really wonderful name. But can you think of another name just as wonderful?"

Chloë protests, "Samantha is the best name *ever*!"

As Chloë is about to protest again, Emily deftly holds the puppy in front of her sister at eye level for a long moment and then returns it to her lap.

Chloë now has both hands clasped over her mouth, and a look of shocked surprise in her eyes. She quickly drops her hands exclaiming, "Sam! Let's call him Sam! Em, isn't Sam the best name in the whole *world*?"

Laughing at her sweet sister's antics, Emily says, "Yes, Chlo, Sam *is* the best name ever." She scratches the puppy behind one ear. "Hello, Sam," she says affectionately and carefully places the puppy in Chloë's lap.

Chloë cuddles him lovingly and says, "Hi, Sam. Hi, little Sam. I'm your new mommy." Saying to Gracie Ann as she picks her up, "Gracie Ann, this is your new little brother, Sam." She presses Gracie Ann's face on top of Sam's head–*smack!*

Gracie Ann seems to smile. She is very pleased to have a new little brother and likes the idea of being a big sister. She thinks he's the cutest thing ever.

Looking at Seth hopefully, Chloë asks, "Can Sam sleep in our room tonight? He really wants to."

Seth chuckles, "Sam has his own very special room where he feels safe, Chlo. It's called a crate. Inside his special room he has his own toys and food and water and a nice warm blanket to lie on. I have two crates for him: one for the house and one for the playhouse. The one in the house is in the laundry room. Come on, I'll show you. "

As they walk to the laundry room so Seth can show the girls the puppy's crate and explain Sam's need to have his own protected space, three things take place simultaneously: Chloë thinks Sam is the handsomest and smartest dog in the whole world; Seth thinks that Sam was certainly a grand slam homerun; and for the first time in her life, Miss Emily Fleming falls in love.

CHAPTER NINETEEN

It is after lunch on Saturday afternoon. Chloë is sitting in a kitchen chair holding Sam, who now sports a big blue satin bow around his neck. Emily is busy painting the puppy's toes. Gracie Ann sits in a chair next to Chloë watching her little brother get a manicure, or would that be a pedicure, she wonders. Both, she proudly remembers, it's a mani-pedi! Seth is casually dressed in a pair of relaxed fit jeans, a blue, long-sleeve, cotton Polo shirt and white Nikes. Both girls noticed that after lunch he came back into the kitchen wearing light cologne. Chloë wanted to ask why he smelled funny, but Emily said it wouldn't be polite, so she didn't. Seth looks at the clock. The time is one-thirty p.m. He anxiously waits for Elena to arrive.

"Ladies, I didn't know boys got their nails painted," Seth says lightly.

"Of course they do," Chloë says.

Emily glances at the clock and smiles at Seth.

Casually, Seth says, "I noticed the door to Sam's crate was wide open this morning. He was nowhere to be seen . . . I wonder how that happened."

"Sam opened it," Chloë informs him. "He's the smartest dog in the whole world. He wanted to sleep in our room last night."

Seth looks at the clock again and says agreeably, "Well, I guess that explains everything."

There is a soft knock at the front door. Emily looks at Seth with a knowing smile and returns to putting nail polish on Sam's toes. Chloë focuses on what Emily does. Seth breaks out in a wide grin.

"Excuse me, ladies," Seth says. "I believe there's someone at the front door." He quickly goes to the front door and opens it.

Elena stands in front of him looking radiant. She is dressed in a pair of tasteful, charcoal, pinstripe slacks, and a simple white blouse; her hair is pulled back and tied with a colorful silk scarf in bright autumn reds, yellows, oranges, and gold; she wears a pair of black Toms. The young woman is stunning with a healthy, all-American, girl-next-door glow.

The moment she sees Seth, Elena breaks into a smile and looks at him with a friendly, warm expression on her face. Seth, in return, grins at her in his customary easy way. He is completely captivated by Elena. He thinks he could stand there all day just looking at this beautiful woman. Sitting on the porch by Elena's feet are three large eco-friendly grocery bags filled to capacity.

"Hi Elena, I'm really glad you came." Seth is scarcely able to contain his excitement.

"Hello, Seth. What a nice home you have," Elena says, still smiling warmly at him; her dark eyes are luminous.

"It's Mom's," he explains. "Katie and I grew up in this house. I'm just staying here for a little while. Mom's away on a women's mission trip this weekend with her church group."

"It's just lovely," she says with genuine sincerity.

"Thank you." He notices the grocery bags by her feet. "What's all this?"

"Oh, nothing much," Elena says in an offhand manner. "Just a few things, I never come empty-handed."

"Well, thank you," Seth says, impressed. "Please, come in. Let me help you."

Seth grabs two bags, and Elena retrieves the third one. Seth feels their weight as they walk through the living room to the kitchen. "Wow, Elena. These are heavy. What do you have in here?" He sniffs the contents, "Oh . . . my . . . gosh . . . it smells so good!"

Elena responds demurely, "I thought I'd save you the trouble of making dinner tonight, Seth. I hope everyone will like it."

"Look at all of this food—thank you. Elena, you must have spent all morning in the kitchen."

"As a matter of fact, I did," she says smartly.

They enter the kitchen with the bags. As soon as Chloë sees Elena she starts shouting, "Miss Hernandez! Miss Hernandez!" She points to Sam proudly. "Look what Seth gave us! His name's Sam! He's the smartest dog in the world!"

"Hi children," Elena says brightly. "Sam, you are the most adorable puppy ever."

"And the smartest!" Chloë chimes.

"I can see he is." Elena agrees.

Elena sets her grocery bag on the counter and goes to the children. Seth does the same with his bags and begins to unload their contents. As he does, he sniffs every dish and relishes everything he smells. Lastly, he removes the cake and licks his chops.

"You're painting his nails, Chloë?" Elena asks excitedly.

"Not really," Chloë says. "I'm holding him. Em's better at painting, but I'm helping."

Elena pulls up a chair next to the children and scratches behind Sam's ear. "I love the color. Is it periwinkle blue?"

"Yes," Emily says. "We found the bottle in Seth's sister's room. It's almost gone. But we have enough for today."

"Well, we'll just have to see about replenishing such critical girl supplies," Elena says, smiling and petting Sam again.

They finish with Sam just as Seth unloads the last items from the bags. The food dishes cover one entire section of the counter.

"Elena, I'm so impressed," Seth says, astonished. "You've brought enough here to feed a dozen people. Won't you please join us for dinner tonight?"

Chloë shouts, "Please! Please Miss Hernandez! *Please* stay for dinner."

Elena shrugs and responds innocently, "I wouldn't want to intrude . . . Really, I wouldn't."

Emily says politely, "I hope you will, Miss Hernandez."

"Yes. Please do," Seth adds, hoping with all of his heart she will say yes.

"Are you sure? I feel like I'm barging in on everyone," Elena offers demurely.

Eagerly, Seth says, "You wouldn't be. Really, Elena, you wouldn't." Then he pauses, his face drops, and his voice sounds discouraged. "But if you have other plans, I . . ."

"I would love to!" Elena quickly answers.

Seth grins, relieved. "I'm glad you said yes."

Chloë hops down and gives Sam to Seth. "Yippee! C'mon, Miss Hernandez, c'mon! Let's go outside. I'll show you what Seth did." Chloë grabs Elena's right hand and starts pulling her towards the back door. Emily follows them.

Laughing, Elena looks back over her shoulder at Seth as she is being kidnapped by Chloë. "Are you coming, Mr. Seth McAllister?" she asks gaily.

"Sure, I'm right behind you. Just let me put Sam in his home so he can rest, and I'll be there in a second." Seth puts Sam in his crate, and he goes out the back door to have fun.

CHAPTER TWENTY

After a couple of hours outside in the backyard, Seth and Elena come through the back door. They are laughing. Emily and Chloë chose to play in the playhouse a little while longer. The clock on the wall reads three-thirty p.m.

"That was so much fun!" Elena says, her beautiful dark eyes glowing. "I love to swing. And Seth, the playhouse is amazing. What you've done for Emily and Chloë is so special. They just love it here. It's easy to see why."

"Thanks," says Seth. "But it was fun for me to fix up everything. Elena, what's incredible is how well you relate to them."

"It isn't hard. They're wonderful girls," she says, smiling at this terrific man and thinking, "Seth's so great with children. He's almost too good to be true—smart, handsome, caring, and a real gentleman. Papa would approve, so would Mama. Three children would be perfect."

Inviting Elena to sit at the table, Seth pulls out the chair for her. He gets cold lemonade from the fridge, fills two glasses, and brings one to Elena. "Thank you," she says.

Seth decides it's too soon to sit next to Elena and instead, just as well, decides to sit across from her so he can gaze at her beautiful features. He can see what a lovely figure she has, and he appreciates the fact that Elena is modest about it. Kathryn had schooled him this was one of the favorable signs, and it was definitely an important box on her checklist. Sitting there looking at her, he can hardly believe his good fortune that Elena is single and he's thinking, "She's so perfect in every way—smart, beautiful, caring, natural, and a real lady. Just the kind of girl Mother would like and one who would jet straight to the top of Katie's approved list. I wonder if she wants children."

Admiring her, he asks, "Elena, how did you get involved with The Children's Sanctuary?"

She responds energetically, "I was home over Christmas my junior year of college. There was a notice on the bulletin board at church about the Sanctuary needing volunteers. I went down, signed-up, loved it, and volunteered every Christmas after that and summers too."

"That doesn't surprise me about you. Then you started teaching there?"

"Yes. I completed my master's and decided I wanted to teach at The Children's Sanctuary's Charter School. It's my second year."

"What's your master's in, Elena?" he asks, making conversation. He can't stop looking at her, and he's wondering if she's noticed.

"Literature. You?"

"I have a master's in Architecture."

Elena brightens. "My dad wanted to be an architect," she says. "But he had a chance to come to America, so he left college and came here. He has a design and construction company now. Papa never finished his degree."

"He must be very good to have his own company," Seth says, impressed.

"He is. He's very talented."

Everything Elena says is interesting to Seth. "Elena," he asks curiously, "why The Children's Sanctuary? You could have gone anywhere."

"Papa's always told me, 'Follow your heart.' When I was volunteering, I thought I was doing something to save the children. It made me feel good about myself." Looking at him, she imagines the future and muses, "He has the prettiest blue eyes I've ever seen and such handsome features. Our children will be beautiful. I bet our first will be a boy; then girl, girl; no, maybe boy, girl, boy would be better."

"You should have felt good about volunteering," Seth says. "It was a great thing to do."

"I did," Elena answers. "But it wasn't until my first year of teaching that I came to understand the true meaning of the Sanctuary. It happened during our Christmas party."

"I'd love to hear about it," Seth says, intrigued.

"And I'd love to tell you about it," Elena says eagerly. "You see, every year at The Children's Sanctuary we have a Christmas party in the gym. The place is packed with donors, cottage parents, sponsor parents, staff members, and, of course, all the children who are running around like crazy. After everyone has eaten at the buffet, we start the Christmas program of traditional skits, songs, and stories. The children can hardly wait because their presents are stacked in huge, bright piles on the floor all around the gym. Their cottage numbers are taped on the wall above each pile, and that's how they know which ones belong to them. When Santa arrives, it's the signal to the children they can open their presents."

"What happens then?" Seth asks, eager to hear more.

Elena laughs. "Seth, it's joyful pandemonium. The children run squealing to their presents and tear into them just like kids do everywhere."

Seth chuckles. "It sounds great."

"It really is," she says. "I was sitting alone, looking at the shining, happy faces of the children. I was watching the people smiling and laughing. They come from every walk of life, you know, and it takes all of their collective efforts to make it possible. And that's when I was suddenly struck by the true meaning of the Sanctuary."

Seth leans forward slightly, giving Elena his full attention. "Please, tell me. I want to hear."

From her heart, Elena says, "Oh, I know the Sanctuary doesn't look like much from the outside. Just a collection of a few nondescript buildings and plain looking homes tucked away in a poor part of the county. Most people who drive by don't even notice us, let alone have any idea what we do there. Some would even argue that caring for eighty children will scarcely make a difference in a world where good is so often trumped by evil. But I know that isn't true. On that evening Seth, I understood completely the true meaning of the Sanctuary: it's the charitable effort itself that is the cause for great hope in the world. I believe this hope is the deeper meaning of the Sanctuary. It shows our better nature as people. I believe it's a testament to a capacity for profound goodness that resides in every human being. Right then I suddenly realized it wasn't these children alone who needed saving but myself as well. Who was saving whom? Why do I teach there? I teach at The Children's Sanctuary because I want to be part of this wonderful hope."

Enthralled with her, Seth says admiringly, "Elena, you're remarkable."

"No, not really Seth," she replies modestly. "I just want to make a difference. All of us can."

"That's why you're remarkable," Seth repeats, as he thinks, "she has the loveliest smile, kindest eyes, and the most beautiful face I've ever seen."

"Thank you," she replies. Elena averts her eyes bashfully. Looking out the bay window, she sees the children swinging. "The children are probably thirsty, don't you think?"

"I'm sure you're right, Elena," Seth agrees. "I'll go outside and get them."

"You don't have to do that," Elena says. She gets up from her chair, walks over to the back door, opens it, sticks two fingers in her teeth, whistles at an ear-piercing pitch, and yells, "Kids! Lemonade! Come and get it!"

The children come running to the door. Breathless, Chloë arrives first with little sweat beads collected above her upper lip and curls sticking to her forehead. "I won!" she yells, "I raced Emily, and I won!"

Elena winks at Emily. "I see you did. You're a fast runner, Chloë. You and Emily go wash your hands, please." Elena turns and sees Seth is grinning at her and shaking his head. "What?" she asks innocently.

"Nothing, nothing at all," he says affably.

The children sit at the table, and Elena pours lemonade into a glass for Emily and into a plastic tumbler for Chloë. Elena sits next to Seth. The children soon finish their lemonade.

"Let's play another game," Chloë says, enthused.

"Chloë never runs out of energy," Seth comments.

Elena laughs. "Okay, Chloë. But let's play something inside. We all need to cool off. What would you like to play?"

Thrilled, Chloë jumps down from her chair and shouts, "Dancing with My Girls!" and she begins bouncing up and down, her big curls bouncing with her.

Elena turns to Seth, perplexed. "'Dancing with My Girls'? I don't think I know that game."

"Emily and Chloë taught me," Seth tells her. "It's a lot of fun— if you like to dance."

"Oh, I love to dance." Elena says excitedly.

Chloë runs to the radio, "I get to be first!"

"What she means is," Seth explains to Elena, "we turn on the radio and Chloë pushes the play forward button. We dance to whatever music it lands on."

"What fun," Elena says, delighted.

"But you have to be quick," Seth adds. "The person controlling the radio can push the play forward button at any time, which makes it really fun and really fast."

"I like it more and more—I like fast," Elena says, and her dark eyes gleam with excitement.

"Who's gonna go first?" Chloë asks. She is energized by the fact she will be controlling the radio.

Quickly getting up from the table, Elena joins Chloë by the radio. "Not me," she says gaily. "I'm going to watch first."

Seth glances at Emily, "Looks like it's you and me, Em."

Emily smiles shyly at Seth. They rise from their chairs and position themselves in the kitchen in front of the table a few feet apart. Seth bows formally to her, and Emily curtsies to him. Emily nods at Chloë for the game to begin.

Chloë switches on the radio, giggles, holds-up her forefinger high in the air, wiggles it for everyone to see, and then dramatically dives it down to the play forward button and gives it a good punch. The radio blasts out a Slovenian-style polka.

Zoom! Away go Seth and Emily in a whirl of energy, dancing to the fast-paced piano and chromatic accordion in a frenzy of fast dips and turns. Elena claps her hands to the beat of the music and shouts encouragement to the dancers. Chloë is buzzed about being boss again. Suddenly the music changes to an even faster pace as the radio blares out Charlie Daniels Band's "The Devil Went Down to Georgia." The pair flies into what can only be described as dance turbocharged, with Emily flawlessly following every quick cross-body lead change and piece of rapid foot work that Seth performs. At this dizzying speed, Seth works up a sweat as they sprint to the racing fiddle while Emily appears as fresh as a morning daisy, totally poised and graceful even in the heat of this tempo.

Elena can't believe her eyes and thinks, "Wow! Look at Emily. She's amazing and so artistic. I've never seen anyone move like her." She already felt Seth was handsome, smart, and giving; and Elena is thrilled watching him now. "And you mean to tell me that boy can dance, too? Yes, definitely three children. *I don't care what order they're in!*"

After two minutes and just as quickly as before, the music switches to "I Need You" by America. Seth pants, thankful for an easy listening tune. Dancing to this beat, the pair moves at a glacial pace compared to the tempo of the previous songs. But being the boss of bosses, Chloë doesn't let this slow song last. It's way too boring for her tastes, and she's got the power. *Punch!* Lenny Kravitz is belting out "American Woman."

Elena can't resist the music and scoots to the kitchen floor, declaring, "C'mon ladies, this is a girl's song! Mr. Seth McAllister, retire to the radio but don't push that button," she orders playfully. Chloë jumps from the chair and joins Emily and Elena in the middle of the kitchen floor.

Seth immediately takes Chloë's place at the radio. He doesn't dare touch that button.

The girls are just being girls, abandoning themselves to the joy of dancing. They show plenty of sassy attitude while swinging their hips, throwing their heads from side to side, acting silly, and giggling as they rock and gyrate to the heavy tempo, totally in sync with the music and with each other. At this moment, in their minds the nearest boy is a thousand light years away. It's all about being a girl and all about feeling the pulsating music. The song ends, and the girls laugh wildly.

Anxious to re-assume her rank as commander of the radio, Chloë eagerly grabs Emily's hand and pulls her towards the counter. "C'mon Em, it's Seth's and Miss Hernandez's turn."

Seth is glad to leave his station at the counter and join Elena. He stands a few feet from her, and his heart is racing. Elena's eyes are dark shining globes, and she gazes directly into his, passionately. He bows politely to her; she curtsies politely to him.

"Ready?" Chloë giggles and quickly punches the radio button. "Have You Ever Really Loved a Woman" by Bryan Adams is just beginning.

At the first alluring chords, Elena swiftly crosses the space be—tween them, places an index finger lightly on Seth's right shoulder, and in one fluid motion circles him before he can move. When Elena comes round in front of him, Seth looks into her half-closed eyes as she parts her rose lips sensually and lightly tosses her raven hair. She draws him down deeply beneath the twin dark pools of her reflective gaze, completely beguiling the man.

Seth can't move. He simply stands there looking at her, bedazzled. There's no possibility that this man can resist this woman; there's no possibility at all, nor does he want to try. He had fallen helplessly in love with Elena the instant he first saw her at The Children's Sanctuary.

Chloë rolls her eyes up at Emily questioningly. Emily smiles at her sister and motions to Chloë not to push the play forward button. Emily wants this song to play out for Seth and Elena.

Looking at him seductively, Elena softly teases, "Well, Mr. Seth McAllister, did you come here to dance or just to occupy that space on the floor?"

Seth cracks a grin, "I came here to dance, Miss Elena Sanctuary who teaches at the Hernandez School," and quickly reaches for her.

She can't wait to be in his arms. The amorous music swells, and the pace increases as Elena effortlessly follows Seth's every lead and his every smooth change. This pair was made in Heaven for each other.

To Seth, the sight of Elena, the sound of her, the touch of her, the warmth of her, the scent of her faint perfume is thrilling and like nothing else he has ever experienced before in his life. He believes Elena is like the Venus de Milo—stunning and classic and inspirational and timeless and completely unique. Seth never wants their dance to end.

Elena wishes the music would go on endlessly. As her feet fly nimbly to the mounting tempo of the strumming chords, her heart flies even faster, winging its way up into the clear cerulean sky above the world, ascending beyond the celestial sphere, soaring past the silver moon, and gliding straight into the star field paradise of Seth's beautiful eyes. His gaze shines like a crystal blue beacon, beckoning her to him and safely lighting her pathway from across the universe. Here in this cosmos, held serenely secure in his strong arms and fixed eternally like the immutable forces of two planetary bodies in harmonious attraction, Elena is blissfully aware she will be dancing with the man of her dreams forever.

CHAPTER TWENTY-ONE

It is now Saturday evening, and the time is eight p.m. Seth has just walked Elena out the front door. The children are inside going through their nightly routine. Soon, Seth will read a bedtime story to Chloë. It has been a special day for everyone. Seth and Elena stand together on the porch.

Elena is hoping for a goodnight kiss. She has purposefully moved close to him, providing the opportunity.

Seth, in his shy way, wonders if it's too soon to kiss this lovely creature. "Boy, I sure would like to," he tells himself. But he worries, "What if that scares her off? Better wait. I don't want to come on too strong." So instead of kissing her, he says politely, "Elena, I'm really glad you came today."

"I had a wonderful time, Seth. Thank you. You don't have to walk me to my car. The children shouldn't be left alone for too long." Knowing he wants to kiss her but seeing his shyness, Elena has artfully moved a step closer to him with her face turned up to his, waiting and hoping and longing. Her mind is shouting, "C'mon boy! I'm right here. Aren't you going to kiss me?"

With her standing so close to him, Seth's reservation quickly melts away. He leans forward to kiss her, but just as he does, Elena suddenly sneezes, "*Achoo!*"

It must be explained that as a little girl Elena sneezed whenever she became too apprehensive, which was only caused by two events: unbearable anticipation, or, more often than not, the result of being caught stretching the truth over some mischief she and Javier had gotten into as co-conspirators. To her brother, his sister's habit of sneezing at such crucial times was a source of sheer frustration, as it meant that they could never get away with anything. To her mother and father, Elena's "telling sneeze" was tantamount to an admission of guilt. It was one of her cute idiosyncrasies made all the more adorable by her habit of holding her breath to prevent herself from sneezing during these critical moments. As a strong-willed child, and anxious not to disappoint Javier, Elena would hold her breath to the point of turning blue. But this tactic of hers never worked because her parents would simply wait her out. When Elena finally burst her breath and gulped fresh oxygen, it was immediately followed by a sneeze. At which point Javier would loudly complain: "*Gee whizz, El. I'm never gonna let you play with me again!*" This little habit of sneezing whenever she was under duress had followed Elena into adulthood.

Standing with Seth under the porch light, Elena is embarrassed at having just sneezed, and she mentally kicks herself for losing the moment. Quickly she reaches into her purse and plucks out a tissue. Patting her nose daintily, she says to Seth lightly, "Must be something in the air." Elena smiles at him encouragingly and adds much too eagerly, "But I'm not contagious."

Seth thinks to himself, "Does this girl know how absolutely adorable she is?" Amused with her antics, he responds, "But you are 'catching,' aren't you?"

Elena blushes at being caught but nevertheless is particularly pleased with Seth's quick-witted comeback. Not to be outdone, she places her hand lightly on his chest and pats him once, saying pertly, "The word is 'catchable,' mister. I'm the lit major here, remember?"

"Okay, Miss Lit Major," Seth teases, "do you have a good story to leave me with?"

"Of course I do. And you shouldn't end your sentences in pre–positions, Mr. Architecture Major."

Seth grins and shrugs.

Elena's beautiful dark eyes glow and her silky black hair has the luster of satin beneath the soft porch light as she begins dramatically, "Once, there was this old Irishman whose best companion was his trusted dog. One day, the dog up and died. The old man was heartbroken. He took the poor dog's body in a box to his parish priest and asked the priest to perform burial rights for it. The priest told the old man he sincerely regretted his loss, but the Church didn't permit its priests to perform burial rights for animals. The old man shook his head mournfully and said, 'Father, I'm really sorry to hear that. I was just about to write you a check for fifty thousand dollars.' Hearing this, the priest quickly says, 'Man, why didn't you tell me your dog was Catholic?'"

Seth laughs out loud. "Is there anything you don't do well?" he asks.

"Not anything I'm gonna tell you about, mister." She quickly kisses him on the cheek. "See ya," she says, and she skips down the stairs before he can budge.

"Hey, wait a minute!" Seth calls after her. Elena twirls around, eyes shining, looking at him expectantly.

"Can I see you again?"

"When?"

"Tomorrow night."

"Sure. I'd love that."

"Great. What would you like to do?"

"Feed me a veggie burger and a malted shake—I'm a happy girl. It's gotta be extra thick, though."

"You like your veggie burgers extra thick?"

"No, Mr. Smarty Pants. I like my malts extra-thick. *Really* extra thick."

"What's your favorite flavor?"

"All of them!" she laughs.

"Pick you up at seven?"

"That's a date. Bring my dishes back—clean."

"I will. Elena, dinner was really great."

On the verge of confessing, she coyly says, "Seth, about dinner tonight . . ."

"You're amazing. It reminded me of my mom's cooking."

She shrugs and smiles. "Thank you. See ya."

Seth calls, "See ya, Elena."

Seth watches Elena get safely to her car and drive off. "This is one of the best days of my life," he says out loud. He turns and goes back into the house, closing the front door softly behind him.

Later that evening, after the bedtime story, *Peter Rabbit*, and after the children are fast asleep, Seth quietly walks into the kitchen carrying the thin leather case Mr. Nakamura gave him on the day of his homecoming. He sits down at the table, opens the case, pulls out a pen and a sheaf of paper, and begins drawing.

CHAPTER TWENTY-TWO

Yesenia and Humberto are in the kitchen. Yesenia stands at the stove stirring some onions and meat in a large skillet with her long-handled cooking spoon. She is in a wonderful mood. Humberto sits at the table intently reading the sports section of the paper. His battered fedora hangs on the back of his chair.

"Humberto, it's love! Our Elena's in love!" Yesenia says, beside herself with excitement.

Focused on his paper, Humberto simply grunts and continues reading.

"That boy's all she can talk about, think about. They've seen each other every night since they met. I'm telling you, mi amor, it's love!"

Humberto rattles his paper and grunts again without looking up.

Annoyed by his inattention, Yesenia cuts a small slice of cake, puts it on a plate, and sets it on the table beneath the newspaper. Humberto sniffs a couple of times and jerks his paper away. Seeing the cake, he grins at his wife.

"Humberto. You haven't heard one thing I've been saying," his wife accuses him.

Humberto stabs a forkful of cake and says defensively, "Sure I have. Every word, mi amor," and he stuffs the cake in his mouth.

Yesenia looks at him skeptically, "So, you know Elena's in love?"

"What?" Humberto says, surprised. "Who said?"

Pointing her cooking spoon at him she says, "You see. You haven't been paying any attention to me. You never do. Our daughter's in love. Ai yai yai, I've never done so much cooking."

Preoccupied with his cake, Humberto comments distractedly, "I thought that was for the church?"

"No, it's been for Elena's young man. She was helping me though," Yesenia says proudly.

Humberto looks up, surprised. "Elena? Elena's been helping you in the kitchen? Is she learning anything?"

"Still a danger, I'm afraid," Yesenia sighs. "But she'll learn in time."

"That boy thinks Elena can cook? Oh, what a web you women weave," Humberto teases, finishing off the last of his cake.

Yesenia huffs, "We women are the beautiful silk threads. You men do your own weaving, and very eagerly I might add."

"True," Humberto agrees, and then adds mischievously, "only at the time, we never realize what we're weaving is a noose for our own necks, mi amor."

His wife smiles at him knowingly. "I remember how eager you were for the noose."

"True, very true," he agrees again. "Yes, try as she might, Elena will never be as good a cook as you. More cake?"

"Humberto!" Yesenia scolds, annoyed with him, "I'm telling you our daughter's in love, and all you can think about is cake? Don't you want to know about the young man?"

Humberto regards his wife impassively. "Sure I do. Does he have a good job?"

Yesenia makes a face at him. "Does he have a good job? That's not what's important." Looking up, a wave of euphoria washes over her as she says dreamily, "You should be asking what's really important: 'does he love Elena with all of his heart and soul? Does he think she's the most wonderful girl in the world? Does he respect and admire her for the person she is? Does he support her in achieving everything she wants to achieve? Is he kind, considerate, and thoughtful of her?'" Then, placing both hands over her heart, she sighs dramatically, "Does his heart *sing* whenever she is near him?" Carried away with her romantic musings, Yesenia suddenly rushes to Humberto, throws her arms around his neck, hugs him tightly, and presses her cheek into his, blissfully.

Grimacing, Humberto protests, "Yesenia, will you stop *hugging* me."

Yesenia releases her husband, looks at him, and blinks innocently. Still euphoric, she asks, "Mi amor, what do you think? Isn't it just wonderful?"

"So the boy doesn't have a job," Humberto says flatly.

Yesenia shakes her cooking spoon at him, complaining, "Why do I even talk to you? He doesn't now, but he will."

Humberto purses his lips to one side and says, "I knew it. The boy's a deadbeat."

"He's not either," Yesenia protests, "if you had been at the Sanctuary's Christmas party last night you could have met him. He's *so* handsome, mi amor. And *smart*. You should see the way they look at each other. It reminded me of us at their age. It's love!" Reveling in happy anticipation of the certain nuptials, Yesenia sings, "There's a wedding coming. A mother know-ohs."

Dubious, Humberto asks, "What makes the boy so smart?"

Eagerly, Yesenia answers, "Elena told me he has a master's degree in architecture from the Boyd School, graduated number one in his class."

Suddenly, Humberto becomes interested, even impressed. "That's the most prestigious school for architects in the country. You said number one in his class?"

"And he's a really nice boy, Humberto. You'll like him." Yesenia begins pleasantly humming to herself.

"He graduated number one?"

His wife doesn't hear him over her happy humming and the song in her heart as she thinks about grandchildren.

Humberto complains, "Yesenia, stop that humming. I'm trying to talk to you. Why aren't you listening to me? Are you sure it was the Boyd School?"

"I'm sure, mi amor," Yesenia answers sweetly. She is neither offended by Humberto's order to cease humming nor does she pay the least bit of attention to him. She continues humming.

Humberto considers it. "Number one . . . the Boyd School . . . that's promising. What's he doing now?" he asks in an upbeat tone, feeling better about Elena's choice.

Without taking her eyes from the skillet, Yesenia answers mildly, "He lives at home with his mother."

Humberto's face sags, and he shakes his head in disbelief, irritated. "What? He lives at home with his mother. Is the boy Italian?"

"No, Humberto, he's not Italian," Yesenia says, exasperated with him. "His name, since you haven't even asked, is Seth McAllister. He's of Scottish heritage, and he was born right here in our town."

Perturbed, Humberto says, "Don't tell me he's a gringo? A gringo who lives at home with his mother. Well that's just wonderful . . ."

Yesenia whirls around and shakes her spoon at her husband. "Stop! You stop that right now," she scolds. "Stop using that G word. You know this family doesn't use that word. You should be ashamed. He's a nice boy. Your daughter loves him, and there's nothing you can do about it except go along and smile."

Humberto knows he stepped over the line with Yesenia when he said gringo. He didn't mean to say it in front of her. It just popped out of his mouth. He and his best friend Casey O'Toole teased each other all the time using it. Humberto called his Irish friend the Jolly Green Gringo, and Casey called his Latino friend the Coffee Bean Gringo. These monikers, not to mention many more colorful ones, were just harmless fun in their minds, even affectionate terms. But Yesenia absolutely didn't allow it in her home. She felt it was disrespectful to their adopted country and just as demeaning to the one who used it as to the one it was describing. She wouldn't have it. Humberto could never understand why Yesenia felt so strongly about this mild epithet. So years ago he had simply shrugged his shoulders, shaken his head, and concluded what all men finally conclude when they can't fathom why a woman feels so strongly about something a man thinks nothing about at all: "It must be a woman thing." Beyond this universal male default rationalization of a woman's curious behavior, he thought no more of it. Humberto quickly apologizes, "You're right, Yesenia. I'm sorry for using that word. But honestly, mi amor, what'll they do? Get married and move in with us?"

Yesenia looks up at the ceiling and says, "Please God, give me patience with this man." She turns to Humberto, saying with for– bearance, "Mi amor, try to remember your precious muchacha bonita. She's in love with this boy, and she's never been happier. You don't want to hurt our daughter's feelings; she'll be here any minute."

"Oh, I won't," Humberto grumbles. "But tell me this, Yes: why couldn't she have fallen in love with a doctor?"

Looking at her husband, Yesenia shakes her head wearily. "Once, you were such a romantic boy."

There's a pleasant, rapid knock at the back door. Just before Elena comes through the door, Yesenia casts a last, quick frown at her husband and shakes her spoon at him in warning. Elena enters. Her whole demeanor is of a young woman in love. She is energetic and dreamy eyed. She kisses her father on the cheek.

"Hi Papa! Hi Mama! Isn't it a wonderful day? Did you like Seth, Mama? Isn't he the best? Papa, I wish you'd been there last night to meet him."

"He was just wonderful, cariño," her mother says. "And so handsome. And such a gentleman. Everything and more you've been telling me about him. I liked him so much."

"He really liked you too. Papa, why didn't you come last night?"

"I couldn't, muchacha bonita. Needed to figure out how to get this new job done on time. I'm a man short."

Elena is excited for him. "You won a new project?"

"It's a small one, niña. Only last a month at the most. Still, it's something to keep us going."

"I'm so proud of you," she says and hugs her father.

Elena's cell phone rings. She sees that it's Seth calling her. She mouths to her mother, "Seth." Yesenia smiles and nods to her. Elena answers her phone.

"Hi. Yes, I'm at my parents right now. Sure, I'll be over soon. The children liked their Christmas gifts from me?" She laughs, "Oh, poor little Sam. See you in a few. Bye babe." She closes the phone and grins at her parents. "That was Seth."

Yesenia, seeing how happy her daughter is, says to her, "I think he's wonderful, Elena."

An idea suddenly pops into Elena's head, and her face lights up. "Papa! You're not a man short. Hire Seth! Mama, did you tell him Seth has a master's degree in architecture?"

"Yes, niña, your mother told me about his fancy degree," Humberto says skeptically. "It doesn't mean he's qualified to do anything. We do hard work for real men."

Unseen by Elena, Yesenia sends a disapproving look Humberto's way. He shifts uncomfortably in his chair.

Elena is unfazed. Still just as enthusiastic, she says, "Seth will do anything to help. Papa, come with me and meet him today."

Humberto hesitates. "I was planning on going to the office and—"

"Elena that's a wonderful idea," her mother interrupts. Yesenia looks sternly at her husband but speaks pleasantly, "Humberto, follow her over there, meet Seth, and then go to the office." She finishes by giving him "the look."

Seeing his wife means business, Humberto responds flatly, "Sure. I'd love to meet him."

His wife nods her approval and decides to reward him. "Go then," she says, "and be home on time for dinner, mi amor. I'm making a fresh batch of chicken ranchero this afternoon."

Oblivious to her father's skepticism, Elena claps her hands, "Oh Papa! You'll like him so much. I just *know* you will."

"I'm sure too, niña. I can't wait," Humberto says, thankful he will at the least be getting his favorite dish for dinner.

Elena beams and says excitedly, "I'm going out to my car. I'll wait for you outside."

Elena gives her mother a quick hug and leaves. Yesenia, pleased with Humberto, walks over to him and places a hand affectionately on his shoulder. He reaches up and pats it sweetly.

"Thank you, mi amor. What did you think?" Yesenia asks.

"Elena does seem very happy," he says. "I suppose this is as good a time as any to meet the young man. I really could use an extra hand for a month."

His wife pats him, kisses him on the cheek, and says, "You see how nicely things are working out? And thank you, mi amor, for taking such good care of our family. You work so hard for us."

Humberto gets up from his chair, wraps his arm around his wife's waist, and looks at her lovingly. "I couldn't do any of it without you . . . Yes?"

"Mi amor?" Yesenia answers playfully.

Humberto's eyes are glowing warmly. "You'll always be the prettiest girl in the room." He kisses his wife on the cheek, grabs his battered hat, and goes out to his car.

CHAPTER TWENTY-THREE

Elena and Humberto have arrived at the McAllister home and are standing at the front door. Elena knocks lightly; in a moment, the door opens, and there is Chloë's happy face looking up at them.

"Miss Hernandez! Miss Hernandez!" she shouts.

"Hi Chloë, this is my father, Mr. Hernandez."

Humberto says kindly, "Hello Chloë. It is very nice to meet you. I understand you have a little puppy?"

Chloë nods excitedly. "His name's Sam. He's the smartest dog in the whole world!"

Mr. Hernandez chuckles. "I'm sure he is."

"Chlo, where's Seth, Emily, and Sam?" asks Elena.

"We're in the kitchen playing, c'mon." Chloë leads them into the kitchen. Sitting on a kitchen chair is Seth. The girls have his hair in curlers and lipstick on his lips, slightly smeared. Emily is busy brushing nail polish on the last of Seth's nails. The color is periwinkle blue. Both Emily and Seth are concentrating on his nails at the moment. When Elena enters the kitchen with her father and sees what's going on, she immediately starts laughing. Humberto stands there in stunned silence. Emily looks up and smiles pleasantly. Seth looks at Elena and grins. Chloë joins her sister and starts adjusting the hair curlers in Seth's hair.

"I see you're getting beautified, Seth," Elena says lightly.

Unconcerned by how his appearance might look to Elena's

father, Seth replies enthusiastically, "Sam ran out of toes. Chloë insisted I be the next customer."

"Love the color," Elena quips.

Seth grins. "Thank you."

Both girls look at Elena and say in unison, "Thank you, Miss Hernandez, for our makeup kits."

"You're so welcome," Elena replies, hardly able to contain her laughter.

During this exchange between Elena and Seth and Elena and the children, Humberto has turned to his daughter and stares at her in dazed disbelief.

Steeped in the hilarity of the moment, Elena says matter of fact, "Papa. Please meet Seth McAllister. Seth, this is my father, Mr. Hernandez."

From the chair, Seth nods and smiles at him and says, as if nothing in the world is amiss, "Nice to meet you, Mr. Hernandez. I'd get up and shake hands with you but my nails are still wet."

Humberto slowly nods his head in response. Flabbergasted, he looks at his daughter in silence and finally manages to say, "Elena, did you know about this?"

Straining to keep from laughing out loud, she replies innocently, "Know about what, Papa?"

Humberto doesn't realize she's teasing him. "It's just that I . . . I mean . . . is this your idea of . . . well . . . I was thinking . . ."

Elena's eyes are filled with mirth. "I know what you're thinking, Papa. How lucky that Seth's a *real* man. A *real* man who isn't afraid to play games with children." She looks at Emily. "Emily, this is my father, Mr. Hernandez. Papa, this is Emily Fleming."

Politely, Emily says, "Hello Mr. Hernandez. Miss Hernandez is my teacher. She's really good."

"Hi Emily," says Mr. Hernandez, regaining his eveness. "My daughter has told me all about you and your sister. She thinks you're both very special."

Excitedly, Chloë tells them, "Me and Emily did the curlers. I did the lipstick by myself. Em's better at painting. But I helped."

Emily puts the final touches on Seth's nails and says to her sister, "C'mon, Chlo. Let's go outside and play in the playhouse." They both leave the kitchen and go out the back door.

Seth gets up and comes over to Elena and Humberto. "Mr. Hernandez," he says beaming, "you've got the most wonderful daughter in the world. I guess you know that already."

Squinting at Seth, Humberto tries to answer, but he just can't find any words. He simply stares at him with a quizzical expression on his face.

Looking at Seth, Elena hands him a tissue and motions for him to remove the lipstick. Seth shrugs, takes the tissue, and begins wiping his mouth.

"Seth," Elena says, "Papa couldn't wait to meet you. He has something he wants to ask you."

Humberto looks at his daughter as if he's lost.

Seeing her father is speechless, Elena encourages him. "Remember Papa? Rememberrr . . . the new job . . . you're a man short . . . you could use Seth's help. It's all coming back to you now, isn't it?"

Humberto, nearly recovered from being stunned by Seth's un-expected appearance, scratches his cheek thoughtfully and looks at Seth, who still has a smear of lipstick in the left corner of his mouth.

Seth looks at Humberto expectantly.

Unsure, Humberto begins, "Uh . . . Uh . . . I run a small design and construction company. I could use an extra man—only for about a month you understand—so you probably wouldn't be interested."

"I'm interested!" says Seth enthusiastically. "Mr. Hernandez, Elena has told me how talented you are. Just the chance to work around you would be a great opportunity, even for a few weeks. I'll do anything you need."

Humberto is pleasantly surprised. "Elena said that?"

"Of course," she says. "Papa, you're the most talented man I know. Seth was really anxious to meet you."

Seeing how enthusiastic Elena is and remembering his wife's warning, Humberto relents, "Well then, be there Monday morning at seven-thirty, young man. Elena will give you the address. You understand it's minimum wage. It'll only last a few weeks."

Seth reaches out to shake hands. "Thank you, Mr. Hernandez. I really appreciate it."

Humberto looks doubtfully at Seth's offered hand.

Seth gives him a reassuring nod. "It's okay Mr. Hernandez. They're dry now."

Cautiously, Mr. Hernandez shakes Seth's hand. "One more thing about Monday morning young man. Probably best not to wear lipstick and nail polish to the office."

Seth answers jovially, "Yes sir, Mr. Hernandez. Not to worry, this is just a weekend thing."

Humberto nods slowly, still uncertain he has made the right decision about hiring Seth. He turns, hugs his daughter, and leaves.

Seth grins at Elena. "He looked a little surprised, babe."

Elena laughs out loud so hard that tears are coming from her eyes. "A little? You don't know my father: Mr. Conservative. When we walked in and he saw you with lipstick, nail polish, and hair curlers, I'm surprised he didn't bolt out of here."

Seth's tone is lighthearted. "So, does this mean I didn't make that all-important, good first impression?"

"Let's just say you made an impression he'll never forget," she says, amused.

He shrugs and looks at Elena affectionately. "Well, he still hired me."

"I wish I could be there Monday morning," she says. "What fun."

"It'll go fine," he says, unconcerned. "I'm really looking forward to it."

She pats his mouth with another tissue. "Here babe, you still have a smidgen in one corner." Elena gently wipes the last of the lipstick away. She smiles at Seth lovingly and then holds his hand in hers, admiring it. "Emily did a wonderful job on your nails. Periwinkle blue?"

"Yes. Blue is for boys. And I like this shade the best."

"Suits you perfectly, honey. Don't forget, your toenails should match. I'll be sure to tell Emily and Chloë to take care of that today for you."

Seth nods good-naturedly. "Great. I want to look my best for you."

They kiss tenderly.

CHAPTER TWENTY-FOUR

It is seven-thirty Monday morning, and Seth is standing outside the front door of a ramshackle building. There is a sign across the top that reads: Humberto Hernandez, Design and Construction. Seth quietly opens the door and walks in the office.

On the floor in front of him is a young, slender Latino about his same age. This man is on his hands and knees with his back to Seth. He hasn't heard Seth come in. The man is concentrating on carefully drawing a line in white chalk and is slowly backing up towards Seth. The line has started from the far back of the office, comes down between two office desks (the left desk is much larger than the one on the right), and continues towards the front door. Against the left wall is a row of metal filing cabinets. Hanging on the wall above them is a large calendar. Pictured on it, a proud-faced matador in gold sequined pants and matching jacket sweeps his red cape aside as a massive bull charges past, hurling its death tipped horns tantalizing centimeters from the bull fighter's groin. There is a large, round clock on the wall above one cabinet. Atop the desk are two framed photos. A drafting table is nearby. Against the opposite wall to the right are more metal filing cabinets, and on this wall hangs another large calendar. This one features fall flowers including bouquets of cyclamens in red, pink, and white mixed with chrysanthemums in white and gold. Below the calendar is the smaller desk, very neat and orderly, and on it is a pot of poinsettias placed in one corner. The left side of the office has a distinctly plain, masculine appearance and is cluttered; the right is stylish, effeminate, and tidy.

Seth observes the man curiously. The Latino is completely absorbed with drawing the chalk line precisely. He backs up, coming closer and closer to Seth. Finally, when the man is about to bump into him, Seth clears his throat.

At this unexpected noise, the young Latino jumps with fright and squeals. He turns his head quickly and looks up at Seth, pursing his lips together in a tight flat line, looking peeved. He hops up from the floor, facing Seth. He is about five feet six inches tall, thin with unusually delicate features, perfect white teeth, and large sensitive eyes. His short, jet black hair is combed straight back. Seth sees he is dressed surprisingly stylishly, even chic. He wears a Ralph Lauren cotton shirt, chino pants, and Delli Aldo loafers. Seth instantly feels there is something very likeable about him. The man places one delicate hand with impeccably groomed nails on his hip and in a slight lisp huffs, "Well! I hope you know you just about scared the living daylights out of me!"

Seth shows his grin. "Sorry, didn't mean to do that. My name's Seth, Seth McAllister. I'm reporting for work."

His accuser relaxes. Now getting a second look at Seth and clearly pleased, he says cordially, "Oh, so you're the new man Mr. Hernandez hired. He told me to expect you this morning, but I didn't know you'd be so tall." He smiles graciously at Seth. He offers his right hand, saying with a flourish, "I'm Juan-Carlos Alberto Donato Buenaventura. Please, call me Juan-Carlos. I'm the interior designer . . . and receptionist, secretary, office manager, and bookkeeper. I also handle special projects." The man is glowing now.

Seth takes the Latino's offered hand in his and presses it gently. He is completely accepting that Juan-Carlos is gay. "Nice to meet you, Juan-Carlos. Is Mr. Hernandez here?" he asks.

Juan-Carlos is instantly fond of Seth because this tall man

is completely non-judgmental and, he must confess truthfully, because he is so good looking. "No," Juan-Carlos replies amiably, "Mr. Hernandez will not come for a few minutes more. He went to the work site first."

Seth nods, "May I ask you what you're doing?"

Holding up the chalk, Juan-Carlos smiles broadly. "Oh, you mean with this?" He points to the floor. "That line separates me and Mr. Hernandez. It becomes faded throughout the week. So, I must re-draw it every Monday morning."

Seth rubs his chin and with friendly curiosity asks, "I see, but why the line in the first place?"

Juan-Carlos begins whispering rapidly as if sharing a big secret, "Because I get overexcited. And when I do, I start hugging everybody. Once, I hugged Mr. Hernandez," he stops and looks sideways at Seth, then confesses modestly, "that wasn't my best idea. After that, he made me draw this line. I have to stay on my side of it whenever Mr. Hernandez is here."

Amused, Seth observes, "I notice it's not drawn down the center?"

"This is true," Juan-Carlos shrugs and sighs. "Mr. Hernandez says the boss deserves a bigger desk and more room. I suppose this must be so."

The door opens behind them and in walks Mr. Hernandez with his crew, Angel and Tomás. Angel is a mountain of a man at six feet four inches and ripped with muscle; he possesses thoughtful brown eyes, a courteous demeanor, and looks to be about the same age as Seth and Juan-Carlos. He doesn't speak a word of English, but the languid movement of his dark eyes takes in everything. Tomás is of average height and build, approximately five feet nine inches tall, with a round face, astute chocolate eyes, a dark complexion, and appears to be in his mid thirties. Tomás speaks reasonably good English and serves as the interpreter for his friend and working companion, Angel. Humberto notices that Juan-Carlos is on the wrong side of the line.

"Juan-Carlos!" Humberto snaps. Juan-Carlos looks down, sees he's an inch inside Mr. Hernandez's territory, and nimbly hops back across, his feathers unruffled. Humberto quickly glances at Seth's nails and mouth. He says in a business-like fashion, "Good. You're on time young man. I see you've met Juan-Carlos. Meet the rest of the crew, Angel Muñoz and Tomás Piña."

In Spanish, Humberto introduces Seth to Angel and Tomás. Seth shakes their hands, and both men say, "Mucho gusto," and nod respectfully to him.

"We've got to get going to the work site," Humberto orders.

"Should I take my car, Mr. Hernandez?" Seth asks.

"Your car?" Humberto says, surprised. "You're not going any—where." Humberto walks over and retrieves a broom that is hidden behind the far metal cabinet, walks back with it, and hands the broom to Seth. "Everyone starts at the bottom, fancy degree or not," Humberto says flatly.

Tomás and Angel look at each other, shift, and remain silent.

Seth takes the broom and says light-heartedly, "I'm glad to start anywhere, Mr. Hernandez."

Humberto is pleased with Seth's willingness and softens his voice. "Juan-Carlos can show you what to do. Juan-Carlos, call Casey and tell him to make that delivery to the work site."

"Yes boss," he dutifully answers.

Humberto and his crew leave the office for the work site. Juan-Carlos goes to his desk and nods to Seth cordially. Seth gestures in a quick circular motion with his broom. "Guess I'll get to work," he says genially.

Juan-Carlos smiles, sits down at his desk, and picks up the office phone. He calls Casey to deliver the load of wood per Mr. Hernandez's orders.

○ ○ ○

The day has progressed quietly, and Seth has thoroughly cleaned and swept most of the office. He is finishing up. The clock on the wall now reads five in the afternoon. Juan-Carlos sits at his desk doing paperwork. Seth sweeps around Humberto's desk and notices the two framed photographs on it. One is of Elena in her high school junior prom dress and the other is of his son, Javier, as a child, standing in a field of bluebonnets dressed in white shorts and a white shirt, with a sweet, innocent look on his face. He picks up

Elena's photo, smiles, and places it back. Next, he picks up Javier's picture and studies it. Holding it, he turns to Juan-Carlos.

"I recognize Elena," he says. "She's so lovely in her prom dress. But who is this?"

Juan-Carlos responds softly, "That is Javier, Elena's brother, Mr. and Mrs. Hernandez's only son."

Seth is surprised. "I didn't know Elena had a brother. She's never mentioned him."

"It is very sad," Juan-Carlos says, shaking his head slowly. "Javier was a marine. He was killed three years ago. A good boy. A very good boy. We all miss him very much."

Shocked and saddened, Seth replies, "I didn't know. I'm so sorry."

"Mr. Hernandez never speaks of it. His heart is still broken. Miss Elena loved her brother more than anything. It is very painful for her. I loved him too. Everyone who knew Javier loved him."

Seth gazes at Javier's photo and notices how much he and Elena resemble one another. He carefully places the picture back in the exact spot on Humberto's desk. He looks at Juan-Carlos and asks, "Juan-Carlos, how did you first come to work for Mr. Hernandez?"

Juan-Carlos folds his hands on his desk and says quietly, "Mr. Hernandez and my father were best friends at the university in Mexico. They studied architecture together. Many years later my father died, and then my mother died a few months after that. I have no brothers or sisters. Mr. Hernandez made arrangements for me to come to this country and work for him. He made my hours so I could go to school to become an American citizen. It's been two years now that I am a citizen. Mr. Hernandez did all of this for me. Señor and Señora Hernandez and Miss Elena are my family now. Javier was the brother I always wished I had. It has been very hard. It has been very sad."

Seth is deeply touched by Juan-Carlos's sensitivity and love for the Hernandez family. "Mr. Hernandez is very lucky to have you."

"No," Juan-Carlos says thoughtfully, "I am the lucky one."

"I'm glad to be working with you, Juan-Carlos," Seth says. He takes the broom and continues his last bit of sweeping.

Juan-Carlos sees the time on the clock, organizes a few papers on his desk, and gets up. "Time to go," he says, now more upbeat. "I must get to class. You've enjoyed your first day?"

"Sure have," Seth answers. "You're working on your degree?"

Juan-Carlos responds proudly, "No. I teach English as a second language at the community center three nights a week. You will be here late?"

"Until six, I have a few more things to do. I'm seeing Elena after that."

Juan-Carlos happily approves, "Oh, you and Miss Elena. That is very good." Making his way to the front door and being careful not to smudge the chalk line, Juan-Carlos pauses, looks back at Seth, and says, "You must understand about Mr. Hernandez. Before he lost Javier, he was always happy. Many times he is gruff now . . . but still, he is a good man, a decent and honorable man. He grieves, that is all." Then turning and leaving, Juan-Carlos closes the front door behind him, barely making a sound.

Seth is left alone in the office. He sweeps a bit more and stops, finished with his work. He places the broom back behind the end metal cabinet from where it came. When he does so, he notices that there is something behind the cabinet, between it and the wall. He reaches behind the cabinet and pulls it out. It is a long scroll. Seth knows immediately what it is; it's a blueprint of some kind. He takes the scroll to the drafting table and unrolls it, discovering it is a remodeling plan. Using paper weights to hold each corner down, Seth begins studying the plan carefully, noting certain aspects of particular interest. The blueprint really intrigues Seth, and he becomes immersed in it. As he scrutinizes the drawing, Humberto comes in the front door.

Seth looks up from the table. "Hello, Mr. Hernandez."

Mr. Hernandez instantly recognizes what Seth is looking at and says sharply, "What are you doing there?"

"I found this when I was cleaning up," Seth explains. "They're design plans for a church sanctuary. Elena told me about this, Mr. Hernandez. This is your design, isn't it?"

Humberto walks over to the table and stands next to Seth, looking down at the design plan. "Yes, it's mine," he says gruffly. "What's wrong with it?"

"What's wrong?" Seth answers, awestruck. "Mr. Hernandez, this is fantastic. It's so original. It's inspired!"

Humberto is surprised and responds cautiously, "You really think so?"

"Yes, Mr. Hernandez," Seth says sincerely. "Where did you learn this?" he asks admiringly.

"Over the years . . . on the job," Humberto replies. He pulls at his chin and studies the blueprint. He is remembering little details about the design.

"Mr. Hernandez," Seth says eagerly, "if you don't mind my asking, how did you figure out the angles and load factors?"

Warming up to Seth's genuine sincerity and professional admiration, Humberto leans over the plans and begins pointing things out to the young man. "It wasn't too difficult. I was working with a limited space, that's true, but there was a good opportunity to redesign it in such a way to accommodate many more people." Humberto pulls a stubby pencil from his shirt pocket, and using it as a pointer, continues, "You see, by taking out this wall here and reshaping this other one, and then angling the pews and pulpit like this, I could increase the floor space without compromising the existing load balance. That saved the church a lot of money and me and my crew a lot of time. Up here, we put in a new and larger stained glass window for the additional lighting I wanted. And over here, two more, smaller stained glass windows that give the entire space a warm, balanced, and comfortable feel. At Mass, the glow from the morning sun through these windows creates a peaceful ambiance and accentuates the new, inlaid wooden floor very nicely."

Paying careful attention, Seth is astonished. "I wouldn't have thought it could be done this way. But now that I see it, I see it is the only way to do it. This is amazing. Mr. Hernandez, I'm working on a design right now. Kind of a freelance project I'm doing at night. When you have time, could I show it to you? Get your advice?"

"I'll look at it sometime." Humberto glances at the clock on the wall. "You're working late, Seth. It's okay for you to go home at five."

"I wanted to finish up a few more things before I left. I'm seeing Elena tonight."

Looking around the office at Seth's work, Humberto is clearly pleased by what he sees. "You've done enough for one day, young man. You and Elena have a good time tonight."

"Thank you, Mr. Hernandez. I'll see you tomorrow."

"Plan on coming with me and the crew to the work site in the morning."

"Yes sir! Thank you."

Seth turns and leaves. He is careful not to tread on the chalk line that Juan-Carlos had so painstakingly drawn that morning.

Humberto watches Seth leave. He has come to the conclusion the young man is very likeable, maybe has more promise than he originally thought. After Seth is gone, Humberto sighs, looks down at the blueprints, and continues studying them for another half hour.

CHAPTER TWENTY-FIVE

Later in the evening of Seth's first day at work, he and Elena sit in the chair swing on the front porch of his home. They are back from their date.

"Thank you for tonight," Elena says softly.

"I had a wonderful time with you. I always do," Seth tells her.

"Me too," she says, looking at him tenderly.

Tentatively, Seth says, "Elena, may I ask you something? Something I know is very personal."

"Of course, honey. You can always ask me anything."

Seth begins quietly, almost reverently. "At your father's office today, there were two photographs on top of his desk. One was of you in your prom dress, and the other was of a boy in a field of flowers." Then, delicately, he continues, "Juan-Carlos told me that boy was your brother, Javier. Elena, why didn't you tell me about him?"

"I was going to," Elena whispers, her eyes beginning to brim with tears.

"Juan-Carlos told me what happened," Seth says with deep compassion. "Elena, I'm very, very sorry."

Thinking about the brother she loved so much, Elena says

calmly, "Javier was wonderful. He was loving, sweet, and very kind, so much like Mama. He was the best brother a sister could ever want."

Seth takes her hand in his tenderly. "I can't tell you how sorry I am it happened."

She smiles weakly at him as a huge tear trickles down her left cheek. "The two of you would have been great friends. Javier is gone now, but I will always love him."

"I wish I had known him," Seth says gently. He pauses, thinking.

Elena can see he wants to ask more but is concerned for her feelings. She presses his hand lovingly, "Remember Seth, I said you can always ask me anything," and she looks in his eyes, letting him know it's all right.

Seth shakes his head slowly and asks, "Elena, this terrible loss? May I ask how you handle it as well as you do?"

"Of course you may," she says contemplatively. "The night before he left to go overseas, Javier came into my room. We sat and talked for a long time. He said if anything happened to him that I should mourn him for just a little while, and then he wanted me to embrace life and live it fully and happily. I was crying. Javier put his arm around my shoulders and hugged me closely to him. Through my tears, he made me promise him I would do this. There isn't a day that goes by that I don't think about my brother or miss him terribly. But I'm determined to keep the promise I made to him. I know it's the best way I can honor Javier's life. It's what he wanted me to do. It's the final gift and the greatest gift my brother ever gave me." Tears are now flowing down Elena's cheeks, and she gently dries them with a small handkerchief from her purse.

Incredibly moved by Elena's story, Seth quietly says, "I would like to tell you something Elena . . . something I've never told anyone. I want to tell you what happened on the day I was shot."

Elena turns fully towards him, taking his hand and holding it tenderly between both of hers. With her eyes she tells him to take all the time he needs, that she will wait patiently for him to begin whenever he is ready. Her entire being invites him to open himself up to her.

Seth's brow furrows, and he drifts off to another time and place as he begins recounting that terrible day. His voice sounds hollow. "We were on patrol. The three of us in a Humvee. A roadside bomb exploded and blew us over on our side. Enemy gunfire erupted. The soldiers in the Humvee behind us started firing back. My buddies, Jake and Marvin, were hurt. Not me. I popped open the passenger door, got Jake out, and carried him to the other Humvee. I went back for Marvin. He was the driver. But I should have been driving that day. It was my turn to drive. Marvin had hopped in ahead of me that morning, took the wheel, grinned, and said, 'Don't worry about it.' Marvin was hurt badly. The cabin was filling with smoke, and he was covered in blood. I grabbed his vest and pulled but couldn't budge him. Marvin was caught on something. I couldn't see what it was because of the smoke. I pulled harder but couldn't free him. Again and again I tried, but couldn't move him. Our faces were inches apart. The smoke was getting thicker. Marvin didn't panic; he didn't say anything. He just looked at me. Bullets were bouncing off the Humvee. That's when a bullet shattered my left wrist. I fell backwards to the ground and rolled away. Just before I blacked out, I heard the Humvee explode. The next thing I knew, I woke up in a small depression in the ground, and my left hand was missing. The battle was still going on all around me, and I lay there for hours until the medics were able to reach me."

Elena is astonished by Seth's story. She squeezes his hand in hers and says devotedly, "Oh, Seth. You did everything you could to save your friend. You must know that."

The sound of Elena's comforting words bring Seth back to the present. "All I know is that I didn't save him. Maybe, just maybe, Elena, if I'd been a little faster, tried harder, had a few more seconds . . ."

"Babe, no. You did all you could."

"Elena, Marvin gave everything for his country. And me? I never discharged my rifle. Not once, not the entire time I was over there. Don't you see? I was given a medal for never firing a shot, in a war where I made no difference, and for a life I didn't save. I feel like such a fraud."

Completely composed, Elena says with quiet assurance, "No Seth, don't say that. It's not true. You made a big difference because you served. You received the medal for your bravery. For saving Jake and doing your best to save Marvin. You gave no thought to your own life."

Seth slowly shakes his head. "We were all soldiers together, Elena. Why Marvin and not me? I was supposed to be driving that day. I've been struggling to make sense of it."

"No one can ever know the answer to a question like that," Elena softly tells him. "It's beyond what any of us can understand, Seth. Only God knows the answer."

Seth nods, pauses, and then continues, "There's something more I don't understand. He knew I couldn't save him, but Marvin was so peaceful. I'll never forget the look in his eyes, Elena, never."

"What did you see, Seth?" she asks compassionately.

"Forgiveness. I saw forgiveness, Elena. An unfathomable, complete forgiveness." His voice cracks with the memory. "How could Marvin forgive me at the very moment he knew I couldn't save him? How could he forgive me for not driving that day?"

Wanting desperately to help him understand, Elena gently presses his hand and says lovingly, "Seth, when you were looking into Marvin's eyes I believe you were seeing his, but he wasn't seeing yours. Your friend was gazing upon the face of God. And what he was seeing put him completely at peace. The forgiveness you saw was divine forgiveness. What you saw was the reflection of God's grace in Marvin's eyes, Seth. Marvin is home now. He's where he is supposed to be, like my brother is home and where he is supposed to be. They are both at peace now."

Elena's tone caresses his vulnerability and her words nurture Seth's inner self. He pauses, thinking about what she has said. He looks at Elena, still with suffering in his eyes. "I just want to know it all meant something—that it counted for something truly important. That the losses mattered."

Elena answers him calmly with steady strength in her voice, "Don't ever doubt that the losses mattered, Seth. Our homes are safer; our families are safer; our country is safer because of every soldier like Marvin, like Javier, and like you. It's the many who are saved that make our spirits soar. It's the one who's lost that breaks our hearts. Your heart is broken for your friend."

"You're right, Elena, it is. I can't seem to get past it," he says.

Looking deeply into the eyes of the man she loves, Elena tenderly implores him, "Oh Seth, let go of it. Please let go of it. Say goodbye to your friend. Forgive yourself, as you are forgiven. Let God take this burden from your shoulders so your heart will heal."

He nods his head, still struggling with it. "Elena, I've been trying to come to terms with everything."

Elena's heart breaks for him. "Let's try together. Life is a wonderful gift, Seth. We've found each other. There never have to be any goodbyes between us."

CHAPTER TWENTY-SIX

It is now one month later. Seth's job working for Mr. Hernandez is coming to an end. It is early evening and Humberto has called a meeting at his home. Everyone is gathered in the kitchen: Humberto, Yesenia, Angel, Tomás, Juan-Carlos, Elena, and Seth. Humberto, Yesenia, and Elena are sitting at the kitchen table. The others are standing. Seth stands on the end next to Juan-Carlos, who is between him and Angel. Tomás stands on the other side of Angel and quietly interprets for him. The gathering has a somber tone. Juan-Carlos dabs at his eyes with a tissue.

"You know the project is coming to an end this week," Humberto says. "I haven't been able to find any more work. The truth is, I don't know when I will."

The Mexican men look down and shift uneasily in their places. Seth and Elena look at each other seriously.

Humberto continues, "What I'm saying is this: I'll have to lay everyone off at the end of this week. It's gotten that bad."

Yesenia, sitting next to Humberto, places her hand on his forearm, supportively. Humberto looks at his wife appreciatively and gently pats her hand.

Humberto scans the men's faces. "This isn't easy for me to say, men. I'd like to keep us together, but if I can't afford to pay you any longer . . . well, I know you all have families to support. Tomás and Angel, the money you send home to Mexico for your wives and children is all that stands between them and hunger. There isn't any choice."

Tomás says respectfully, "Señor Hernandez. Angel and me, we have talked; we will work for the pay you can do."

Humberto nods, "Tomás, I appreciate it. I appreciate both of you. But I can't afford to pay anything."

"Still, Señor Hernandez, we wish to stay with you. Maybe something good will come."

Touched by their loyalty, Humberto says sympathetically, "I can't let you do that. You're both fine craftsmen. I'll start calling around tomorrow, see if I can find work for everyone at different places. My friend Casey says he'll help me."

Juan-Carlos weeps quietly at the news. Angel places a massive arm around his shoulders to comfort him.

Humberto sighs deeply and concludes the meeting. "That's all there is to say, men. You're a fine crew. I'll see you at the work site in the morning. We still have a few more days together."

Angel, Tomás, and Juan-Carlos depart somberly, going out the back door and closing it quietly behind them. Seth remains standing. He has folded his arms across his chest. He glances anxiously at Elena. She nods back, reassuring him. Yesenia observed this exchange between them and senses something is about to happen.

"Mr. Hernandez? May I show you something?" Seth asks tentatively.

"Yes, of course," says Humberto. "What is it?"

"You remember that freelance project I'm working on at night? I asked you if you would give me some advice."

Emotionally drained, Humberto answers tiredly, "Yes, I remember, but now's probably not the best time."

"Papa," Elena says, "please give Seth a chance to show you. I have it right here." Elena produces a tightly rolled-up scroll tied neatly with a blue satin ribbon.

Humberto and Yesenia look at each other questioningly. Seth goes and sits at the table next to Elena.

"I suppose it won't do any harm," Humberto says. "Let's see what you have."

Elena smiles at Seth as she hands him the scroll. Seth unrolls it on top of the kitchen table. He and Elena are enthusiastic, and they use coffee cups to anchor its corners.

Humberto and Yesenia are curious to see what they have laid out. They both lean forward, looking at it.

Mr. Hernandez studies it and says curiously, "It's a design." He looks at Seth. "It's a design for a home."

Seth nods eagerly. "That's right, Mr. Hernandez. It's a home. It's a new home for The Children's Sanctuary. I got the idea when I went to the campus to get Emily and Chloë the first time." He looks at Elena adoringly, she the same way at him. "That's the day Elena and I first met."

"Papa," Elena says energetically, "you remember. We have cottages for the children at the Sanctuary. But we never have enough homes for all the needy children."

Humberto looks at the plan and begins to take a greater interest in it, rubbing his chin thoughtfully as he carefully studies it. "Yes, I remember your telling me about these things," he says.

Seth glances at Elena, she smiles encouragingly, and nods for him to continue.

With optimism in his voice, Seth continues, "Mr. Hernandez, I'm sure you can help me. There's a limited amount of space to work with. I need at least four bedrooms and two bathrooms in the children's area, and then, another bathroom, bedroom, and small living area for the cottage parents. Plus a common living room, dining room, and kitchen. And there has to be enough natural lighting to give the home that real 'family feel' I want to create." Seth looks anxiously at Elena.

Watching them, Yesenia realizes this is an event the two of them have been planning.

"So, Mr. Hernandez," Seth concludes, "what do you think?"

Yesenia notices that Elena is holding her breath.

Humberto doesn't answer right away. Instead, he continues to study the plan. Elena begins to turn blue. Finally, taking a stubby pencil from his shirt pocket and without looking up from the plan, Humberto asks Seth, "Do you mind?"

At this, Elena blows out her breath, sucks in new oxygen, and stifles a sneeze. Her color begins to return. Humberto, being fascinated by Seth's design, hasn't noticed his daughter's drama.

"No, please do," Seth encourages him.

As Humberto begins to mark on the plan with his pencil, Elena and Seth look at each other and grin with relief. Elena wrinkles her nose at Seth.

Watching the young people, Yesenia knows they had planned this out very well.

Humberto talks to Seth as he studies the design and makes a few corrections. "Seth, this is a fine design. You've thought of many good things. Really, I'm very impressed. Let me make a few suggestions."

Seth leans over the plans as Humberto continues, "You see? If you move this support column over here, and take out this wall, that frees up more open space for the living room. Instead of two small windows on the east and west, combine them into one larger window for greater light. Here, add an overhead skylight. This will give you that 'family feel' you're wanting. Move this wall at more of an angle, like this. Now you have the same amount of space, but it flows seamlessly and feels more spacious."

Seth pays close attention and nods his head. He is enthusiastic over Humberto's suggestions. "What about the kitchen and dining room, Mr. Hernandez? I feel like I'm missing something there."

"Try using a large island so that it forms a natural separation between the two rooms." Then, drawing with his pencil, Humberto says, "You see, if you do it like this it will create more open space and usable light."

"Yes, yes! I see exactly what you mean," Seth says excitedly.

Mr. Hernandez eases back in his chair. "Glad I could help."

"Thank you, Mr. Hernandez. I really do appreciate it."

"Papa," Elena says, "there's something else Seth wants to ask you. Go ahead, babe."

Humberto looks at Seth expectantly. "There's something else?"

"Mr. Hernandez," Seth begins haltingly, "we'll be finishing the project we're on now in a few days. I was hoping—once we're done, I mean—I was hoping . . . well, the truth is, Elena and I were hoping . . . we were hoping Humberto Hernandez Design and Construction would build this new cottage for The Children's Sanctuary."

Mr. Hernandez looks at him kindly. "I wish we could, Seth. There's no money for the materials. And besides, I couldn't pay you or the crew. It's a wonderful idea, especially with this design. Very creative. But I'm afraid it's impossible."

Undaunted, Seth continues with gathering enthusiasm, "The foundation's already been poured, Mr. Hernandez. Everything we need to build the home is stored at the campus."

"Seth's right, Papa!" Elena eagerly joins the conversation every bit as excited as Seth. "Another builder started it but went out of business. All the building material was donated. Everything's in the barn."

"But the problem remains about paying the crew," Humberto explains patiently. "There's just no money."

"Mr. Hernandez, I have savings to pay the crew for at least a month," Seth says. "It'll only take us about two and a half months to build the new home, if the weather holds."

Humberto points out sympathetically, "What about the other month and a half? I appreciate your offer, Seth. It's very generous. But keep your savings, young man."

"The rest of the money can come from our savings," Yesenia says softly.

Humberto is not surprised by his wife's declaration. "It would take all of our savings, mi amor," he informs her affectionately. "We would have no money left. And if no work comes after that . . ."

Without hesitation, Yesenia says with quiet, faith-affirming strength, "If no work comes after that, I can go back to sewing until work comes, mi amor."

"We'd be broke, Yesenia," Humberto explains caringly.

Yesenia looks lovingly at her husband; he looks at her in the same way. They know each other so well after thirty-five years of marriage. "Needy children will have a home," she says considerately.

"We will have each other. And we won't be broke, mi amor. We just won't have any money. We started out that way and have always managed."

Humberto nods his head thoughtfully in agreement. "This is true, mi amor." He smiles at her, remembering all of the tough times they've been through together. "I've managed because I've always had you."

Yesenia responds warmly to him, "We've managed because we've always had each other, mi amor."

"Papa, everyone would be kept together," Elena encourages. "Seth says the home could be finished by early April. And in the spring, construction picks up. The chances for work will be better then, practically a sure thing."

Thinking about what his daughter just said, Humberto tilts his head to one side, observing her. He says deliberately, drawing out her name for effect, "E—le—na, how long have you two been planning this?"

Caught in the glare of her father's knowing gaze, Elena suddenly looks like she's five years old again. She sneezes, "*Achoo!*"

"Aha!" her father says. "I knew it!"

Elena grins, shrugs her shoulders, and confesses impishly, "A few weeks, that's all. Seth came to me with the idea. I encouraged him, and we've been working on it together every night since then."

"Was your mother in on this?" Humberto asks, casting a discerning look at Elena.

Seth quickly defends her. "Honestly, Mr. Hernandez, Mrs. Hernandez didn't know anything about it until now."

Humberto looks at his wife, saying lightly, "*Yesenia?*"

"This is the first I've heard," she says, rolling her eyes innocently and nodding at her daughter.

Mildly, Humberto prods his wife, "But if you had known, mi amor, you would have sided with them, no?"

"Of course, mi amor," Yesenia answers cheerfully.

Humberto taps the stubby pencil against his lower lip, thinking, and says, "I see . . . Yes, what should we do?"

Yesenia reaches for her husband's hand and presses it affectionately, "Whatever you want to do, mi amor. I know you'll make the right decision. And you know I'll be by your side no matter what comes."

Humberto looks down, studies the plan, and rubs the back of his neck. The others are watching him and waiting anxiously. Finally, Humberto looks up at Seth. "Young man, I don't accept charity."

"It's not charity," Seth quickly says. "It's an investment, Mr. Hernandez. I would learn so much from you that it would be worth twice what I paid for graduate school. Please, won't you think of it this way?"

"Well, that's a generous way to look at it, Seth," Humberto responds politely. "If I were to do it, you understand it'd be a loan? I'd pay you back." He rubs the back of his neck again. "Of course, this doesn't make any business sense. None at all. You all can see that, can't you?" He thinks through it, talking out loud to himself, "There are children who need a home, a crew that needs work, a wife who loves me broke or not, a daughter and her boyfriend who don't care if they have a dime." He pauses for a long moment and then sighs, "And what this all means is we'll start the children's home next week, and I must be the dumbest Mexican in the world."

Elena, Seth, and Yesenia are thrilled. Yesenia hugs Humberto's neck telling him, "Oh mi amor por siempre!" Seth and Elena are embracing too.

Humberto doesn't complain. He smiles at his daughter, "Niña, you encouraged Seth, and the two of you have been cooking this up for several weeks? What made you think I would do it?"

Elena's eyes are glowing as she says, "I know how sweet you are, Papa. And it's for needy children. I told Seth if we said it was for the children and you started showing interest in his design, we had you." Elena wrinkles her nose at Seth, and she smiles at her mother, who nods and beams back.

Humberto turns to Seth and says instructively, "Did you hear that, young man? Let that be a lesson to you: Elena and her mother? Those two have always been plotters."

Seth grins at Elena, who shrugs and wrinkles her nose at him again. They both laugh easily.

Humberto says, "Yesenia, please remind me to call Juan-Carlos.

I should tell him that we'll all be together for a few months longer. If I don't, he'll just cry himself to sleep tonight."

Elena whispers to Seth excitedly, "You're making progress, babe. Papa called you my boyfriend. That means he approves of you." To her parents she says sweetly, "Mama, Papa, Seth and I have to go. We have reservations for dinner tonight." She and Seth rise to leave.

"Mr. Hernandez," Seth says, pumping his hand eagerly, "I really do appreciate this opportunity."

"You're welcome, Seth. Your design's very good. Excellent, in fact. I'll see you in the morning."

Seth helps Elena with her coat. "Honey," she asks him, "did you order the ballet tickets for Emily's birthday?"

"Sure did."

"You made certain they're for the performance on her birthday?"

"Yes, babe, double checked. Her birthday all right, February twenty-eighth."

As they leave, Elena hugs her parents. Seth hugs Mrs. Hernandez and shakes Mr. Hernandez's hand again.

Once the young people are gone, Humberto turns to his wife and says, "I have to admit, Yesenia, I approve of that young man. The truth is, I like him very much—very, very much."

Yesenia wraps her arm around Humberto's waist and hugs him affectionately. Her eyes sparkle, and she sings gaily, "There's a wedding coming. A mother know-ohs . . ."

CHAPTER TWENTY-SEVEN

It is now the morning of February twenty-eighth, Emily's birthday. The clock on the wall shows the time is ten o'clock. Seth, Elena, Emily, and Chloë are in the kitchen at Seth's house. There is excitement in the air. The girls prepare to go out.

"Ladies, are we all ready?" Elena asks delightedly.

The children nod enthusiastically. Chloë has been ready and waiting for an hour. Much to Gracie Ann's disappointment, her mommy has told her she must stay home. Gracie Ann is sitting in a kitchen chair, pouting and looking quite unhappy.

Elena turns to Seth. "Babe, we'll be gone for three or four hours—picking up the girl's dresses for tonight, having lunch, shopping for shoes and handbags, and a few more last minute girl things. Be back around two."

"Have fun, honey. I'm headed to the cottage site for a few hours. See everyone later. Happy birthday, Emily."

Elena and the children leave to go shopping. Seth heads for the construction site.

o o o

It is three in the afternoon on Emily's birthday. Elena and the children have returned to Seth's home from their shopping. She and Emily sit before the vanity mirror in Kathryn's bedroom. Asleep on the bed with Gracie Ann under her arm, Chloë lightly snores.

Emily gazes affectionately at her little sister. "Chlo really needed a nap."

"Yes," Elena agrees. "She's already had a big day, and there's a bigger night coming. The nap will do her good."

Emily looks at herself in the mirror and concern clouds her eyes. Timidly she asks, "Miss Hernandez? I know I could never be pretty like you. But do you think . . . I mean . . . am I a little bit pretty?"

"Emily, sweetheart, you're beautiful," Elena says energetically. "You are an absolutely beautiful young lady."

Emily looks at Elena questioningly and asks in a whisper, "Does Seth think so?"

"Of course he does," Elena assures her.

Looking at herself in the mirror, Emily lightly traces the scar above her left eyebrow. "How can I be, with this?" she says, distressed.

"That's nothing to worry about," Elena says lightheartedly. "We'll make it disappear. No problem."

Emily instantly brightens. "You can do that?" she asks, happy and hopeful.

Elena untwists the lid of a small jar. "A little concealer will do the trick," she says. "I use it all the time. Every girl does, you know. We all depend on it to make those boys think we're perfect—which, of course, we are!" Elena laughs. Emily smiles and begins to relax. She has been anxious about tonight.

"Now," Elena says enthusiastically, "let me show you some real magic." Emily turns and faces Elena. Elena expertly applies the concealer to the scar area above Emily's eyebrow. In less than a minute Elena says, "Poof! All gone!"

Emily gazes into the mirror, amazed. She can hardly believe her eyes. "It's not there! It's really gone!" She turns to Elena, excited. "Thank you! Thank you, Miss Hernandez! I didn't think I could ever be pretty."

Holding both of Emily's hands tenderly in hers, Elena says confidently, "Emily, you're beautiful. Don't ever think you're not. Now, we have three hours to get you ready. And I have a little surprise for you. Just you wait until you see the jewelry my friends have let us borrow for the evening. By the time we're done, you'll be so beautiful, that handsome fellow down the hall that we call Mr. Seth McAllister will think you're a royal princess."

Breaking out into a broad smile, Emily is openly excited for the first time; for the first time in a very long, long time. Elena and Emily hug and giggle as they begin to get Emily ready for her birthday evening out.

o o o

The clock on the wall reads six p.m. on Emily's birthday. Seth stands in the kitchen dressed in a black tuxedo waiting for the ladies. He hears Elena's voice from the hallway.

"Announcing, Miss Chloë Fleming!"

Chloë enters the kitchen dramatically in a beautiful pink gown and pink patent Mary Jane shoes; she holds a small, sequined, pink satin clutch. There is light rouge on her little round cheeks and faint red on her lips. Elena has had Chloë's hair cut shorter in a frisky, sassy style to match her perky personality. Chloë's unruly curls are tamed and hang in harmony, framing her little face and making her appear, dare Seth think it, cherubic. She pauses theatrically, waiting to be admired, grins at Seth, and then comes and stands next to him on his left.

"Chloë, you look *so* pretty," Seth compliments.

"I know," she says sprightly. Then standing at attention, Chloë says, "Announcing, Miss Elena Hernandez!"

Elena enters the room. The moment Seth sees her, his heart stops. Elena is absolutely stunning in a simple, black, strapless evening gown. She wears a thin, herringbone gold necklace with matching earrings and a delicate gold bracelet on her left wrist. She carries a black evening clutch with a gold clasp. Her ebony hair is done in a lovely chignon. With her hair pulled back this way, Elena's classic looks are accentuated exquisitely. Seth thinks he's never seen anything so beautiful in his entire life. He can't stop looking at her.

She smiles graciously at him as she approaches and stands next to him on his left, where Chloë has made room for her.

"Elena, you're gorgeous!" Seth whispers excitedly.

"Hush," she says affectionately.

She and Chloë stand at attention and say in unison, "Announcing, Miss Emily Fleming!"

Emily enters the kitchen. If Seth was stunned by Elena's elegant appearance, he is completely astonished by Emily's transformation. "This isn't a little girl coming into the room," he thinks. "This is a lovely young lady." Emily's blonde hair is swept up on her head, emphasizing her Grecian facial structure. Her large, expressive emerald eyes are highlighted by the light eye shadow and liner that Elena has expertly applied. The scar has vanished. Seth hadn't realized how beautiful Emily's eyes were until this very moment. The rest of her makeup is perfectly done, and there is a soft rose tint on her lips. Emily's dress is a magnificent, dark green, full-length satin gown with long sleeves, and her shoes are black, satin, short pumps. She carries a stylish, matching black clutch with a gold clasp. Around her neck is an attractive gold necklace with a faux emerald drop, and dainty hoop earrings of gold hang delicately from her ears. Emily's left wrist is adorned with a gold cable bracelet.

As Emily crosses the room, poised and elegant, something new and important is happening to her. For she is not simply crossing the kitchen floor, she is stepping through one of life's many portals in a girl's ever-changing existence, this time leaving the last vestiges of her little girlhood behind and passing into the next phase of her life's promising journey. Emily is radiant. She has a new confidence about herself that hasn't been there before. This confidence is confirmed by the most important male figure in her life. She sees it in Seth's admiring eyes. Emily knows she is pretty.

"Wow! Wow! Wow!" are the first words from Seth's mouth. "Emily, you are *so* beautiful. Yesterday, when you were nine, you were a pretty girl. But today, today you're ten, and you're a beautiful young lady."

Glowing and smiling as she gazes up at him, Emily softly says, "Thank you."

Seth offers his right arm to her with a flourish. "Miss Fleming, may I escort you?" Emily beams and slips her arm through Seth's.

He offers his other arm to Elena. "Miss Hernandez, may I escort you?"

"Yes, please," and Elena slips her arm through his.

Elena holds her hand out to Chloë. "Miss Fleming? May I escort you?" Chloë smiles playfully and grabs her hand, eager to go.

Seth grins, stands at attention, and says, "Announcing! I have the three prettiest ladies in the world with me tonight. Let's go to the ballet and make everyone insanely jealous!"

○ ○ ○

It's eleven-thirty on the night of Emily's birthday. The back door leading into the kitchen opens. Seth enters the kitchen, carrying Chloë. She is sound asleep with her head on his shoulder. Chloë wears a golden tiara on her head and holds a little gold wand topped with a star. He is followed into the room by Emily and Elena who are whispering excitedly to each other about the ballet and the late dinner that followed. After they enter, Emily takes the sleeping Chloë from Seth.

"Thank you for tonight, Seth," Emily says demurely. "It's been my happiest birthday ever."

"You're welcome, birthday girl. You looked beautiful tonight, Emily. I was so proud to be with you."

Emily smiles modestly, thanks him, and turns to Elena. "Miss Hernandez, thank you for everything."

Elena hugs Emily. "You're welcome, sweetheart. Remember how I showed you to remove your makeup?"

"Yes, ma'am."

"Good. See you and Chlo tomorrow, okay?" Emily nods and Elena gives her a quick kiss on the cheek and whispers, "Never forget how beautiful you are."

Emily beams, "I won't, Miss Hernandez. Thank you again."

Emily, carrying the sleeping Chloë, turns and goes out of the kitchen and down the hall to their bedroom.

Elena watches them go. She is thankful for Emily's happiness.

Seth leans against the kitchen counter. Pleased with the evening, he says, "That was a big success, I'd say."

Elena smiles at him. "Yes, babe, it couldn't have been better. Thank you. Wasn't Emily beautiful tonight?"

"She was absolutely lovely. Honestly Elena, I couldn't believe the transformation. When she grows up she'll be a rare beauty, just like you."

"You're such a charmer, Mr. Seth McAllister. You must want something," she says playfully.

"I'm just calling it like I see it, babe. Would you come in the living room for a sec? I want to show you something new about the cottage."

"Sure," she replies. The two young people walk into the living room and sit together on the couch. Elena asks, "Honey, what did you want to show me?"

Immediately Seth drops to one knee and pulls out a ring. Gazing up at her, he says with all of his heart, "There could never be anyone else in the world for me but you. Not in the past. Not in the future. Only now, only you. If I had lived in a different time and place, I never would have known real love, true and everlasting love, because you wouldn't have been there for me. I love you, Elena. I will love you forever. Will you marry me and make me the happiest man in the world?"

Elena is so stunned she can't speak. For a dazed moment she stares at Seth as if she doesn't quite recognize who he is. Then she cries out, "Yes! Yes! Yes! *Yes!*" She throws her arms around his neck and hugs him so tightly she doesn't realize she's choking him. Still with one knee on the floor, Seth waits patiently, straining his neck to one side so he can breathe. She releases and smiles at him, happy tears pouring from her eyes.

Seth says softly, "Elena, please hold out your left hand."

She holds out her left hand, and he gently slips the engagement ring on her finger. As he does, Elena is so elated that she literally bounces on the couch.

Seth rises from his knee and sits next to his fiancée, holding her hand. Elena admires her ring. She gazes at Seth and kisses him tenderly. She holds her left hand out in front of her, admiring again the simple, lovely ring.

"I wish I could have gotten you something nicer," Seth says.

"Nicer?" Elena responds, surprised. "Darling, this is the most beautiful ring in the world. I'm never going to take it off. Never!" and she hugs him tightly.

"You're happy then?" he asks.

"I'm the happiest girl in this whole big wide world!"

"Remember, I'm just a guy who makes minimum wage."

Still admiring her ring, Elena says with carefree abandon, "Not for long, babe. Papa will have to fire you soon if there's no more work." She turns to him excitedly, "Oh Seth! Isn't life wonderful?"

Seth can't help but laugh. "All you'll have is me."

"You're all I'll ever want." She puts her arms around him again and hugs him, burying her face in his neck. When she releases him, Elena gazes adoringly at her ring once more, holding it out in front of her.

But in the midst of her joy, a look of distress suddenly registers on Elena's face. Her shoulders sag. She cheerlessly folds her hands in her lap, stares down at them, and bites her lower lip, childlike. "Oh, no . . . oh . . . oh, honey," she says plaintively.

Alarmed, Seth quickly asks, "Elena, what's wrong?"

Feeling contrite, Elena faces away from him, saying, "Oh Seth, I don't know how to tell you . . . tell you something . . . something that's really awful . . ."

Seth asks anxiously, "Elena, what? Is it your health? Darling, are you ill?"

She looks at the ring, slowly shakes her head, and meekly replies, "No, nothing like that," and she lightly taps her right palm nervously against her knee, protesting the self-imposed dilemma.

Anxious, Seth asks tenderly, "What is it, then? Please tell me, Elena. You can tell me anything. I'll understand. I promise I'll understand."

Looking truly pitiful, Elena responds miserably, "Good, because I want you to remember you said that." Turning to him, unsure of just how to proceed, she says, "I have something to tell you . . . but before I do, I want you to know I've always told you the truth—I just haven't been honest about it. I mean, mostly I have . . . but not every single, itty, bitty time." Elena sneezes. "Oh!" she reacts and reaches for a tissue from the box on the coffee table, pats her nose daintily, rolls her eyes, and stalls for time. She admires her ring once more and then deftly tucks it under her leg, sitting on it.

Seth is completely confounded by her strange behavior and looks at her perplexed. He doesn't have the least idea of what to expect next.

Elena takes a long, deep breath, gathers herself, and glumly confesses, "I can't cook."

Seth pauses; he looks at her, mystified, and asks, "What about all that food?"

Shrugging her shoulders, she answers woefully, "Mama . . . Mama made it all."

Still bewildered by her behavior, Seth ponders Elena's admission. He calmly repeats Elena's confession back to her, "You can't cook."

Thinking it's a question, Elena replies dismally, "No."

Trying his best to understand why Elena is so stressed out, Seth simply repeats, "You can't cook." He says it again for clarification and not as a question, so he's certain he hasn't missed something truly important at this moment.

"What does he think of me now?" Elena worries. She believes the poor boy, being wholly stunned by her revelation, can't comprehend it. "Which is why," she thinks with a tinge of irritation, *"he keeps repeating the same silly question!"* Elena slowly shakes her head back and forth saying pitifully in a quiet, guilt-ridden voice, "No, I can't. The truth is, I'm lucky to get water to boil without blowing up something." Sighing heavily, she pokes out her lower lip and lightly taps her palm against her knee.

Seth is quiet as he sorts things out. He begins to understand now, or at least he hopes so.

Elena feels like the seconds of silence from Seth last a million years. She waits anxiously, unconsciously holding her breath. She rolls her lovely, guilt-laden dark eyes up to meet Seth's baffled baby blues. She keeps her engagement ring tucked underneath her leg and rocks slightly back and forth in dreary anticipation.

Seth looks at her puzzled and wonders, "Why is Elena turning blue?" He shrugs, cracks a leisurely grin, and says, "Babe, that's why they have something called, 'takeout.'"

The worry instantly vanishes from Elena's face. All in one

motion she blows out her breath, gulps down oxygen, sneezes, and vaults into him, knocking Seth back and pinning him on the couch and kissing him all over his face, saying, "You wonderful, wonderful man!"

Seth laughs, "Are you always going to be like this?"

Her arms hang around his neck, and her body presses into him. "Pretty much," she happily admits.

"Why did you hide your engagement ring under your leg?" he teases her. "Did you think I was going to ask for it back?"

Grinning up at him she says, "Forget that mister, you're never getting this ring back."

The two lovers share another long kiss and sweet embrace before Elena says it's time for her to go. Seth helps her with her coat, opens the door, and walks his fiancée to her car. Elena turns to him in the romantic moonlight, and they kiss warmly by the car door.

"We're still going to the park tomorrow?" she asks.

"Sure. The girls are looking forward to it," he says.

"I can't wait. See you in the morning at ten-thirty. I love you, Seth."

"I love you too, Elena."

○ ○ ○

While Seth is proposing to Elena in the living room, Emily is busy getting her sister undressed, into her pink pajamas, and tucked into bed. Chloë never even woke up.

Emily carefully places Chloë's golden tiara and magic wand safely on the dresser. She is very tired. When Emily gets into bed next to her sister, she falls asleep immediately. All is still.

Emily dreams. In her dream, she appears on stage as a beautiful prima ballerina. Her hair is up in a tight, shimmering bun. She wears a glittering white tutu over a dazzling white costume and a sparkling, jeweled tiara on her head. As Princess Aurora, she dances a solo in *Sleeping Beauty*.

Once her solo performance ends, a handsome prince appears at the far end of the stage. He is tall, broad shouldered, handsome, and strong. The young man is striking with his shock of blond hair, mesmerizing blue eyes, and angular jaw—her hero. Swiftly, he is by her side with a firm arm around her narrow waist. As they dance a pas de deux, he lifts her effortlessly, high into the air. She floats above him unafraid, confident of his skill and certain of his love for her. He would never let her fall. She is free to soar. And soar she does! The music rises to a thrilling crescendo. Her prince holds her tightly in one last stunning spin. The music stops. Exhausted by the demanding routine, she and her partner pant. They gaze at each other like two lovers. She looks out at the adoring crowd. Emily curtsies. Then, hand in hand with her prince, she runs off stage to the thunderous applause of an audience thrilled by her electrifying performance.

CHAPTER TWENTY-EIGHT

It is the morning after Emily's big birthday night. Seth and Chloë sit together at the kitchen table. Chloë concentrates on the star-shaped origami piece that she has been learning how to make with the squares of pink paper Seth purchased for the child. Seth patiently encourages her. Standing by the counter, Emily puts apples into a picnic basket. Out in the backyard a Blue Jay squawks, complaining about being chased by Sam. This morning, Emily wears a white leotard with a short, gossamer ballerina skirt. Wearing play clothes for the park with her golden tiara fixed firmly on her head and with her trusty magic wand by her side, Chloë is ready to go. The clock on the wall reads ten-fifteen.

"Oh, I'll never do it," Chloë says, discouraged.

"Sure you will," Seth says. "You're almost there. See, just fold it here, and here, and there you are." He holds up a perfect pink star.

"It's too hard to remember," Chloë complains.

"Just keep trying, you'll do it," Seth encourages her. Then he asks, "Hey Chlo, where's Gracie Ann this morning? Is she going to the park with us?"

Employing her motherly tone, Chloë responds, "Yes, she can't wait to go. It's all the child's talked about this morning. She's outside on the steps, waiting for Miss Hernandez. Gracie Ann really likes her."

"I do too. She should be here soon," Seth says, showing his excitement.

Chloë eyes him, puckers her lips, and makes two quick smooching sounds saying, "Kissy! Kissy!"

Seth shrugs and grins at the child. He is amused and, he must admit, pleased to see that overnight Chloë's curls have rebelled against their coiffed constraints; the unruly ringlets have returned, shorter yes, but returned nevertheless in full riot, sassy and defiant.

While Emily fills the picnic basket, and while Seth and Chloë work on the star, and while Gracie Ann sits on the steps outside waiting for Miss Hernandez, a Joseph and Sons taxi pulls up to the curb of the home. Emond Slagg, sinister and troll-like, steps out of the cab. Even in the light of day he looks disheveled and menacing. Slagg wears the same drab coat and pants he wore when he visited his wicked brother at midnight on the day of Seth's homecoming. The grizzly man slams the cab door shut, looks around furtively, and takes a step forward on the sidewalk. The cabbie leans his head out of the window.

"Hey mister."

Slagg whirls around, glaring at him and rudely demanding, "What!"

"You gotta sign, mister. Company rules." The cabbie sticks a clipboard out of the window to the scruffy man. He grabs it, hastily scratches his name at the bottom, and then thrusts it back at the cabbie.

Slagg turns to walk away, but the cabbie calls again, "Wait a second, bud. I gotta give you a receipt. Company rules." The cabbie offers Slagg the receipt out of the window.

Snarling, Emond snatches it out of his hand.

"Thanks bud," the cabbie says and drives away.

Slagg turns around and studies the home like he's casing it. Contemplating something known only to him, he scratches his right cheek thoughtfully. Then he remembers the receipt in his hand and crushes it. Taking a few steps forward, he stops at the mailbox. Jerking open its hatch, he angrily throws in the wadded receipt, and pounds the hatch shut. With his head lolling side to side, hyena-like, he moves cautiously up the walk, limping slightly.

Slagg reaches the porch steps and begins climbing them, guardedly stopping on each step and casting his eyes about cautiously. He doesn't notice Gracie Ann sitting on the third stair. Slagg steps on her, which causes him to falter. Furious, he reaches down and grabs Gracie Ann, squeezing and shaking her violently. He stares at her with blood-red rage in his eyes and angrily throws the doll child to one side. She slams against the lower left panel of the front door and bounces off, landing face up with her right leg under her at an unnatural angle.

Hurt and frightened, Gracie Ann whimpers, "I don't understand. Why did he do this to me?"

The beastly man approaches the door with stealth, carefully places both hands quietly against it, presses his right ear to the wood, and listens intently for any sound. Momentarily, he steps back, smoothes his rumpled coat, and raps loudly on the front door with his heavy ring.

At the knocking sound Emily looks up quickly from the picnic basket. She and Seth glance at each other.

"That's Elena. She's here early," Seth says enthusiastically.

"I'll get it," Emily offers happily.

"Thank you, Em."

Emily moves lithely from the kitchen into the living room. As she traverses the living room, she deftly performs two quick pirouettes. Halfway through her second pirouette there are two more impatient knocks. Emily stops abruptly. She becomes concerned. There is something about this heavy knocking that alarms her. Instead of going directly to the door, Emily carefully approaches the front window, cautiously sweeps the curtain aside, and peers out.

Alerted by the rustling of the curtains, Slagg's instinct is to crouch down low. He pivots to one side just below the window sill. Quickly, he springs up in front of the window. He and Emily stare at each other with only the thin window pane separating them.

Emily gasps in terror with a scream caught in her throat and jumps back. Her hand whips up to her scar. Suddenly, she remembers how it got there. She remembers what this man did to her. The events of that horrible night come flooding back in a rampage. The child remembers everything. Emily collapses to the floor on her knees, petrified. Her mind is racing, "*Chloë. I must get to Chloë!*" is her first thought, and it jolts her to her senses. She leaps to her feet and looks around frantically. Emily runs into the kitchen. She grabs Chloë, ordering her, "Come on, Chloë. Come on now!"

"I haven't finished," Chloë complains.

Emily becomes firmer. "Chloë, we're playing hide-and-seek. You've got to come with me now!"

"I don't wanna play," Chloë whines, pulling back.

"What's wrong, Emily?" Seth asks, concerned by her panicked state.

Her eyes wild with fear, Emily screams, "It's him!" She forcefully lifts Chloë out of her chair, "You have to play!"

"You're so bossy!" Chloë wails.

Carrying Chloë in her arms, Emily flees out the back door.

There are two heavier, impatient knocks on the front door. Seth turns his attention from the children and looks in the direction of the sound. He bounds from his chair and strides to the front door. He opens it.

Emond Slagg stands there on the porch, his mouth agape.

Seeing Slagg makes every muscle in Seth's body go tense. He instantly recognizes him from the photo in Emily's file. Seth steps out quickly and firmly closes the door behind him. He towers over this little hyena-like man who has taken a step back at the daunting sight of Seth.

Emond parts his lips, conjures his counterfeit smile, and says solicitously, "Sorry to disturb you folks. I was beginnin' to think nobody was home." He offers his hand to Seth. "Slagg's the name, Emond Slagg. I've come to see my darlin' girls." He bows and bares his yellow teeth. "The Missus and me, sure been a missin' 'em."

Seth doesn't make any move to shake the ugly man's hand, nor does he say a word to him. He stares at Slagg, drilling into him with his fiery eyes.

Discomfited by Seth's stare, Slagg retreats a half step more and glances around nervously. He looks for the best avenue of escape.

Without saying a word, Seth motions to the man to take a seat at the small table on the porch. Seth's direction is unmistakably an order, not an invitation. Taking the chair closest to the stairs, Slagg sits down. Keeping his eyes on the man, Seth seats himself in the chair across from him. The two men are just a couple of feet apart now, directly facing each other. Slagg's elbows are on the table, and he clasps his fingers together and pulls them apart apprehensively. His heavy ring is prominently displayed. Seth's right hand is on the table; his left is resting on his knee hidden beneath it.

Slagg is the first to speak. He sounds like a carnival huckster confident of his conniving talents. "Don't rightly know if I caught your name, young feller."

In an emotionless, steady voice, Seth answers, "Seth McAllister."

Slagg relaxes, smiles, and extends his hand again. "Well now, pleased to meet ya, young Seth," he says sociably.

Seth doesn't move a muscle. He continues to stare at Slagg; heavy storm clouds gather in Seth's eyes.

Slagg's swagger waffles. His eyes become restless, he slowly withdraws his outstretched hand, cocks his head to one side, and slug-like drags his tongue across his cracked lips, laying down a glistening trail of slime.

"Well now," Slagg continues affably, "maybe there ain't no need fer introductions after all. Ya already know'd who I was. But I'm a changed man now. Yes sir! A changed man. Reformed and truly penitent!"

Seth leans forward, closing the distance between them by a few more inches. He doesn't say a word. He continues to stare directly into the man's lifeless eyes.

Slagg pulls at his chin, scratches his throat, tilts his head, and attempts a slicker tactic. "What I done was wrong—real wrong," he says, falsely contrite. "But you got to know I stopped the drinkin', and my probation done ended yesterdee. That's why I come right off. Hurried I did. Come in a taxi. Yes sir. Spent my last dollar. Couldn't hardly wait to see them darlin' girls." His eyes search furtively past Seth's shoulder, "They around?" His voice is gravelly.

Seth leans forward again, closing the distance between them by another few inches. In an ominously calm voice, like the eerie blue stillness a split second before lightning strikes, he says, "That's an unusual ring."

Hearing this, Slagg relaxes in the mistaken belief that his deception is working. He holds up the grotesque ring, admiring it and proudly showing it off to Seth. "You like it?" he smiles, baring his tobacco-stained teeth. "I won this ring from a Haitian feller in a poker pot. He said it was cursed. Was glad to be rid of it. Them crazy Haitians believe in voodoo magic, ya know." He pauses, looks at Seth for any effect, and continues rapidly, "It's brung me nothin' but luck!" Pointing to the ring's crest, he brags, "This here growlin' gargoyle? Looks like the devil, don't he? You see them snarling lips? They's razor sharp. I been in many a bar fight where wern't nothin' tween me and perdition 'cept this ring. Then *whack!* I'd bring it a crashin' down on some poor soul's skull. There'd be a loud crack, and he'd collapse in a heap." Relishing the story, he swings the ring with a sweeping backhand flourish through the air. "Or raked across a sailor's cheek? Why man, I'ma tellin' ya, this little feller's sneer will slice him open to the bone quicker than a parin' knife." Boasting fiendishly, Slagg taps the heavy ring's crest on the metal table and laughs, "I guess it's a curse all right—to other people! Yes sir," he gloats, "it comes in real handy to have a hunk of brass on your hand."

The beast sitting across from Seth is so engrossed in telling the story about his monstrous ring that he hasn't noticed that Seth is looking at him now as if he is about to destroy him. When Slagg finally focuses on Seth, he is visibly startled by the lion-like man across from him who is now, he realizes, frighteningly close. Cold sweat breaks out in a ridge across Slagg's forehead. He swallows nervously and squirms in his seat. He stares back at Seth in fear, no longer looking menacing but suddenly looking less like a beast and more like a frightened little sewer rat that realizes its life is in peril.

"Emily has never been in a bar." Seth's voice is apocalyptic.

Stalling for time, Slagg swings his head to one side and points to his left ear. "Little hard of hearin'. Wha'd ya say?"

"Emily has never been in a bar," Seth repeats, and his tone is so foreboding that it completely unnerves Slagg.

"Why, no . . . no . . . I ain't never said she was," Slagg replies feebly, barely audible.

"Then why did you hit her?"

"I . . . I didn't . . . she fell."

"I don't believe you. The scar?" Seth challenges.

A tempest of anger storms up in Slagg and makes him forget his fear and his façade. Showing his true colors, he says angrily, "You mean that little mark above her eye? That ain't nothin'!"

Seth brings his left hand up and slams it down hard on the metal table with a terrible boom. "Steel. Steel is stronger." Seth's voice is like cracking thunder.

Instantly quieted, Slagg is truly horrified now, so terrified he is on the verge of complete panic. "Wha . . . What?" he squeaks, and he cowers before Seth.

"Steel is stronger than brass, I said." Seth's tone is now that of Judgment Day. He leans closer so their faces are only a few inches apart, truly looking like a lion that is about to pounce and rip Slagg to pieces.

The little man can no longer stand the tension. He bolts and rushes towards the stairs and, ape-like, grabs a wooden support column for leverage to swing down the steps to escape.

But Seth is much quicker. He thrusts the steel hooks into the column beside Slagg's face, cutting off his retreat. Darkly ominous in tone and intention, Seth says, "Thought you would leave?"

Slagg is completely terrified. Bulging and full of fear, his eyes roll nervously towards the steel hooks. He sweats profusely. The man is too frightened to move.

Reaching up with his right hand, Seth grabs Slagg by the throat, pinning him hard against the wooden column. Then he raises his hooks and rests them on the right cheekbone of Slagg's petrified face. Slagg issues another pathetic squeak.

"In Special Forces," Seth says in a low, terrible voice, "I was trained to kill a man quickly." He taps Slagg's cheek with his steel hooks, "Or, very slowly."

Slagg's eyes widen in fear, and he licks his dry lips.

Seth looks at Slagg as if he is a destructive, insignificant insect that should be exterminated for the betterment of the world. "With a little more pressure I could crush your cheekbone," he tells him. "With the flick of my wrist I could scoop out your eye . . . and then the other." Seth drops the hooks to the man's stomach. "With a quick thrust I could rip out your liver." He brings the hooks to Slagg's chest and taps menacingly. "And your heart, Slagg? If you have a heart. Before you could flinch, I could drive this steel through your sternum and split it in two." He leans his face closer to Slagg's. "Or, now that I've got you by the throat, why not crush your windpipe? See your face slowly turn purple and then black. Watch you wheezing and writhing on the ground as you desperately gasp for air . . . sweet air that will never come."

Slagg has gone completely limp but manages to whimper, "Please, please don't hurt me."

"Your ring hand is free Slagg," Seth reminds him, his voice rumbling. "Go ahead. Raise it up and use it against me. It's what I want you to do."

Frozen with fear, Slagg cannot move nor does he dare.

Seth rebukes him contemptuously, "I see. It's just for drunken sailors and little girls."

At this moment, Seth really seems as if he is going to kill Slagg. He could easily do it with just a quick snap, and he wants to finish the man with every fiber of his being. As he is on the brink of succumbing to this murderous impulse, Seth stops. He gathers himself and blinks his eyes as if clearing his head. He becomes conscious again of his whereabouts. Still holding Slagg by the throat, Seth realizes that the very evil he abhors is a power that craves to seduce and contaminate him. In disgust, Seth flings the vile man off the porch.

Slagg hits the ground with a thud and is stunned. He quickly recovers and stands up, wobbly.

Seth issues an ominous warning, "If you ever try to see the girls again, Slagg—in any place, at any time—not even your father in Hell will be able to hide you from me. I'll seek you out, and I will find you. If we ever meet again, I'll finish you. I promise!"

Slagg retreats a few feet to where he feels a safe distance away. He spins around and has a demonic, twisted look on his blotchy face; his eyes pop with rage. Shaking his fist threateningly, Slagg screams, "You can't treat me like this! Ain't nothin' you can do! Ain't nothin' nobody can do! I got the law! You'll see! I got the law!"

Seth takes a step forward, as if he is coming down the steps after him. Slagg whirls and rushes down the walk. As he passes the mailbox, in hot fury, he hits the top of it with his heavy ring. The force of it sounds like a mini explosion. He beats a hasty retreat down the street and out of sight.

Seth returns to the small table and sits down, breathing hard, realizing he could have done something terrible. He sees Elena coming up the walk and stands. Waiting for her, he works hard to recover his composure.

As Elena approaches, she looks over her shoulder in the direction of Slagg and glimpses his back as he retreats in the distance. She climbs the stairs to Seth's side. "Who was that horrible man?" she asks, concerned. Before Seth can answer, alarmed by his obvious distress, Elena says, "Babe, what's wrong? Where are the children?"

"That was Emond Slagg," Seth says.

Looking in Slagg's direction, she says, "You mean that was him. The man who hurt Emily?"

"Yes, that's right. Slagg came here today looking for the children. He's off probation."

Elena has never seen Seth like this before. She says anxiously, "Babe, you look like you wanted to kill him."

Sounding bewildered, Seth answers, "Elena, I had my hand around the man's throat, and I honestly think I was about to kill him. I could have snapped his neck like a twig. But then a calm voice spoke to me and said, 'Don't.' Just that single word, 'Don't.' But its serene, authoritative command was enough to bring me to my senses."

"I'm glad it did, honey. The man's not worth it." Fearful, Elena asks again, "Where are the children?"

"I'm sure they're hiding in the playhouse," Seth says. "Elena, Emily was terrified. She remembers everything now."

Elena entreats him, "Go to her, Seth. Go now. I'll wait for you in the kitchen."

Seth and Elena start to enter the house. As they go in the door, Seth stops, reaches down, and rescues Gracie Ann. He tenderly brushes her off, gently straightens her bent leg, and cuddles her in the crook of his arm.

Gracie Ann is glad someone cares about her. Most of all, she needs and wants her mommy.

Once in the kitchen, Seth leaves Gracie Ann with Elena, and he quickly goes through the back door and into the yard.

CHAPTER TWENTY-NINE

Seth strides across the backyard to the playhouse. He approaches the adult door of the playhouse and stands in front of it. He doesn't knock. Instead, he calls out reassuringly, "It's Seth. May I come in?"

In a weak voice, Emily responds, "Yes."

Seth opens the door gently and walks in. The girls are sitting on the small couch. Emily and Chloë are looking at pictures in a children's book.

"I told you this wasn't a good hiding place," Chloë says petulantly. "Seth found us right away. You're so bossy!"

"Miss Hernandez and Gracie Ann are waiting for you in the kitchen Chlo," Seth says calmly. "She has milk and cookies."

"Goody!" Chloë says happily. She jumps off the couch and hurriedly leaves through the children's door.

Once Chloë is gone, Emily begins shaking with fear.

"He's gone Emily," Seth says gently.

Emily gazes at Seth but says nothing. She bites her lower lip, and her hands are clasped together tightly in her lap. Seth approaches the small couch to comfort her. But as he does, Emily rises and moves away from him. Sensing that it's the right thing, Seth decides to take her place on the edge of the little couch and observe her.

Emily has moved a short distance away and stands by the large window. The light of the mid-morning sun streams through the clear panes, and the shafts of sunlight softly illuminate Emily, bathing her in a subtle, rich hue. In this light, dressed in her white leotard and white, gossamer ballet skirt, she appears angel-like—angel-like and also delicate, fragile, vulnerable, and utterly alone in the world.

"Emily, he's gone," Seth repeats softly. "He'll never hurt you again."

Her shoulders shudder. Trembling by the window, Emily turns towards Seth and whispers something frightening, "It wasn't me that night . . . it was Chloë . . . he was going to hurt Chloë."

Seth is shocked by her words. He is riveted by what he has just heard. For the first time, he fully grasps how unbelievably brave this girl is. He knows now that Emily shielded Chloë that terrible night and absorbed a blow that could have killed her. While bleeding profusely, she placed herself in harm's way between her sister and a monstrous attacker. Then, with unimaginable courage and heroic determination, she successfully fought off the drunken brute, saving Chloë. Seth believes Emily is as brave as any soldier he has ever met. He realizes she is the most extraordinary young girl he will ever know.

In complete awe of her uncommon strength of character and courage, he speaks quietly and reassuringly to Emily, "Neither of you will ever see him again. Not ever. I promise you, Emily."

Without saying a word, Emily stares at Seth as if in a trance. She turns away from him. Emily carefully brings her hand up to her left eyebrow and with her fingertips lightly traces the scar, feeling its length. She rests her fingers on it as she remembers the horror of that night and shudders again.

Removing her fingertips from the scar, her hand sinks limply to her side. Emily whispers out loud in a tone of stunned disbelief, as if trying to grasp the awful thing that happened, "He hit me . . . suddenly, he hit me . . ." She pauses and looks about the playhouse as if lost. The heartache in her voice is numbing when she cries out, "I miss my mommy and daddy!" Weeping now, she drops her chin and pleads forlornly, "I want them back . . . I want them back . . . Mommy, I'm so afraid. What's going to happen to us?"

Watching her from the couch, Seth realizes this remarkable child is mourning the loss of her parents, her shattered world, and everything she once knew, everything she doesn't understand and can't comprehend. But he also sees she is not weeping uncontrollably. Emily does not crumble under the weight of her tragic loss. There is an inner strength in her that even she does not fully understand. With tears staining her face and her arms hanging loosely by her sides, Emily lifts her head, and, as if appealing to the whole world, she implores, "Can't you see me? Can't you see us?" The girl stays very still, staring silently ahead as if listening and waiting for an answer.

Emily is statuesque as she stands gracefully by the sunlit window. The soft sunlight streams through the glass and sheaths her in a halo of heavenly radiance, turning her blond hair golden. Closing her eyes, Emily seems to fall under an enchanted spell. With her eyes closed, she says prayerfully, "When I'm so afraid, I close my eyes, and you come to me, Mommy. You come, and for a little while we're together again. Please come to me now, Mommy, please come." Stillness descends upon the playhouse, and it becomes as peaceful as a house of worship.

Her eyes remain closed as Emily raises her arms and threads them across her chest, gently hugging herself. Her body relaxes, and she releases her arms, letting them slide slowly to her sides. She opens her eyes, smiles warmly, and becomes like a little girl again. Emily begins speaking to her mother. "Mommy, you're here. I'm so happy you've come. I knew you would. I'm never afraid when you're with me, Mommy, never. There's no one else like you—no one."

Emily giggles, "I love when you hold me. I hear you laughing . . ." She touches her face gently with her fingertips. "I feel your warm kisses on my face. Mommy, your skin's *so* soft," she whispers.

She pauses briefly. Then Emily brightens and says, "Remember? Remember Mommy when you and Daddy went to parties? You would come into my room all dressed up and kiss me goodnight. You were so beautiful. I can still smell your perfume, Mommy. Oh, how I loved your perfume!"

Emily listens for a moment and then says hopefully, "I am a good big sister? I'm trying to be a strong girl like you taught me. I'm trying the best I can, but it's so hard without you. Mommy, I miss you *so* much."

Again she listens, and her hopes are lifted. "I am strong? You are very proud of me? Oh, I hope so. I want you to be proud of me. Mommy, when I grow up, I want to be just like you."

The little girl smiles and nods in understanding. Then, with her voice aching, she gazes up and pleads, "Mommy, please don't go . . . not yet . . . stay with me a little longer, please."

Unseen hands gently caress Emily's upturned face. Unheard words tenderly soothe her anguished heart. Trustingly and tearfully, she says, "You'll love me always and forever? I know you will. I love you, too. Yes Mommy, I can be strong a little longer."

Emily becomes inspired. "I'm not alone? I don't have to be afraid? There's someone special protecting me and Chloë? I know who he is Mommy. I know!"

There is a long pause; then Emily speaks wistfully, "You have to go now? I understand . . . goodbye, Mommy, goodbye. I love you, Mommy." Emily rises on her toes and calls after her mother, "I love you . . . I love you . . . I love you . . ."

When her mother's spirit has left the room, Emily turns and gazes out the window. She stands artistically; her delicate hands are now clasped together loosely in front of her; Emily's right leg is gracefully bowed in a relaxed ballerina pose. The sunlight sparkles like diamonds in her golden hair, her gossamer skirt is aglow, and her white leotard is luminescent. Slowly, she breathes deeply in and deeply out. Purposefully, she repeats this process several more times. When she is fully composed, Emily turns from the window and takes a step forward out of the sunlight. Gone now is the luminescence. She looks directly into Seth's eyes and calmly asks, "Where is Chloë?"

Seth knows he has just witnessed something truly divine. He, too, had felt another presence in the room, a presence that radiated absolute love. He believes the room has been graced by an angel, its afterglow briefly enveloping Emily. A flame of Seth's own faith has been rekindled by what he just saw. He answers her with quiet assurance, "She's safe in the house with Elena. Emily, you'll never see that man again. I promise you."

Emily's emerald eyes steadily focus on Seth. "I know," she says softly, "because you never break a promise."

"No. Not ever, Emily, especially to you," Seth whispers, astounded by this extraordinary girl and the remarkable moment. "Emily," he asks, "what would you like to do now?"

"Go to the park and play," Emily answers.

CHAPTER THIRTY

It is the Monday following the weekend of Emily's tenth birthday and Seth's proposal to Elena. The humidity is low, and it is a beautiful March day, cool and clear. On the grounds of The Children's Sanctuary, Angel and Tomás work side by side on the new children's cottage for girls. Not far from them is Humberto, who stands over a work table absorbed in studying the design plans. Occasionally, he plucks the pencil from his shirt pocket, scribbles notes on a pad, and makes some quick calculations. Seth arrives and approaches the men with his characteristic ambling stride. He carries a book in an open satchel. This happy young man is running late on this lovely morning. As he gets close, Humberto lifts his head and sees Seth coming. Dramatically, he raises his wrist to eye level and taps his watch.

"Sorry about being late, Mr. Hernandez," Seth apologizes, "but it was a big weekend. Maybe you've heard?"

Humberto cracks a wide grin and greets him warmly, pumping his hand and patting him on the back vigorously. "I guess I can let it slide this one time," Humberto says. "Congratulations! You and my Elena! I'm glad for you both!"

"Yes sir! Yes sir! Me too!"

"My muchacha bonita is so happy. And of course her mother, and yours, and Elena and Kathryn have been tying up the phones all morning making wedding plans. Yesenia shooed me out of the house first thing, as quick as she could. She even bribed me with a couple of cinnamon churros to get me out the door."

"We're pretty excited, that's for sure, Mr. Hernandez."

Tomás and Angel have stopped their work and come over to congratulate Seth, shaking his hand and earnestly patting his back. Humberto gestures to the book in Seth's satchel. "What's that book you've got there?" he asks.

Pulling it out, Seth replies, "It's something I picked up this morning on my way to work. It's why I'm late. It's a book about men and marriage, kind of an advice book. I want to get started off right."

Humberto's eyes fill with playfulness. "May I see it?" he asks innocently.

"Sure." Seth hands him the book.

Tomás and Angel stand next to them, watching. Humberto reads the title and mischievously glances at the two Mexican men. Tomás interprets for Angel as Humberto reads aloud: "*How to Have the Perfect Marriage: What Every Man Should Know.*" Humberto begins eagerly thumbing through the pages of the book. He stops and reads again, quoting theatrically, "'If your wife is upset with you and you don't know why, sit down with her, ask what's wrong, and she will tell you. Then, you can reason with her, and all will be fine.'" Humberto stops abruptly and stares at Tomás and Angel. The three of them burst out laughing.

Humberto is having fun. He leafs through more pages and stops. He reads silently to himself, nodding his head in amusement. "This is a really good one," he announces, grinning. "Now listen carefully everyone. 'Honesty is very important for every successful marriage. Always tell your wife the complete truth.'" Humberto, Angel, and Tomás start laughing again, only this time much harder.

Seth is beginning to understand the book is not so practical. He smiles wanly as the men have fun at his expense.

Humberto doesn't want to give up the game just yet, it's too entertaining. He thumbs through a few more pages, stops, and reads to himself. Not satisfied, he flips through more pages, stops, reads, and nods his head, saying enthusiastically, "This is the best of them all! Seth, you should remember this one, so pay very close attention." In his most dramatic voice yet, and pronouncing every word with precision, he begins, "'If you do something or forget to do something, or say something or forget to say something, and your wife's feelings are hurt as a result, simply apologize sincerely, and she will quickly forgive and soon forget.'" The three men immediately burst out laughing to the point of tears. Humberto hands the book back to Seth.

Tomás and Angel walk off teasing and back slapping each other about the book's advice. Angel can be heard saying to Tomás, "El autor, está completamente loco de la cabeza!"

Seth stands awkwardly with the book in his hand, waiting for Mr. Hernandez to stop laughing. "Not such a good idea, I guess," he says.

Humberto wipes tears from his eyes. "I'm glad you want to make my Elena happy. But the man who wrote this book knows nothing of marriage."

Seth looks at Humberto naïvely, "Can I ask your advice, Mr. Hernandez? You and Mrs. Hernandez have a wonderful marriage. What's your secret?"

"You want to know my secret?"

"Yes sir."

Humberto regards Seth for a long moment and then says wisely, "You can be right . . . or you can be happy."

"That's it? That's your secret?" Seth says, perplexed.

"No, it's not mine," Humberto admits. "It's Dr. Phil's. I watch him whenever I can. Trust me. It's everything you need to know. I wish I had known it the first fifteen years of my marriage to that woman."

Seth scratches his chin thoughtfully. "Okay . . . thanks, Mr. Hernandez."

Humberto grins at Seth. "You're welcome, young man. Now remember, we're going to the courthouse later. Need that last permit. I'll be inside the field office in the meantime." Humberto stops and admires the construction work. "The house is coming along nicely, more quickly than I thought. But that's part of the brilliance of your new design. It's the most efficient design I've ever seen, and it doesn't skimp on the amenities."

Seth politely corrects him, "You mean *our* new design, Mr. Hernandez. Without your suggestions and changes, I'd like to think it would still be good, but it wouldn't be brilliant. You put the 'brilliant' in it."

Humberto nods, appreciating the young man's respect and recognition. "Our new design," he agrees. Then he studies the pad on which he made the computations and says, "By my calculations, we'll most likely be short a load of wood."

"Yes sir, I know. I'm looking into that now."

Chuckling, Mr. Hernandez shakes his head. "You and my muchacha bonita. I couldn't be happier," he says and walks off in the direction of the field office.

When he leaves, Seth goes to the cottage to start work. As he passes by the trash barrel, he tosses in the advice book.

○ ○ ○

Around noon of that same day, Elena, Emily, and Chloë appear at the construction site for the new cottage. Elena carries a tray balancing a pitcher and several glasses. Emily looks especially pretty today, having taken extra care to look nice for Seth. Elena has helped her apply just a touch of translucent powder and light lip gloss. Emily is carrying a bag of cookies and holding Chloë's hand.

Busily working, the men do not hear them approach. Elena sets the tray down on the work table and pours a glass of lemonade, handing it to Chloë and encouraging her to deliver it to Angel. Chloë takes the glass, approaches the massive Angel, and pulls gently on the loose trousers of his right leg to get his attention. The little girl looks incredibly small standing next to this gentle giant. Angel turns and looks about but doesn't notice Chloë. Annoyed by his failure to see her, Chloë gives Angel's pant leg several more quick tugs to get his attention. Angel looks down at Chloë and smiles broadly. Beaming up at him, Chloë offers Angel the glass of lemonade, which the man gratefully accepts.

Speaking to her cordially in Spanish, Angel says, "Ah, una
señorita. Mira Tomás! Es como mi niña chiquita. Muchas gracias,
señorita, por la limonada deliciosa!"

Curious and bold as always, Chloë asks, "What's he saying?"

Tomás nods in a friendly gesture and says, "Una señorita means
lady in the Spanish. My friend also said you remind him of his own
little daughter. And, he is thanking you for the delicious lemonade."

Chloë shouts to her sister excitedly, "Did you hear that, Em?
Angel said I'm a . . ." She turns quickly to Tomás, with a questioning
expression.

Tomás repeats slowly, "Señorita."

"Señorita!" Chloë shouts. "That means lady! Em, everyone
thinks I'm a lady!"

"You are a lady, Chlo. You're a wonderful little lady," Emily calls
to her. Hearing Chloë shout to Emily, Seth turns and waves to the
girls. Chloë rushes back for another glass that Elena has poured.
Emily has approached the men too, and in her characteristic graceful
manner she offers the open bag of cookies to Angel and to Tomás.
They both take a cookie from the bag and thank her. She nods
formally to them. Chloë joins her sister and hands Tomás the glass
of lemonade. Emily nods to the men a last time, and Chloë smiles
broadly and waves goodbye as they return and stand by Elena.

"May I take some cookies and a glass of lemonade to Seth?"
Emily asks Elena.

"Of course you may."

Emily smiles modestly at her. She takes the glass of lemonade
that Elena has just poured, and along with the bag of cookies, she
goes to Seth. Elena watches them.

"Hi Seth," Emily says softly. Beginning to blush, she offers him
the lemonade and the open bag of cookies.

"Hi Em, thanks for the refreshments. It's just what I needed."
Seth takes the glass and helps himself to a cookie. He enjoys a long,
slow drink of the cold lemonade and then devours the cookie in
one bite.

"Do you like everything, Seth?" Emily asks hopefully.

"It's wonderful, Em. The cookie's terrific—my favorite,
chocolate chip. You and my mom make the best ones."

"I know they're your favorite. That's why I made them this morning. I really hope you like them."

"I do, Em. I really do; thank you. Okay if I have another one?"

Pleased with his compliment, Emily smiles shyly and holds open the bag. He fishes out another cookie and thanks her again. Emily turns and rejoins Elena and Chloë by the work table where she offers a cookie to her sister.

At this moment, Juan-Carlos arrives. He is dressed very hip in skinny jeans, a long sleeve Versace white cotton shirt and navy blue Hogan sneakers. Juan-Carlos believes one could make a fashion statement regardless of the environment, and as he scurries across the dusty work site he proves this place is no exception. He carries a large, unwieldy binder full of wall paper samples and paint swatches. Excited about creating the interior design of the new home and delighted with the news of Elena's engagement, Juan-Carlos hurries over to the girls and dramatically says, "Hi to everyone. Miss Elena. Miss Elena. Let me see. Let me *see!*" He gushes over her ring. "Scrumptious, scrumptious, simply *scrumptious!* I knew that man was right for you the moment I saw him. I'm so happy I could cry!"

Elena laughs at Juan-Carlos's unabashed joy, wonderful sweetness, and kind generosity. She has always loved him and felt he was part of the family since her father brought him to America. "Thank you. That means so much to me coming from you, Juan-Carlos. You're right at the top of our list for wedding invitations. Promise me now that you'll come."

Juan-Carlos is thrilled and becomes overly excited. He beams broadly and places one hand on his hip, saying rapidly and practically falling over with glee, "I was hoping so. You know I'll be there. You know I just will! And you ladies *must* let me help with the planning. I know all the best florists!"

Elena laughs, "Of course you can help plan things, Juan-Carlos. I was counting on you."

Switching to his samples, Juan-Carlos gushes again. "Now, I want to show everyone. I'm *sooo* excited! Today, I'm all about the joy." He hoists the binder onto the table and frantically motions for them to gather round. He begins to quickly thumb through the binder and stops, pointing proudly. "Don't you just love this wallpaper for the children's rooms, Miss Elena? And look at these borders I found. Aren't they darling?"

Elena is very impressed and enthusiastic about his selections. "It's wonderful. It's perfect. Juan-Carlos, you've worked your magic again."

Juan-Carlos shines with pride and presents a small paper sample of the paint color. "Look at this. Just *look*. It's absolutely perfect with the wallpaper, if I say so myself." Then sighing dramatically, he adds, "It was such a struggle. Honestly, Miss Elena, I just about worried myself sick to tiny pieces over every little detail. It had to be perfect for the children. But then, voilà! It all came together!"

Elena compliments him, "Kudos to you, Juan-Carlos, only you could have done it so well. The children will love it."

"I know. I'm so proud of myself, too, Miss Elena." Then in a hushed, animated whisper he adds, "But these are only a few of the samples. They're bringing my absolute best selections from the showroom just any minute. Oh, speak of, here they come now."

Juan-Carlos points to a tall, trim, Latino who is in his late twenties. He wears tight, black leather Versace pants with a light blue Versace long-sleeve shirt with a cream-colored, cashmere sweater draped over his shoulders, its long sleeves looped loosely across his chest. His shoes are expensive, highly polished, black leather Ralph Laurens with pointed toes and elevated heels. His hair is pulled back in a tight, slick, short ponytail. The expression on his face is that of someone who has just smelled something rotten.

Trailing this man is another Latino who struggles to keep up. This other Latino is the man's personal assistant; he is in his early twenties, and is much shorter at around five foot two, is as skinny as a flagpole, and is quite delicate-looking. But as fragile as he appears, this has not deterred his boss from loading him down like a pack burro; the poor man can hardly walk, burdened by the bulk and the weight he is carrying. He looks as if he might collapse and collide with Mother Earth at any moment.

Juan-Carlos waves enthusiastically and calls excitedly to the taller man. "Alejandro! Alejandro! We're here. We're over here-ere!"

Alejandro insists on being addressed exclusively by his given name because he fancies it's more impressive to his clientele. He is the owner of the interior design boutique, "Alejandro's!" This is the interior design boutique Juan-Carlos is using for his selections. Juan-Carlos and Alejandro have known each other for years. They had met at the community center where Juan-Carlos first taught ESL. Naturally, because of his likeable demeanor and endless patience, Juan-Carlos had been the most popular instructor, and his classes were always full. Years ago, Alejandro was in one of his classes. Unlike his friend Juan-Carlos, Alejandro has a surly attitude and inflated ego. But despite this, Juan-Carlos respected the man's abilities in many ways and chose his boutique because he knew Alejandro carried the best selections in town and would have what he wanted in stock. That, plus the fact that Alejandro owed him so many favors for referring business his way, he knew he could demand, and get, a hefty discount. Still, it was hard for anyone to get past the man's overblown ego. This failing kept the boutique from tripling in size, in the opinion of Juan-Carlos, and he often told Alejandro so. Today, Alejandro is particularly perturbed by having to pick his way carefully through the rubble of the construction site to avoid getting his fancy shoes sullied or his designer sweater soiled.

Glancing at Juan-Carlos, Alejandro grimaces, turns, and snaps his fingers at his personal assistant. "Chop! Chop! I can't be here all day! Come along, now. How hard can it be to just follow me?"

His assistant nearly buckles under the heavy load, but Alejandro doesn't offer to help him, such a charitable thought would never enter the man's head. Elena and Emily exchange amused glances as the two men approach. Chloë moves in front of her sister and leans into her, eyes glowing at the commotion. Emily drapes her long, delicate arms crisscross over Chloë's front and gives her a loving pat. Elena, Emily, and Chloë become interested observers.

Juan-Carlos is electrified with excitement over the arrival of his other selections. "Everyone, this is Alejandro."

The tall Latino introduces himself with an egotistical flourish, "I'm Alejandro!" Then he adds, like an afterthought, "Oh . . . this is my new personal assistant, Mauricio."

Mauricio smiles pathetically at them and sets his burdens down, relieved.

Juan-Carlos looks surprised. "Alejandro, you've hired yet another new personal assistant?"

"It's impossible to get decent help these days," Alejandro complains. "One must make do," he sniffs. Then, snapping his fingers impatiently, he turns on his assistant, "Get that binder off the ground. Chop! Chop! No, no, not that one, the other one, you idiot. Put it here. Hurry up. Be careful. Don't tear *anything*!"

Mauricio dutifully picks up the correct binder and places it on the table. Alejandro leafs through it quickly, selects the samples he's decided on, and lays out four large squares of wall paper on the table.

Light-headed with excitement, Juan-Carlos stares lovingly at the samples that have just been placed on the table. His face immediately drops. Juan-Carlos is mortified by what he sees. "This is not what I ordered," he says in shocked disbelief. "This is not at all what I selected." Crushed, he looks at Alejandro and says plaintively, "This must be some terrible mistake. You brought the wrong samples by mistake, Alejandro."

"No mistake. I do not make mistakes!" Alejandro admonishes him in a surly and dismissive tone. "With the discount you de–manded and the exquisite selections you made, it was simply too expensive for me. I decided it was a waste. What I brought is close enough. If you don't like these four, I brought plenty more like them you can choose from. After all, it's just for a bunch of kids."

Juan-Carlos is stunned. He's practically in shock and is finding it hard to breathe. "But this won't do at all . . ."

Condescendingly, Alejandro quips, "It will have to do. It was mega headaches for me fighting the traffic to get to this out-of-the-way backwoods place from my boutique in midtown. Now choose!"

Alejandro's 'now choose' was just the cold slap in the face that Juan-Carlos needed. Feeling put down and betrayed by this upstart, Juan-Carlos's initial shocked disbelief is instantly replaced with acrimony. He responds slowly and deliberately, each word rising in crescendo for emphasis, "Just . . . for . . . a . . . bunch . . . of . . . kids? Oh, I see. Choose, you say? All right, Alejandro. I will choose." Juan-Carlos methodically picks up each sample and dramatically rips every one of them in two. Every time he tears one apart, he carelessly tosses each half into the air. "This will not (*rip!*) do (*rip!*) for the children's (*rip!*) rooms (*rip!*)." Staring at his friend, Juan-Carlos barks, "Now, pick up this trash Alejandro! Then you will go to your boutique, get what I ordered, and be back here in two hours!"

It is Alejandro's turn to be shocked. Having yelped like a puppy with every dramatic act of destruction of his second-rate samples, the man is in tears. Alejandro cringes and quakes in his designer shoes and shivers under his designer shirt. He is speechless. While Juan-Carlos looks at him sharply, poor Alejandro shakes his head sadly, snivels, and manages to recover to some degree. He sniffs haughtily and purses his lips so tightly together that the veins in his forehead pop out. Then he snaps his fingers rudely at his assistant and orders, "Chop! Chop! Pick up this trash . . . uh, samples."

Mauricio quickly moves as ordered. "Stop, Mauricio!" Juan-Carlos commands. Then, carefully and precisely, he says, "I know who you are, Alejandro. I recommended you for your first job. A lowly personal assistant . . . and you were fired for incompetence. You can't fool me with your conceited airs. I said *you*, Alejandro, *you* pick up this trash. And don't you get prissy with me!"

Alejandro's shoulders collapse. He drops his head in shame and dutifully picks up the torn samples. After collecting them, he tries to salvage some dignity by sniffing haughtily, turning swiftly on his heels, and departing quickly, followed by his personal assistant who once again struggles with his heavy load.

When Alejandro is a dozen feet away, Juan-Carlos calls after him, "Remember, Alejandro, two hours." Then he claps his hands smartly, "Chop-chop!" Alejandro stops and his back stiffens, but he does not turn around. However, his personal assistant, who enjoyed that his arrogant boss was brought down several notches, looks back at the last moment and waves happily to Juan-Carlos. Juan-Carlos waves back merrily to him. Elena laughs, and the children giggle.

After they have gone, Juan-Carlos puts one hand on his hip, turns to Elena and the girls, and says petulantly, "That Alejandro, he's never been anything but a cheapskate. Sometimes he makes me *so* mad I could just spit!"

Again, Elena laughs out loud, and the kids giggle. Elena says, "Juan-Carlos, I'm so proud of you for sticking up for the children.

Why don't you show Emily and Chloë the other things you have in mind? Would you like that, children?"

Emily and Chloë nod their heads enthusiastically.

Juan-Carlos grins, happy and eager to show them all of his plans for decorating the cottage. He hoists his binder from the table and leaves with the children following him.

Elena strolls over to where Seth is working. He is standing on a ladder, hammering. "Hi babe," she says.

Seth looks over his shoulder and puts down his hammer. "Hi honey. Thanks for the refreshments."

"You're welcome. It was all Emily's idea." Elena admires the work. "You're making a lot of progress."

"Yes, even faster than I thought. If the weather holds, we'll be finished by early April, a week ahead of schedule, thanks to my friends."

"That's wonderful. By the way, do you know Emily's in love with you?"

"I love Emily and Chloë, too. We all do."

"No honey, that's not what I mean," Elena tells him patiently. "I'm saying Emily is 'in love' with you."

Seth is surprised. "Why do you say that?"

"It's true, babe. You're her Prince Charming. It's very special because you are Emily's first love. And it's also a big responsibility because a girl never forgets her first love, not ever."

"Oh, I didn't know."

"Seth, you really didn't know?" Elena asks, bewildered that the man could miss it, particularly since he was so much better than most males at picking up on female feelings.

"No honey, I really didn't. Is there something special I should do?"

Elena shakes her head sympathetically, reminding herself that all men, even her beautiful, sensitive Seth, have certain blind spots that are common to their gender. She concludes it's simply a DNA flaw and forgives him. Then, gently instructing him, she says, "No honey, there isn't anything a man can do about a girl who's in love with him. I just wanted you to know. Please be sensitive to her feelings."

"Of course, I will. I'm glad you told me."

Elena switches the subject and asks coyly, "Did you call Casey about the extra wood you need for the cottage?"

Seth cuts his eyes at her. "No, as a matter of fact, he called me. Said he'd heard. Now, I wonder who he could possibly have heard it from?"

Elena wrinkles her nose at him. "You're ending your sentences in prepositions again," she says teasingly.

"And you're dodging the question," he counters lightly.

Elena shrugs, looks angelic, and twirls her hair distractedly, saying, "It's one of those great mysteries. Guess we'll never know."

Seth looks past her. "And here comes the wood now."

A large lumber truck is arriving, slowly rumbling onto the construction site. It comes hissing to a halt, its brakes squealing. The air shimmers with heat waves around the silver exhaust pipe which extends several feet above the cab. Humberto appears, attracted by the sound of the truck's arrival.

With amused anticipation, Elena announces, "And here comes Papa."

"What is this?" Humberto asks.

"Looks like wood to me," Elena answers innocently.

"I didn't order any wood. Did you, Seth?"

"No sir. Not me."

Humberto turns to his daughter and eyes her suspiciously. Drawing out her name for emphasis, he says, "E—le—na?"

Elena has a mirthful look of mischief and laughs as she denies having any knowledge of it. Her father observes her closely to see if she's holding her breath. Satisfied that she's not, Humberto pulls his cell phone from his pocket and taps a number.

His friend Casey answers, "Casey here."

"It's Humberto, Casey."

"Top of the morning to ya."

"A load of your wood just arrived."

"You don't say?"

"Thanks, Casey, but I can't afford it."

"It's not for sale."

"You can't be giving it to me."

"Who said anything about *you*? It's for the children."

"You can't afford this."

"You're right. I can't. It'll probably bust me. So that's exactly why I'm doing it. Now, you got anything important to say 'cause you're taking up my valuable time over here. Some of us have to work for a living, ya know."

Humberto slowly shakes his head. "I always knew I was the dumbest Mexican in the world. But I didn't know my best friend was the dumbest Irishman."

"You are a slow-roasted coffee bean. My wife's been telling me that for thirty-five years—except this morning. When I told her I was delivering the wood you needed for the children's cottage, she kissed me and said maybe I had a few brain cells after all."

Humberto smiles appreciatively, thinking about his friend's generosity at a time when he knew he could least afford it. "Thanks, Casey. It's just what we needed. I really appreciate it. We all do."

"Don't mention it. Goodbye."

"Adios, amigo."

Humberto slowly closes his cell phone, feeling very thankful for his friend. From the start of construction Humberto had begun to feel there was something very special about this new cottage; extraordinary things kept happening. As it turned out, not all of the building material they needed was stored in the barn. They were short critical materials in several key areas. But quite unexpectedly, these shortages were resolved of their own accord, or so it seemed. First, somebody anonymously donated the extra electrical wiring they had to have; then one day, some badly needed tile appeared out of nowhere; next, a guy he never knew sent him a flatbed loaded with drywall that was absolutely essential; and one morning, a bunch of Seth's friends showed up and stayed for three weeks to help with the construction, all of them fine craftsmen in their own right, who insisted on being paid for their work in Mrs. McAllister's chocolate chip cookies and a midday meal from the Hernandez household kitchen; and now, Casey's load of wood.

Humberto turns to Seth and asks, "You ready to get that permit?"

"Yes sir," Seth answers.

"Angel and Tomás!" Humberto calls, "show 'em where to unload this truck." Humberto looks at his lovely daughter, thinking how precious she is, and wags his finger playfully at her. "Muchacha bonita, you and your mother have been plotting again." He pauses and then says, grinning, "Muchas gracias, niña," and he hugs his daughter tightly.

When he steps back, Elena notices her father has tears in his eyes. "Papa's such a sweet man," she thinks as she smiles tenderly at him.

Walking over and kissing Elena on the cheek, Seth says, "Thanks for the refreshments, babe. See you later tonight."

The two men leave.

Elena goes inside the unfinished cottage to join the children and Juan-Carlos. She is anxious to see his artistic vision for the cottage's interior.

○ ○ ○

With Seth driving, he and Humberto leave the cottage site in the dented, worn-out pickup truck that Humberto has owned for twelve years. Shortly, they arrive at the annex courthouse. They park in front. The men have gone there to get a final building permit. As they are about to exit the cab of the pick-up, protesters appear on the sidewalk carrying large, homemade signs and begin picketing. Their signs read, "Illegal Aliens Are Stealing Our Jobs!" and "You Are Not Welcome Here!" and "Mexicans Go Home!"

Seth is appalled and deeply embarrassed. "Mr. Hernandez, I'm so sorry. They don't know," he says apologetically.

Humberto stares at the protesters. He suddenly looks much older. "No Seth, they don't know," he says sadly.

Seeing Mr. Hernandez's pain, Seth becomes angry. "I'm going to say something to them," and he opens his door.

"No," Humberto responds calmly and places his hand on Seth's forearm to stop him. Without any bitterness in his voice, Humberto observes sorrowfully, "That's not the answer, Seth. Do not say anything to them, please. They have the right to express themselves freely. It's one of the great things about our country."

Shaking his head in disgust, Seth relents and looks silently ahead for a moment before saying, "Mr. Hernandez, the only thing I can think of to say is to tell you I'm sorry; I'm so sorry. This isn't fair to you and your family."

Mr. Hernandez nods, letting Seth know he appreciates his concern but doesn't answer. Humberto continues watching the protesters for a long time, not displaying any anger towards them. Finally, he says quietly with somber observation, "We know this is a problem. We know a solution needs to be found, one that respects the sovereign rights of America while giving the poor access to the opportunities here. I came here believing this is the greatest country in the world. I still believe that. If we work together to achieve a solution, a just balance can be found. We might find it more quickly if people would begin by remembering all of the names of the soldiers who are buried beneath America's soil. All of them helped secure America's freedom, many with their lives. Names like Sullivan, Russo, Cohen, Khan, Nguyen, and Washington. And resting beside these brave American soldiers are other brave American soldiers with names like Garcia, Lopez, Gomez, Rivera, Salazar . . . and Hernandez."

CHAPTER THIRTY-ONE

It is the first Saturday in April. The new cottage for girls is completed and being dedicated on this bright clear morning. The time of day is eleven o'clock. Attending the ceremony and seated inside are Humberto, Yesenia, Elena, Seth, Mrs. McAllister, Kathryn and Terry, Juan-Carlos, Angel, and Tomás. Mrs. King is in the front at the podium and is about to speak. Also attending the dedication is a new couple who are first-time visitors to The Children's Sanctuary: John Goodman and his wife, Mary. Mr. Goodman is in his late forties; his wife is a few years younger. Mr. Goodman wears an expensive, conservative suit and his wife wears a lovely tailored dress. They are seated at the back of the room, a little apart from the others, quietly observing and holding hands. Mr. Goodman appears to be preoccupied, intently studying the construction elements and design features of the home. Just as Mrs. King is about to speak, Mrs. Goodman gently squeezes her husband's hand, signaling him to pay attention. Mr. Goodman smiles at his wife, straightens, and gives his full attention to Mrs. King.

Mrs. King begins, "Welcome everyone, and thank you for being here today. The dedication of a new cottage is one of the happiest days of all at The Children's Sanctuary because it means we are able to care for more children who need us. All children who find their way to this new cottage will also find a safe and loving home. For some, it will literally save their lives. For all, it will ensure a future free of abuse and neglect. Here, they will know only kindness, tenderness, and love."

The audience breaks out in spontaneous applause. Yesenia leans into Humberto, pats his hand affectionately, and says, "I'm so proud of you, mi amor." Humberto nods and fights back tears.

Mrs. King smiles and speaks directly to the crew. "Mr. Hernandez, Seth, Juan-Carlos, Angel, and Tomás, I have watched your tireless efforts as you built and decorated this beautiful new cottage for little girls. All of us are truly thankful for what you've done, but none are more thankful than the children who will live here. There's something I want each of you to always remember. In this cottage, every time a child receives a hug, those will be your arms around her. Every time a child is tucked into a warm bed, those will be your hands tucking the covers under her chin. Every time a child hears a voice sing out 'Sweet dreams,' that will be your voice she hears."

Elena dabs tears from her eyes with a handkerchief, slips her arm through Seth's, and whispers to him, "You're so wonderful." She lightly pecks him on his cheek and hugs his arm.

Mrs. King holds up a wall plaque to show the audience. "I conferred with the staff, and we all agreed that that this was the most meaningful way to show you our lasting appreciation. This plaque will hang on the wall inside the cottage by the front door for the children to see every day. It reads: 'Under this roof you are safe. Within these walls you are loved. This is your home. It is your home where all of your dreams can come true.' Each of your names is inscribed below."

Interpreting for Angel, Tomás wipes his eyes with his sleeve. The massive Angel sits stoically as boulder-size tears roll down his cheeks. Juan-Carlos weeps openly. Angel places an oak-like arm around his narrow shoulders to comfort him.

Mrs. King announces cheerfully, "Now everyone, there's punch, coffee, and cookies"—she nods to Yesenia—"and four wonderful cakes in the dining area. Help yourselves." Mrs. King smiles broadly and leaves the podium, going out the front door. Mr. and Mrs. Goodman follow her out.

Elena turns to Seth sitting beside her. "Honey, we need to talk."

"Sure. What about?"

"Did you notice the couple in the back of the room?"

"Yes, I saw them when they came in. Nice-looking couple. I haven't seen them before."

"Oh honey," Elena says tenderly, "this is such a special day, with the dedication of the new cottage. You've all done an incredibly wonderful job. I'm so proud of you. But there's other news that makes this a special day, too. But maybe, I'm afraid, the kind of news that could be a little bit sad for you, babe. That couple in the back of the room was Mr. and Mrs. Goodman. I've been told they are two amazing people who are interested in adopting Emily and Chloë. That's the real reason they came today. By sheer coincidence it was on the same day of the cottage dedication. So, Mrs. King invited them to attend. They are meeting with Mrs. King in her office now. They would like to meet you, too."

Seth is stunned, trying to grasp the idea. "They want to adopt Emily and Chloë?"

Elena places her hand on his forearm and says lovingly, "Babe, you've been wonderful for them. It was going to happen. From what I've heard, I believe this couple will make the perfect parents for the children."

"They want to meet me?" Seth is nearly in a daze.

"Of course they want to meet you," she says encouragingly. "Mrs. King has told them how special you are to the children."

"When do they want to meet me?"

"They're waiting for us now."

Elena and Seth leave the room and go to Mrs. King's office. When they arrive, Mrs. King is sitting behind her desk and rises to greet them. The Goodmans are seated in front of her beside two open chairs and also rise for the introductions.

Mrs. King says warmly, "Mr. and Mrs. Goodman, I'd like you to meet Elena Hernandez, Emily's teacher, and Seth McAllister, the children's friend."

Elena offers her hand to Mr. Goodman, and, smiling at her, he gently shakes it.

"Mrs. King has told us so many nice things about you both," says Mr. Goodman. Please, let me introduce my wife, Mary."

The two women instinctively hug. They immediately feel they are kindred spirits.

"Not just nice things," Mrs. Goodman compliments her sincerely, "Mrs. King has told us what a wonderful teacher you are, Elena. How you inspire all of your students. From what I've heard, you're just incredible."

Mr. Goodman shakes Seth's hand heartily, "Hi, Seth, John Goodman, and this is my wife, Mary." Mary smiles at Seth, offering her hand, which he takes and lightly presses.

"I understand congratulations are in order. You two are getting married?" Mrs. Goodman says with genuine interest.

Elena glows and looks at Seth. "Yes, June fourth."

"You two make a beautiful couple; the perfect pair, if you don't mind me saying so," Mrs. Goodman adds.

"Thank you, Mrs. Goodman," Elena responds happily.

"Please, Elena, call me Mary."

"Thank you, Mary. I will."

"Let's all have a seat, shall we?" Mrs. King says.

Elena notices that the Goodmans are holding hands again, just as she had observed them doing at the dedication a few minutes ago. They seem to be in perfect harmony with each other.

Mrs. King begins, "Seth, I've told Mr. and Mrs. Goodman about the special relationship you have with Emily and Chloë. I think it would be a really good idea for the children to meet them at your house. They're most secure and comfortable there with you. Of course, Emily and Chloë have no idea about the true purpose, not yet."

Elena watches Seth. She reaches for his hand and presses it affectionately, looking at him reassuringly.

Mrs. Goodman notices what Elena has just done and says considerately to Seth, "Mrs. King has told us all about you and the children, Seth. It's a remarkable story. They were so lucky to find you. I'm sure you have mixed emotions about this whole thing. It must come as a big surprise."

"I was the lucky one, I'd say," Seth replies, his feelings catching in his throat. "You're very perceptive, Mrs. Goodman. It is a surprise.

I wasn't expecting this, but, of course, I want the best for Emily and Chloë . . ."

"But you'll miss them. You'll miss them terribly, won't you?" Mrs. Goodman says kindly.

"Yes, I'll miss them very much." Seth never knew that one small word could stir such heartache. He is so thankful that Elena is sitting beside him. The touch of her hand and the love in her eyes support and reassure him in the very way he needs it at this critical moment.

Mrs. Goodman speaks softly, "Seth, I've always wanted to be a mother." As she continues, her husband places his arm around her shoulders. "After I miscarried with my first pregnancy, the doctors told me I could never have children of my own. It's been the greatest disappointment of my life." She looks at her husband lovingly. "It took me a while. John has been so supportive. But I'm ready now. When I read the file on Emily and Chloë, I have to say I immediately fell in love with them. We both did."

Seth is very moved by Mrs. Goodman and now thinks she reminds him a little bit of his own mother. He says, "Mrs. Goodman, the children are coming to my house today and will stay for the rest of the weekend. We'll be leaving shortly. You're both welcome to come this afternoon. Elena will be there, too."

Elena looks reassuringly at Seth. Again, she squeezes his hand affectionately.

"Yes, please come," Elena says to Mary. "Seth, don't you think three o'clock would be right? They can also stay for dinner."

"Three's perfect. And I hope you will have dinner with us," Seth says, beginning to get over his initial shock. Elena's support has given him the emotional strength he needed. He is also developing a positive feeling about this couple. His first impression is that they are very loving and caring of one another.

Mrs. Goodman is so excited there are tears welling up in her eyes. "We'd love to," she says. "We'll bring dinner though. I insist. Three o'clock, then?"

"Yes. Be sure to wear your play clothes," Elena adds cordially.

Mrs. Goodman looks at her husband, who is just as excited as his wife is at that moment. "We'll have to go buy some," she laughs. "John, we have just enough time, if we hurry."

CHAPTER THIRTY-TWO

Seth, Elena, and the children sit together at the kitchen table. Seth helps Chloë with her origami star. Elena assists Emily with a school paper. Gracie Ann lies face up on the table and feels a little nervous about meeting the new friends her mommy told her were coming today. Sam rests in his crate. The clock on the wall shows the time is three p.m. There is a light knock at the front door.

Chloë is excited. She looks up from the table and jumps down. "That's the new friends."

"Yep," Seth says. "Let's go meet 'em."

"You and Chloë go," Elena says. "We're almost done here."

Emily smiles in agreement. Emily and Elena remain at the kitchen table while Seth and Chloë go to the front door. In less than a minute they return with Mr. and Mrs. Goodman, who are now dressed much more casually. They are carrying presents for the children. Chloë has latched onto Mrs. Goodman's hand and in her excitement is practically dragging Mary into the kitchen. The Goodmans are instantly smitten with Chloë. Elena and Emily rise from the table.

"Em! Em! Look! They brought us presents!" Chloë shouts.

Elena formally introduces Emily. "Mr. and Mrs. Goodman, I'd

like you to meet Emily Fleming, Chloë's sister. Emily, this is Mr. and Mrs. Goodman."

Warmly, Mrs. Goodman says, "Hi, Emily. I'm Mary Goodman, and this is my husband, John. We're so glad to meet you." She offers her hand to Emily.

Emily smiles politely, takes her hand, and says, "It's very nice to meet you too, Mrs. and Mr. Goodman."

Chloë is beside herself with joy, bouncing up and down. "They brought presents, Em! Can we open them?"

Everyone laughs, and Mrs. Goodman says, "Yes, I want you to."

The children sit at the table and open their presents. There are hair ribbons, barrettes, and nail polish for Chloë, and a beautiful silver-handled hair brush with a matching silver inlaid hand mirror for Emily.

Chloë reacts with her all-out brand of enthusiasm and shows her presents to Gracie Ann. "Look, Gracie Ann! See what we got! Mrs. Goodman, this is Gracie Ann. I'm her Mommy."

"Hi Gracie Ann," Mrs. Goodman says. "What a pretty girl you are."

Emily responds to the couple, "It was very nice of you to think of us this way. Thank you."

Excited, Chloë jumps off her seat and grabs Mrs. Goodman's hand. "We have a dog and everything! At first his name was Samantha, but he's a boy. So I named him Sam. He's the smartest dog in the whole world! You wanna meet him?"

"I certainly would," says Mrs. Goodman energetically.

Chloë gets Sam from his crate and brings him in to meet Mrs. Goodman, who dotes over him, saying, "Sam's not just smart, he's *so* handsome. Why Chloë, I bet he's both the smartest and the handsomest dog in the whole world."

"He is!" Chloë beams. "C'mon, let me show you the backyard. We've got birds, and swings, a playhouse, and everything. Seth made it all for us." Chloë begins tugging on Mrs. Goodman's free hand. Laughing, Mary hands Sam to Seth as Chloë pulls her towards the back door.

Emily has been quietly observing. She approves of Mrs. Good–man.

Mrs. Goodman looks over her shoulder as she goes out the door, saying excitedly, "C'mon John, let's go, let's everybody go!"

Mr. Goodman grins, pleased that his wife is so happy. He is thrilled with the children.

All of them follow Chloë and Mrs. Goodman out into the backyard.

CHAPTER THIRTY-THREE

The entire afternoon has been a huge success, much better than anyone could have imagined. Mrs. Goodman feels like it's her most wonderful dream come true. The clock on the wall reads seven-thirty p.m. The Goodmans have stayed for dinner and everyone, including the children, pitched-in to help clean up. It was a lot of fun.

Elena asks, "Mary, would you like to help with bedtime?"

"I would love to. What can I do?"

Glancing at Emily for permission, Elena says, "After their baths, I could brush Emily's hair with her new hairbrush, and you could do Chloë's."

Emily nods her head in agreement.

Thrilled, Chloë asks, "Can I wear one of my new barrettes to bed? The pink one is my favorite."

Mrs. Goodman hugs her and says, "Of course you can, sweetheart. It'll be so pretty on you."

"And will you read us a bedtime story?" Chloë pleads.

Elena glances at Seth sympathetically.

Seth smiles weakly and looks away.

"I was hoping I could," Mrs. Goodman says, gazing at Chloë with motherly love.

Cheerfully Elena directs, "Okay children. Let's get started for bedtime. It's getting late."

Chloë jumps down from the table. Emily rises from her chair and graciously addresses Mr. and Mrs. Goodman. "Thank you again, Mr. and Mrs. Goodman, for dinner." She raises her eyebrows at Chloë.

"Thank you," Chloë echoes. She holds up Gracie Anne and bubbles, "Gracie Ann says thank you, too."

The children go out of the room together followed by the women. Seth and Mr. Goodman get up from the kitchen table and retire to the living room. Mr. Goodman sits on the couch, and Seth sits in the chair across from him.

Mr. Goodman says wholeheartedly, "I haven't seen my wife this happy in a long time, Seth. Emily and Chloë are angels." Mr. Goodman is overtaken by emotion and begins wiping tears from his eyes with a handkerchief while he continues to talk. "I mean, Mary is an angel herself, you understand, always has been. I'm so lucky to have her. For years, I've been waiting and hoping for this day to come for her, for us, and now it's finally arrived. This afternoon I saw my wife become, once again, that happy, sweet, joy-filled girl I married. What you have done for these children is incredible. How can I ever thank you?"

"Mr. Goodman, it's not me you should be thanking," Seth says. "It's Emily. She's simply remarkable. Emily changed my life for the better when I needed it the most. And, of course, Chloë is the icing on everyone's cake."

"Elena told us the story. From what I've heard, you've done a tremendous job with the children. Elena? Now there's a special girl."

"I'm the luckiest guy in the world," Seth says.

"I feel the same way about Mary," Mr. Goodman responds, "always have." He puts away his handkerchief and changes the subject. "Seth, I've wanted to ask you something. The home that was dedicated today, I was told you designed it."

"The initial, rough design, yes," Seth answers, "but the finished design was mostly Mr. Hernandez. He's Elena's father."

Mr. Goodman continues amiably, "I understand you have a master's degree in architecture. Elena told us you graduated first in your class from the Boyd School."

"Yes sir, I did."

"That's very impressive, Seth. The Boyd School is the top architectural school in the country. You say the design was a collaborative effort between you and Mr. Hernandez?"

"Yes sir, Mr. Hernandez is the most naturally gifted architect I've ever seen. He corrected my design flaws and added new designs of his own. He was absolutely right in his suggestions and calculations. The brilliance of the finished design really belongs to him. The man's a true genius."

Mr. Goodman has been paying very close attention to Seth. "I suspect you're being a little too modest, young man. But I appreciate that attitude in someone your age. Please tell me about Mr. Hernandez. Where did he graduate from college?"

"He doesn't have a formal college degree," Seth answers.

"Even better; neither do I," Mr. Goodman says, pleased. "He's a man after my own heart—learned on the job like I did. It's the best education in the world. Listen, I have to tell you, I was thoroughly impressed by what I saw today. More than thoroughly impressed, I was astonished. The optimal use of light and space are incredible. Everything flowed together perfectly. It gave a sense of spaciousness and family warmth that was completely harmonious. Seth, it's exactly the kind of new, family home design I've been wanting for my next major project. What I'm trying to say is, young man, would you consider coming to work for me?"

"Coming to work for you?" Seth repeats, surprised.

Mr. Goodman chuckles, "I'm getting ahead of myself again. Mary tells me I do that all the time when I get excited. I'm the founder of The New Millennium Family Home Company in Dallas. We're the largest privately-owned family home construction company in the country. I have plans to move into the Houston market in a big way soon. Your design would give us a great competitive edge."

Seth tries to wrap his mind around Mr. Goodman's proposition. "You're offering me a job, Mr. Goodman?"

"That's exactly what I'm doing! I'll start you off as a senior designer. It won't be long before you make manager, and within ten years after that, who knows? Maybe even vice president. I know exceptional talent when I see it, young man. I'll double your salary. How does a hundred thousand sound?"

Seth is overwhelmed. He stammers, "Well . . . Mr. Goodman . . . I don't know . . . I'll have to talk it over with Elena. I wasn't considering a job change. I'm getting married soon."

Mr. Goodman is enthusiastic. "Driving a hard bargain, hey? I like that in a person. How about a manager's title right off and a hundred and ten thousand dollars, guaranteed bonus of twenty percent the first year, and a paid moving package. I'll even fly you and Elena to Dallas for a three-day house hunting trip, all expenses paid. You can start two weeks after you come back from your honeymoon. I'm not going to let my competition get you. No sir!" He offers to shake hands. "What do you say? Do we have a deal?"

Seth can't believe his ears. He's really excited now about this new career opportunity. "Mr. Goodman, it sounds great. Really it does—thank you—and I'm happy to shake your hand. But if it's okay with you, I still need to talk to Elena about it, just to make sure. Can I get back to you in a week?"

Mr. Goodman says enthusiastically, "Of course, *of course*. That's the right thing to do. Take it from an ol' married guy like me. You want to make sure the wife, I mean, fiancée, agrees. That's always the best course."

Elena and Mrs. Goodman walk into the room. Both men politely stand. Mrs. Goodman is positively glowing. "Oh, John, the children are even more precious and adorable than I ever dreamed possible." She asks anxiously, "Can we get the paperwork started right away?"

"Sure we can, sweetheart," Mr. Goodman assures her. "First thing tomorrow morning we'll fill out the petition and have it filed. Mrs. King said she would do everything to help expedite the process on our behalf. She's already talked to the judge and given us a strong recommendation." They hug each other tightly while Seth and Elena look on, holding hands.

Mrs. Goodman turns and hugs Elena. Both women are teary-eyed. "Thank you, Elena. I don't know what more I can say. I'm just so happy."

Elena hugs her again. "That says it all, Mary."

Mrs. Goodman looks at Seth and throws her arms around him, hugging him tightly. "Thank you so much for everything, Seth. I promise you; I promise you from the bottom of my heart that I will be the very best mother in the world to Emily and Chloë."

"I know you will be, Mrs. Goodman," Seth says softly.

They exchange handshakes and hugs. The Goodmans depart.

Seth stands next to Elena, subdued. Elena takes his hand and holds it affectionately. Concerned for him, she says, "You doing okay, babe?"

"I suppose so," he says. "Which story did Chloë pick out?"

Elena hugs him. "Oh honey, I'm marrying the sweetest man in the whole world. *Peter Rabbit*, she fell asleep after a few pages."

"That's one of our favorites." Seth pauses and sounds let down. "They took to Mrs. Goodman right away . . . even Emily. That surprised me a little."

"It's because they were here with you in this beautiful, safe, and loving home you've made for them. Emily believes in you completely, Seth. She knows anyone you invite into this wonderful home is a friend and someone she can trust. Did I tell you Mary isn't flying back to Dallas? She's going to stay in town and spend as much time with the children as she can. She's even volunteered to be my teacher's aide at school. We're meeting at the school first thing Monday morning. Don't you think that's wonderful?"

Seth nods in agreement but is unable to hide his sadness. An important change is coming, and even though he knows it's the right thing for Emily and Chloë, he can't help but feel melancholy about it.

Elena says encouragingly, "Did you see how happy the Good-mans are? They'll be perfect parents for Emily and Chloë, don't you think?"

"Yes, I really think so," Seth says, beginning to accept in his heart what he knows is best for the children. "I believe Mrs. Goodman will be a wonderful mother and Mr. Goodman will be a wonderful father. By the way, Mr. Goodman offered me a job tonight. Said he'd double my salary."

Elena blinks at the sudden news and asks innocently, "He offered you fifteen dollars an hour?"

"Yep, something like that," Seth says nonchalantly.

"What did you say?" She asks curiously.

"I said I'd have to talk to you about it first."

Elena playfully pats him on the chest. "That was the right answer, dear. Now that you've told me, decide what you think is best. I know you'll make the right decision for us." She gives him a quick peck on the cheek.

Seth shifts his stance and responds with his easy grin. "That's the grin I was hoping to see," Elena says cheerfully. They kiss tenderly.

CHAPTER THIRTY-FOUR

Judge Peters, dressed in his robes, sits behind his desk and reads a report. He is an elderly, distinguished-looking man with a head of white hair, a thoughtful face, attentive eyes, and wears spectacles that are perched low on his nose. Across from him sits Wickham Slagg, dressed all in gray, black hair slicked back. With his fingers pressed steeple-like against his lower lip, Wickham studies the judge. There is an uneasy tension in the air between the two men.

Wickham says solicitously, "Your Honor, I believe you can see that everything is in order."

Without looking at him, Judge Peters raises one hand to silence Slagg as he continues to read the report. After another minute, Judge Peters finishes the report and places it down on his desk. He leans back, takes off his glasses, and thoughtfully considers what he has read.

Unctuously, Wickham offers, "Judge Peters, as I was saying, I believe the reports from the lab, Child Protective Services, and from the court's own appointed psychologist, Dr. Fitzholder, leave no question that the children should be placed in the full custody of my clients. After all, Mrs. Slagg is the children's only living relative." Slagg sweeps his tongue slowly across his teeth as he measures the judge.

Judge Peters regards Slagg briefly before responding, "On the surface it would appear so. But the file on your clients causes me to suspect there's domestic violence, in addition to this one violent act by Mr. Emond Slagg against Miss Emily Fleming. This troubles me. It troubles me considerably to release children into his keeping."

Wickham is quick to agree. "Rightfully so, your Honor, rightfully so. But I can honestly tell you my client—my dear, dear brother—is deeply sorry for that one time incident. And, no formal charges about domestic violence have ever been filed. May I point out that Dr. Fitzholder recommended him unconditionally? She concluded he would be a very loving parent. It's all right there in her report."

Judge Peters is skeptical. "I read Dr. Fitzholder's report. I see the lab results. No sign of alcohol or drugs. CPS concluded the family environment has stabilized. Somehow, it all seems too good to be true for a man with his history. I don't abide child abusers."

Wickham is oily and obsequious. "Child abuser is rather harsh, I believe, sir. Still, your Honor is right to question. May I emphasize that all the reports are in agreement and that all are quite positive. Dr. Fitzholder's credentials are impeccable. And let's not forget that Mrs. Slagg is the children's only living relative. She longs to be a loving mother to the children. Her legal standing is unassailable." Slagg whisks his lapel and glances at his nails.

Judge Peters stares at Slagg. "Yes, the reports carry substantial weight. I have to seriously consider them. And Mrs. Slagg has preferential rights under the law. We both know that. I have found nothing in her history that causes me concern."

"Well then," Wickham oozes, "may I suggest we move forward right away so the children can be returned to their loving home as quickly as possible? Knowing how busy the court is, and in light of these glowing reports, is there really any need for a formal hearing? Your Honor could simply sign the order today and be done with it. There are no other interested parties involved."

Judge Peters looks at him warily. "You seem to be very anxious to conclude this matter, Mr. Slagg."

Wickham answers, affably sly, "Not at all, your Honor, I was only thinking of the children."

Judge Peters eyes Slagg suspiciously. "I see . . . That's very considerate of you. You are wrong, however, about there being no other interested parties. Another couple has petitioned to adopt these children."

Surprised, Wickham reacts with a flash of anger. "That's ridiculous!" He quickly catches his temper, smiles considerately, and continues courteously, "Another couple wishes to adopt, you say? Your Honor, in a case such as this, they have no standing."

Judge Peters observes Slagg distrustfully. "No, the couple doesn't. But the children are currently in the custody of The Children's Sanctuary, which does have standing." Then looking carefully at Slagg the judge adds, "The director, Mrs. King, whom I highly regard and respect, has recommended this couple without reservation. In fact, she was quite enthusiastic about them. Her endorsement means a lot to this court, Mr. Slagg."

Wickham can barely contain his outrage and says derisively, "The Children's Sanctuary can make a recommendation, certainly. But the law clearly supports Mrs. Slagg. As the only living relative, she has preferential rights. There's no doubt about the final outcome in this case, your Honor. The court's time shouldn't be wasted."

Judge Peters immediately responds sternly, "Mr. Slagg, I'll make the decisions about the court's time." He searches Slagg's face. "What reason do you have for wanting this ended so quickly?"

Wickham regains his composure and says smoothly, "No reason, your Honor. I only have the children's best interests at heart." He burnishes his perfectly manicured nails on his lapel and adjusts his silk handkerchief.

"I'm glad to hear you say that," Judge Peters says. "You asked for a formal hearing in April, and that's what you're going to get. You're right about the court's time. The docket is full except for one day, Good Friday. I'm going to schedule it that morning, two weeks from now."

Wickham protests, "Your Honor, Good Friday? Easter weekend? Isn't that a bit out of the ordinary?"

Judge Peters responds in a business-like fashion, "It's unusual, I know. But there's nothing more important than children. Making the right decision, and making it as soon as possible, is the best thing to do, even if the timing is a little inconvenient. Will you be calling witnesses?"

"Yes, I'll be calling two witnesses: Mr. and Mrs. Slagg. May I ask who is representing The Children's Sanctuary?"

"He's a fellow by the name of Terry Mason," the judge replies.

Wickham draws a deep breath and says, "Haven't heard of him. He's a family law specialist?"

"No. I understand environmental law is his specialty. He's working on this case pro bono, you know. The Children's Sanctuary couldn't afford to pay an attorney."

The corners of Wickham's mouth curl up in a sneer. Scarcely able to mask his contempt, he scoffs, "Really? Pity them."

Judge Peters pauses, regards Slagg dubiously, and remarks, "You know, Mr. Slagg. There have been rumors about you for years. Never lost a case, hmm . . . My senses tell me there's something more to this matter than meets the eye. I may be bound by the law, Mr. Slagg, but I am still allowed a private opinion. I don't like child abusers or the people who shield them. If I find out there are any shenanigans going on concerning these children, it won't go well for your client, or for you, I might add."

Wickham rises from his chair, flashes a counterfeit smile, fastidiously brushes off his suit, and tidies his handkerchief before saying, "Those rumors are planted by my jealous opponents who always lose to me, nothing more. Thank you for your time today, your Honor. May I take my leave?"

Judge Peters remains seated and responds formally, "You may."

The two men do not shake hands. Judge Peters continues to observe Slagg as he turns to leave the chambers. When Slagg reaches the door and opens it, he looks back over his shoulder at Judge Peters. "In two weeks, your Honor. Good Friday. I'll be ready."

Judge Peters gives Slagg a slight nod. Slagg leaves and closes the door behind him. The wise judge continues staring at the door for a moment, questioning Slagg and his true motives. Then, he returns his glasses to their proper place at the end of his nose, picks up the report from his desk, and peruses it again.

Outside the judge's chambers, a visibly upset Wickham Slagg stops, scrubs his teeth with his tongue, checks his manicured nails, fiddles with his handkerchief, flicks an imaginary speck off his suit, and hastily departs.

CHAPTER THIRTY-FIVE

Seth, Elena, Kathryn, and Terry sit at the kitchen table at the McAllister home. Seth is riddled with concern.

"Terry," Seth says, "it's unthinkable that there's any chance Emily and Chloë could be sent back to live with the Slaggs. Something's broken with the system. It can't be."

"I know how strongly you feel about this, Seth," Terry sympathizes. "I agree. It's not right. But I have to tell you, after reading the reports in this case and studying the law, there's a high probability the court will do just that. Judge Peters may not have a choice."

Seth is argumentative. "But you saw the pictures. You saw what Slagg did to Emily. How could any judge award custody to the Slaggs?"

Elena places her hand on Seth's forearm to calm him.

Worried, Kathryn asks her husband, "Are you sure?"

"Yes," Terry says, "the law's really one-sided here. Family takes precedence. Mrs. Slagg is the only living blood relative. The court must abide by the law."

Seth can't contain his anger. "The court can't ignore the abuse, can it? How will they get around that?"

"No, the court won't ignore it," Terry answers calmly. "But

it was a one-time event. I'm afraid these reports heavily favor the Slaggs. In fact, after reading her report, it seems to me this Dr. Fitzholder goes out of her way to recommend the man."

Elena's heart breaks for Seth's distress. She says to him, "Honey, everyone's going to do their best. I just know something good will happen. Terry, we have one more week to get ready for the hearing, don't we?"

"That's right," Terry says. "The hearing is a week from today. It's highly unusual the judge would set the hearing on the morning of Good Friday. It signals to me he's developed a very strong interest in this case. That's favorable, in my view. Judge Peters has an excellent reputation."

Elena reassures Seth. "See, that's something in our favor already."

Seth remains dismayed and frustrated. "I still can't believe it. Terry, I really appreciate your stepping in on such short notice to help us. I'm sorry we can't pay you."

"Don't mention it. I'm happy to help. Katie and I are very fond of the children. I'll do my best, but family law is new to me. It's really complex."

Kathryn speaks lovingly to her husband, "Sweetheart, we all know you'll do your best. You'll be wonderful. I know you will be."

CHAPTER THIRTY-SIX

It is Good Friday, and the time is nine a.m. The court hearing regarding custody of the Fleming children is about to begin. Seated at the table in the front of the courtroom is attorney Slagg. Seated next to him is Emond, and seated next to Emond is his wife, Nadine. Attorney Slagg is neatly dressed in his all-gray attire with his black hair slicked back. He carefully brushes off his expensive suit, adjusts his silk handkerchief, checks his polished finger nails, and sweeps his tongue across his teeth. Emond Slagg wears a cheap, ill-fitting brown suit and his same worn, scruffy shoes. The suit cannot disguise his brute-like features. Nadine Slagg, a thin and pale woman with dishwater blonde hair, wears a second-hand, bone-colored dress that accentuates her washed out appearance. Across from them at the other table is Terry Mason, sitting alone with a stack of papers in front of him. He is dressed in a dark blue suit, white shirt, and conservative tie. In the courtroom gallery are Kathryn, Elena, Seth, Humberto, Yesenia, Mr. and Mrs. Goodman, Juan-Carlos, Angel, Tomás, and a representative from Mrs. King's office. Also among them are a half-dozen other spectators who know Judge Peters professionally and are curious about a case he would schedule to hear on Good Friday. At the last moment, Mr.

Nakamura enters silently and takes a seat far back in the courtroom.

With his sleek smile, attorney Slagg nods to Terry. Terry acknowledges him.

Judge Peters enters the courtroom. The court bailiff asks everyone to rise. The judge sits down and motions for the gallery to be seated.

Judge Peters speaks, "First, I want to thank everyone for being here today. I know it's quite unusual to have a court hearing on the morning of Good Friday, but I feel the welfare of these children is so important that it is warranted. Secondly, I'll do my best to move this hearing along as quickly as possible. Counsel for Mr. and Mrs. Slagg, are you ready?"

Wickham stands, "Yes, your Honor."

Judge Peters looks at Terry. "Counsel for The Children's Sanctuary, representing Miss Emily Fleming and Miss Chloë Fleming, are you ready?"

Terry stands, "Yes, your Honor."

"Then let's begin. Mr. Slagg, you may call your first witness."

Wickham says, "Yes, your Honor. I would like to call Mrs. Nadine Slagg to the stand."

Clearly nervous, Nadine rises, crosses the short distance, and sits in the witness chair. She is sworn in. She looks small and fragile on the witness stand.

Wickham politely asks, "Mrs. Slagg, have you ever been in a courtroom before?"

Nadine answers meekly, "No sir, this is my first time."

"I thought so. It's understandable you're nervous, Mrs. Slagg. Anyone would be. I'm just going to ask you a few simple questions, and then we'll be done. Understand?"

"I understand." Nadine's response is barely audible.

Wickham nods graciously, "Thank you, Mrs. Slagg. Now, let me please begin by asking how long you and Mr. Slagg have been married?"

"Twenty-five years." Nadine's voice is shaky.

Breaking out in a wide grin Wickham says, "Congratulations, Mrs. Slagg, on such a loving, stable, and successful marriage. Are there children?"

With heartbreaking regret in her voice, she answers, "No sir. No children."

Considerately, Wickham asks, "Did you want children, Mrs. Slagg?"

Nadine's anguish is palpable. "Very much, I wanted children more than anything."

"I know this is a sensitive subject, Mrs. Slagg." Wickham brings a hand up and places it over his heart. "But would you please tell the court why you and Mr. Slagg never had children?"

Nadine begins tentatively, "My husband, he was away at sea for months at a time. My health ain't been so good during our marriage. Time got away . . . it was probably my fault . . ." She looks pitifully at Wickham.

Wickham nods and offers her false compassion. "Now, now, things like this aren't anyone's fault. Has your doctor told you that you can't have children? I mean—I'm sorry, but I have to ask this question—that, physically, you can't have children?"

Nadine struggles with her emotions. "I could when we was first married. But . . . I had this accident . . . I cain't have children no more."

"I'm so sorry, Mrs. Slagg," Wickham empathizes, "I know you would be a wonderful mother. Emily and Chloë Fleming came to live with you and Mr. Slagg, didn't they?"

Nadine brightens, "Oh yes, yes they did."

"Tell us about that, won't you Mrs. Slagg?"

"They's wonderful children. I fell in love with them girls right away. I was happy. I was a mother. It was my life's dream."

Wickham is pleasantly surprised by Nadine's unmistakable sincerity and thinks, "This mouse of a woman is coming across great. Her mousiness is an asset for us. The judge must love her already!"

"I can see you love the children, Mrs. Slagg." Wickham turns, and with his arms sweeping expansively, he theatrically addresses the gallery, "I believe we can all see that." Then turning back to Nadine, he confidently delivers his final winning question. "You love the children. Is this why you want them to come live with you and your loving husband?"

Wickham is surprised again, but this time it's anything but a pleasant surprise. Nadine doesn't answer his question. Instead she hesitates, drops her head, and stares down at her hands that are folded in her lap. Wickham is caught off guard and thinks, "Could this be a subtle display of defiance? Wasn't Emond supposed to keep this little woman in line?" He glances at Emond and clears his throat, stalling for time while he sorts out what to say next.

Wickham shifts his stance uneasily and speaks with solicitous concern. "Mrs. Slagg, again, it is perfectly understandable that you are nervous. I know some of my questions have been very personal in nature, quite sensitive, in fact. I apologize. I apologize most sincerely, ma'am. Perhaps you didn't hear my last question? Let me please restate what I asked. You love the children. You have longed to be a mother. These are the reasons why you want this court to award custody of the children to you and your husband. Isn't this correct?"

Again, Nadine hesitates. She lifts her head and looks nervously around the courtroom. She glances at her husband sitting at the table. When she does, Emond places his hand with the grotesque ring on it against his right cheek. Nadine visibly shudders.

Wickham grows anxious. He looks nervously at Emond.

Judge Peters says, concerned, "Mrs. Slagg, are you all right? Bailiff, please bring Mrs. Slagg some water." The bailiff brings a glass of water to her. Her lips tremble on the rim as she takes a sip. "Mrs. Slagg, please take all the time you need to compose yourself," the judge says.

Nadine takes another sip of water. Once more, she glances at her husband. Imperceptible to everyone else in the courtroom but Nadine, Emond taps his ring ever so slightly against his cheek.

"Are you feeling better now? Are you ready to go on?" Wickham asks generously.

Nadine answers in a submissive voice, "Yes, I think I'm better."

Flashing a false smile, Wickham says, "I'm so glad. Do you re–member my last question, Mrs. Slagg? I would be happy to repeat it."

Nadine is obviously upset, and her voice remains low and weak when she answers, "No sir, I remember it." She stares ahead and speaks as if to herself, "I do love them children. More than anything, I want to be a mother."

Wickham is relieved, but unable to completely mask his irritation. "Thank you, Mrs. Slagg. No further questions. Pass the witness."

Terry has been closely observing Nadine, as has Judge Peters. They both sense there is something wrong but can't quite grasp what it might be. It's hidden just under the surface, its menacing presence roiling the water.

Terry is very gentle with Nadine as he asks, "Mrs. Slagg, you seem to be upset. Are you frightened of something?"

Nadine hesitates. She is so anxious that her voice is barely audible when she feebly answers, "No sir."

Terry nods and continues considerately, "I believe you do love the children, Mrs. Slagg. And because I believe this, I just have one question for you: Mrs. Slagg, do you think it's in the best interests of the children, in the best interests of Emily and Chloë, to come and live with you and Mr. Slagg?"

Nadine is silent. She drops her eyes, looks down at her hands, and does not answer.

Terry waits patiently.

The hapless woman raises her head and glances fearfully at Emond and Wickham. Emond's face is dark with fury.

Tense and indecisive, Nadine looks nervously at Terry.

Judge Peters watches her closely. He grows more concerned.

"Mrs. Slagg?" Terry asks politely, "are you sure you're feeling well enough to continue?"

"Yes . . ." Her voice is shaky.

"Mrs. Slagg," Terry says softly, "let me please repeat the only question I have for you. Do you think it's in the best interests of the children to live with you and Mr. Slagg?"

Nadine looks at him pathetically. Fearing for her life, she responds in a whisper, "I do love them children." She drops her head in shame and sorrow, looks down at her hands, and appears to shrink into nothingness.

Terry realizes the woman didn't answer his question directly. However, out of compassion for her, he chooses not to pursue it. He sees she is terrified and about to become ill. "Thank you, Mrs. Slagg," he says. "Your Honor, I have no further questions for this witness."

Wickham also realizes the woman didn't answer Terry's question. But it was good enough in his estimation, particularly since Terry was a fool for not pressing Nadine on it. He thinks, "There's possibly more to this mousy woman than I thought. Well, no matter, that's Emond's problem. Once I get the money it's good riddance to the both of them."

Judge Peters regards Mrs. Slagg with concern. "You may step down, Mrs. Slagg," he says.

Nadine steps down from the witness chair. She rejoins Wickham and Emond at the table but is too frightened to look at them. The diminutive woman trembles. She hangs her head, stares down at the table, and makes herself smaller.

Judge Peters asks, "Mr. Slagg, do you have another witness you wish to call?"

Wickham responds, "Yes, your Honor. I would like to call Mr. Emond Slagg to the stand."

Emond rises from his chair and makes his way to the witness stand, limping and lunging forward with a hyena-like stride. As he is sworn in, he slouches in the witness chair and stares out at the gallery with malicious, compassionless eyes, appearing like an agitated predator confined, without bars, in the civility of the courtroom. The man looks crouched and ready to spring from the witness chair and rip out someone's throat.

Observing his brother on the witness stand, Wickham is already aggravated with him and thinking, "Sit up you fool, like I told you, and try to look less threatening, if that's possible!" Wickham clears his throat, rakes his tongue across his teeth, and speaks in a clipped manner to his brother. "Mr. Slagg, I know you can't hear well out of your left ear—a childhood accident. So if you don't hear a question clearly, please ask me or Mr. Mason over there to repeat it, and we will, all right?"

"Yes sir, I will."

Wickham begins, "I'd like to get right to the point of something that I believe is most critical to the court. You did push one of the children, did you not? I believe it was Emily."

Emond answers, feigning regret in his voice, "Yes sir, to my ever lastin' shame, I did. I'll regret it fer the rest of my days. I kin promise everone, it won't never happen no more."

Wickham pans around the courtroom. "I, for one, believe you, Mr. Slagg. Tell us what took place that night, please."

"I'd been out drinkin'. Got in the habit of drinkin' on them long, lonely voyages—a missin' my wife 'n' all. That demon rum gets a hold of ya. It can do terrible things. Turn a peaceable man like me inside out, it surely kin."

"To put it plainly," Wickham asserts, "you were drunk when you came home that night."

"Yes sir, I was. But ya gotta know I didn't hit Emily. I sort of pushed her. She fell. Hit herself on the bed frame. Jest an accident, it was. Weren't my fault."

"I understand," Wickham says. "The court has a record of that bed frame accident. Mr. Slagg, this is a very important question: do you still drink?"

Incredibly, Emond sounds sincere when he answers, "No sir! Nary a drop. I'm done with that demon rum forever, and that devil's done with me."

Wickham continues pointedly, "Mr. Slagg, you served a jail term of three months, and you were on probation for a year. Did you successfully complete your probation?"

"Yes sir. Never no problem keepin' to the straight and narrow. No sir, not now. I'm a reformed man!"

Wickham turns, smiling gratuitously at the gallery, enjoying his own performance. "Again, I believe you, Mr. Slagg. When did your probation end?"

Emond grins, exposing his fierce, yellow teeth. "February. End of February."

"I see," Wickham says, pleased with how the trial is going and confident now that his brother can pull this off. All the coaching helped. "And what was the first thing you did after your probation ended?"

Emond now plays his part perfectly as rehearsed and answers fervently, "I'da been a missin' them darlin' girls awful and jest couldn't wait to see 'em. The day after my probation ended—I mean the very next mornin' you understand—I hurried over to see 'em."

Wickham slyly follows up. "Why?"

"The gospel truth is, I fell in love with them sweet girls when they was living with me and Nadine. They was the light of my life, and Nadine's, too. We was both so happy. I was sorry for what I done. I wanted to see 'em as soon as I could, to start makin' up 'n' all."

"That makes perfect sense to me, as I'm sure it does to all of us, Mr. Slagg. Any good parent would feel the same way," Wickham says. "And would you please tell the court what happened when you went to see the children that morning?"

"It was like this," Emond begins. "First, I went to The Children's Sanctuary whar they was supposed to be and learnt they wern't thar. They was a stayin' with this other family 'cross town. So I went to find 'em. Spent the last of my money on a cab doin' it, too."

Wickham proceeds politely, "Now wait a minute, Mr. Slagg. How did you know to go to that address? I'm sure that information isn't something The Children's Sanctuary gives out to just anyone who asks, now is it?"

Emond's expression looks positively hurt as he answers, "Oh, no sir; at first they wouldn't give me nothin'. The girl at the front desk said I'd have to wait for her boss to get back. It was on a weekend, and she was thar all by herself."

"Well then," Wickham asks amiably, "how did you get this information?"

"I showed her the legal paper you gave me saying I had a right to see 'em. Then I told her she could get in a lot of trouble if'n she didn't tell me right off. I said I wasn't gonna wait around for no boss to get back neither. So the girl finally told me."

"That was quite an ordeal for you I'm sure, Mr. Slagg. Please tell us what happened that day when you arrived at the home where the Fleming children were staying."

"Well sir, I knocked on the door, real gentle like. I saw sweet little Emily look at me out the front winda. Then, before I'd know'd it, the door swings open and out steps this big man. He roughed me up some and threw me off the porch. Lucky I didn't break my neck. Then he threatened me. Said if I ever tried to see Emily and Chloë agin he'd find me and finish me."

"I see," Wickham says sympathetically. "That must have been pretty frightening for you. Were you frightened, Mr. Slagg?"

"Yes sir, 'n' terrible so. But more scart fer the children. I mean, what kinda place is that Children's Sanctuary anyways? Sendin' them little children to stay with such a violent man."

"What happened after that, Mr. Slagg?"

"Nothin'. I figured thar'd been enough trouble fer my sweet girls. I jest stayed away."

"Has that been hard for you?"

"It's been awful fer me and Nadine. All we want is to have our little family together agin. That ain't askin' fer too much, is it?"

"No, not too much at all," Wickham says considerately. "In fact, Mr. Slagg, I think it's the right thing for you and Mrs. Slagg to want, and it's clearly in the best interests of the children. Thank you, Mr. Slagg. Pass the witness, your Honor."

During Emond's testimony Nadine has continued to stare down at the table, frozen with fear and sinking further into her chair. Judge Peters and Terry have been observing her behavior. They each now believe that something is very wrong. Judge Peters suspects it's a domestic violence issue, yet another case where the victim has never filed charges, he thinks sadly.

Terry begins his cross examination. "Mr. Slagg, I heard you testify about the night Emily was hurt. The night you struck her and—"

Emond interrupts forcefully, "I ain't never said that! I ain't never said I struck her!"

Judge Peters reacts sternly, instructing Emond, "Mr. Slagg. Do not interrupt Mr. Mason when he is asking you a question. If your counsel objects to anything that Mr. Mason is asking you, he will announce his objection to the court, and the court will rule on his objection before you are required to answer the question. Do you understand?"

"Yes sir." Emond's voice sounds like a low growl. His eyes are hostile slits, trained on Terry.

"I'll rephrase, your Honor," Terry says. "Mr. Slagg, on the evening Emily was hurt, do you recall what time of the night it was?"

Emond replies craftily, "Uh . . . it's hard to remember. Wait, I know. It was ten o'clock. Yes sir, ten all right. I remember cause thar's a lighted clock radio in me and Nadine's bedroom. Thar was music playin'. It was ten, all right."

"I see. And when you pushed Emily, where did it happen?"

Emond becomes testy. "Whatta ya mean, whar? We was at home."

"I understand it happened at your home, Mr. Slagg. I'm asking you, what room in your home?"

"In them girls' room. Away from me and Nadine. At the back end of the house." Emond is agitated.

Wickham's eyes sternly focus on Emond, hoping he'll look his way. He had rehearsed Emond that this was the signal for him to calm down immediately.

Terry continues, "When you went down the hall into the girl's room, what was your intention?"

Wickham jumps up, saying, "Objection! Your Honor, we concede it happened at home. Counselor's on a fishing trip."

"Objection overruled," the judge says succinctly. "Answer the question, Mr. Slagg."

Emond stalls for time. He points to his left ear. "What'd ya say?"

Patiently, Terry repeats the question. "You walked down the hall and went into the girls' room. It was ten o'clock at night, and you were drunk. Why did you go into their room?"

Emond's temper spikes. "They was supposed to be asleep. They know'd the rules. I heard 'em in thar a laughin' and a movin' around. They was being real quiet about it, but I heard 'em jest the same. I went to see. They was dancin' in thar."

Terry looks at him evenly. "And that made you angry, Mr. Slagg?"

"Yeah, sure. Like I said, they know'd the rules. In bed by nine, and no whinin'!"

"So you got angry at them for disobeying your rules, Mr. Slagg, and that's when you pushed Emily?"

"Yeah, I guess. Somethin' like that."

Terry picks up a report from his desk. "The hospital report, which I have right here in my hand, states that in addition to the deep gash above Emily's left eyebrow that required extensive repair, there were multiple hematomas on both of her legs. The bruising was so severe that the little girl couldn't even walk for several days. You did that to her, didn't you Mr. Slagg?"

Emond responds angrily, "It wern't intentional. She fell and started a bleedin' everwhar. Fer some reason she and her sister hid under the bed. I was jest tryin' to pull her out to hep the child."

Terry presses him, "That's not true. Emily was terrified, wasn't she, Mr. Slagg? That's why she hid under the bed with her sister. You were forcefully grabbing at Emily, clamping your strong hands on her legs, pressing into her flesh with your fingers, grabbing and pulling on her."

"That ain't true!" Emond shouts.

Passionately now and his voice rising, Terry openly contests Emond's story. "Emily was struggling against you, wasn't she? She was scared to death—scared to death of what you would do to her or to her sister if you dragged her out from under the bed. Isn't that true?"

Emond's face is red with rage. "No! That ain't right! I wern't going to hurt her! Like I done said, I was tryin' to hep the child!" Emond glances at Wickham for help and sees his brother's austere countenance drilling into him. He remembers it's the signal that he must control himself. Emond lowers his voice and huffs indignantly, "Yeah. Some thanks I got. The girl kicked me in the face and more'n once. She was wearin' them shoes of hers with metal on 'em. She kicked me in the mouth and busted my lip."

During Terry's cross examination of Emond, Tomás has been quietly interpreting for Angel, whose face has steadily darkened as he listened. The gallery is riveted by the disturbing testimony and people feel uneasy.

Terry stares fiercely at Emond, knowing the man is lying at every turn. Terry works hard at regaining his own composure and then continues. "Mr. Slagg. You just testified on the night you pushed Emily that you came home drunk. It was ten o'clock because you remember seeing the lighted clock radio in your bedroom, and there was music playing. Is this correct?"

Wanting to bash the lawyer with his ring, Emond answers grudgingly, "Yeah, but I don't drink no more. I done said that."

Concerned about this exchange between Terry and his brother,

Wickham grows anxious again, thinking, "When is that stupid brother of mine going to do something right. He's about to blow it!"

Nadine continues to stare down at the table, rigid and white, looking like a marble statue.

Terry finds everything about Emond repugnant. He does his best to check his emotions and continues methodically. "Mr. Slagg, you were drunk; the music was playing; your bedroom is at the opposite end of your house from the children's bedroom, and you're hard of hearing. Yet, in your drunken state, you still heard the children quietly playing at the back of the house. I'm going to ask you this question again. When you walked down the hall into the girls' bedroom that night, what was your real intention? And this time, tell us the truth."

Wickham springs from his chair, crying, "Objection! Objection! Objection! Your Honor, counsel is clearly badgering the witness with wild speculation. Mr. Slagg's already testified that he heard them down the hall, and that's why he went to the children's room. Their home is small and has wooden floors. Tap shoes make a lot of racket on wooden floors. That's what the girl had on, tap shoes."

Terry stands immediately, glaring and shouting at Wickham. "Counsel is leading his client. He's already been well-coached. I'd like to get one honest answer out of this witness!" Terry breathes hard.

Judge Peters speaks critically, "That's enough from both of you. Sit down."

The attorneys sit down as ordered. They glare at each other from their chairs.

Addressing Terry, Judge Peters continues, "Mr. Mason, I under-stand you feel passionately about this case. But the fact is, you are speculating, and I can't allow that. I'm going to sustain Mr. Slagg's objection. However, let me add that the court is troubled by the witness's testimony." Then he turns to Wickham. "Mr. Slagg, as an officer of the court, I expect you to conduct yourself professionally at all times in this courtroom."

"Yes, your Honor. I apologize for my outburst," Wickham says.

Judge Peters glances at the clock. He takes off his glasses, rubs his eyes, and says, "Mr. Slagg and Mr. Mason, I've heard testimony and observed things this morning that compel me to re-examine the reports more carefully. I want to see if I may have missed something. It's Good Friday. I'm going to adjourn early. We'll finish tomorrow morning."

Wickham stands and addresses the judge, "Your Honor?"

"Yes, Mr. Slagg?"

"Your Honor, with all due respect, everyone wants what's in the best interest of the children, and we want it as quickly as possible. May I point out that, in this case, the law is perfectly clear. As a family member, and the only surviving one at that, my client, Mrs. Slagg, has a preferential custody right. Additionally, all of the reports in this case support my clients, without exception. Even the court's own appointed psychologist has recommended them very highly. There has been nothing offered here today by Mr. Mason that is really meaningful. He has provided no proof whatsoever to support his irresponsible speculation. May I ask your Honor to rule now in favor of my clients?"

Judge Peters looks at Terry and arches his eyebrows, "Mr. Mason?"

Subdued, Terry responds respectfully, "Your Honor, I still have a few more questions to ask Mr. Slagg."

Wickham becomes annoyed. "Your Honor, please, this farce should not be allowed to continue. The law is clear. May we have your ruling?"

Judge Peters is wise and wary. "Still in a hurry, Mr. Slagg?" he says cautiously. "People make mistakes when they get in a hurry. No, Mr. Slagg, more reading and reflection is the right thing for me to do in this case. Too much hangs in the balance for these children. I know it's unprecedented, gentlemen, but we'll begin again tomorrow morning at nine a.m. I expect we'll be finished in less than an hour. I'll adjourn for today unless one of you objects."

Believing he has won, Wickham answers smugly, "No objections from me, your Honor."

"No objections, your Honor," Terry responds, restrained.

Judge Peters addresses Terry. "Mr. Mason, before I adjourn for the day, you need to know I will only give you a few more minutes tomorrow morning to conclude your cross examination of this witness. Then, I will rule. As Mr. Slagg has pointed out, the law is clear, and I am bound by the law, whether I like it or not. Perhaps you'll have some hard evidence tomorrow morning that this court can consider."

"Thank you, your Honor," Terry says appreciatively.

Judge Peters turns to Emond on the witness stand. "Mr. Slagg, you may step down now. But remember, you will still be under oath when Mr. Mason continues his cross examination tomorrow. You are excused for today."

Emond slinks from the witness stand and limps to the table. Nadine does not look up as he approaches. He casts a bullying glare at her.

Judge Peters retires to his chambers. Silently, the participants in the case, and the people in the gallery, file out of the courtroom.

CHAPTER THIRTY-SEVEN

Seth, Elena, Terry, Kathryn, John and Mary Goodman, Margaret McAllister, Humberto, and Yesenia are gathered in the McAllister living room. The atmosphere is somber.

Terry is speaking. "I wish things had gone better in court today. But we have until tomorrow morning. I'll be reviewing all aspects of the case again tonight."

Seth is frustrated and deeply discouraged. "I know you will, Terry. I just can't understand it. How can everything be in their favor?"

"I don't know," Terry responds. "If it's any consolation Seth, I really believe Mrs. Slagg loves the children."

"I think she does, too," Elena agrees, and then adds with concern, "that woman was terrified. Didn't you see how she looked on the stand?"

"I know she was afraid. But there wasn't any way for me to explore the reasons for that," Terry explains.

"The reason for it was plain," Kathryn says adamantly. "Mrs. Slagg is a battered wife who is scared to death of her husband. The man's a brute. He ought to be put away."

"Honey," Terry says, his voice sounding tired from the day,

"I need something concrete, something indisputable to present to Judge Peters. Slagg's drug screen was clean; he completed probation without a hitch; the psychologist was adamant about her recommendation of the man, and CPS gave him and Nadine the all clear."

"What about Judge Peters?" Kathryn asks hopefully.

"I think we have reason for optimism there, honey," Terry answers. "Like the rest of us, I'm sure Judge Peters feels there's something really wrong here. He's trying to put his finger on it. I'm certain that's why he wanted more time. He has a very strong interest in this case. Everything the judge has done is completely unprecedented. I've never even heard of a judge continuing a case on a Saturday morning, let alone on Easter weekend."

Mary is encouraged by what she just heard. "You think Judge Peters will help the children?"

Considerately, Terry says, "He will if he can, Mary. But Judge Peters will not allow himself to be swayed by his personal feelings, no matter how sympathetic he may be. Only the evidence before him and the law will guide his final ruling."

"Do we have evidence that's favorable to us?" Mary asks, struggling against her growing despair.

"I haven't been able to find any," Terry responds softly.

Seth is angry. "What are you saying?"

Identifying with Seth's concern, Terry shakes his head sympathetically and tells him what he knows he needs to hear, "What I'm saying is, unless we can find and present hard evidence to the contrary tomorrow morning, Judge Peters has no other choice but to rule in favor of the Slaggs."

Mary begins to cry and buries her face in her husband's shoulder. Her husband shakes his head sadly, hugs his wife lovingly, and does his best to comfort her. The other women come to Mary's side to comfort her, too.

"No!" Seth shouts defiantly. "I promised Emily she would never see Slagg again. I won't break my promise to her. I can't!"

"Honey, honey," Elena calmly reassures him, "it's not over yet. Something will turn in our favor. I know it will."

Seth is nearly in tears. "But I promised her, Elena." Seth re–

members how confidently Emily answered him that afternoon in the playhouse: *'I know, because you never break a promise.'* Seth looks forlornly at Elena and says in a hushed tone of despair, "Emily believes in me."

"We still have until tomorrow morning, Seth." Terry encourages him. "I'll go over every detail of this case again tonight. I'm not giving up."

"Neither am I!" counters Seth, practically shouting his frustration. "They must have made a mistake somewhere. I'll find it. Even if it takes me all night, I'll find it!"

"Call me if you do," Terry says evenly. "I'll be up." He turns to his wife. "Sweetheart, are you ready to go? Good night everyone. I'll see you tomorrow Seth."

Kathryn and Terry leave through the front door. John Goodman nods to his wife that it is time to go. Humberto motions to Yesenia that they should leave as well. The men shake hands, the women hug, and they leave the house.

Mrs. McAllister, Seth, and Elena remain in the living room. There is a soft knock at the front door. Mrs. McAllister is puzzled, as she is not expecting a visitor. She goes to the front door and opens it. Mr. Nakamura stands there, holding a plant in a lovely white porcelain pot. It is his new variety of Easter lily.

Mrs. McAllister is surprised. "Mr. Nakamura. Please come in."

Mr. Nakamura bows to Mrs. McAllister. He steps into the room with his plant and places it on the floor beside him. He bows again to Seth and Elena.

Mr. Nakamura speaks with gentleness in his voice. "Good evening, Mrs. McAllister. Good evening, Seth. This lovely young lady must be your fiancée?"

"Yes, Mr. Nakamura," Seth says, "please let me introduce my fiancée, Elena Hernandez."

Mr. Nakamura smiles graciously at Elena. She smiles warmly in return and says, "I am so pleased to finally meet you, Mr. Nakamura. Seth has told me you've been travelling this past month."

Mr. Nakamura nods and says, "Thank you, Miss Hernandez. Yes, my annual trip to California to see firsthand the many new varieties of hybrids my friends have developed. I am most glad to be home now."

"That sounds so exciting," Elena says as she squeezes Seth's hand and nods genially to the old man.

Mrs. McAllister asks, "Mr. Nakamura, may I offer you some–thing to drink, some tea, perhaps?"

"Thank you, but no, Mrs. McAllister."

"I saw you in court today, Mr. Nakamura," Seth says.

"Yes, I was there."

"What did you think?"

"I do not think Mr. Slagg was telling the truth. I believe Mrs. Slagg is a woman of great strength who has endured much pain and sorrow."

"Yes," Seth agrees, "we all suspect she has suffered a great deal."

"That poor woman," Mrs. McAllister observes gravely. Then hoping to lift the mood, she changes the subject, points to the plant, and says, "Seth told me you were developing a new variety of Easter lily. Is this one?"

"Yes, the first one," Mr. Nakamura answers modestly. "It would bring me much honor if you would accept it as an Easter gift, Mrs. McAllister."

"Thank you, Mr. Nakamura. You are so thoughtful. Yes, I would love to have it. It will be beautiful right here in the living room."

Mr. Nakamura bows and, declining Seth's offer to help, picks up the plant and places it on the floor by the coffee table. The flowers have not opened but appear ready to bloom at any moment.

Mr. Nakamura turns to Seth. "Deshi, you are much distressed?"

"Yes, I'm afraid for the children," Seth responds with strong emotion in his voice. "It looks like we could lose tomorrow. I can't let that happen."

Mr. Nakamura nods understandingly, contemplates the passion in the young man's voice, and looks Seth directly in the eyes, saying wisely, "Seth, the darkest place in the world is at the foot of a lighthouse. To find the light, all people must do is lift up their eyes."

Seth is emphatic. "There's more to it than that, Mr. Nakamura. I've got to find answers tonight that support our side. Time is running out."

Mr. Nakamura observes Seth closely for a long moment before responding placidly, "Perhaps you should be still, dwell upon your faith, and allow the answers to come to you. Might not that be better?"

Seth answers impatient and agitated, "It doesn't work that way with the law, Mr. Nakamura. It's up to me to get hard evidence. I have to find it."

Mr. Nakamura simply nods. "I see," he says serenely. "Mrs. McAllister, thank you for your hospitality. Miss Hernandez, I am so pleased to meet you." He bows and prepares to leave.

Mrs. McAllister says kindly, "Thank you for the Easter lily, Mr. Nakamura. It will be beautiful, I know."

"Mr. Nakamura, I enjoyed meeting you," Elena says. "You'll be receiving a wedding invitation soon."

"Thank you, Miss Hernandez. I look forward to attending the wedding." Mr. Nakamura smiles and bows once again to the ladies. He bows to Seth, who bows deferentially in return.

Mrs. McAllister shows the elderly man to the front door and opens it for him. Mr. Nakamura pauses at the door and turns back to Seth. "Remember, Deshi, this is a weekend for miracles." He bows once more, turns, and leaves.

Closing the front door behind him, Mrs. McAllister says to Seth and Elena, "He's such a gentle, wonderful man." She reflects upon Mr. Nakamura for a moment, then continues, "It's been a long day, and if you don't mind, I'm going to bed now. There's so much to do tomorrow morning with my ladies group. We're getting the church ready for Easter services on Sunday. Good night, Elena. Good night, son." Mrs. McAllister hugs Elena and kisses Seth on the cheek.

"Good night, Mrs. McAllister," Elena says sweetly.

"Good night, Mom," Seth says.

Seth and Elena are left alone in the living room. They sit on the couch. Elena reaches and holds Seth's hand and says, "Babe, if there's an answer, I know you'll find it."

Seth is filled with anxiety. "I've got to, Elena. I can't let the children down. I can't let you down."

Elena cannot hide her worry for him and presses his hand for emphasis. "You could never let me down, never. I love you with all of my heart, Seth. Nothing could ever change that. No matter what happens tomorrow, I believe things will turn out for the best. I really do."

"I hope so. Will you be there?"

"Of course I will be. I'll be right beside you, tomorrow and always." Elena kisses him softly on the cheek and rises to leave. She picks up her coat from the back of the chair. Seth helps her with it, and they walk to the door. Elena speaks tenderly to him. "Seth, I believe Mr. Nakamura is right."

"You mean about not doing anything?" he responds incred— ulously.

"He wasn't saying that, honey. He meant if you depend on your faith and rely on God completely, God will be faithful."

Seth remains upset, and his distress is getting the better of him. "No, the answer's in that stack of case material on the kitchen table. It's somewhere in there. It has to be. I'll go over it again and again, line by line, until I find it!"

Elena smiles lovingly at him and gently says, trying her best to be encouraging, "If it's there, I know you'll find it. Good night honey, and remember, no matter what comes, I'll always love you. You get started. I'll walk myself to my car. It's just in the driveway."

Seth opens the door for her. They embrace.

As Elena walks to her car, her overwhelming concern for Seth causes a swell of tears to spill from her eyes and trickle down her cheeks. She has decided not to go straight home. Instead, she is going to church to pray for Seth, for the children, and for a miracle.

CHAPTER THIRTY-EIGHT

After Elena leaves, Seth immediately pours over the case material. He is now sitting alone at the kitchen table reading, focusing on a page of a report, intently studying every line. The clock on the wall reads three-thirty in the morning. A chaos of single sheets of paper are scattered across the table. Seth looks haggard, weary, and literally at his wits' end. Frustrated, he throws the report aside and angrily slams his fist on the table. "I can't find anything!" He picks up another report and scans it quickly. Finding no help there either, he flings it to one side, disheartened. "There's nothing here. Nothing! How can that be?" Panic is breathing down his neck. But he refuses to give up, believing he can find the answer. Seth grabs another case binder he's reviewed many times already and frantically flips through the pages, desperately searching for clues.

Suddenly, he stops. Seth slowly sets the binder to one side and stares ahead hollowly. At this moment, he realizes he will not be able to find any evidence in these files to support his side. The full weight of it falls on him like a thousand pound sledge hammer. Seth is crushed. He knows he is powerless to do anything about it. The young man crosses his arms on the table in front of him and rests his face on his forearms. He is exhausted. Every ounce of his strength and will have been drained from his body. Seth weeps. He feels abandoned and completely alone. He feels like he's deep underground in a labyrinth, hopelessly lost in just one of a million dark mazes where neither God nor man can find him. As he weeps with his head down on his arms, like in a dream, he hears Mr. Nakamura's voice and Elena's voice calling to him from far away:

"To find the light, all people must do is lift up their eyes."

"If you rely on God completely, God will be faithful."

Seth lifts his head, and rivulets of tears course down his cheeks. He turns in his chair and stares at the cross on the wall behind him. He rises from his seat and stands before the cross, continuing to gaze at it. Then, kneeling down on both knees on the kitchen floor, he clasps his hands together in front of him, looks up at the cross, and prays with an open and contrite heart:

"Dear God, please help me. Please God, I need You. I cannot do this alone. The children need saving, but I cannot save them. I alone have never been able to save them. I know that now. Only You, Lord, only You are capable. Please forgive me my human pride. I place it all in Your hands. Not mine, Lord, but Your will be done forever and ever. Amen."

CHAPTER THIRTY-NINE

It is the next day, Saturday morning of Easter weekend. The clock on the wall in the McAllister kitchen reads eight o'clock. Mrs. McAllister has prepared breakfast. She is dressed and waits for her friends from the ladies group to pick her up for their two hours of work preparing the church for Easter Sunday. There is a large stack of mail piled on the kitchen table. Seth comes into the kitchen looking tired. He is dressed in a navy blue suit for court and sits down at the table, subdued. Mrs. McAllister brings him a cup of coffee.

His mother tries to be cheerful. "Good morning, sweetheart; is everything okay?"

"I guess," he answers, downcast. "Thank you for the coffee. Mom, are you leaving for church soon?"

"Yes sweetheart, my ride should be here in a few minutes. Are you sure you're okay, dear? You look a little tired."

"I'm fine, Mom." Seth looks at the large stack of mail on the table and begins sorting through it, disinterested. "Looks like an awful lot of mail for today," he says, absently.

"Heavens no," his mother says. "It's too early for Saturday's mail. That's three day's worth. I've been so busy I completely forgot about it. There was so much of it, there wasn't enough room on the counter. What a funny dream I had last night. I was sleeping and suddenly woke up. I sat straight up in bed, worried about the mail. It was three-thirty in the morning! Imagine that. Before I started breakfast I went to the mailbox and brought it all in."

Seth meanders through the mountain of mail. "It sure piled up. The usual pieces of junk mail and bills, I see."

Suddenly animated and fussy, his mother says, "The mailbox was stuffed full. I had to reach way back to get the last little bit, and it was nothing but a piece of trash. Now who would do a thing like that? Throw trash in our mailbox! And did I ever tell you someone put a big dent right on top of it? What is the world coming to?"

Seth looks up from the pile and smiles weakly at his mother. He continues sorting through the mail. He begins to unfold a wadded up piece of paper. "That's it," his mother says. "That piece of trash I was telling you about. Now who would be mean enough . . ." She trails off in mid-sentence, staring at Seth.

Seth has unfolded the crumpled paper and placed it on the table in front of him, smoothing out the wrinkles. He carefully reads it, wholly absorbed. His face suddenly changes to joyful elation, and he lets out an ear-splitting *whoop*! Mrs. McAllister is so startled her mouth drops open. Seth jumps up from the table and hugs his mother tightly.

"Mom! Mom! You wonderful, wonderful woman you!" Ecstatic, he begins dancing her around the kitchen.

"Seth. Honey, stop," his mother cries. "For Heaven's sake, what did I do?"

"For Heaven's sake? Yes, for Heaven's sake all right." He hugs her again.

"But what dear? Please tell me what I did," she asks, completely at a loss.

"Just everything!" Seth is practically leaping for joy.

Placing one hand up to her mouth, Mrs. McAllister says, awestruck, "I did? Are you going to tell me what it is?"

"Mom," he says hurriedly, "I don't have time to explain now. You're the best though. I love you."

He grins at her as he picks up the kitchen phone and begins punching in a number. "Terry?"

"Hello Seth," Terry answers wearily. "I was up most of the night. I'm sorry to tell you this, but I haven't been able to find anything that will help us."

Seth exclaims, "Terry, I have it! I've got what we need. I know it. You will too when I show it to you. No time to talk about it now. I'll meet you in court."

"That's great news! You know as much about this case as I do, so I'm sure you've found what we need. I'm ready to give that guy Slagg a real kick in the pants—him and his brother, both. Hurry though. Court's in session in thirty minutes."

"I'm leaving now."

They each hang up. Mrs. McAllister continues to gaze at Seth, baffled. Seth picks up the phone again and quickly taps in another number. Elena answers on the other end.

"Hello?"

"Babe, it's a miracle!" Seth is practically shouting.

"Seth! You found what you needed." Elena says, echoing Seth's enthusiasm.

"I'm sure of it, Elena. But I didn't find it. It found me."

"That's wonderful. Tell me about it, honey."

"I will later, when there's more time. I've got to meet Terry in court right away. This is how you can help me. Instead of coming to court this morning, would you please go to the Sanctuary and get Emily and Chloë and take them to your parent's home. I'll meet you there after court, all right?"

"Of course, I'll do whatever you need me to do. I'll leave right away."

"Thanks babe. I love you very much."

"I love you too, Seth. Goodbye, I'll see you soon."

Mrs. McAllister stands there bewildered, looking at her son. Seth hugs her another time and quickly kisses her on the cheek. "You're the best, Mom. The absolute best! I love you." Seth places the crumpled piece of paper in his pocket and hurriedly leaves for court.

Mrs. McAllister, still completely mystified, watches her son go.

When he is gone, she lightly touches her cheek where he kissed her and says pleasantly, "I love you too, sweetheart."

As Seth hurries to the car, he punches another number into his cell phone. The voice on the other end answers, "Joseph and Sons Cab Company, may I help you?"

CHAPTER FORTY

In the courtroom Saturday morning, Judge Peters sits at his bench. He wears his glasses on the end of his nose and studies papers. The Slagg brothers and Nadine are seated at their table. Wickham and Emond are supremely confident. Nadine looks down, troubled and muted. Today she wears a simple, navy blue blazer over a light blue blouse that softens her otherwise blanched appearance. Terry sits at his table, glancing anxiously towards the entrance, waiting for Seth to arrive. Kathryn, Humberto, Yesenia, Tomás, Angel, Juan-Carlos, and John and Mary Goodman are in the gallery, speaking softly to each other and waiting for court to begin. The representative from Mrs. King's office is there, and the other half-dozen interested spectators have also returned. Alone, far back in the gallery, Mr. Nakamura sits, unnoticed.

Whispering in his brother's good ear and bragging in an egoistic, smug tone, Wickham says, "Emond, we've got this judge right where we want him. He'll follow the dictates of the law, regardless of his personal feelings. Watch me; I'm about to take that hard streak of stubborn morality of his and hit him right between the eyes with it."

"Yeah, a real goodie two shoes," Emond growls.

Wickham, giddy with hubris, adds, "That guy Mason's a

featherweight. Just answer his questions, dear brother, and we'll be out of here quick. It's time you started thinking about how you're going to spend your share of the trust money."

Emond's eyes fill with gluttonous anticipation. "Yeah Wickham, them double rum shots and warm sandy beaches sound awful nice."

Judge Peters puts down the papers he is reading and looks out over his spectacles, surveying the courtroom. He clears his throat, signaling he is ready to begin, and says, "Thank you, ladies and gentleman, for coming here on a Saturday morning. I know it's highly unusual. Even more so being Easter weekend. I won't keep you long this morning." The judge looks at Emond. "Mr. Slagg, please re-take the stand. Remember, you are still under oath."

Emond lumbers to the witness chair and sits down. He looks every bit as menacing now as he did yesterday. He's wearing the same suit and hasn't changed his sweat stained shirt. Wickham folds his hands under his chin, holding his fingers steeple-like and pressed under his lower lip. He observes shrewdly and swishes his tongue across his teeth.

Judge Peters asks, "Mr. Slagg, are you ready?"

Wickham rises and says solicitously, "Yes, your Honor, and thank you, your Honor."

Unimpressed, Judge Peters says dismissively, "Sit down, Mr. Slagg." The judge turns to Terry, "And you, Mr. Mason. Are you ready?"

Terry scans the doorway, stands, and answers, "Your Honor. If it pleases the court, may I have five minutes more before beginning? I'm expecting some important information to arrive. It'll be here any moment."

Wickham rises immediately. "Your Honor, I must object. Counsel has had plenty of time to prepare his case. He doesn't deserve any special favors."

Seth enters the courtroom as Wickham finishes his sentence. Terry motions to him to come over to the table.

Not having noticed him in the gallery yesterday, Emond sees Seth enter and stand next to Terry. Emond's nostrils widen, his face reddens, and he glares at Seth with cold hatred in his eyes.

"Your Honor," Terry says respectfully, "it's just arrived. May I have two minutes to look at it, please?"

"Mr. Slagg, two minutes?" Judge Peters inquires.

Wickham shrugs and says derisively, "Of course, your Honor, two minutes won't change a thing." Wickham sits down in his chair and winks at his brother that there's nothing to worry about.

Seth shows the wrinkled paper to Terry and explains its significance. Terry is careful not to display any emotion and shakes Seth's hand. Seth goes to the gallery and sits in the front row. Terry looks at Judge Peters and nods that he is ready to continue his cross-examination.

"You may begin, Mr. Mason," the judge says.

"Thank you, your Honor." Terry begins, "Mr. Slagg, you testified yesterday that you went to see Emily and Chloë Fleming, whom I will refer to as 'the children,' as soon as you could. Is that correct?"

Emond is uncharacteristically cordial. "Yes sir, right away, cause I jest couldn't wait to see them darlin' girls. I hurried right over."

Wickham is delightfully pleased by Emond's convincing tone and thinks, "He's going to be just fine up there today. That final bit of coaching last night did the trick."

"When was that, Mr. Slagg?" Terry asks.

"Whatta ya mean, when?"

"You testified that you went to see the children as soon as you could, Mr. Slagg. When was, 'As soon as you could?'"

"That'd be the very next mornin' after my probation done ended."

"Mr. Slagg, please remind us, when did your probation end?"

Emond answers comfortably, "The end of February. Like I said, I hurried right over to see my girls."

"Yes. I believe you said you took a cab?"

"Yes sir, and spent my last dollar doin' it, too. But what's money?"

"Mr. Slagg, do you remember the name of the cab company that took you to the home where the children were staying at the time?"

Emond snorts, "Nah, jest some cab company. Could've been any one of 'em."

"Yes, it could have been," Terry says, disarmingly friendly. "But if I told you it was the Joseph and Sons Cab Company, would that be correct?"

Emond rubs his chin thoughtfully. "Yeah, now that you mention the name, that was the one. Sure was. Sure enough was."

"Do you recall signing a receipt, Mr. Slagg?"

"Yeah, I signed one. Don't know what happened to it though."

Wickham stands and with a dramatic hand gesture speaks impatiently, "Your Honor, please, this witness has already testified he went to see the children. If Mr. Mason has some important information, which obviously doesn't exist, let him present it. He's wasting everyone's time."

"Mr. Mason, where are you going with this?" Judge Peters asks.

"If your Honor will please allow me to continue a moment longer, I'm getting to that, sir."

"Please continue, Mr. Mason," Judge Peters instructs.

Wickham shakes his head in disgust, sits down, and glances at his watch. He resumes his former posture with his hands folded together under his chin and fingers formed steeple-like and pressed beneath his lower lip. Feeling aggravated and impatient, he continues to observe.

Terry continues smoothly, "Yes, Mr. Slagg. You did sign a receipt, and I have it right here."

Wickham stands again and speaks in a condescending tone. "Your Honor, this is counsel's new piece of information? Well, good for him! It only proves what we've been saying all along; my client couldn't wait to see the children because he and his wife love them."

Surprising his opponent, Terry agrees, saying apologetically, "Mr. Slagg is correct, your Honor. I concede it's not much. But I'd still like to enter it into evidence, if that's all right with Mr. Slagg."

Judge Peters asks, "Any objections, Mr. Slagg?"

Wickham quickly replies contentiously, "A receipt that proves our case? Of course not. Please enter it—anything to hurry up this hearing." He glances impatiently at his watch again and sits down.

Terry hands the cab receipt to the court reporter, and it is entered into evidence. Then he continues his cross examination. "Mr. Slagg, the day after your probation ended, you went to the home where the children were staying. When you arrived, please tell us again, what happened?"

Emond glances at his brother. The lawyer smiles and nods for him to answer. Now appearing bored, Wickham whisks his lapel, looks critically at his cuticles, and brushes his tongue across his teeth.

"I knocked on the front door real gentle like," Emond says. "Emily come to the winda, looked out, 'n' disappeared. The next thing I know'd this big fella comes out, pushes me around, 'n' throws me off the porch." He points at Seth sitting in the front row of the gallery. "That's him! Sittin' right thar!" Mocking him, Emond taunts, "'The next time I see ya it'll be the end of you.' Ha! I'm still here, ain't I?"

Terry ignores Emond's taunt and continues, unruffled. "Mr. Slagg, you were at the front door, and Emily came to the window. You saw her. You're absolutely sure it was Emily?"

"Yeah, course I'm sure. We was jest a few feet away."

"A few feet away," Terry repeats. "And by the terms of your probation, you were ordered to stay at least one thousand feet away from the children. Isn't that correct, Mr. Slagg?"

Venom seeps into Emond's tone. "Yeah, so what? I wern't on probation no more."

Terry turns to Judge Peters. "Your Honor, may I ask the court to please hand the cab receipt to the witness."

"Bailiff," orders Judge Peters, "take the receipt from the court reporter and please hand it to Mr. Slagg."

Emond glances furtively at his brother, who winks again, signaling that there is nothing to be concerned about.

"Mr. Slagg, is that your signature at the bottom?" Terry asks.

Growing more belligerent, Emond answers, "Yeah, it's mine. I signed it. So what?"

"You're sure, Mr. Slagg?"

"I done said I signed it!" Emond insists, his temper flaring.

"Thank you, Mr. Slagg. Now you testified that your probation was over at the end of February. Correct?"

"Yeah, that's what I said all right."

Terry eyes him carefully. "When exactly was that, Mr. Slagg?"

"I done said that." Emond starts contentiously and then glances at his brother who gives him an instructive look. Emond turns slyly sociable and says, "And it was a blessin' to the Missus and me. February's the shortest month. Ever'one knows that. So I hurried right over thar the very next mornin' after the twenty-eighth."

Terry is cool, calm, and collected. He nods amiably, "Yes, we finally agree on something Mr. Slagg, a blessing indeed. There, in the upper right hand corner of the receipt, is the date. Would you please read it out loud?"

Emond scowls angrily at Terry and then searches the receipt, bringing it close to his face, squinting and peering at it. He stares at something on it for a long time. Slowly, his face becomes grotesque and goes purple with rage. His mouth gapes open like a sinkhole, and he looks up, mortified; his face filled with a mixture of fury and dread. He stares at his brother in shock and anger.

Wickham looks back at him, bewildered and suddenly alarmed. His face is a confused question mark.

The gallery is completely silent.

Terry studies Emond carefully. "Mr. Slagg, what is the date on the receipt?"

Emond doesn't answer. He stares malevolently at his brother, and his face has now gone black with unbridled ferocity. He holds the receipt to one side in his white-knuckled fist.

Judge Peters instructs sternly, "Mr. Slagg, answer Mr. Mason's question."

Emond stares down at the receipt and then looks up slowly and glowers coldly at his brother. Speaking to Wickham, he answers with murder in his tone, "February twenty-ninth."

The gallery shifts in their seats and begins whispering excitedly. Judge Peters taps his gavel, asking for order in the court. The gallery quiets down immediately.

"Yes," Terry says pointedly, "that's correct, Mr. Slagg. February twenty-ninth. Once every four years the shortest month of the year has one additional day. This is one of those years, a blessing indeed!"

Wickham jumps up from his chair in full panic. "Your Honor, this is some kind of trick!"

Terry answers confidently, "No trick, your Honor. I've just been told that Joseph and Sons Cab Company has corroborated that it drove a passenger by the name of Emond Slagg to the McAllister address on February twenty-ninth. They have a record of the date and time. This receipt proves that Mr. Slagg went to see the children while he was still on probation. Mr. Slagg himself testified that he was within a few feet of Emily Fleming, clearly a violation of the terms of his probation."

Wickham pleads, "Your Honor! It was just an honest mistake! Surely this court cannot . . . it will not . . . allow just one day . . ."

Judge Peters interrupts him harshly, "Mr. Slagg. Sit down, and be quiet. You needn't be instructing me on what this court can and cannot allow. The law is the law. You know how I feel about that."

Wickham has turned ashen and dutifully sits down, his head drooping and his eyes staring at the table. His tongue has gone dry. He doesn't have the energy to rake it across his teeth.

Nadine remains silent. She hasn't flinched, and she hasn't lifted her head.

Emond stares balefully at his brother, his face boiling with anger.

Judge Peters instructs, "Bailiff, please take the evidence from Mr. Slagg, and hand it to me." The bailiff does so; the judge reads it and places it in front of him. Looking down at Emond, Judge Peters says severely, "Mr. Slagg, this court believes any violation of probation is a very serious offense. You were on probation for abuse of a child, a crime I consider to be one of the most heinous."

Emond hasn't shifted his eyes from his brother.

The judge turns his attention to Wickham. "Mr. Slagg, I've heard testimony in this hearing that causes me great concern. You can be certain that I will apply the letter of the law. Your client is looking at a long jail sentence, to be sure."

Emond snaps at the judge's words. Terrified, he panics and begins shouting wildly at his brother in an uncontrollable rage. "This is your fault, Wickham! Them snotty kids ain't been nothin' but trouble fer me! If'n you think I'm going to jail all alone . . ."

Wickham stands abruptly and shouts back, "Shut up, Emond!"

Emond mocks him and screams, "Shut up? Shut up? You're the one that told me the fix was in on everthin'! The psychologist, the lab, everthin'! We couldn't lose!"

"Be quiet, you fool! You're making things worse!" Wickham yells.

Emond howls back, "Fool, am I? A fool for listenin' to you, brother! This is your fault! I ain't goin' down without you!"

Wickham completely loses control and shrieks, "My fault? No! You Emond! You! If you hadn't hit that child with your ring, none of this . . ."

Realizing what he just said, Wickham stops at once, sits down stiffly, and stares at the table.

Emond's eyes are wild with fright. He jumps off the stand and rushes down the aisle towards the courtroom exit. Angel stands up quickly, blocking his way with his massive, muscular body. Emond stops in his tracks and looks up at Angel, quaking. Angel's wrath-filled eyes blaze into Emond's petrified eyes. Silently, Angel raises his colossal right arm and points toward the judge. Slinking back, Emond cowers from the vengeful Angel, turns around, skulks slowly to the front, and stands before Judge Peters with his head hung low. This wife beater, this child abuser, is totally defeated. His brother Wickham is slumped at the table with his face in his hands.

Judge Peters says pointedly, "That was a very enlightening outburst, Mr. Slagg. Bailiff, please handcuff and shackle Mr. Slagg. But first, remove his ring. It's important evidence now."

The bailiff does as the judge has ordered. Then he takes Emond, handcuffed and shackled, to a chair by the door that leads to jail.

"Now bailiff," the judge orders, "please handcuff and shackle the other Mr. Slagg."

Wickham jerks up his head, his face ghostly white and terrified. "Me? Why me, Judge? I haven't done anything wrong. It was all Emond's fault!"

"You haven't done anything wrong, Mr. Slagg?" Judge Peters challenges. "From what I've just heard your client say, you're deeply involved with evidence tampering, witness tampering, bribery, obstruction of justice, and, oh yes, perjury—that child fell and cut herself on the bed frame, indeed. Mr. Slagg, you and your kind represent the worst in the legal profession. And even though your group is small in comparison to the many fine lawyers and judges who practice and serve with integrity, still it is the people like you in our midst who do such great harm to their clients and to the legal profession. It may be that betrayal of trust happens to some extent in every area of society, and for this reason we must always be vigilant. But it is particularly loathsome when it occurs in those professions where innocent children, desperate people, and guileless clients are betrayed in the worst ways by the very people whose positions and titles alone invoke inviolable trust and confidence. The law is one of those professions, and so are the clergy, the medical profession, and the financial services sector. Mr. Slagg, I believe Hell reserves a special place for people like you. But in this life, there is another special place reserved for you. Bailiff!"

The bailiff quickly handcuffs and shackles Wickham and puts him in a chair next to his brother. Judge Peters addresses the brothers severely, "You both will answer for your crimes; I assure you. But that can wait until Monday. Remove the prisoners."

The bailiff removes the Slagg brothers from the courtroom and takes them to jail. Emond shoves his brother as they go through the door.

Judge Peters looks at the gallery and continues, "Now, we still have important business to finish, and that is the custody of two children. Mrs. Slagg, may I ask you to take the stand again?"

Nadine looks up from the table where she has been sitting in stony silence the entire time. The slight woman rises from her seat and walks slowly to the stand, looking like she is in agony as she seats herself.

"Mrs. Slagg, there is no reason to be alarmed, I assure you," Judge Peters says compassionately. "I will be the only one asking you questions, and they will be few. Would you like something to drink?"

Nadine, with Emond and Wickham out of the courtroom, relaxes perceptibly and responds quietly, "No thank you, your Honor."

Judge Peters says, "Mrs. Slagg, I can't help but believe you were forced into this hearing by your husband and his brother. Would that be correct?"

"Yes sir. I was afraid of what Emond would do to me if I didn't do what they said."

Judge Peters nods sympathetically, "I thought so. Mrs. Slagg, this court is in a position to recommend counseling and refer you to a women's treatment facility. There would be no expense to you."

"Could Emond get at me?" Nadine softly asks.

"No, Mrs. Slagg. Mr. Slagg will be in prison for at least twenty years, I should think. You needn't be afraid of him ever again."

Nadine looks at the judge gratefully. "Then, yes sir, your Honor. I would like to get help. I know I need it. Most days I cain't hardly get out of bed no more. I'm sick-like. I been this way a long time."

"I'll see to it right away," the judge says. "Mrs. Slagg, there is still the matter of the Fleming children. Another couple has petitioned the court to adopt them. They are here today, sitting in the gallery. But you are the Fleming children's only living relative, and the law gives you preferential rights. Do you wish to assert your rights over the children?"

Nadine hesitates, then says, "Your Honor, I ain't told the complete truth. I was afraid to."

"Mrs. Slagg, if you didn't tell the truth because you were afraid, the court understands," Judge Peters promises her. "But it is very important that you tell the truth now. What part of your earlier testimony do you wish to correct?"

Nadine answers softly, "All I ever wanted to be was a mother, a good mother. It weren't no accident . . . It weren't no accident at all where I couldn't have children. When Emond was away on one of them long boat trips, I had my tubes tied. I couldn't bring precious children into this world with that monster." She begins to cry quietly. "If Emond had found out the truth, he would have killed me. He would have killed me for defying him."

Gripped by Nadine's poignant testimony, the gallery has gone completely silent. They realize the woman is speaking from the depths of her soul.

Judge Peters responds sympathetically, "I'm sorry, Mrs. Slagg. Truly, I am very sorry. Still, you have an important decision to make today. Please, what do you wish to do about the children?"

As if pleading, Nadine responds, "You have to understand. I'd lost all hope of ever being a mother. Then Emily and Chloë come to our home. I was a mother. I was a *good* mother. I was living my life's dream. They's wonderful children. Your Honor, I ain't got much education. I cain't always say things in a pretty way. But I know right from wrong. I know what's best for my darling Emily and my sweet Chloë."

Bravely, at this moment, Mrs. Goodman rises from her seat in the gallery. She stands silently, steadily gazing at Nadine.

Judge Peters remains observant and silent, wisely discerning that these two good women, if left alone, will make a decision that is truly in the best interests of the children. He intends to allow them all the time they need.

The two women locked eyes the instant Mary stood. Mary knows this petite woman of limited education and meager means, who has suffered years of spousal abuse, holds the future of her motherhood in her hands, her heart's greatest hope and greatest desire. Nadine realizes that this well-dressed woman and the well-dressed man sitting by her are the couple that wants to adopt the children. Intuitively, she divines they are very good people, a loving couple. Nadine sees all the hope-filled expectation in Mary's anxious eyes. Mary sees the agonizing, maternal instinct struggling within Nadine's eyes.

The courtroom is hushed in cathedral-like silence. They wait in reverence.

Mary and Nadine face one another, two women who appear on the surface to be as different and distant from each other as two women could possibly be, but, in truth, they are like sisters in their shared and selfless love for the children. Looking at each other, they both understand this immediately. In this pivotal moment, with no words spoken between them, something wonderful happens, something so wonderful it even surpasses the sacred spirit of sisterhood. It is the great equalizer among women that transcends culture, transcends race, and transcends status. In that moment, Nadine and Mary synchronize as *mothers*. As mothers, their eyes simultaneously exchange every feeling of love, every longing of hope, and every wonderful dream for Emily and Chloë that all good mothers, in every known time and in every place since the world began, want for their children. In this, all mothers share an unassailable bond as old as the moon and as eternal as the stars. God has made it so.

The courtroom remains quiet in respectful silence. Nadine closes her eyes and bows her head. A full minute passes. Then, slowly lifting her head, she opens her eyes and stares at Mary. Mary hasn't moved. Nadine's eyes are now free of all anxiety. She is at peace with her decision. As the two women gaze at each other, Nadine calmly answers the judge, but she is looking at and speaking directly to Mary. "Your Honor, I want to give up all of my rights to the children."

The gallery stirs, and grateful tears pour from Mary's eyes. She reaches for her husband's shoulder to steady herself and mouths a profound "thank you" to Nadine. In return, Nadine gives a respectful nod of acknowledgement to Mary. Mary sits down and leans into her husband. John slips his arm around her shoulders and hugs her tightly. His face is streaked with tears as well.

Judge Peters asks quietly, "You are certain, Mrs. Slagg?"

"Yes, your Honor. I am certain," Nadine responds in a steady and secure voice. "I know it's the right thing for the children."

Judge Peters hands Nadine a document. "Mrs. Slagg, by signing this document you will release all claims to the children. It will be final. Would you like to consult an attorney? You have that right."

Nadine simply shakes her head and takes the document from the judge. She signs it and hands it back to him.

"Thank you," Judge Peters says. "And Mrs. Slagg, may I tell you it's what a person says that matters and not how pretty she says it. You've been extraordinarily eloquent today, and you're one of the most incredible women I have ever had the pleasure of meeting in this courtroom. One thing more, Mrs. Slagg: always know you are a good mother. It's true; you are a very, very good mother. We've all witnessed a good mother's remarkable sacrifice today. You are excused, Mrs. Slagg."

Nadine steps down from the witness stand. With her shoulders back and her head held high, looking neither to the left nor to the right, and with profound dignity and uncommon strength of character, Nadine walks down the aisle of the courtroom and out the front door.

Judge Peters looks at the gallery and says, "Mr. and Mrs. Goodman, would you please approach the bench."

The Goodmans stand and come before Judge Peters. They are holding hands.

Judge Peters addresses the couple. "Emily and Chloë Fleming

are now the wards of this court. I have complete and final authority over them. I have read your petition for adoption and thoroughly reviewed your file. I am happy to tell you that I believe it is in the best interests of these children to grant your petition, which I will sign immediately. Congratulations on being the proud parents of two beautiful little girls."

The gallery erupts in applause. Judge Peters lifts his gavel to call to order, but decides against it. He sits back and enjoys the festive scene.

Elena enters the courtroom with alarm on her face. She sees Seth, Terry, Kathryn, her parents, and the Goodmans shaking each other's hands and hugging each other excitedly. She hurries over to them.

Seth sees her coming and immediately hugs her, exclaiming, "Elena, we won! The children have been adopted by Mr. and Mrs. Goodman."

"Honey, that's wonderful news," Elena says. "I knew you'd come through. But I'm worried, Seth. When I arrived at The Children's Sanctuary, Emily and Chloë were gone. No one knows where they are."

Hearing what Elena's said, the entire group is alarmed, but especially Mary and John Goodman. They cling to each other.

As if a revelation was sent to him, Seth knows at once where the children are. "Don't worry," Seth assures them, "the children are safe. Everyone, come to the house. I'm leaving now. Elena, please have your parents follow you in their car. Mr. and Mrs. Goodman, please don't be concerned. I promise you; the children are safe."

CHAPTER FORTY-ONE

Seth has arrived home from the courthouse and is in the kitchen. He picks out a half dozen chocolate chip cookies from the cookie jar and stacks them neatly on a plate. He fishes out several dog biscuits from a box on the counter next to the cookie jar and lines them up on the plate across from the cookies. Carrying the plate, he walks through the back door, into the backyard, and goes directly to the playhouse. Something new has been posted on the door for big people: it is a sign in large block letters that Chloë's made in her lopsided printing with Emily's able assistance:

```
┌─────────────────────────────┐
│                             │
│   NO BOYS ALLOWED           │
│   EXCEPT FOR SAM            │
│                             │
└─────────────────────────────┘
```

He smiles and knocks gently on the adult door.
Chloë responds in a sing-song voice, "Who's there-er?"
Seth grins broadly. "It's me, Seth," he calls out.
"No boys allowed-owed. Read the sign-ign." He hears giggling inside.

"I'll pay," Seth bargains.

"Whatcha got?" Chloë responds, curiously.

"Cookies."

"Not enough for a boy-oy," Chloë replies, and he hears more giggling.

"I've got cookies . . . and dog biscuits."

"Okay, you can come in," Chloë agrees.

Seth opens the door and enters the playhouse. Chloë sits in a chair ladylike, while Emily calmly brushes her hair. Sam is in his crate, chewing on a toy. Gracie Ann rests on the table with her face up and a red barrette in her hair; she seems to smile. The children are happy and blissfully unconcerned.

Seth looks quizzically at Emily, and she smiles at him.

"So, how are you ladies today?" Seth asks mildly.

Eyeing him, Chloë says playfully, "No way! You gotta pay first. Hand over the cookies *and* Sam's biscuits, please."

"Of course, Chloë," and Seth grins at her as he hands her the plate and takes a seat on the couch. He says casually, "Elena went to the Sanctuary this morning looking for you ladies. She was a little worried when she couldn't find you there."

While brushing Chloë's hair, Emily responds confidently, "I had a dream last night. I was told we should come here this morning and wait. Wait for something wonderful."

Seth is amazed. "In your dream, Emily, was it a person?"

"No, it wasn't a person. It was a voice. The nicest voice I've ever heard. When I woke up, I wasn't afraid anymore. I knew I'd never be afraid again."

"But how . . . how did you get here this morning?" Seth is fascinated.

"In my dream, I was told we should walk to the end of The Children's Sanctuary driveway this morning and wait. A car would come for us. The driver would ask for us by our names, and that's how we would know it was safe to go with him."

"What happened?" Seth asks in a near whisper.

"Just like the voice told me," Emily says, "a car stopped for us. It had letters and a light on top. The driver asked, 'Are you Emily and Chloë Fleming?' I said yes. We got in, and the nice man drove us here."

WOMEN OF UNCOMMON STRENGTH

"You came in a cab," Seth says, now understanding. "How did he know to bring you here? How did you pay him?"

Emily stops brushing Chloë's hair and looks at Seth untroubled. "He said he already knew. He didn't ask for money. When he let us off, he just smiled and drove away."

Seth slowly nods, reflecting deeply on Emily's dream, his mother's dream, and remembering the time on the kitchen clock when he knelt and prayed. He realizes the connection between all three and is profoundly grateful. He knows the true source of Emily's strength; it is the same as his own. Even when he felt the most alone, he understands now that he was never actually alone. All he ever needed to do was make the decision to lift up his eyes to see the light, to listen with his ears, to hear the knock, and to open the door. Seth comprehends that he has been granted a glimpse of the grander plan for his life and is genuinely humbled.

"Well, did it?" Emily gaily asks.

Momentarily lost in his thoughts, Seth says, "I'm sorry, what?"

"Did something wonderful happen?" Emily asks again, brightly.

Seth smiles and nods his head. "Yes, Emily, it did. Your dream was real. The most wonderful thing in the world has happened. Mr. and Mrs. Goodman are going to be your new parents. They'll be here soon."

Chloë jumps up from her chair squealing with delight, and the two sisters hug each other. Chloë quickly hops back into the chair. "Hurry, Em! Finish brushing my hair! I want to look pretty for Mommy and Daddy. The pink ribbon, please."

Emily brushes her sister's hair another stroke and then reaches for the pink ribbon. As she places it in Chloë's hair, Emily smiles at Seth. "I knew. You promised me."

"Yes Emily, I did promise you," Seth answers, remembering that special day in the playhouse and the image that will forever be in his mind of a radiant Emily in the streaming sunlight, her hair golden and her garments glowing.

Emily ties the ribbon into place and hands Chloë the silver inlaid hand mirror that Mrs. Goodman gave her. Chloë takes the mirror and quickly checks herself for perfection. Very pleased that all is just right, she hands the mirror back to Emily and hops off the chair, eager to go. She grabs Gracie Ann.

329

"I'm ready!" Chloë announces.

Seth can't help but laugh and says, "Great, Chloë. If you're ready, we're all ready. Everyone's probably here by now."

Seth retrieves Sam from his crate, and they leave the playhouse. Emily and Chloë walk ahead, holding hands and talking excitedly. When they enter the kitchen, everyone is there waiting anxiously for them to arrive: The Goodmans, Kathryn, Mrs. McAllister, Elena, Humberto, and Yesenia.

As soon as Chloë enters the room, she runs to Mrs. Goodman, crying, "Mommy! Mommy! Mommy!" She buries her face in Mrs. Goodman's waist and hugs her tightly. While this new mother hugs Chloë, she motions for Emily to come to her, too, which Emily does, and the three of them embrace.

"Mommy," Mary whispers to her husband, "it's the most beautiful word in the world."

John smiles broadly and hugs his wife. With a paper table napkin he attempts to stem the flood of tears streaming from his eyes, tears of pure joy.

Mrs. McAllister announces, "Everyone. The ladies are going to help me with the food and drinks." Shooing at the men playfully, she continues, "You men go into the living room. We'll call you when everything's ready."

Humberto, Seth, and Mr. Goodman retreat to the living room. Seth and Mr. Goodman sit on the couch. Humberto sits in the chair facing them.

Mr. Goodman beams, "I've never been so happy." He gestures towards Seth, "Mr. Hernandez, I suppose you know you've got great son-in-law material there."

Humberto says proudly, "Yes, he has my approval. He will make a fine husband for my Elena."

Looking apologetic, Mr. Goodman says, "Well, I hope you won't hold it against me for trying to hire him, Mr. Hernandez. I've been searching for an exceptionally talented architect like Seth for a long time."

Humberto is surprised by what Mr. Goodman just said, but doesn't let on. "No, no, not at all, Mr. Goodman," he responds, and he glances at Seth.

"Did the best I could," Mr. Goodman continues cheerfully, "offered him a hundred and ten thousand, annual bonus, and all his moving expenses. I was going to start him off as a manager. You know what he told me? Said he appreciated my offer, but he already had the job he wanted."

"He did?" Humberto answers, looking appraisingly at Seth.

"He sure did," Mr. Goodman laughs cordially. "But I've been thinking. We're moving into Houston in a big way soon, going to build several thousand new houses over the next twenty years. Mr. Hernandez, with your company and fine team in place, and with Seth here, well . . . what I mean is, I think it's a much better idea if I have an exclusive joint venture partnership with a local company like yours. I've seen your work already. You designed and built a beautiful home for The Children's Sanctuary. Our customers would love a family home like that. You and Seth would create all the new designs and oversee construction, of course. What do you say? Do we have a deal?"

Humberto is stunned. "Yes . . . yes, it sounds very appealing, Mr. Goodman, very appealing." Humberto pauses, thinks about it seriously, and then says politely, "However, under the circumstances, I must tell you that I have to turn down your offer. Please understand; I appreciate your offer. It's very generous, and I would like to accept it, but I don't have the money for operating expenses—salaries and the like. If I can't hold up my end of the bargain, I wouldn't feel right about accepting your offer. I just couldn't do it, Mr. Goodman, but thank you anyway."

Appreciating the man's integrity and character, Mr. Goodman is all the more excited. "Mr. Hernandez, you're a man after my own heart. I've always felt the same way myself. We're gonna make a great team. But there's no problem here that I can see. If you will agree to it, I expect you'll have plenty of money for operating expenses once I buy your design plan. I want that design for my own company. We'll build thousands of homes with it." Mr. Goodman pulls a pen and a note pad from his pocket. Pleased with himself, he quickly jots down a figure for the purchase price of the design and hands it to Humberto. "What do you think?" he asks, almost giddy with excitement.

Humberto looks at the price, considers it, smiles, and nods his head. "Mr. Goodman, I'd say we have a deal."

"Great. That's great!" Mr. Goodman is ecstatic. "The hardest thing is finding the right people. And I know you're the right people. Let's shake on it here and now. Mr. Hernandez, my word is my bond."

The two men shake hands cordially. Mr. Goodman turns and pumps Seth's hand.

Mr. Goodman continues agreeably, "And from now on Mr. Hernandez, please call me John. My name's John."

"I will, and please, John, my name's Humberto."

"Wonderful, just wonderful," Mr. Goodman says. "You know, we'll need a local lumberyard to handle the volume. Serve as the main distribution center in this region. Is there one you can re–commend?"

"I know the right one," Humberto says, thinking of his friend Casey.

"I thought you might. It's your decision," Mr. Goodman says. "Of course, we'll also have to have a major environmental impact study. We always do things right by the environment, you know. The best family home is the most environmentally-friendly home I've always said, even before it became fashionable. Can you recommend a local attorney who specializes in environmental law?"

"You've already met one of the best, Mr. Goodman," Seth tells him. "It's Terry Mason."

"You mean that sharp, young attorney who represented my children in court? Hire him right away. Pay him whatever he asks. We've got at least five years worth of steady work, and, after that, we'll keep him on retainer. I hope he's not too busy to handle us. And Seth, please call me John."

Mrs. McAllister enters the living room and announces that the food is ready. The men rise and start towards the kitchen. Mr. Goodman is leading the way but stops by Mrs. McAllister and says, "Ladies first." She smiles and nods respectfully and goes into the kitchen with Mr. Goodman following behind her.

Humberto places his hand on Seth's shoulder and stops him in the living room. Seth turns to him. Humberto is looking at him with astonishment. "You turned down a hundred and ten thousand dollars to keep an eight dollar an hour job?" he asks incredulously.

"You're paying me seven-fifty an hour," Seth corrects him good-naturedly.

"I know, I know," Humberto says. "But I was thinking about raising you. Still, you turned down a hundred and ten thousand dollars?"

"Plus an annual bonus and paid moving package. Don't forget that, too," Seth teases.

Humberto lets out a long, whistling breath and says affectionately, "You know, I'd just about gotten used to the idea of my muchacha bonita marrying a gringo. But I didn't know she was marrying the dumbest gringo in the world."

Seth grins, "Guess you're stuck with me. Of course, I could go in there and tell Mrs. Hernandez what you just said. You know, about me being the dumbest gringo in the world and all. If I did, she'd probably put you back on Dr. Fuentes' rabbit diet—for life. I'd sure hate to see that happen." Then, drawing it out for effect, he adds, "Yes sir, I . . . sure . . . would."

Humberto's face scrunches up as he considers the very real possibility of Yesenia doing just that if she found out about his G word comment. He quickly grins and pats Seth fondly on the shoulder, saying affably, "Now, now. You know I was just kiddin'. I kid like that all the time. You know I do. Just ask Juan-Carlos. Besides, I meant gringo in a nice way." Then lowering his voice and cutting his eyes past Seth towards the kitchen, Humberto says conspiringly, "No need to say anything to that woman in there, okay?"

Just as Seth nods that Humberto's secret is safe with him, the front door opens. Terry walks in. "Hi Terry," Seth greets him. "About time you got here. Where've you been?"

"With Judge Peters," Terry says. "You won't believe what's happened. I was in the judge's office wrapping up some paperwork, and his phone started ringing off the wall. He asked me to stay and help him take notes."

"What was it about?" Seth asks.

"Word has spread fast among Slagg's cronies," Terry says. "They're ratting on him as fast as they can before he rats on them, trying to cut their own deals to avoid going down with his ship. The first call was from Dr. Fitzholder. She admitted falsifying her report. That guy's web of evil is unbelievable: payoffs, kickbacks, bribery, witness tampering, evidence tampering, obstruction of justice, client abuse."

"I believe it," Seth says. "What panicked his so-called buddies?"

Terry grins, "They realized Judge Peters has a record of all the key people mixed-up with Slagg. Last year, Slagg bribed them to send supportive letters to the judge, asking for lenience when his brother was placed on probation. These letters are a laundry list of Slagg's closest allies. A case of real and poetic justice: Slagg bribed them to send the letters, hanging himself, and all of them, in the process."

"Yep," Seth says, "I'd say they all have a pretty good reason to worry."

"Right away," Terry continues, "the judge started making calls to the other members on the board of the state's special commission for ethics and legal reform, turning the names over to them. They'll all be out of business soon and, for many of them, a lot worse."

"Terry, why were the Slagg brothers really after the children?" Seth asks.

"It was money. We learned from a caller that the children have a large trust fund. The original bank handling it failed, and when the new bank took over, things were in such a mess that the paperwork fell through the cracks. The only ones who knew about the trust fund were the Slagg brothers and the caller Wickham had confided in." Terry looks seriously at Seth. "There's no telling what those evil men had in store for the children, but it's safe to say you saved them from something terrible."

"Thank you. But it wasn't me. I was only the instrument. What about Wickham Slagg?"

"He'll never practice law again. That guy is going to prison for a long, long time. Be keeping company with his brother every day for years to come."

"Couldn't have happened to a more deserving pair," Seth says.

The three men move into the kitchen. The rest of the group visits over coffee and dessert. Chloë sits in Mrs. Goodman's lap with Gracie Ann. Elena and Emily stand off to one side, talking quietly.

After an hour, Mrs. Goodman says, "John, darling. If we leave now we'll still have time to stop at the department store and buy our daughters new Easter dresses for church services tomorrow."

"Did you hear that, Em?" Chloë says, thrilled. "New Easter dresses! Let's go!"

"Sounds like fun to me," Mr. Goodman says, excitedly. "I'm ready when you are, sweetheart."

"What about Sam?" Chloë asks with concern. "Can he come, too?"

"Chloë," Seth says, "the hotel won't let Sam stay there. You and Emily can come back here after church tomorrow. He'll be fine with me tonight. Sam will be waiting for you and ready to go," he assures her.

"Okay," Chloë says happily, eager to leave.

Chloë takes Mrs. Goodman's hand and Mr. Goodman's hand, and they walk into the living room. Seth, Elena, and Emily follow. Mr. Goodman helps Mrs. Goodman with her coat, and they are ready to leave. Emily looks at Elena, her eyes full of anguish.

Elena says politely, "John and Mary, Emily and I want to talk for just a minute, if you don't mind. I'll bring her out in a moment, if that's okay."

Mary immediately senses there's something important going on between them and says, "Of course, Elena. You and Emily take all the time you need. Seth, would you mind walking us to our car, please?"

"Happy to," Seth says.

Seth, Chloë, and the Goodmans go out the front door. Elena and Emily sit on the couch together. Elena holds Emily's hand as big tears begin to roll down the girl's cheeks. Emily sits very still, and her head is slightly bowed. Elena waits patiently.

Emily looks at her and says tentatively, "Can we talk . . . woman to woman?"

Elena smiles at her compassionately and says, "How about friend to friend?"

Emily whispers, "It's about Seth."

"Emily," Elena says softly, "Seth is very happy for you and Chloë."

Emily struggles to find the right words to express deep feelings that are new to her. "I know. Only . . . it's just that . . . I don't know how to tell him . . ." Emily cannot finish her thought. It is too painful for her. Huge tears slide down her face.

Elena places her arm around Emily's shoulders, pulling her close. Emily leans into Elena for comfort. Speaking to her tenderly and gently stroking her hair, Elena says, "I think I understand, sweetheart. You don't know how to tell Seth goodbye. How to tell him that he'll be in your heart forever. That you will never forget him and that you will always love him."

Unable to speak, Emily nods her head, and Elena hugs her more tightly. "I'll help you, Emily," Elena assures her. "Tomorrow afternoon, when you and Chloë come for Sam, I'll have everything ready."

"How will I know what to do?" Emily worries.

Elena says encouragingly, "You'll know, Emily. I promise, you'll know. Tomorrow, just follow your heart. Can you do that?"

"I think so," Emily softly answers.

"Of course you can," Elena says cheerfully. Straightening up, she hands Emily a Kleenex.

Emily takes it, pats her eyes, and gently blows her nose.

"Come now, sweetheart," Elena says optimistically. "We girls have got to stick together. It'll be fine tomorrow. Are you ready?"

Emily breathes in and out deeply, recovers a bit of her composure, and nods her head. Elena and Emily leave the couch and walk to the front door. As they do, Seth returns through the door. He holds it open for Emily, smiling at her as she passes through. But as she leaves, Emily looks away without acknowledging him.

Seth closes the door, surprised by Emily's behavior, and looks at Elena, puzzled. "Is Emily upset?"

"Yes."

"But why? I thought she'd be happy."

"She is happy."

"I don't understand."

"Babe, there are some things only a girl's heart feels and only a woman's heart knows."

"Oh."

Elena takes his hand and holds it tenderly. They walk into the kitchen where Terry, Kathryn, Margaret, Humberto, and Yesenia are talking.

Humberto feels a peace at this moment that he hasn't felt in several years. He rises from his chair and politely says, "Yesenia, Margaret has been hosting us long enough. Perhaps it is time for us to go."

Yesenia smiles pleasantly at him, gets up from her chair, stands next to her husband, and says, "Whenever you wish, mi amor."

Mrs. McAllister protests mildly, "You don't have to leave. I'm enjoying everyone's company."

Humberto replies modestly, "Thank you Margaret, it is very kind of you. But Yesenia and I should go." He looks at his wife affectionately, and taking her hand in his, quietly tells her, "We have much to do at home . . . and we don't want to be late for church tomorrow morning."

Yesenia gazes at her husband, and tears of happiness flood her eyes. She hugs Humberto, "No, mi amor. We don't. Father Michael will rejoice. He's never given up believing that he would welcome you back one Sunday to your church home."

"Seth and I will walk you out," Elena says, overjoyed for her mother and father, and for them all. She knows now that her father is healing. The four of them walk into the living room. Elena hugs her parents. Yesenia hugs Seth, and the two men shake hands.

Yesenia and Humberto walk to the front door. As they near the door, Humberto stops and turns around. Yesenia slips her arm through his and waits. Humberto holds his old, battered fedora in both hands. Elena threads her arm through Seth's as they wait for Humberto to say what's on his mind.

"I was thinking," Humberto says to Seth deferentially, "I was thinking I'd like to start on the new sign . . . it'd be ready about the time you and Elena are back from your honeymoon."

The women look at each other, puzzled.

"A new sign?" Seth asks, not fully comprehending Humberto's meaning.

Humberto hesitates, shifts uneasily, looks down at the floor self-consciously, and then back up at Seth. In a humble tone that gives voice to a broken heart that yearns for a way to heal, Humberto answers softly, "Yes, the new sign. The one that will read: Humberto Hernandez and Son, Design and Construction. We would be partners . . . if that's all right with you."

Yesenia is filled with jubilance beyond words and leans lovingly into her husband. Elena hugs Seth's arm and looks at him tenderly. Overwhelmed by the man's generosity, Seth answers from the bottom of his heart, "I'd like that. I'd like that very much, Dad."

Humberto nods appreciatively to Seth, and without saying anything more, he opens the door for his wife. When he and Yesenia step out onto the porch, Humberto closes the front door quietly behind him. In doing so, this very good man closes the door on the most painful loss in his life and opens his heart to closure and the promising possibilities beyond. Unseen to the young couple inside the house are the soothing tears that Humberto and Yesenia share as husband and wife. They walk down the sidewalk, hand in hand, on their way to their car. On this day, a son has been restored to a father, and a father has been restored to a son.

CHAPTER FORTY-TWO

It is early afternoon on Easter Sunday, and it is a beautiful spring day. Elena is in the living room of the McAllister home, having come straight from church services with Seth. Looking lovely, she wears a tailored, yellow, silk dress with a scalloped neckline and matching yellow leather pumps. Around her neck hangs a beautiful, sterling silver four way cross with a dove center that dangles from a dainty sterling Rolo chain, and gracing her ears are tasteful, sterling silver linear knot earrings. On her left wrist, she proudly wears the silver, antique Omega ladies watch that Mrs. McAllister presented to her; the one that had once belonged to Mrs. McAllister's own mother. Elena has just placed the portable disc player from her classroom on the living room lamp table. Seth enters the room from the kitchen wearing his dark navy blue suit with a cream-colored button down shirt, striped navy and gold tie, and black Whalen dress oxfords.

Seth asks, "Honey, can I help you with anything?"

"No babe. Thank you, everything's done. The children will be here any minute. Is Sam ready?"

"Yes, he's ready and waiting in his crate with a big blue bow."

There's a child's rapid knock at the front door. Elena and Seth smile knowingly at each other.

"That sounds like a Chloë knock, to me," Elena says cheerfully. "I'll get the door." Elena goes to the door and opens it. Chloë skips in energetically, followed by Emily, who hangs back. The children are dressed in beautiful Easter dresses: Chloë's dress is pastel pink; Emily's dress is pure white. Elena hugs Chloë.

"Miss Hernandez," Chloë says starry-eyed, "see my new dress!" She flips-up her dress above her knees, showing off. "See, it's got a petticoat and everything!"

"Yes, I see. You look so beautiful." Elena laughs and claps her hands for Chloë.

Chloë runs and jumps into Seth's outstretched arms. Emily looks up at Elena with a tentative, questioning expression. Elena smiles and nods her head, assuring Emily that everything is ready. They watch Chloë and Seth.

"I have something special for you," Chloë giggles. "Close your eyyyy-eees."

Seth closes his eyes as instructed and waits.

Chloë produces a pink paper star. She is thrilled with herself. "Open!" she commands.

Seth opens his eyes. "Chloë, you did it!" he brags. "That's a beautiful star. I'm so proud of you."

"You told me to keep trying," Chloë chortles, pleased. "It's easy now. I can make bunches of them. It's like the paper is magic. This is my first one. It's for you." She offers it to Seth.

Seth takes the star and presses it to his heart. "I'll keep it forever and ever Chloë. And every time I look at it, I'll think of you. You kept working and working at it, and you finally did it. But always remember Chlo, the magic isn't in the paper. The magic is in you." He kisses her on her head.

"That's awesome," Chloë whispers wondrously. "The magic's in me." She giggles and asks, "Where's Sam? Is he ready?"

Seth puts her down. "Yep, the smartest and handsomest dog in the whole world is waiting for you in his crate. He's ready to go. His leash is by his crate. Take him out the back way and around to the front, please."

Chloë wiggles her finger for Seth to bend down. When he does, she quickly kisses him on the cheek—*smack*! "Bye Seth!" She spins, runs giggling into the kitchen, and is gone. Seth turns to Emily.

Emily glances up at Elena. Elena smiles down at her reassuringly.

"If you both will excuse me, please," Elena says politely. As she walks towards the kitchen she stops briefly by the lamp table, switches on the disc player, and then leaves the room.

There is a brief moment before the music starts. Emily and Seth look at one another. The music begins. It is Andrea Bocelli and Celine Dion singing a duet, "The Prayer." Seth and Emily continue to look at each other, both unsure of what to do next. Then, Seth bows formally to Emily. In turn, Emily curtsies formally to him.

They come together and dance for the last time. Emily flawlessly follows Seth's every lead. She is so light and graceful on her feet that Seth can hardly feel her in his arms. They dance beautifully together as the music and the lyrics fill their hearts, fill the room, and fill the Easter air. Emily is lost in the moment. Dancing with Seth, she steadily gazes at him; her eyes do not veer from his for a single second. When the song finishes, they stop dancing, but continue holding each other.

Without taking her eyes from his, Emily releases Seth and takes a step back. She curtsies to him. He bows to her. Emily turns away and takes a step towards the front door.

Seth remains perfectly still and waits. He watches her closely, hoping Emily will turn around, understanding it is her decision, and knowing that if she does, he can be certain that this girl of uncommon strength will mend.

Emily stops. She turns around and faces him. Emily looks deeply into Seth's eyes . . . she hesitates . . . and then rushes to him. She reaches her arms around his waist and holds him tightly, burying her face in his shirt. Emily's tears are unleashed in a torrent. Her pent-up feelings burst forth freely with a force that's meant to wash away the hurt, the unfairness, and the confusion over the loss of her parents, her former life, and her struggle to survive. An ocean of innocent tears flood her wounds, anointing them and cleansing them and preparing them to heal. Like a surging tide, these tears channel the way to her new life; their purifying waters blessing her with the means to recapture a fragment of her lost girlhood; their unstoppable swell bringing peace to her brave heart.

Looking down at Emily with compassion and love, Seth gently strokes her hair. He admires Emily as he could never admire anyone else and knows she is remarkable in every way.

Their love is chaste; it is vestal.

Elena, with handkerchief in hand, has come quietly back into the room. She remains discreetly in the background, observing, and patting her eyes.

Emily lifts up her face to Seth's and whispers, "I love you, Seth."

"I love you too, Emily," he whispers back.

Emily presses one side of her face into his shirt and holds him gently. She is no longer crying. Seth can feel her against him, drawing in her breath rhythmically in long, slow, deep breaths, and letting it out in long, slow, measured cadences. He recognizes Emily is in the process of gathering her composure and releasing her pain. Seth is patient, allowing her all the time that she needs. He stops stroking her hair and caringly places an arm over Emily's shoulders, hugging her lightly in a protective way.

The front door opens a crack, and Chloë sticks her head in, eyes shining. Then, opening the door all the way, she steps into the room holding Gracie Ann, who is dressed in her own little pink Easter frock with a petticoat, looking very pretty and very happy indeed. Forgetting to close the door behind her, Chloë takes another step forward and stops a few feet from Emily and Seth, observing them quietly. Hesitant and in a soft voice, she says, "Are you ready, Em? Mommy and Daddy are waiting."

Emily lifts her head from Seth's shirt, and with a radiant smile on her face gazes up at him for a last time, saying nothing. Seth now sees something in Emily's eyes that fills his heart with joy; he sees true happiness.

Emily releases Seth, turns, and goes to Chloë. Reaching and holding both her sister's hands in hers, Emily says brightly, "You're right, Chlo. Mommy and Daddy are waiting. Let's go. . . . Let's go home." Holding hands and without looking back, the children rush through the open front door. They skip down the stairs and run down the sidewalk straight into the loving arms of their waiting parents.

Seth watches them go. Once the Goodman's car drives out

of sight, Seth gently closes the front door. He stands gazing at the closed door, feeling the memories beyond it, and something inside him begins to hurt. Seth turns to Elena, shrugs, and smiles weakly, fighting back tears. Elena, now sitting on the couch with handkerchief in hand and her eyes puffy, pats the cushion next to her. Seth goes and sits by her, their bodies touching.

"I can't believe they're really gone," he says, with an unmistakable sadness in his voice.

Elena reaches for his hand and says softly, "Seth, in Emily's heart is the purest love you'll ever know."

"And your love?" he asks quietly.

"In this woman's heart is the greatest love you'll ever know."

"I believe you, Elena. With every beat of my heart, I will always believe you."

Elena nuzzles into him, rests her head on his shoulder, and says, "Seth, as remarkable as Emily is, there's even more to her than you may realize. Do you remember her white sweater? The one I brought to her that afternoon in the Sanctuary's office? We met that day because of it, remember?

"Yes, I remember," he answers.

"Her mother knitted that sweater for her, honey. Emily would never have left it in the classroom by mistake."

Seth shakes his head slowly and whispers, "Emily . . ." He gazes at the front door. "Elena, I'm going to miss them so much."

"Of course you are, babe," she says, patting his hand reassuringly. "But Mary told me she plans to invite us to all of the children's birthdays and recitals. And they'll also be back for our wedding in June. Emily will be a lovely bridesmaid. And Chloë, our little flower girl, will probably steal the show completely."

"Yes, she probably will," Seth agrees. "And I suppose Sam, with painted nails and wearing a big blue satin bow, will come scampering down the aisle as the ring bearer." Then he says, "Elena, I've learned so much these last few months."

She lifts her head from his shoulder and looks at him. "Tell me what you're thinking, honey."

"My mom once told me, 'Life wounds every person. It's what we do with our wounds that matters.' I've learned how true that is.

But I've also learned that life blesses every person, and it's what we do with our blessings that matters more."

"Even our wounds can become blessings," Elena observes softly.

Seth nods in agreement and presses her hand affectionately. "It's remarkable," he says, "even the most miraculous things can happen when you least expect them and under the most ordinary circumstances."

"Yes," Elena quietly agrees. "You walk into a room, and your life changes forever." She slips her arm into Seth's.

"That afternoon at Katie's," Seth says reflectively, "when I first met Emily, she observed me for a long moment, considering something. Then, all of a sudden, she offered a delicate hand to me. Her hand was just out of reach. Emily knew it was. But she simply stood there unmoving, watching me and waiting patiently. I leaned forward to close the small gap between us. As I reached for her hand, just before our fingers touched, I hesitated. I hesitated for an instant. Looking back on it, I realize that I knew by taking that little girl's hand, I was making an important decision." He pauses, thinking, and then continues, "What seemed like an ordinary event at the time wasn't ordinary at all. Emily offered her hand to me. But it was really much more than that. Here was a child, and every child like her, not offering her hand but offering a prayer: a prayer for hope, a prayer for recognition, a prayer for understanding, a prayer for love. But it was up to me to hear her prayer, to understand it for what it was . . . and to act. Emily was watching and waiting and hoping. What I decided would define the true me. I see that now. It was up to me to bridge the gap between us because children cannot save themselves."

"No," Elena says thoughtfully, "they only have us for that. God places them in our care."

"Yes, Elena. We just need to open our eyes, listen with our hearts, and reach forward a little. In this small effort everything is possible. I hesitated for an instant. And now I understand in that fraction of time before we touched, within that tiny sliver of space between my fingertips and Emily's, floated every virtue in the universe. Then we locked hands and held on tightly. And that has made all the difference."

"Sweetheart, there was never any doubt you would answer Emily's prayer. It's who you are. It's why I fell in love with you."

"I had lost that belief in myself, Elena. But I found it again. I found it again because of the children and because of you. I was given a second chance."

Elena notices the Easter lily in its lovely ceramic pot on the floor at the end of the coffee table. The plant is now in full, magnificent bloom. "Look, Seth. The Easter lily, I've never seen one so beautiful."

Seth contemplates the plant's glorious blooms, the pure white, horn-shaped lilies that, in form and fragrance, trumpet joy and hope and herald everlasting life on this most special of all special days.

"Mr. Nakamura's latest success," Seth says quietly. Then, he adds, "Once I was lost but now am found."

Elena lays her head on Seth's shoulder again and snuggles into him, feeling safe and secure for a lifetime. "You were their man of steel, and now you're my man of steel," she says softly. "Honey, do you remember when Chloë asked you if you could fly?"

Seth chuckles as he fondly recalls that day. "Yes, I remember. It was the first time Emily and Chloë came to the house. We were in the kitchen. Right after she asked me if I could fly, she hit me with a spoon."

Elena raises her head from Seth's shoulder. Gazing into his beautiful blue eyes, she says lovingly, "You can fly, babe. You've been flying all along."

ABOUT THE AUTHOR

Gladney B. Darroh has been interested in creative writing since college. He majored in English Literature initially, before switching and earning a degree in economics, but continued to study and develop his creative writing skills privately.

Best known for his many achievements in community service and professional awards in his industry, Gladney draws his inspiration for writing from his personal beliefs and experience. He is interested in writing about ordinary people and how their unyielding devotion to family, beliefs, community, and service, together with the sacrifices they endure along the way, are what make seemingly ordinary individuals great.

The author has two children and is a native of Houston, Texas, where he still resides. This is his first novel. He welcomes reader's comments on his Facebook page: www.facebook.com/gladneybdarroh

Made in the USA
Charleston, SC
08 September 2012

WOMEN OF UNCOMMON STRENGTH

GLADNEY B. DARROH